Tedra ~ (mom's best

FATE
Loves

TWIST OF FATE
Book Three

TINA SAXON !

Enjoy the read !

xoxo

Fate Loves

Copyright © 2017 by Tina Saxon

ISBN Digital: 978-0-9987762-4-8
ISBN Print: 978-0-9987762-5-5

Cover design by: Damonza
Edited by: Max Dobson @ The Polished Pen
Proofreading by: Elaine York @ Allusion Graphics
www.allusiongraphics.com
Formatting by: Elaine York @ Allusion Graphics
www.allusiongraphics.com

FATE
Loves

Prologue

Aiden

Of all the nights to ruin, she had to ruin this one–the night I asked Addison to be my wife. I can't believe it. My chest tightens as confusion and anger wage a war inside me. I pace my apartment, practically pulling my hair out. Why is Jessie doing this to me?

Addison won't answer my fucking calls, and I can only imagine what she must think. Five sets of eyes watch me wear a hole in my floor as I walk back and forth. Cuss words fly out of my mouth as my feet drag across the hardwood floor.

"Aiden ..." Ryan clears his throat from the couch and leans forward on his knees. "Are you sure you didn't—"

"What the fuck kind of question is that? I think I know where I dipped my stick," I grit through my clenched teeth. He knows what Addison means to me. I would never have cheated on her.

His eyes bore into me like he knows something. *Clue me in, asshole, because I don't know where you're going with this.*

"Aiden, you saw Jessie eight months ago."

"I fucking did not," I bark, crossing my arms over my chest.

He stands up, stuffing his hands in his pockets. "When I came to the beach house, when you decided to use the walls as a punching bag...when I got there, Jessie was leaving the house and she made it pretty clear you two had just finished fucking."

"What the hell? I don't even remember seeing her."

Ryan shrugs one shoulder. "You were so shitfaced when I got there, I'm surprised you remember anything."

"If I was that bad, I'm positive I wouldn't have been able to fuck anyone." I drop onto the couch and slouch back against the cushion, rubbing my hands over my face. A bitter laugh escapes my lips. "Back when Addison first met Jessie, she said she wouldn't be surprised if Jessie showed up one day saying she had my child. I was mortified. I never thought Jessie would do something like that." I stare up at the ceiling, shaking my head. "Fuck, was I wrong."

Addison

"I warned him she'd end up doing something like this..." I walk into my apartment, pull my shoes off, and chuck them across the room. "I knew something was off with her. She was up to something." A deep growl comes out as I stomp around. Harper, Sydney, and Bryn sit down in the living room.

"Do you think there's any way she's telling the truth?" Bryn asks.

I stop pacing and look at all of them. Tilting my head, I think about it for a minute. I guess I hadn't thought that it might actually be a possibility. She certainly looked pregnant. I remember Ryan saying she left town around the time I was kidnapped, but Aiden told me he didn't see her when he was at the beach house.

"I think she's lying." I cross my arms over my chest. "I mean, she's obviously not lying about being pregnant, but I don't think it's Aiden's."

"Are you sure?" Harper asks hesitantly, biting her lip.

"Do you know something I don't?"

"Well...when Jessie made her announcement I was standing next to..." she pauses, trying to remember a name, "...Jessie's best friend, I think."

"Macie."

"Yes, Macie. Right after the announcement, I said, *'There's no way Aiden cheated on Addison...'*" she winces, "...and her reply was, 'Well, it could be...they did get together at the beach house before she took off.'"

My eyes bulge out, and I clench my hands into fists. "What!" I snap. My gaze darts around the room. When I spot my purse on the floor by the door, I scurry over and frantically dig through it. "Where the hell is my phone?" I glance around the room and everyone shrugs. "Can this night get any worse?" I scream, falling to the floor. "I need someone's phone."

Syd walks over and hands me her phone, looking apologetic. I take a few breaths before dialing his number. There has to be an explanation. Jessie is lying; I just need to prove it.

"Syd, where is Addison?" Aiden answers right away.

"It's me. We need to talk."

Chapter one

L iving in limbo somehow makes the world slow down. Every day feels like it's never going to end and when it finally does, the next day you wake up just to start all over again. Sitting at my dining table, I bring a spoonful of warm, cinnamon raisin oatmeal to my mouth and mull over the night two weeks ago that changed everything.

Aiden swears he didn't see Jessie, but Ryan says she was there; he actually physically saw her. Is there a possibility the child is his? Aiden's not sure. His uncertainty is driving a wedge between us. Although, I'm not the one backing away this time. It's him. I place my hand flat on the wood table and stare at my gorgeous ring.

He feels conflicted and guilty he can't remember, so he's pulling away from me. It's the first time since we've met that he isn't fighting for us. I hate being on this end, but that's okay. I can fight for us. It's time he sees how much I want this. Nothing will get in our way. *Even a lying bitch like Jessie.*

"Hi, Addie," Lexi says, yawning and stretching as she walks out of her room. She comes over to me, and I pull her in for a hug.

"Good morning, Lulu." I place a kiss on her forehead. She's Lulu to everyone except Aiden. I think she'll always be Tater Tot to him, and she loves it.

"Is Aiden coming over today?" She misses him. *Hell, so do I.*

"I don't know, sweet girl. He's been busy with work. We'll see him soon though." I sigh and hug her again. I'm going to call him and tell him he needs to come over. We haven't seen him in three days, and it's not beneath me to guilt him into coming over either.

After we finish eating, I send Lexi to go take a shower and get ready to go to the park. My hope is I can talk Aiden into going with us. I pick our empty bowls off the table and place them into the sink. Singing fills the air, so I know Lexi is in the shower. I smile, remembering when someone asked her if she sang in the shower. She was really confused, but ever since then she's demanded to take showers and sings while she does it.

I glance around the room, spot my phone on the entry table, and walk over to pick it up. My finger hovers over his number. *Please, say yes.* I press my finger down and put the phone against my ear. I close my eyes and hope he wants to see me today.

"Hey, Addison." His voice trails off, and I swallow the uneasiness I'm feeling.

"Are you doing anything today?" My tone is hopeful. When he doesn't answer right away, I continue. "Lexi was asking if we were going to see you today. We're going to the park. It'd be great if you went with us." My words are out quick, maybe a little desperate. I don't care. *I am desperate.* Goddammit, I just want see my fiancé.

After a few beats, he says, "You had to pull the Lexi card, didn't you?"

"I shouldn't have to. I miss you, Aiden." I walk to the windows and look down at the people enjoying the outdoors. Leaning my head against the glass, I wish he'd tell me he missed me, too.

If I couldn't hear him breathing, I'd think he had hung up. I keep quiet and let him work through it in his mind. Deep down I know he wants to say yes, but the guilt he harbors has put up a wall that so far has been impenetrable. God, I've tried to break it down. Right now, he feels more guilt over being away from Lexi than the whole Jessie situation. He would do anything for his Tater Tot. I hate that I've had to use her like this, but he hasn't given me any other choice. I've tried showing up at his work, banging down his door at his apartment...I even stake out his apartment so he *has* to see me when he leaves. Unfortunately, it's always the same response: *I just need to figure this out.* And every time he says it, my heart twists in pain.

"Okay...when?" he finally answers. A huge smile spreads across my face, and I throw an arm in the air. *Yes!*

"Ten. I told Lexi I'd take her to the zoo so she can feed the penguins. We'll meet you outside the entrance?"

"I'll be there."

"I love you, Aiden."

"I know, babe. I love you, too." His words are sad, but at least he said it. I'll take what I can get right now. We hang up and I peek down at the time on my phone. Nine-thirty. Crap! Why didn't I tell him ten-thirty? I run into my room and yell for Lexi to get out of the shower. I have learned that when you have a child, you need to always tack on an extra hour of prep time. Kids are not fast when you need them to be. I don't understand it; they run around like flies on speed *all day* but the second you tell them to do something, they immediately turn into sloths. Thankfully, when I tell Lexi we're meeting Aiden, she manages to get ready in record time. I guess I need to start using Aiden, too. I wonder how long I can use them as motivational tools to get what I want from each of them. They're bound to catch on eventually.

***

"Where is he?" Lexi asks, skipping around outside the zoo. I'm sitting on a brick wall, watching her twirl all around. Glancing at my watch, it's ten after ten. I refuse to think he would bail on us. When I look up to answer her, Aiden comes into my view outside the ticket booth. Our eyes lock. All the air around us gets sucked into the large breath I take. It's not until Lexi sees him, runs and jumps into his arms, that our eye contact breaks and I can exhale. It feels like I haven't seen him in forever.

Six foot two of pure, male hotness stands there with his arm muscles flexed as he holds Lexi. The black T-shirt he wears is taut around his arms and chest but fits loosely around his middle. I haven't touched his body in two weeks. My fingers tingle wanting to go over and run them under his shirt, feel the ripple of muscles I've memorized and missed. His beige cargo shorts hang low on his hips and the band of his underwear peeks out from where Lexi's leg has lifted his shirt slightly. I bite my lip as my mouth waters. God, I hate Jessie more and more each minute.

I sigh as my gaze trails back up to his eyes. He flashes a knowing smile. *Yes, you stubborn jerk. I want you and I'm not ashamed to show it.* Putting my hands on the brick wall, I hop off and walk toward him. My lips curl into a sly smile when his eyes move down my legs. Knowing it drives him crazy, I threw on a pair of cut-off shorts. When I'm standing right in front of him, he puts Lexi down. He hesitates to reach for me so I take the lead. I stand on my toes and wrap my arms around his neck. The second our bodies touch, his arms fold around me. He squeezes me like he's holding on for dear life. He buries his face in the curve of my neck, and I feel him take in a deep breath. Relief flows through my body. *He missed me.* I run my hand through his hair.

"I miss you so much, Aiden."

"I'm sorry, Addison. I'm so sorry," he mumbles into my hair.

I swallow the words that I know won't make a difference. He doesn't want to hear them. He's not one hundred percent sure, and he won't be until we get a paternity test.

"Hey, guys!" Lexi says, grabbing our hands, trying to pull us toward the entrance. "Let's go. I want to feed the penguins."

We pull apart and Aiden looks down at me with watery eyes. He blinks back his tears and looks down at Lexi, managing to flash her a smile.

"Then let's go, Tater Tot, but you have to watch those fingers of yours. I hear penguins like tater tots," he says, leaning down and nibbling on her fingers. She squeals and pulls her hands back.

"No, they don't," she says seriously, putting her hand on her hips. "They like fish sticks." Aiden and I bust out laughing. He's so carefree. This is how it should be, every day. I twist my ring around my finger. It'll happen...as soon as we prove Jessie is lying.

We walk around the park, hand in hand. I can feel Aiden's eyes on me periodically. I want to meet his gaze and let him see the vulnerability between us, but I'm afraid he'll pull back again. Lexi goes from animal to animal, and we laugh when she tries to mimic them. When Lexi runs off to play in the children's playground area, we find an empty bench in the sea of parents who are also sitting and watching. The sun shines bright above and is hot, so I'm thankful the bench is under an awning.

Aiden sits back, legs spread wide, as he keeps a keen eye on Lexi. I cross my legs and play with my ring. It's become a nervous habit these past couple of weeks, especially when I'm thinking about Aiden. A hand covers mine. I look up to Aiden, and he watches me with an intense stare.

"Tell me where your head is right now," I say. He pulls my hand to his lap and holds it.

He inhales deeply and then sighs. "What if it's mine?"

"If, *and that's a big if*, does it change how you feel about me?" I didn't want to ask this, but I need to. It's my biggest fear that keeps me up at night.

"Addison, I never wanted kids before. Then when I met you, I never imagined having kids with anyone but you, and now I *really* want them." He glances at Lexi as she climbs on top of a bronze turtle with two other little girls. "Especially after having Lexi around."

"Okay," I say slowly, wondering where this is going.

"If she ends up being mine, I could never turn my back on her."

I jerk my head back a little, confused. "Do you think I'd make you choose? Or are you saying you'd be with Jessie because she has your baby?" Both options make my chest tighten.

His lips curl like he just ate a lemon. "God, no. I love you. You're the only woman I want to be with."

Then he thinks I wouldn't want him to be a part of his daughter's life? My eyes dart around as I tell myself not to be hurt. He's not thinking clearly.

"Aiden, if she happens to be yours, it's because Jessie manipulated the situation somehow. I know you wouldn't willingly cheat on me." He starts to say something, but I hold up a finger. "Wait, I'm not done. But she's still your child and a part of you. I would expect you to take responsibility, and I would be there for you one hundred percent."

"Even if that means Jessie would be a part of our lives forever?" he asks, his voice pained.

I swallow the lump of hate stuck in my throat. "Yes," I squeak out. He looks at me with a lopsided grin. "I don't have to like the woman." I shrug.

He looks away and finds Lexi again. She smiles and waves. He waves back. "I don't know if I could do that to you. It'd be a constant reminder of what happened."

"Aiden," I pause, waiting for him to look back at me. "If I had gotten pregnant from..." My stomach twists, and I clench my hand in my lap just thinking about it. I clear my throat before continuing. "Joe...would you have loved me or my child any less?"

He turns toward me and grabs both my hands. "Addison, never."

"I feel the same way." I pull my hand out from under his and run it against his jaw. "Nothing has changed for me. I love you and want to marry you. And if this kid is yours, then I'll love her because she'll be a part of *you*."

He smiles softly and his dimples deepen. I glance at his full lips and silently pray that he kisses me. His smile grows larger as he leans down.

"I haven't lost my ability to read you," he says as his lips brush mine. The sounds of kids screaming and playing in the background fades as my lips part and I let out a soft mewl. He presses down harder, but the kiss is simple and sweet. I pull back when a kid's cry grabs my attention. I look for Lexi and find her crawling through a tunnel. Satisfied Lexi isn't the one hurt, I look back at Aiden. He picks up my legs and turns me so they are in between his. His thumb grazes my thigh, and I bask in the feeling of his touch.

"Have dinner with me tonight?" he asks. "See if Syd can take Lexi."

"She can," I respond quickly. He chuckles. "And, yes, I'd love to have dinner."

He links his hand with mine, and we stand together. While I'm dusting my shorts off, I notice a couple of other moms checking out Aiden. I'm not surprised. He's gorgeous, but he's mine, ladies. I lean up on my toes and place a soft, chaste kiss on his lips. He shakes his head and a smug smile rests on his face. I was waiting for a smart-ass comment. Instead, he pulls me into his hard chest and kisses me passionately. My body melts into his. His hand is splayed on my back, and I can feel him add pressure. I don't even care we're in the middle of a kid-friendly zone with a million parents around us—who I'm sure are now gawking. I've waited for two weeks for this man to kiss me like this again.

"*Eww.* Are you done kissing?" Lexi says, covering her eyes with her hand. We look down at her. She peeks through her fingers. "I'm ready to go feed more animals."

"Alright, Lulu, show us the way," I say. She gets in between us and grabs hold of our hands, skipping while we walk to the giraffes.

Chapter two

"**K**eep the change," I say, handing the cabbie a twenty-dollar bill. I look up at Aiden's building and anticipation sends butterflies fluttering through my body. The eight-story building in Tribeca faces One World Trade Center. I love my apartment, but I *really* love this area. Some of the best restaurants and shops are down here. My place is conveniently located near where I work and Central Park, one of my favorite places to go in New York City, but I could easily live here.

It's about an hour until dusk so the sun reflects brightly off the building's glass windows. Aiden told me to be here at seven. I glance at my watch and it's six fifty-five. Digging in my purse, I pull out a mirror and check my makeup and lip-gloss one last time. Walking up the couple stairs to the entrance, I'm greeted by my reflection in the glass doors. I'm wearing a simple, white, above-the-knee swing dress with spaghetti straps. It's August and too hot to wear my hair down, so it's in a loose French braid, off to one side. The beige, wedge sandals make my tan legs look longer. Aiden's a leg man, so I made sure to show them off tonight.

When I walk in, the security guard greets me by name. "Good evening, Ms. Mason." I tilt my head in confusion because

I've never met this guy. "Agent Roberts showed me a picture of you." I smile at the thought of Aiden showing my picture to people. "You can go on up."

I thank him and walk to the elevators. I press the fifth-floor button and wait for the doors to close. I hope being together today proved to him that I'm here for him. As I rock back and forth on my feet, I impatiently wait for the elevator doors to open. When I walk off the lift, I see a note taped to his door. *Meet me up on the eighth floor.* What is he up to? He never ceases to amaze me when he does things for me. I was stupid pushing him away, always keeping him at an arm's length. Thank God he pushed back. He's always known what I was too afraid to admit: we were meant for each other. I always thought Fate was being cruel by causing our two worlds to collide, but now I think she knew Aiden was the only guy who would complete me. And I'm not about to lose it now after everything we've been through.

I step off the elevator onto the eighth-floor foyer and notice only two doors. I look at both doors, assuming this is the penthouse floor. One door has a note taped to it. *Open the door.* I walk to it and slowly turn the knob, wondering what's on the other side.

The view freezes me in place. It's one of the most beautiful terraces I've ever seen. The view is phenomenal, but it's the actual terrace that has me stunned. It's huge. The ground of the entire terrace is tiled with very large, cream-colored tiles. Trees and shrubs line the terrace in varying shapes and different-sized pots. Each pot also has a light, which creates a romantic ambiance all around. One part of the terrace has a royal blue-colored, L-shaped couch and the other part has a table and chairs. In between the two areas is a large wall made with planks of teak. Three rectangular pots sit in front of a trellis that has vines growing up it. It's a very modern and clean design.

"Are you ever going to shut the door?" Aiden stands off to the side, chuckling. I laugh when I notice I'm still holding onto the door.

"Wow, Aiden." I turn and close the door and face him. "It's gorgeous."

His eyes gleam. "That's exactly what I was thinking," he says, his gaze pinned on me. I blush as he appraises my body. One look and I'm already turning to mush. I've never been dependent on a man before, but it's been hard to even breathe without Aiden here these past couple of weeks.

He's holding a tumbler with whiskey-colored liquid in one hand. His other hand is in his pocket. As he brings the glass to his mouth, his eyebrow raises over the brim. His Adam's apple moves as the liquid slides down his throat. I feel the burn he must feel from the liquid wash over me. My body shudders with desire. I take a deep breath and saunter over to him, taking the drink from his hand and take a sip.

"*Mmm...Jack.*"

"No," he rasps, taking the glass from my hand and placing it on the bar behind him. "I guess I need to remind you who I am."

I gasp when he wraps his arm around my waist and thrusts me forward, slamming me into his chest. I bite my bottom lip in response to the desire spiraling in his dark, intense eyes. My pulse quickens and my lips tingle, knowing he's about to devour them. He flashes a cocky, knowing smile before he fuses his lips to mine. There is nothing gentle about this kiss. One hand is on my back and the other grabs my ass. His tongue moves with mine. A deep moan reverberates into my mouth and sends the vibration through my body.

Falling farther into him, I run my hand through his hair. I release all the pent-up frustration from the last couple of weeks into this kiss. His frenzied pace is proof he's doing the same. He bites my lip and pulls back, our chests heaving.

He puts his forehead against mine. "And don't you ever forget it," he muses, kissing me on the nose.

I exhale loudly and look up at him. "You can remind me whenever you'd like."

"Every day, sweetheart. For the rest of my life." The smile I give him reaches my eyes. Those words make my heart swell. "But right now, we need to eat before I lose control and remind you what I feel like inside of you, out here in the open."

Desire tickles deep down into my belly, and I almost tell him to screw dinner. When I see the decorated table with a setting for two and lit candles, I don't want to ruin his plans.

"Whose terrace is this? It seems too nice to belong to the residents of the building." We have a rooftop at my apartment, but there are only a couple of fold-up chairs and a plastic lounger. It's mainly used as a smoking area. Nothing fancy, and *nothing* like this.

"The man who lives in the penthouse owns it," he says, pulling out my chair for me to sit. "He's out of town. When he leaves, he tells me so I can keep watch over his place. I have a key, but I've never really cared about coming up here before, but I thought it'd be the perfect spot to bring you."

"It is perfect up here." The sun has settled below the buildings, and lights from surrounding offices and apartments glow around us like fireflies. Some flicker off while others turn on.

Aiden made chicken piccata for dinner, one of my favorite dishes ever. The slight lemon tang and creamy butter sauce is perfection. I think I'll keep him just for this. Our conversation is light during dinner. I sense he is avoiding the conversation we need to have. *Jessie.* I'd like to sweep her under the rug, too, but we need to talk about what's going to happen when the baby is born. Jessie is due in two weeks. I don't even know if Aiden has talked to her other than the night she showed up to ruin my birthday and engagement party. I've only seen him three times since that night, and I don't really want to spoil dinner, but it's time. I pick up my wine and take a sip. I stare at my half-full glass and twirl it around a couple times. *Screw it.* I swallow the remainder of the wine in one gulp. When it comes to Jessie, I'm thinking the more wine, the better.

Aiden sits back in his chair, head angled as he watches me with an intense expression. I smile innocently and shrug. "Wine is really good," I say. He nods and sits forward to pour some more into my glass.

"Let's go sit on the couch," he says, standing and reaching for my hand. I slip my hand into his large hand, and he squeezes it lightly. "I love you so much, Addison. I'm sorry for the last couple weeks." He sighs. Regret swirls in his eyes. It's hard to see the strong confident man I know and love look like he's lost control.

I push up on my toes and kiss him softly on the lips. "C'mon, let's go sit," I whisper.

We stroll over and sit down on the deep cushions. They're pretty clean for being outside, exposed to the elements. Aiden swings my legs around and places them in between his legs like he did at the zoo. He leans back against the cushions and stares up to the dark sky.

"Have you talked to her?" I ask, breaking the silence.

He shakes his head and then turns toward me. "I don't want to talk to her. I don't think what I have to say will be healthy for a woman who is eight months pregnant." I flash a lopsided smile. He's probably right. "Max has talked to her, though," he says, absently brushing his thumb on my inner thigh.

"I think she's lying," I blurt out. He twists his lips and nods. "If you were so drunk that you can't remember, I have a hard time believing she was able to...or you were able to—"

He places a finger on my mouth to stop me from talking. "I think the same thing, but I can't ignore that she was in my house." He clenches his teeth together and leans forward on his legs. I can physically see how much this is messing with him.

"Has anyone confirmed her due date?"

He looks over to me again with furrowed brows. "What do you mean?"

I shrug. "I mean, she *says* she's due in two weeks, but is she?"

He stares at me for a beat, letting the question sink in. "Wouldn't that be hard to lie about?"

"I guess...We'll see if she's induced or has her naturally." Aiden's confused expression intensifies. He turns his body toward me. "Let's just say, if she's trying to trick you, how she has the baby will definitely be a key factor."

"Okay," he draws out. "I have no idea about pregnancies, so whatever you say I believe."

"*Exactly*. That's what she's counting on, too." He blows out his cheeks. "But if the baby is yours, we'll deal with that. Together," I say, linking my fingers through his.

"Together," he repeats. Our eyes hold, and I search for the confident man I know in the depths of his green eyes. *He's in there.* Aiden raises a brow, asking if I've found what I'm looking for. *Not yet.* He winks at me before breaking our connection. I watch his hand dig into his pocket and pull out his phone. When his eyes find mine again, he flashes a hesitant smile. "Dance with me?"

"Always," I respond. It kills me that he's questioning if I *want to.* He usually demands it, doesn't wait for me to say yes. I want him to pick me up, throw me over his shoulder, and take what he wants. Take, not ask.

He looks down to his phone, avoiding my pleading eyes, and searches for a song. "In Case You Didn't Know" by Brett Young fills the terrace space. I look around for the speakers, but they're hidden. Aiden stands, grabbing my hand on the way up, and draws me to his chest. I wrap my arm around his neck, and he brings my other hand up to his heart. I can feel the beating of his heart under my hand. The constant rhythmic vibration is like Morse code, and he's telling me that he's here with me.

Our bodies sway to the music and the deep timbre of his voice sings to me, telling me so much more than what the words say. I wrap my hand around his and place it on my heart. I want him to feel what he does to me, to never doubt that again. My heart races and I want to scream *"only you can make me feel this way."* Instead, I stay quiet and let our hearts do all the talking.

After the song ends, Aiden tightens his hold on me. "Jesus, Addison. I want you so bad."

"Why are you talking, then?" I bite my lip. *Take, don't ask.*

"Because I can't do that to you." I pull my head back and look up with a questioning expression. "I can't make love to you while I'm wondering if I'm having a baby with another woman." He looks away and sighs. *Is it wrong that I don't care?*

"I'm pretty sure you won't be thinking about anything except me if we make love." My lips curl into a smile. He softly chuckles and shakes his head. "You know I can change your mind." My hand starts to move down his chest. He stops me with a pained look.

"I know you can. Please, don't, sweetheart." The sting of his rejection hurts. My hand tightens, gripping his shirt. "I'm just trying to do the right thing here," he pleads.

My brow furrows. "Right for who? Me? Because it's *not* right. It's. Wrong. So...*so wrong.*" I dig my head into his chest so I can't see his regret. I feel his chest shake. I jerk my head up and he purses his lips to stop himself from laughing. I smack him on the chest. "It's not funny. You can't sing to me, tell me that you love me and that you *want me,* only to reject me. *'Come here, little girl, I have some candy for you',*" I say sarcastically and roll my eyes.

He can't hold back his laughter anymore. I shake my head. I can't believe he thinks this is funny. He leans over and gives me a chaste kiss on the lips but pulls back quickly. "I promise I'll make it up to you."

"I'll hold you to that. Next time, I'm not stopping," I warn. I am not too proud to beg.

"I love you, Addison. With every part of me. Please, don't ever question that."

I exhale, releasing my hurt feelings. I'm being selfish. I don't know why I'm so petrified he'll forget about me. Maybe because I've been burned by Fate before. More than once. Aiden wraps his hand around my neck. His thumb runs along my jaw.

"You're beautiful," he whispers and pulls me to his lips. My lips part and I let out a small moan. He deepens the kiss. Our tongues dance to their own music, a passionate, slow song.

"Well, it looks like you took my advice." I gasp at the sound of a man's voice behind me. I whip my head around and an older man stands there, staring at us with a huge grin. Aiden chuckles. His hand falls from my neck, and he strolls over to the man. The gentleman is dressed in black slacks with a white, button-up shirt. A tie hangs loose around his neck, like he just got off work. I tilt my head, looking at him a little harder. He looks familiar.

"Hey, Mack, what are you doing back so early?" Aiden asks while he shakes hands with him. Why does he look...oh, shit! My eyes widen in surprise.

Mack Livingston, Texas billionaire oil tycoon, is standing a few feet in front of me. I blush thinking about what he just walked in on. I bite my lip and spin around in embarrassment. I run my hands down my dress, take a deep breath, and turn to face him. My steps are light as I walk up and stand by Aiden's side. He reaches for my hand, interlocking our fingers. Mack's smile reaches his eyes when he looks over at me. The soft lines around his sparkling blue eyes reflect years of wisdom and life. His white hair is styled perfectly, not a hair out of place.

"I assume you're Addison?" he asks, holding his hand out for me to shake. I release Aiden's hand and shake the hand of the older man standing in front of me. His handshake is welcoming, yet powerful. Just like him.

"I am," I say, returning his smile. "It's an honor to meet you." I remember doing a report on him in high school for my economics class. I can regurgitate his life history back to him, but I stand here, not knowing what to say. He's a freaking billionaire.

He waves his hand around. "The honor is mine. I was sick of seeing Aiden mope around the last couple of weeks." I look over at Aiden, and he rolls his eyes. "I'm glad he pulled his head out of his ass and finally called you."

"Well, it didn't go quite that way," I tease.

"No, she used Lexi to guilt me."

"Good," he boasts. "Your priorities should be Addison and Lexi right now." My smile grows when I hear him talk about Lexi like he knows who she is. It means Aiden must talk about her. "You know how many women have accused me of being the father of their child?" He throws his hands out. I don't know the answer to that, but I know how many kids he has. Zero. He can't. When he was a child, he had an infection that made him unable to have children of his own. It's public knowledge so I'm surprised any woman is stupid enough to try to pass a child off as his.

He claps and points at me. "Aww, you already know," he says, grinning. I nod. "There are some really desperate women out there and it sounds like one finally caught up with this guy." He jerks his head in Aiden's direction. *Finally?* It sounds like they've known each other for a while.

"Watch it, old man. Addison doesn't need to hear about any of my past indiscretions. She's had to deal with one too many."

"It's good to see you happy, Aiden," he says. His endearing tone surprises me. He and Aiden must be close. "I'm going to leave you to your woman now before I say something that'll put you in the dog house." He reaches over and pats Aiden on the back.

"That's probably a good idea. How long are you in town?"

"Mack, I'm getting lonely," a woman's high-pitched voice rings out. I glance over to the terrace door at a petite blonde wearing a silk robe and five-inch stripper heels. I can tell by her perky nipples that she's not wearing anything under it. She can't be much older than thirty. My mouth is agape for a few seconds before I catch myself gawking and snap it shut.

Aiden reaches over and squeezes Mack's shoulder. "And you wonder how you keep getting yourself in situations," Aiden chuckles.

He shrugs. "What can I say? I'm a sucker for beautiful women."

He's a billionaire man-whore. I bite my cheek so words don't fly out of my mouth. I shouldn't be surprised. He's been married five times—at least, at the time of my report it was five. But seeing it first-hand is eye-opening.

"I'm in town for a couple days. I'll call you tomorrow. Stay up here as long as you'd like," he says, walking away. He turns toward us. "Addison, it was a pleasure to meet you." He smiles wide, and I return the smile.

"You too, Mr. Livingston." *I think.*

"Mack, please, call me Mack." I nod and he winks before turning back around.

After he's out of sight, Aiden turns to face me and grabs a piece of hair between his fingers and tugs. "I guess you know who he is?"

"Well, right now 'sugar daddy' comes to mind," I say with sarcasm. Aiden drops his head and laughs. "Outside of that, yes. How long have you known him?"

Aiden looks up, calculating in his head. "I guess a little over five years. Since I've lived here."

"You guys seem close?"

Aiden nods. "I guess so. He's a great guy. We catch up whenever he's in town, which isn't often. We usually have a beer or dinner. He leads an interesting life."

"I know. I did a report on him in high school. He's a hot topic in Texas. I obviously didn't read about how much of a man-whore he is, though," I murmur. Aiden stifles his laugh.

"You'd be surprised about what you *didn't* read about."

I hold my hand up, shaking my head. "I don't want to know. I have great respect for the guy...which may be slightly tainted right now. He's accomplished a lot, including all the charitable things he's done. Don't ruin that for me." I smirk.

He grabs my hand that's still in the air and steps forward into me. "Where were we?" he murmurs as he kisses the curve of my neck. My eyes flutter closed and my breath catches as the heat of his kisses sends tingles down my back. It takes me a second to focus on where we were. *Damn him.*

I take a step back out of his grasp, and he arches a brow. "You were apologizing that we can't be together, so stop making me want you," I say dryly. He grins.

"Will you sit up here with me for a little longer?" He reaches forward for my hand again.

"Of course." We walk back to the couch and sit like we were before. "How is it that we're engaged and you've never mentioned Mack, yet he knows about me *and* Lexi?"

He looks away briefly, scrubs his hand over his jaw, and then looks back to me. "I'm pretty sure I've told you before that we've gone to dinner." I tilt my head as I run through my memory. I know he has mentioned going to dinner with a friend here and there. "I probably never said Mack Livingston, probably just Mack. He's only in town once a quarter, so we don't get together often," he explains. "He's been in town the last two weeks for a business acquisition, so I've seen him more than normal—seeing as I've been home more than normal."

We talk a little more about Mack but then sit back and listen to the city. Horns from taxis blare below us and music from a neighboring rooftop bar adds a melody to the sound. Two spotlights in the distance sweep across the night sky. The nights here have a language all of their own. I lean my head down on Aiden's shoulder.

"Do you like it here?" Aiden asks.

"Here, as in New York City?"

"No, this area." I lift my head and look at him.

"I love this area," I answer. He nods his head. "Why?"

"I'm just thinking about where we'll live when we get married."

"This area is great, but your apartment is only one bedroom." I scrunch my nose. "But I might be tempted to make it work with access to a terrace like this."

"Good to know," he chuckles.

"I guess I just figured because of space, you'd move into my apartment."

"That's an option," he says looking down at me. "Or we can find a place close to here."

I nod in agreement. "Aiden, I will go anywhere as long as we're together."

Chapter three

"**H**ave we received the data on the prints we collected on the Spring case?" I ask Harper as I peek my head into her office. She looks up at me from her computer and tilts her head. I lift my eyebrows, waiting for an answer she's not giving me. "Well?" I ask impatiently.

Her lips twist. "Addison, we just took those prints yesterday." Her words come out slow and unsure. I roll my eyes and let out an exasperated sigh. Can't people do anything quickly around here? I spin on my heels and stomp to my office. Who can I call to get things moving? I grab my office phone and bring it to my ear while I hold down the receiver button, thinking of whom the best person to call would be. *Hmm.*

"Addison, put down the phone." I look over to Harper as she walks into my office. She walks up to me, takes the phone out of my hand, and hangs it up. "Is today the day?" she asks, sympathetically.

I fall back into my chair, digging the heels of my palms into my eyes. "Yes," I murmur. I sit up straighter and cross my arms. "I've done everything I can possibly do in here," I say, looking around. My desk is spotless; all my paperwork has been filed away or put in my file holder on my desk. I even cleaned my keyboard. Ugh, that was disgusting. I have got to clean more often. "I can't stop thinking about Jessie having Aiden's baby today. It pisses me off even more because I don't even believe it's his!" I push off my chair and it rolls back against the wall, making a *thud*. A growl escapes my lips as I run my hands through my hair.

Harper leans up against my door, shakes her head slightly, and looks down at her watch. "It's four. I'm sure CJ will understand if we took off an hour early. Like you said, you're caught up with everything. Let's go grab a drink." *You don't need to ask me twice.*

"I only have two hours before I have to pick up Lulu, so don't let me drink too much," I say as I open my desk drawer and grab my purse. I wish I could say that I would stop myself, but right now I'm not so sure.

We walk into O'Malley's and Vinnie greats us as we take a seat at the bar. I look around and notice only a couple of other women here. I bet they're not here because their fiancé might become a father by another woman. I slap my forehead. *Stop thinking, Addison.*

"Vinnie, we'll take two glasses of merlot," Harper orders. I'm thankful she didn't order shots. That's a black hole I don't need to fall into tonight, no matter how bad I want to jump headfirst into it. He places our drinks in front of us, and I immediately bring the glass to my lips. I focus on the warm yet smooth red liquid that coats my throat, and it's the first time today my mind isn't focused on Jessie. I slowly put my glass down and stare at it. My mind is blank, and I revel in the emptiness because I know it's not going to last long. Harper allows me this time in silence.

I exhale loudly and turn toward Harper. "Thanks."

"Anytime," she replies. "So, has he talked to her at all?"

I nod my head. I'd encouraged Aiden to talk to her. I know he didn't want to, but he needed to. He reluctantly called her and found out she's staying here in New York, which I'm still not sure why. Aiden has no clue either. I wonder if she's been in New York City this whole time. He's under the assumption the less he knows, the better. I don't like to live like that. I need to know details. She's up to something. Why did she wait eight months to tell him she was pregnant? Where has she been since she left Newport? There are so many unanswered questions. I guess it only matters if the baby is Aiden's. If not, she can pack her bags and get the hell out of our lives forever.

Unfortunately, that's what's bugging me. She knows Aiden is going to have a DNA test done, and I'm almost certain it's not Aiden's. Call it intuition or hope...I just don't believe it's his. What does she get out of this whole thing, knowing it's not Aiden's? What's her next move? I'm certain she has one planned. She's not a stupid woman. I've looked into her a little more these past few weeks. She earned a Master's Degree in Interior Design and owns her own successful interior design business. She owned her own home but sold it seven months ago. She comes from money, so she's not looking for a payout.

"He told her to call him when she goes into labor," I say, propping my head up with my hand and resting it on the bar. Harper picks up her glass and takes a sip. "She's called him five times today just to tell him she felt the baby move." Harper's head falls, and she shakes it. "I know, you think I'm bad. He's a basket case right now, and every time the phone rings with her just telling him the baby moved, Max has to intercept before he blows his shit."

I told him I would take today off to be with him, but he's being stubborn, not wanting to inconvenience me with Jessie.

Too late. We're good right now, so I didn't push it, but he still carries the weight of that guilt inside of him.

***

A week late.

A week of insane anxiousness of waiting for *one* phone call.

The call that hasn't come. I can't say I'm surprised. Jessie never tells Aiden when she's going to the doctor; she only calls him *after* her checkup.

"*Everything is fine,*" she says. "*The baby just doesn't want to come out yet.*"

Right. I want to scream at her, *maybe it's because you're lying about your due date.* Aiden says it doesn't matter because they'll get a DNA test done, regardless. Of course, Jessie has been milking this because she has Aiden's full attention. But the end is in sight. If she doesn't have the baby by next week, they are going to induce her.

"Let's go," Aiden says, walking into my apartment, slamming the door behind him. I freeze midway from putting a glass in the dishwasher and turn to look at him. He throws his keys on the entry table and strides toward me.

"Um...where are we going?"

Sydney called earlier and said she would take Lexi overnight so Aiden and I could have some downtime. When I talked to Aiden, we decided we would just hang out here and watch a movie.

"Go pack an overnight bag." He claps his hands and rubs them together. I watch him for a moment before finally putting the glass in the dishwasher. He's awfully *happy*. I lean against the counter as he traps me with a hand on either side of me.

I cock an eyebrow, wondering what has his mood so light. A carefree smile spreads across his face. "We're getting out of here. Running away from *life*."

I look at him like he can't be serious. "And where would one run to in order to get away from this so-called *life*?" The playfulness in his eyes that's been missing these last few weeks flickers. My hands run up his arms and over his muscular biceps.

"It's a surprise."

"You and your surprises," I say. "Are we going skydiving?"

"No." He taps my nose with his finger. "But nice try. Go pack an overnight bag."

"But Lexi. I didn't tell Syd—"

The incredulous look he gives me stops me. "You don't think I took care of that already?"

"I just needed to make sure."

"Okay, you made sure. Now, go." He grabs my hand and leads me to my bedroom. Whatever he has planned, he's excited. I'll take it over how he's been acting. I grab a bag and throw in an outfit for tomorrow, a swimsuit, and a pair of panties with a matching bra. I giggle to myself, thinking about the last time he told me to pack an overnight bag. I'd debated if I should bring pajamas. *I definitely didn't need them.* That seems like ages ago. The first time he took me to his beach house. The first time I told him I loved him. There were some other firsts, but I am *not* thinking about those.

I find a small makeup bag and put some toiletries in it then zip it up, tossing it into the big bag. Excitement bubbles inside me because we're getting away. We need this break. I wonder if he plans on still being stubborn about doing the *right* thing. It's been over a month since we've been together, and I'm not sure I can stop myself if we're sleeping in the same bed.

"Let's go, woman. Get your sexy ass out here now." Damn, he's in a hurry. I thought I was making good time. I grab my bag and walk into the living room.

"Alright. I'm ready."

He's at my side instantly, taking my bag out of my hands. "I just need to get out of here," he murmurs. The helplessness in his voice pulls at my heart. "I need to reset. And I need you there with me." I slightly nod. I get it. Waiting for *one* moment in time to happen that will change your life forever is consuming. When your vision gets so clouded you can't see straight, you need take a step back and refocus.

This is us. *Refocusing.*

We listen to music in the car rather than talk. I figured we were going to the beach house, but when we drive in the opposite direction on Interstate 78, it's obvious we're not. I open my mouth numerous times to ask where we're going, but then stop myself. *Let him feel in control*, I remind myself.

Aiden's deep voice fills the air sporadically as he sings along with the radio. I turn my head and watch him. His size dominates the small area of the car. I watch as he taps his thumb to the rhythm on the steering wheel. My gaze follows his muscular arms to his taut chest, which is hidden by a worn-out, heather gray T-shirt. FBI is printed across it in black letters, and I'll bet he's had that shirt since Quantico. It looks that old. *I wonder if he'd give it to me?*

"I like when you look at me like that." Aiden's voice interrupts my shirt envy. I look up at him. He's watching the road, but a sly smile creeps across his face, deepening his dimple.

"Actually, I was just thinking I want your shirt." I grin.

He cocks his head my direction. "Is *that* what you were thinking?"

"It was," I reply innocently. "You're the one who always has the dirty thoughts." I pull my leg up under my knee and look forward. Tall trees wrap the sides of the highway, and the setting sun peeks through for the last time tonight.

"Sweetheart, if you only knew." He chuckles. "This is my favorite shirt."

"I can tell."

"It'll be my new favorite shirt on *you* if you wear it and nothing else all day tomorrow." His tone is flirtatious. Heat streaks up my body at the thought of him wanting me naked. My inner goddess jumps up and down, screaming that her god is coming home. *Finally.*

I roll my head to the side, looking at him. "You want me to walk around naked all day with only that shirt on?" I ask coyly.

"Well, technically, you wouldn't be naked." He flashes a wicked smile.

"And what would we do all day, while I'm not *technically* naked and you're not *technically* going to touch me?" *Please, tell me you'll fuck me seven ways till Sunday.* Forget your stupid rule. I reach over and run my index finger down the outline of his obvious bulge.

His body tenses and a low growl erupts from the back of his throat. He takes off his sunglasses and slides them onto the dashboard. When he glances over at me, the heat in his eyes sends flurries of burning need into the pit of my stomach. His hand covers mine, and he pushes it down harder on his cock. It's straining against his jeans, begging to come out. I wet my lips and swallow, my mouth dry from my heavy breaths. I slide my hand out from under his and unbutton his pants. He hisses as I pull the zipper down and free his hard erection. A soft mewl escapes my lips when I see he doesn't have any underwear on.

The sexual tension sucks up all the air in the car, and I feel like I'm drowning. Right now, breathing is the last thing on my mind.

I run my hand down the length of him, and he gasps. "Fuck, Addison," he growls. "You're going to finish what you started. Put your fucking gorgeous mouth on me." His demanding voice lights a fire inside me. I've missed it more than I care to admit. I watch him pull off an exit on the freeway.

I unbuckle my seat belt and lean over his armrest. His hand weaves through my hair. I lick the tip of his cock before I open wide and slide down his shaft. Darkness flows into the car and only the dashboard lights illuminate our bodies.

"Jesus, I've missed that mouth of yours." He slams the car in park, and I'm transported to the first time we did this. His grip tightens around my hair, jerking me back to the present, and I suck harder. His groans spur me on as I work my way up and down. I can feel dampness in between my legs.

It doesn't take long before he's grunting my name, and I can feel his warmth slide down my throat. While he recovers, I lie in his lap, looking up into darkened eyes filled with need. His finger traces my swollen lips.

"We're almost there, so I need you to get in your seat and buckle up because we're not going slow. I need to taste you like I need air right now, but I'm not doing it here. I want to take my time with you. Fuck not touching you." *Thank God.* My body shudders as his hand moves over my breast, down my torso to my groin. He cups my sex, and I arch my back off the seat, moaning from the feel of his fingers digging into me through my shorts.

"I don't think I can wait," I pant. My pent-up desire is so painful, the second he touches me I know I'll explode. I sound like a sex addict right now, craving my next fix that I'd do anything to get it.

After muttering a few curse words, he pushes me up back in my seat and tucks his already hard cock back into his pants. He leans over and kisses me hard then slams the car into drive. As the tires squeal, I grab the handle to hold on, trying to grab traction from his acceleration.

He was right, we were only fifteen minutes away. When we pull into the parking lot of a resort lodge, I look over at him. "You could have told me we were almost here."

"Sweetheart, I have no willpower when it comes to you and that mouth. I will stop whatever the hell I'm doing if you're offering. *Always*." I want to respond "*not* always," but then again, I didn't offer him a blow job two weeks ago.

I cock my head to the side. "I don't remember offering," I tease, biting my lip.

His laugh echoes in the car. "Baby, you whip out my dick and lick your lips like you're about to eat a steak dinner, you damn well are offering." His crass words don't help ease the ache. I hop out of the car and grab my bag from the backseat.

Our steps are hurried to our room. The sexual tension is so thick it's blanketing our surroundings. Everything we pass is a blur and the only thing in focus is our room. I don't have to look up to see the desire and need in Aiden's eyes. I feel it and hear it every now and then when he growls from the back of his throat. His hand is hard in mine as he leads me with purpose.

I'm thrown on the king-size bed, and I sink into the down comforter before the door clicks shut. "Take off your clothes," Aiden demands. He reaches behind his head, tugging off his shirt in one fell swoop. I *was* unzipping my shorts, but I stop short and gawk at his chest and move my gaze down. The muscles in his lower stomach that form a perfect V-shape...it's like a sign saying look down. *So, I do.* He unbuttons his pants and his cock springs free. I lick my lips, still remembering how he felt in my mouth not that long ago.

"Are you going to finish?" Aiden says, looking at me.

"I thought I had, but if you'd like me to go again, I'd be happy to oblige." I smile up at him.

"Woman," he growls. "I was talking about you getting undressed."

Oh. *Oops.* I lift my butt off the bed to pull my shorts down over my hips and he grabs them, yanking them off the rest of the way. His patience is waning, so I whip off my shirt, throwing it on the ground. He hooks his fingers inside the waistband of my panties, pulling them down at a slower pace. I arch my back, reaching underneath to unsnap my bra. When I'm completely bare, he stares down at me. The hunger in his eyes makes my desperate body ache even more. *Touch me, dammit.*

"I feel like I've been on a diet," he rasps. "But I'm about to fucking binge on the taste of you." He falls to his knees, pushing his arms under my thighs and yanking me to his waiting mouth. I cry out at the first swipe of his tongue. He circles my clit and then sucks, sliding two fingers inside me, pumping in and out. I look down my torso and it's sexy as hell to watch him devour me. I run my hand through his hair, gripping it when my body explodes into an abyss of stars.

"I'm sorry, babe." I frown as he stands up, fisting his cock and pumping it once before lining it up at my entrance. I wait for him to tell me what he's sorry for because if he feels he did something wrong just now, I'll let him try again. Instead, he slams into me, and I scream out in pleasure. "Fuck, you're tight," he growls. "I wanted to take my time, but I don't think I can go slow."

"Fuck me, then," I breathe out. His fingers dig into my hips, and he does just that. Our bodies slap together. I lift my hips, meeting his thrusts, and he lets out a guttural groan, watching himself disappear inside of me. He reaches up and grabs my breast in his hand, pinching the nipple, and I cry out. Sweat beads on his forehead.

"Fuuckk, Addison," he roars, throwing his head back. His stomach muscles clench and his body pulses as he empties himself inside of me.

"There is not a sane man in this world who could resist this." He pulls out slowly, watching his cock at my entrance, and then presses it back inside me. I moan as my eyes roll back. "I was fucking insane," he mutters to himself. He pulls out and walks to the bathroom, returning with a towel.

When he lies down beside me, he rolls onto his side and holds his head up with his hand. "Where are we?" I ask, pushing up on my elbows and looking around the room. There is a wall of windows, but it's dark outside, so I can't see anything. It's a typical hotel room, so there is no telling where we are.

"We're in the Poconos."

"*Hmm.* Room is nice." Not like I've seen anything else. I roll to my side, facing him. "You know, there are hotels in the city." The air conditioner kicks on, and I shiver when it blows on my naked body.

Aiden sits up to pull the comforter down, and I crawl underneath. He slips in beside me, and I snuggle against the warmth of his body. "I wanted to get out of the city. You'll understand when you see it in the daylight."

It's quiet here. Even in the dead of night, I can still hear cars outside in the city. I guess I've gotten used to it because I don't notice it anymore—until now, where the silence is unpolluted. My stomach grumbles, and Aiden looks down at me. "Hungry?"

"Yes, but I don't want to get up."

"I want you to see the stars here." His lips graze mine in a quick peck before he rolls over, throws the covers off, and stands up, showing off his magnificent backside. *I want to stay here and watch your gorgeous ass.* He looks at me over his shoulder, waiting for me to move.

I roll my eyes and remove the covers. "I was so warm though," I whine, shivering. "What is it with hotels thinking everyone wants to freeze?"

He chuckles. "You weren't complaining earlier."

I pull up my shorts and look at him. "I guess when you have a ten-inch cock pumping inside of you, you tend to heat up a bit," I quip.

He flashes a megawatt smile, stepping into me. "God, *I love you.* Can you repeat that to me every day, especially when the guys are around?" I laugh and push on his chest so I can finish getting dressed. He takes two steps back, still smiling wide.

"Do guys really *compare?*"

"Fuck yeah," he says.

"Guys are a different breed." He chuckles and I push my head through my shirt, tugging it down over my breasts and tucking part of it into my shorts. "C'mon, I'm hungry and I have some stars to look at."

"Wow," I say in amazement, looking up. We grabbed dinner at a restaurant in the hotel and now we're sitting on a couple of Adirondack chairs on a dock, staring up into the star-filled sky. I forget how bright stars can be without the light pollution drowning them out. "It reminds me of the night we laid on the lawn, watching the stars at Travis's place." I chuckle. "Well... minus the handcuffs."

"I can fix that if you'd like," he teases.

"So, was that officially our first date?" I ask, looking over at him. The beginning of our relationship has been so screwed-up, I don't even know what to call it.

"No," he responds, staring up to the sky. "I'd like to think when I took you to Central Park was our first date. Since you didn't *have* to go with me."

I stare at him for a beat until he turns to me. "As I recall, I don't remember you giving me much of a choice then either, *Mr. Top Gun.*"

"I see nothing wrong with going after what you want." He shrugs. "You should have seen your face."

I pull myself up in my chair and look over at him. He's watching the stars, hands behind his head, legs spread wide.

"I was mortified," I snicker. I still can't believe he did that.

He glances at me and the playful smile on his lips along with his relaxed body makes coming here worth it. I sit back and enjoy the clean night air. The sounds of crickets and frogs echo off the still lake surrounded by tall, lush trees. My eyes close. The serene environment relaxes me to the point of sleep. I hear Aiden's chair creek. I open my eyes, and he's standing over me.

"Let's go, I'm starving," he says.

"We just ate."

The wicked gleam in his eyes tells me he's not referring to food. "I told you, I starved myself for the past month and I'm making up for it this weekend." My body tingles and my pulse quickens. His words are like a circuit to my body and he just hit the on button.

***

The air conditioner kicking on wakes me up. I roll over, looking at Aiden sound asleep. It must be morning because I can see slivers of light coming through the blinds. He's lying on his back and his dark hair is messy and wild against his pillow. I'm not sure if that's from sleeping or *me*. My fingers twitch to touch it again. His five o'clock shadow has turned into a sexy stubble. Dark hairs line his defined jaw. My mind takes me back to last night, how that scruff felt against my most sensitive area. *Fan-fucking-tastic.* I close my eyes and my breath vibrates as my body starts to hum.

I move off the bed as quietly as I can and go to the bathroom. My face is flushed when I look at my reflection in the mirror. I quickly go to the bathroom and brush my teeth. When I step back into the cold room, I spot Aiden's FBI shirt. My mouth curls into a smile as I tiptoe over to it and slip it on. It drapes over my naked body. *Mmm.* It still smells like him. Aiden's asleep when I crawl back on the bed. The movement jostles him, and he moves his arm behind his head but remains sleeping. I pull the sheet down so it uncovers his cock. I bite my lip, drinking in his sexy body. *Thank God for morning erections.*

I want him to feel as worshipped as he makes me feel every time he touches me. I straddle him, wrapping my fingers around his already hard cock and pump once. A low groan falls from his lips. When I look up, vibrant green eyes stare at me. I align him at my entrance and slide down until he's sheathed from root to tip, moaning from the fullness of him inside me. I lift up from my knees and grind my hips back down. My body quivers from the sensitive nerve endings.

"Fuck, that feels good." His voice is still raspy from sleep and the deep sound makes me move faster. His fingers move up my thighs, and he seizes my hips. He holds my hips higher as he pistons below me, spearing me with his cock. I lift the T-shirt I'm wearing and grab my heavy breasts, pinching my nipples. I cry out with pleasure. When he loosens a hand from my hip, I continue riding him. His shirt covers both of us so he reaches under and finds my swollen clit, circling it with his thumb.

"Yes," I scream out. I'm almost there. The fire building inside of me is about to explode.

"Ride me hard, Addison," he commands. The way his cock swells inside of me, I can tell he's almost there, too. I slam down on him, grinding my hips back and forth as I do. We get there together and any coherent words disappear in the grunts and cries and deep groans. I fall on top of him, breathless. Our labored breaths are all we can hear over the air conditioner.

"Can I make that a mandatory wake-up call from now on?" he pants.

I put my chin on his chest, looking up at him. His face is red, and he's sporting a sexy half-grin. He wags his eyebrows, and I laugh. I take another deep inhale and exhale and kiss his chest before pushing myself up.

"I've decided you can't have my shirt," he says unapologetically. I huff, looking down at him. "I thought it was my favorite shirt before, but now it's my *fucking* favorite shirt. Whenever I wear it, I'll think of you riding my cock." He shakes his head and sits up. "Sorry," he murmurs against my lips. *I guess I'll just have to steal it.*

After breakfast, Aiden leads me back to the dock we sat on last night. I couldn't see the magnificent view in the darkness, but in daylight I can see why Aiden wanted to bring me here. The tranquility fills my body, pushing out all my anxiety and worries.

He tells me to stay on the dock. I watch him walk up to a little shack and talk to a guy. When he comes back, he's carrying a couple oars. He flips his hat backwards and then bends down to pick up a canoe lying in a row of others. When he wears a hat, he looks younger. It takes the edge out of his FBI-agent persona. Now I know why he wanted me to wear my bathing suit.

We carry the canoe to the dock, and Aiden tells me to get in. The little boat sways with my steps, and I sink down into it, holding onto the sides. *Shit.* It feels like it's going to tip. Aiden chuckles so I flip him off. "Just make sure to sit in the middle," he says, watching me scoot from seat to seat. *In the middle.*

When he steps into it, I try and steady the damn thing. "Do you know what you're doing," I say, panicking a little.

"You know how to swim, right?" he says, grinning.

"You dump me over, I'm going to kill you." I narrow my eyes at him. His laugh echoes all around us. He sticks the oars in the water and starts rowing. We're facing each other and since he seems to know what he's doing, I sit back and relax. His arms flex each time he rows, and I can't seem to stop staring at them. Aiden clears his throat. My eyes find his, filled with amusement. I shrug, not caring that I was caught. You'd have to be blind not to appreciate his gorgeous arms.

He stops rowing and I look around. We're in the middle of the lake, not another boat in sight. It's just us. "It's gorgeous out here," I say. Aiden takes off his hat for a second while he slips his shirt off and leans back, putting his hands behind his head.

"*Mmm-hmm.*" He takes a few deep inhales, pulls his hat down low, and closes his eyes. The heat of the sun shines on his tanned chest. I twist my lips, watching his chest move up and down. *Is he asleep?* I look around, wondering what to do. I think about grabbing the oars, but I'm afraid to move.

"Aiden," I say. He doesn't move. I sigh. I can't believe he brought me in the middle of lake and then fell asleep. Maybe a little water will wake him up? I slowly lean over, trying to reach the water but the boat leans, too. "Shit," I mutter under my breath, sitting back up.

I look at Aiden and the boyish grin on his face pisses me off. I kick him with my foot. "What do you think is so funny? Stop pretending to be asleep." His grin widens. He rights his hat and leans forward, crawling over the seat that separates us. The canoe starts to rock, and I grab the sides again. "Okay, stop moving. Go back to sleep," I quip. A wicked gleam flickers in his eyes as he continues to slink toward me.

"What's wrong? You usually like to rock the boat." His eyebrow shoots up.

"Maybe metaphorically," I snap as he rocks the canoe more. "Aiden." My voice rises an octave in warning. Does he stop? *No.* The bastard grabs the sides and rocks it more. The closer he gets to me, his wicked smile grows. I know it's coming before it happens, but it doesn't stop the scream that escapes my lips when we're tossed from the canoe.

When I surface, I spit the lake water out of my mouth. *Gross.* I tried to snap it shut before hitting the water, but I was too late. Aiden bobs up beside me, wiping the water from his eyes and putting his hat back on...backwards. I splash him in the face, and he chuckles.

"Asshole," I laugh. I kick my feet to stay afloat. The water feels refreshing from the heat. Aiden swims up to me, wrapping his hands around my waist.

"I like you wet." He bites my lip and grins as his hand moves down to my ass. I slap him in the chest and push off him to swim back to the canoe.

"We are not having sex in this dirty lake water, so don't even think about it."

He swims behind me. I turn around, swimming backwards, keeping my eye on him. I don't trust him to keep his hands to himself. He smirks before he dives under water. The murky water makes it hard to see where he is. I nervously laugh, spinning around looking for him. Adrenaline rushes through me and my pulse picks up. I feel like a shark is about to attack me. I look to the banks to see if I'm close enough to swim.

Suddenly, I'm pulled underwater. I snap my mouth closed and try to release the hold Aiden has on my foot. *I'm going to kill him.* I reluctantly open my eyes. He's grinning at me under water. He releases me but grabs my waist before I can get away. I let out a scream and take in some water. He must see me choking because he pulls me up. When we break the surface I'm already coughing. He swims us to the canoe, and I grab hold of the side

He pats my back. "You weren't supposed to drink the water."

I turn and glare at him. "Really?" I say through my coughs.

He holds on to the side of the canoe beside me. When I stop coughing, he inches toward me. "I'm sorry," he says softly.

I clear my throat. "It's okay. I'm alright. You just surprised me."

He smiles, inching closer. "You know, since you *already* have lake water *inside* of you, what's a little more?"

My mouth falls open, and I roll my eyes. "You are insatiable."

"*That* should not surprise you."

I hold my ground about not having sex in the lake. But the rest of the day, I can't say I resisted his advances. He certainly made up for the month of abstinence. By the time we leave, I'm fully sated and the tenderness between my legs is a reminder of our time spent together.

It was perfect.

Unfortunately, we have to go back to *life*.

Chapter four

Aiden

I was hoping my time with Addison could get me through this mess. Make today easier. It fucking didn't work. I could become a dad today. The weight of it is so heavy I can barely catch my breath. I glance over at my clock on the nightstand. It glows five o'clock. My eyes burn from being wide open the entire night. Jessie is supposed to be at the hospital by nine this morning to be induced. She asked me to be there with her to watch *our* little girl, Presley, be brought into this world.

My heart pounds just thinking about it. If she ends up being mine, I want to be there. How horrible would that story be? *Sorry, Presley, I wasn't there to see you born because I didn't think you were mine.*

Fuck.

Can't breathe.

I roll over and pound a pillow with my fist. Deep down, I don't think she's mine. I don't remember seeing Jessie the entire three days I was there. And if something happened the night Ryan got there, I just can't believe I wouldn't remember. Even as fucked up as I was, I remember Ryan being there so why would I not remember Jessie, or better yet...fucking her?

The same questions fill my head that fill Addison's. If she's not mine, what's the point of all of this? I have a feeling if I find out she's not mine, this isn't the end. Jessie has a plan. Fuck! I make plans, I'm not the target of them.

I throw the covers off me and swing my legs around to the floor. I need to hit the gym to burn off some of this negative energy before I head to the hospital.

The sun is barely peeking over the horizon as I walk to the gym. For a city that never sleeps, this is probably the quietest time of the night. *Or morning.* A few people are out jogging and vendors are starting to set up their carts. In another hour, this place will be packed.

I take in a deep breath of fresh morning air. At least fresh for New York City. I pull out my phone and type out a text to send to Addison but then erase it. I have no idea what to say to ease her mind, so I stuff my phone back in my pocket. She's probably going out of her mind, too. The all-too-familiar feeling of guilt rises inside of me. We should be planning a wedding, not planning a DNA test to find out if I cheated on her.

Lexi is the only daughter I planned on having anytime soon. I requested information on adoption and planned on showing Addison the night I proposed, but that blew up in my face. I haven't changed my mind about Lexi; I would be honored to be her father. Like the wedding, any talk of adoption will have to wait. This sucks. Two innocent children are stuck in the middle of this out-of-control situation.

How the hell did my life get to this point?

I look around the gym when I get there, debating over what I should do first. Run. *As fast as I fucking can.* Getting situated on the treadmill, I crank up the speed and my feet hammer down with each step. If only I could run faster than my thoughts.

***

"I'm here for Jessie Carver," I tell the front desk receptionist. She motions for me to go on back. After getting home from the gym and showering, I received a text from Macie saying what room Jessie was in. I swipe my sweaty hands down my jeans as I walk down the hallway. *I can do this.* We don't know if she's mine, and we won't know for a couple days. I steady my breathing before rounding the corner into Jessie's room.

"Aiden!" Jessie squeals. "You're here." A voice that I once enjoyed sends chills of disgust down my spine. Even though she could be the mom of my daughter, I will never forgive her for what she has done. I will play nice for the sake of Presley, but if she thinks we're going to play house, she's crazier than I thought.

"I'm here for Presley, Jessie. Let's get that straight," I remind her. She rolls her eyes and huffs.

"Did you bring your fiancée?" she says, her voice dripping with sarcasm. "Because I don't want her anywhere near our baby." I swallow the words, wanting to jump out of my mouth. I suck in a deep breath, letting it out slowly through my nose.

"Jessie..." I pause to get a better handle on my emotions, "... if Presley is mine, Addison *will be* a part of her life."

"You think so, Aiden?" Jessie sits up straighter in her bed. "You know, maybe I don't want my baby to have a paternity test. *Maybe* you don't deserve to be her father if you're going to have a dangerous person around my little girl. I mean, she tried to kill me." Her voice raises a couple octaves.

"She did not, Jessie. And if you want to play this game, I'll get a court order to have the DNA test. No matter what, we will find out the truth, so stop fucking with me," I spit out.

"Okay," Macie says, intervening. "Aiden, why don't you go wait in the waiting room?"

I glance at her and then back to Jessie. "You know where to find me," I mumble and then stalk out of the room. I stomp down the white halls of the hospital, mumbling incoherently. People walk past and look at me like I'm crazy.

No, I'm not crazy, I'm fucking pissed.

If she thinks Addison won't be a part of my daughter's life, she's insane. And now she doesn't want a DNA test? That shit isn't surprising. I walk into the waiting room and spot Ryan and Max sitting down at a table in the corner, talking. I'm glad to see them. Maybe they can talk me off this ledge.

"Fuck. Fuck. Fuck." I shrink down in one of the empty chairs; the guys stop talking and stare at me. "What?"

"You look like shit," Max says.

A bitter laugh comes out. "I've had better days."

"Did you go see Jessie?" Ryan asks.

My jaws clench. "Yes," I hiss. They both tilt their head. "Can you believe this shit? She told me Addison couldn't be anywhere near *her* child and *maybe* she doesn't want a DNA test done."

Max stares at me for a moment and nods his head slightly. "Do you want to know what I think?"

"I know what you're thinking. The same thing I am. She's supposedly two weeks late and now she doesn't want a DNA test. Well, fuck that. She's torn my world inside out for the last couple months. I'm going to get a DNA test done even if I don't think this baby is mine just for confirmation."

"You want me to call Jaxon?" Ryan says, sitting forward with his elbows on the table with his phone in hand. It comes in handy having a best friend as an attorney.

"Probably a good idea."

"If you go that route, you know it can take weeks," Max chimes in.

"I don't think I have a choice."

"You always have a choice. It just might not be Jessie's choice." I catch the undertones to Max's voice. Max has people who can run the DNA test, we would just have to secretly get Presley's DNA.

"Do it. I'm not waiting weeks to get an answer. She brought this on herself."

A few hours later, Macie appears and tells us Jessie's almost ready to start pushing. She talks about things I have no clue about. Like effacement and dilation. *I don't even want to know.* She looks expectantly at me, waiting to see if I want to be a part of that. My eyes shift away.

That would be a no. She's not taking that experience away from me with a child who isn't mine. The more minutes that tick by this morning, the more convinced I become that Presley isn't mine anyway.

She shakes her head in disappointment. She thinks it's mine. I hate that Jessie has used her best friend. It's going to crush Macie when she finds out.

"I guess I'll keep you updated," she says and spins around and stomps off.

"She just can't see Jessie lying to you about the baby," Ryan says apologetically.

"What do you think?" I ask, staring at him right in the eyes.

"At first, I didn't know. I saw her leave your house, Aiden. I know she was there. But the fact she's two weeks late, *supposedly*, and now trying to delay a DNA test, I have my suspicions, too."

I nod and scrub my hand over my face. "Have either of you thought about if Presley isn't mine...what could be the reason she did all this, other than to cause a lot of problems between Addison and me? She had to know I would run a DNA test."

"Hmm..." Max says, sitting back in his chair, arms crossed. "I've tried, but I'm coming up blank. She's gone through a lot of trouble to make you think Presley is yours and to have it blow up that fast seems too easy."

"My thoughts exactly."

"Not much we can do about it other than wait it out," Ryan states matter-of-factly. I'm not sure how much more waiting it out I can take.

"Can we talk about something else?"

"I hear Jaxon is going to Florida next month for a couple weeks." Amusement fills Ryan's face.

"You're an asshole." I chuckle. As much as I hate Jaxon and my sister together, there are bigger problems in my life right now. "I guess if my sister is going to fall in love with someone, at least it's with someone I trust."

"Wow," Ryan says, surprised. "I never thought I'd hear those words come out of your mouth." I shrug. Katie's an adult now, and I can't stop her from loving someone, even if it's one of my best friends. He's fully aware if he hurts her, he'll have to deal with all of us.

We bullshit the rest of the morning while we wait. The guys try to keep the conversation light, but no matter what, they can't lighten the load straining my body. My knee bounces up and down in anticipation. I've looked at my phone a million times, even though it sits on the table, laying right side up. Even if I weren't paying attention to it, I still wouldn't miss a call or a text because it's right in front of my face.

I sigh, looking at it again. I wish Addison would call me. Should I call her? I've already brought so much shit to her door with Jessie, I don't know. She's been amazing being there for me these last couple weeks. Especially after I got my head out of my ass.

"Just call her," Max says in his no-nonsense voice. I glare at him. It's not that simple, is it? He lifts his brow as if to tell me, *yes, it is that simple.* I growl, snatching my phone off the table as I push up out of the chair. I hear laughter behind me as I walk out of the sliding doors. *Bastards.*

"Hi," Addison answers quickly. I close my eyes and lean against the building, savoring her sweet southern accent.

"Hey, beautiful," I say, soberly.

"How's it going?"

I sigh. "It's supposedly going."

"You're not in there with her?" She sounds surprised. My shoulders drop. *Fuck.* Is that what she's been thinking all morning?

"No, Addison. The *only* person I'm going to experience that with is you." Silence fills the phone line for a few moments. Why isn't she saying anything? "Sweetheart?"

She clears her throat. "Sorry." I can hear the emotion in her voice. "I just...I just had this picture in my head..."

"I'm sorry. I should've called you earlier," I say quickly. "I just had to calm down a bit. Max and Ryan are here with me."

"Why were you upset?"

I groan in frustration. "Jessie's threatening not to do a DNA test."

She lets out an audible gasp. "I knew it! I knew once the time came she would start with excuses. She is so predictable. You know why she's doing it, right?" she asks, her voice escalated with each word.

"Yes." I sigh heavily.

"What are you going to do?"

"I'm taking care of it. We'll know by tomorrow."

"Got it," she says in understanding. "I love you, Aiden, no matter what."

"I love you, too, Addison. I'll call you with an update later."

I touch the end button and my hands fall slack at my sides. A lady who looks like she's about to pop and her significant other are walking up to the front doors. The man looks like he's about to cry, and the woman is taking in quick breaths, releasing a long one at the end.

"Grow some balls, Jason. I'm the one in labor. Stop crying," she screams, hitting him in the arm. I bite my lip, holding in the chuckle trying to escape. I can imagine Addison saying something like that. God, I can't wait for her to have my children.

I watch the doors shut behind them only to open again. Max is standing there with his hands in his pockets.

"She had the baby," he says.

This is it. Even though I'm almost positive she's not mine, I can't be one hundred percent sure. I might be a dad at this very second, and I'm about to look into the eyes of a child who might be mine. I push off the wall with my foot, sticking my phone into my back pocket and walk back inside.

"How are they?" I ask as we walk toward the nursery.

"Both are doing well. They're cleaning Presley up right now," Ryan says, pointing at a huge piece of glass in front of us. We walk up and watch nurses tend to the babies. Some are sleeping and some not so much. One of the not so much ones is Presley. She is pissed off and beet red. I would be, too, baby girl, if they were smearing greasy crap in my eyes. They weigh her in front of us and boy does she have a set of lungs. It's not until they clean her up and wrap her in some white blanket that she settles down. She's wrapped so tight, I'm surprised she can breathe.

"Don't you think that's a little too tight," I ask the guys, not taking my eyes off her.

"Fuck if I know," Max answers. "It doesn't look comfortable."

"I'd hate not to be able to stretch my arms. It looks like they Saran Wrapped her. It doesn't look right," Ryan comments.

We all stand there and gaze at the baby. And then she opens her eyes and looks right at me. Blue eyes stare up at me. She blinks a couple times. She has little dark blond hairs on top of her head. She's beautiful. She reminds me of...

"Is it weird I'm thinking she looks like Addison? God, that's messed up." Holy shit, this baby thing is messing with my head.

"No, she kind of does. But all babies are born with blue eyes. Not sure where she got the light hair, though," Ryan answers, looking over at me and then back to her. Jessie's natural hair color is dark brown, just like mine. "She doesn't look anything like you."

My eyebrows furrow, looking at Ryan. "She looks like a raisin right now. I don't think you'd be able to tell who a kid looks like when they're first born." One thing is for sure, we're all mesmerized by her.

"Isn't she beautiful?" Macie coos from behind us. Ryan turns to her and pulls her to his front so she can see.

"She is," Ryan replies, resting his head on top of hers. "Hopefully we'll have one soon."

I whip my head in their direction. "Are you guys trying?"

Macie sighs. "We've been trying," she says, defeated. "For what feels like forever."

I slap Ryan on the back. "It'll happen. You guys will be great parents." How I wish we were staring at their baby right now.

"Thanks," he says quietly.

"Do you want to go hold her?" Macie says, clearing her throat and glancing up at me. She tries to hide wiping away a tear by rubbing her whole face.

"Macie," I say, looking away.

"Aiden, *you don't know*. You'll regret it for the rest of your life if you find out you are."

I turn my attention back to Presley. She's wide awake and so small. I'm afraid I'll break her. At least with Lexi, I can play around with her, throw her in the air. I don't ever feel I'm going to hurt her. I've never held a baby before.

"I will. Just give me some time." She lays her hand on my back, so I reach around and pull her into my side. We stand there for a few more moments in silence before she speaks.

"I'll go check on Jess. She should be cleaned up by now. They moved her to room 410."

"Thanks, Mace." I kiss the top of her head before she turns out of my arms and walks away.

"How are we going to do this?" Max asks. He's back to business.

"I'll go into Jessie's room and hold Presley. I'll need a swab on hand, so I can do it when she's not looking." My voice is hushed. Both guys nod in understanding. I look back at Presley and wonder. *Who's your daddy, little girl?* Holy shit! I look up to the ceiling and grimace in disgust. I'm not sure if I'm madder that I thought that just now or because I have used that line on a grown woman. *Never again.*

Max's hand slaps my back. "Let's go get some lunch, then we'll come back."

After lunch, our plan goes off without a hitch. Max distracted Jessie for a few minutes by showing her pictures he took of Presley when she was in the nursery. I was caught off guard, too busy staring into the eyes of Presley. She's beautiful. Her head fits into my entire hand. When my brain finally caught up to what he was doing, I took the swab without anyone noticing.

Now, we wait.

Chapter five

Don't get mad, I tell myself over and over. But this sucks. A few minutes ago, Aiden's phone dinged with a text. He's in the shower so I just glanced at it to make sure it wasn't important. The picture caught my attention so I opened it. *This is what you get for being nosey!*

It was from Jessie. A picture of Aiden holding Presley, and she captioned it with "she misses her daddy." Spear through my heart. I *hate* that woman, but I can't look away from the picture. My eyes start to mist. Looking at this huge man, *my man*, holding a beautiful, tiny baby that isn't mine is heart wrenching. And the worst part, she looks like a child we would've had together. I'm staring at the picture when Aiden walks in, towel around his waist.

"What's wrong?" Aiden asks.

I take in a deep breath and let it out slowly. "Jessie texted you a picture," I say, holding out his phone for him to take. When he reaches to take it from my hand, his hand extends to my wrist and he pulls me to him. He takes the phone with the other hand and throws it on the bed without looking at it. I guess he doesn't need to look at it since he was there.

My arms wrap around his taut chest. Water still drips down his muscular back. I dig my fingers into his back as he draws me so close there isn't an ounce of space between us.

"I'm sorry. I'm sorry for all of this," he says, letting out a soft sigh.

A flood of emotions bubble up inside of me. My eyes fill with tears I can't control. He holds me tighter. "Before she was here, I felt like I could handle it. It wasn't real yet." My throat clogs with emotion. "But now...seeing her in your arms...I'm so jealous, and I don't know how to stop feeling this way," I say, anger taking hold. "And to top it off, she doesn't look like either of you! She looks like me! How ironic is that?" I feel his chest shake, and I pull away to see his face. "Why are you laughing? It's not funny."

"I thought the same thing." One corner of Aiden's mouth twitches. "I don't expect you to be okay with this." His expression turns serious. He pushes my hair behind one ear, cupping my neck as his thumb caresses my cheek. "Did I look at Presley in amazement and wonder? Yes. But the whole time I was thinking I can't wait to have this with you. *She's not mine. I know deep down, she's not."

Aiden's hands glide down my body, and he lifts me up. I wrap my legs around him, loosening his towel and it falls to the ground. He backs us up and lays me on the bed. My mind takes a pivot as heat rushes down to my core, feeling his arousal between us.

"You mean everything to me and nothing will get in the way of us," he says, slowly unbuttoning my shirt. His lips follow his hands, and he places tender kisses on my bare skin as my shirt is opened. He keeps going down to my pants, undoing them and pulling them off, kissing his way back up. A text dings on his phone, but he ignores it. Then it rings. I look down at him, and he flashes a salacious smile. "Nothing. Will. Get. In. The. Way," he says, stopping and kissing me between each word. Goose bumps spread across my body.

He drags his fingers up my thighs, and I shiver from his touch. He kneels on the bed, positioning himself between my legs. He leans over, taking my breast in his mouth, lapping it with his tongue and sucking. I arch my back and moan. I can feel his heavy cock at my entrance. I wrap my legs around his waist and move my hips against him.

He leaves a trail of kisses up my chest, moving to my neck. I lift my chin, giving him easier access. His intoxicating touch always leaves me craving more. He nips my earlobe and groans. My fingers score his back as I try to position my hips so he can slide inside of me.

"You don't have to ask..." he rasps into my ear. "Just take." He thrusts his cock inside of me. I cry out, and my eyes roll back at the overwhelming sensation of pleasure bordering on pain. He sits back on his knees, his fingers grip my hips. His eyes rake over my body and the hunger in them makes my nerves tingle from head to toe. Little electrical sparks explode on my skin, making me writhe underneath him. I place my feet down on the sides of his legs and grind my hips, begging him to move. He lets out a guttural moan, driving in and out of me. His arms are flexed, his stomach muscles tight as he takes control. My breaths quicken and my cries increase. He reaches down in between us. His thumb circles my throbbing clit. My back lifts off the bed, and I scream out his name as my orgasm rips through me. He picks up his pace, pounding inside of me.

"Fuck!" he roars, falling on top of me. His whole body convulses. I can feel his chest heaving while he comes down from his climax. He stays quiet longer than I expect him to. His nose nuzzles my neck.

"You okay?" I whisper. I feel him shake his head.

"You don't *ever* have to ask me if I'm okay when I'm inside of you." He pulls in a deep inhale and lifts his head to let it out. Pushing up on his elbows so he's inches from my face, he flashes a half-grin and pushes his hips into me. I moan softly. "Because when I'm inside of you, everything is fucking perfect."

Unfortunately, *perfect can't stay perfect forever*. Life doesn't stop, but it's the moments of perfection that can get us through anything. The key is to remember them and not let obstacles stand in the way of finding our way back to each other.

After Aiden cleans us both up, he slips on his jeans and winks at me. He pulls out his phone from his front pocket. "It was Max," he says, looking at his phone. He puts it up to his ear and listens to a message. I watch his expression for any clues, but he gives nothing away.

"What'd he say?" I ask after he listens to the voicemail.

"He wants both of us to meet him at his hotel room." He picks up his wallet off the bedside table and sticks it in his back pocket. "He got the results."

"And he didn't tell you?"

"Max doesn't leave information on voicemails." I roll my eyes as I stand up.

"Mr. Spy Man could've just said yes or no. Nobody would've known what he was talking about."

Aiden cracks a smile and slaps my ass. "Get dressed. Something's up because he sounded serious." My body freezes. What if she *is* his? I'll have to deal with Jessie my entire life. This is the first time I've had this feeling that maybe she is his. "Addison, don't."

"But what if—"

"We're not speculating anything. We'll deal with actuals. And if you get your ass moving a little faster, we'll find everything out quicker." He stares at me with a lifted brow.

"Okay! I'm moving."

When we knock on the door to Max's hotel room, Aiden squeezes my hand. I look up to him. "You okay?" Our drive here was in silence. I don't doubt both our minds were too busy flashing images of *what ifs*.

I let out a deep exhale. "Yes. You?"

He nods slowly, unsure. "You're here, so yes."

"I love you." I offer a reassuring smile.

Max opens the door, holding it wide so we can walk in. The room is a suite, so it has a living room and a separate bedroom. Ryan is sitting on the couch, his knee bouncing up and down. That's a bad sign. Aiden pulls me with him into the room, and we sit in the couple chairs Max has set up around the coffee table. I sit down slowly, feeling like we're walking into an intervention. Ryan glances at Aiden and then his gaze lands on me. There's something wrong. Aiden must feel it, too.

"What the hell is going on?" He narrows his eyes at Ryan and then turns his attention to Max, who sits down on the couch.

"You're not the father," Max declares. Aiden's body deflates like a balloon was just let loose. I want to stand up and jump up and down. *I knew it.*

"Holy shit," he rasps, grabbing my leg. Relief settles into his face, and he manages a soft smile. I put my hand over his and squeeze.

"But..." Max starts, pulling our attention back to him. *But, what?* We only needed a yes or a no. There shouldn't be a *but*.

"I told my guy to run a familial DNA test since we were pretty sure Aiden wasn't the dad. You just never know." He looks at me and I nod in understanding. I would've done the same thing. We run familial DNA tests all the time. "There was a match."

"That's good. At least Jessie can't lie about who the dad is then," I say.

"It wasn't an exact match. The match is a relative of the father. Of course, you know we can't determine which relative though," Max says to me. I nod again, wondering where this is going. Max leans forward on his knee, weaving his fingers together. The seriousness of his expression is almost frightening.

"Max, you're not one to usually beat around the bush. What the hell are you holding back?" Aiden asks, mimicking Max by sitting forward.

"Presley is related to Travis."

Wait. What? I jerk my head to Aiden and then back to Max. I don't think I heard that right. I couldn't have heard that right.

"What did you say?"

"She is somehow related to Travis, which means—"

"I know what the hell it means," I snap, standing up and walking around. My eyes bounce from spot to spot. Never in my wildest *what ifs* did this scenario ever go through my mind. How? *Who?* I spin around, looking back to the guys. Ryan has a look of guilt as he fidgets with his watch, Max is staring at me, and Aiden's head is lowered. "What don't I know? What am I missing here?"

Aiden jumps up and walks to me. "Sweetheart." There's panic in his eyes. I take a step back.

I put up a hand to stop him. He knows something. "No! If Travis isn't the father, who else is related to Travis other than me? Because I'm sure the fuck not the father!" I scream, frustrated they're holding something back.

Aiden runs his hands through his hair, looking up briefly before our eyes lock. He blows out a sigh. "You have a brother."

The words suspend in the air like time stopped right as he said them. I gasp and my eyes widen in disbelief. "What?" My voice is barely audible.

Aiden swallows, looks at the guys, and then back to me. "I... forgot." His voice trails off and his eyes plead for understanding.

My head cocks to the side. I'm taken back by his answer. "You forgot?" I say sarcastically. "How do you forget something like that, Aiden?"

I feel hurt and betrayed by the man I love more than anything. I don't understand. How could he keep this from me? I open my mouth to say something but snap it shut. The tightness in my throat prevents words from forming. I shake my head, whip around, and storm out of the hotel room. I just had the air knocked out of me, and I'm having a hard time breathing.

"I have a brother," I say out loud to no one. The words are foreign on my lips. It feels like I'm lying to myself. I pace the hotel floor hallway and hear a door open behind me, but I don't turn around. I know it's Aiden. When I get to the end of the hallway, I look out the window and see nothing. I'm blinded by deceit. My mind is too busy trying to grasp this new information thrown at me. After a few moments, I turn back toward Aiden. He leans against the door, hands in his pockets, eyes cast down.

My feet move like I've got weighted shoes on. I'm trying to understand why he wouldn't tell me, but I can't come up with anything. When I finally make it to him, I whisper, "Why?"

"Addison..." he pauses for a beat and lifts his head, meeting my eyes. "You have to understand. See this from where I stand.

I found out about Travis's son when I first started working for him. He had me check up on him every few months to make sure he was fine. He was one of many people in Travis's world that I checked on for him." I cock my eyebrow at the word *many.* "He's his only son. Anyway, fast forward two and a half years later when I finally find out Travis was your father, it was the furthest thing on my mind at the time."

I think back to that day, how we've come full circle. We're here because of that week. After he found out Travis was my father, Aiden went to the beach house and that's when Jessie claims they created a baby.

"And then you were kidnapped."

He stops talking and lets me gather my thoughts. I pushed him away for months. And when he came back, we had the Lexi situation. I drop my head. We've had a rough couple of years.

"Addison, I truly am sorry I didn't tell you. But, please, believe me when I say I really didn't remember." He reaches out for my hand, and I don't stop him this time. "As soon as he said Presley was related to Travis, it all came back to me."

"How sure are you he's the father, though?"

"Travis doesn't have any living relatives, except you and your brother."

"You didn't know about me at the time...there could be more of us out there." I shake my head at the absurd thought. I can't believe I have a brother, let alone think I could have more.

"It's definitely a possibility." He lifts one shoulder in a shrug.

"But either way, Presley is my niece," I say slowly. Aiden nods. How the hell did Jessie pull this stunt off? I can't imagine she randomly found the one person in this entire world who is related to me. Was this her plan all along?

"How did she know?"

"Let's go inside and I'll explain." I nod and he holds the hotel key to the reader and it clicks open. The cool air from the room feels good on my heated body.

"Are you okay?" Max asks as soon as we walk inside. *Define okay?*

"I can't believe I have a brother," I say. "Does he know Travis is his father?" I glance at Aiden.

"Yes. He was put up for adoption when he was born."

"Where does his live?"

Aiden groans a little. "Here."

My eyebrows shoot up. "Here, as in New York City?"

"Yes."

I slap my hand down on the kitchen table. I have a brother who has been living in the same city as me and I never knew about him. My mind can't process this all at once. I rub my temples. My head freaking hurts.

"His name is Brooks Handley." My head jerks up.

The name sounds familiar. I know I've heard it before. I twist my lips, thinking. Where though? I'm leaning against the kitchen table, my finger tapping against it as I search my mind. And then it clicks.

I gasp, covering my mouth with my hand. "I've met him."

Aiden's brows crease. "There was a murder suicide in his apartment building. I remember him coming out of his apartment, asking us questions about what happened. He wasn't too happy when I told him we couldn't give him any details. In fact, he got in my face demanding answers." I think back to how much of an asshole he was. *Huh.* I was face to face with my brother and I had no idea. "How does Jessie know Brooks?"

Aiden looks at Ryan to explain. "The night I saw Jessie, I didn't watch her actually leave. I just assumed she was on her way out. When I saw the shape Aiden was in, I was more concerned with him. He was a blubbering mess. It was hard to understand everything he was saying, it was so jumbled. He told me Travis was your father. He also told me about his father. And then he told me you had a brother. He mentioned his name in the conversation because I remember it, I just don't know at what point in the conversation we were at. Like I said, talking to an inebriated Aiden was a little difficult." He takes a deep breath and then continues. "I'm thinking Jessie may have never left and heard everything."

Panic rushes through me, and I turn to Aiden. She knows Travis is my dad. *Shit. Shit. Shit.* That's all I need is for her to have that power to tell everyone. I look around the kitchen and head for the fridge. I need a drink. "Max, you have to have something to drink in here somewhere, right?" I go searching frantically for anything to help drown the panic rising inside of me. Aiden grabs my arms, stopping me. He pulls my back into his chest and leans his head down.

"It'll be okay, Addison."

"No, it won't. Jessie is a conniving bitch who will obviously stop at nothing to get between us. She'll use this information," I say, turning in his arms. My voice is panicked. "I can't have the world know I'm Travis's daughter. I've already lived through one revenge; I don't want to find out what the next one will be. And now I have Lexi to worry about."

"We don't know how much she knows. She might not have any idea who Travis is. Especially if I just said his first name."

"Well, she sure as hell had no trouble finding Brooks and getting him to get her pregnant. I'm pretty sure she can put two and two together." I lean my head into his chest.

"Let's just take this one step at a time." Aiden's hand runs down my long hair.

I look up to him. "Okay, what's the first step?"

"Finding out if Brooks knows Jessie."

I inhale sharply and stare up into his eyes. I'm going to meet my brother. I know we've already met, but then he was just a nosey asshole bystander. This time he's my brother and he might have a child. I can't imagine this meeting will be any better than our last. I blow out my cheeks and nod.

Chapter six

"**C**an I help you?" A beautiful, tall, dark-haired woman standing behind her desk asks Aiden as we walk into the foyer of Handley and Rice, Inc.

Brooks and another guy, Jared Rice, started a marketing firm around three years ago, right after graduating college. They hit the jackpot with a few big-name accounts and it skyrocketed their exposure in the marketing world. It's now a multimillion-dollar company. Numerous business magazines have written about the young duo and their quick success.

When I did a search to see who he was last year, I didn't bother looking at who he *really* was. I just made sure he didn't have any outstanding warrants because I would have loved to turn him in. God, he was such an asshole. Looking at his picture now, I see the resemblance to Travis. In fact, their facial features are almost identical except for their eye color. Brooks has hazel eyes.

"We're here to see Mr. Handley," Aiden responds, leaning forward on the tall ledge in front of the desk. Miss *I'm About to Kick Her Ass* is looking at Aiden like she wants to have him for lunch.

I clear my throat, interrupting her gawking. "Is Mr. Handley available?" She licks her lips as she looks at Aiden one last time before turning her attention to me. I shake my head. When her eyes find mine, her expression changes to annoyance. I flash her an obvious fake smile.

"Do you have an appointment? Mr. Handley is a very busy man." She snickers and looks down at what I assume is an appointment book. I notice Aiden moving in the corner of my eye, reaching into his pocket.

"I think this will suffice." He flashes his FBI badge. She looks back up to his face after inspecting the badge. You'd think she'd...*I don't know*, call Brooks and tell him FBI is here. Nope. She drags her teeth slowly over her bottom lip and her cheeks flush. You have got to be kidding me. I jerk my head to Aiden. He looks down at me and laughs. The asshole laughs! I grit my teeth, forcing back the words that want to come out. He's going to pay for this.

"Miss...?" Aiden asks.

"Torres," she purrs.

"*Ms. Torres*," I say between clenched teeth.

Aiden stops me by grabbing my hand. "Will you please let Mr. Handley know we'd just like a few minutes of his time?" Her eyes glance down at our joined hands, and she rolls her eyes. Yes, bitch, *he's mine*.

"I'll be right back." The clack of her heels echoes the entire distance to Brooks's office.

"*Mmm*, I love it when your feistiness comes out."

I jab my elbow into his side. Thoughts of Secretary Skank escape my mind when I hear her coming back because then I hear another pair of shoes walking with her. I crack my knuckles as nerves flow through me. This is weird. I'm about to be face to face with someone who shares my DNA. Flutters in my belly make me thankful we decided to eat after this meeting.

When Brooks rounds the corner and we lock eyes, a look of recognition flashes through his. His lips pull up to a sly grin. *Oh, shit*, he remembers me.

"Ms. Mason," he says. "What brings you here?" He stops in front of us, his hands in his black slacks. He doesn't even glance at Aiden.

"I guess you remember me?" I say, clasping my nervous hands in front of me.

"I do." My mouth gapes open at the seductive way the words slide out of his mouth. I don't know if I should laugh or be horrified. "You're a beautiful woman," he says, unapologetically. "You're hard to forget."

"*Eww.*" The words are out of my mouth before I can stop them. Horrified wins.

I look at Aiden right away, and he shrugs. "He's right."

I narrow my eyes at him. Aiden's enjoying this a little too much.

"I didn't think I was that bad of a catch," Brooks says sarcastically. I turn back to him. This is wrong and it's going in a direction I hadn't expected. I open and close my mouth a couple times as I struggle for words. What do you say to your brother who is hitting on you?

"Mr. Handley, I'm Agent Aiden Roberts. You obviously already know Addison Mason," he chuckles. I roll my eyes. "Do you have a few minutes we can talk in private?"

He looks at me once more. I flick my gaze away, avoiding his eyes. My brother *likes* me. It's not the *like* I was shooting for.

"Follow me."

We follow him into his office, and he shuts the door behind us. His office is on the eighteenth floor and faces the Empire State Building. I don't think I'd get much work done if this was my office because I'd be too busy staring out the window all day. We stand and wait for him to direct us on where he wants us to sit. There's a couch and two seats on one side of the office and there are two seats in front of his desk. He chooses the desk.

We sit and Aiden doesn't waste any time pulling a picture out of his pocket. "Do you know this woman?"

He hands a picture of Jessie to him. Brooks looks it over, flicking the corner of the picture with his finger. He studies it for a minute and shakes his head. He releases a sharp exhale and then looks up at Aiden.

"Do I need to get my lawyer in here?" His tone is sharp. He holds out the picture for Aiden to take back. Well, that answers our question. *He knows her.*

"You might. But it's not what you think," Aiden says, putting the picture back into his back pocket. "Her name is Jessie Carver."

"I know Jessie," he says.

"When was the last time you saw her?" I ask.

"What is this about? Is Jessie hurt? In trouble? Dead? What?" he demands, leaning forward with his elbows resting on the desk. Aiden hesitates and looks at me. I can tell he's having a hard time telling him. He knows how it feels to be blindsided when someone tells you that you might have a child.

I sigh. *Just rip the Band-Aid off.* "Jessie just had a baby," I blurt out. Brooks' eyes open wide. "And we think it's yours." He stands so abruptly I jump. His chair rolls back, hitting the window. He stalks to a bar in the corner of his office, pulls out a glass, and pours himself a drink. Lifting it to his lips, he swallows the entire drink. He puts the glass down and grips the edge of the bar so tightly his knuckles turn white. I can see the muscles in his back tighten through his shirt. He's calculating the possibility in his head.

"I haven't seen her in five months," he grates out. He stares down at the bar as he speaks. "She blew out of my life as fast as she blew into it." He turns and leans against the bar, crossing his arms and feet. "Why are you coming to me about this? Why isn't she?"

Aiden sits up taller, crossing his foot over his leg. "She told me I was the father."

"There you go," he says, throwing his hand in the air. "Why are you bringing this to my door? Congrats, man."

Aiden nods. "We did a paternity test. It's not mine."

Brooks runs his hands through his hair haphazardly. "She told you it was mine, then?" His voice raises as he starts to panic.

"Not exactly," Aiden responds.

He looks like he's about to explode, so I stand up and walk toward him. "We did a familial DNA test." He glares at me like I have two heads. "It's a DNA test that looks for a match of people already in the system," I explain. "There was a match."

"I've never had a DNA test, so I shouldn't be in any system. You guys have the wrong person."

Aiden stands up now. "No, but your biological dad is."

Brooks stares at Aiden—hard. His face turns to stone. "How the fuck do you know who my biological father is?" he sneers. He drops his arms to his side and clenches his hands into a fist. He reminds me of Travis when I wouldn't tell him my real name. *Dangerous.*

"I was undercover, working for Travis. He had me check up on you every now and then," Aiden says, shrugging.

"This just keeps getting better and better." He starts to pace. *Oh, little brother, just wait. We're not done.*

He mumbles a few things under his breath. He stops pacing and lowers his head. "Why did she try to pass it off as yours?"

"Because of me," I whisper. He looks up and pins his hard stare on me.

"I don't understand."

Aiden starts talking before I can explain. "Jessie and I were friends *with benefits* in college. Nothing else. I went away on an assignment..." Brooks raises a brow in question. "Yes, *Travis*. Addison and I met during that time and when I got back into town, we ended up reconnecting. Long story short, Jessie freaked out, thinking we would be together someday. Did some stupid shit but nothing too crazy. *Until now.*"

Brooks nods his head. "Until now," he says slowly. "So, I'm an innocent bystander in this fucked-up situation? I might have a kid because someone is trying to get revenge on you?"

"You are innocent," I say, sighing. "But she sought you out specifically."

Brooks head tilts to the side. "Why?" His voice turns defensive. I swallow hard. I take a few deep breaths and ready myself. My mouth feels like I just ate a cracker. Why am I so nervous? It's not like *I've* kept this secret from him.

Aiden starts to say something, but I jerk my head at him and shake my head.

"Okay, somebody needs to start talking," Brooks says.

"When Aiden was working for Travis...that's when we met," I say.

"Yes, Agent Roberts already covered that," Brooks states matter-of-factly.

"*I know.* What he didn't say was how we met. My mom was killed when I was ten. I knew Travis had something to do with it, I just didn't know how." I stop, wondering how much Brooks knows about Travis. When he doesn't say anything, I continue. "I went to find out who Travis was. Another long story short, Travis didn't kill my mom." As if the pieces of the puzzle start fitting into place, Brooks narrows his eyes at me. I nod my head and flash a lopsided smile. "Travis is my father, too."

Brooks spins around and pours himself another glass of whiskey. I hear him murmur, "Talk about an insta-fucking-family," before downing his drink.

***

"What now?" I say as Aiden holds the door open for me, and we walk out of Brooks's building.

Aiden slips his hand through mine, stopping me, and glances down into my eyes. "I think we have a wedding to plan." He wags his eyebrows.

I drop my shoulders and my lips turn downward. "Really? That's it. You're moving onto the next thing?"

He looks around and shakes his head slightly. "Addison, that up there," he says, pointing up at the building, "*that* is not our problem now. That is between Brooks and Jessie."

"But Presley is my niece. And soon to be yours, too."

"This is exactly what Jessie wanted. Don't let her come in the middle of our life."

"I'm *not.* We're still going to get married, Aiden. But..." I pause, wondering why I feel like I need to do something, "...I mean I haven't even seen her in person."

"No. We are not going to the hospital." I stare at him. His jaw is set and his eyes have me pinned. I cross my arms and huff at his domineering posture. A loud horn pulls my attention toward the street. People are starting to get off work, crowding around us.

"Fine," I snap when it's obvious he's not going to back down. "But *that* up there..." I point up, mimicking him, "...that's my brother, and we just turned his world upside-down. We left him pissed off and confused. I feel like I should *do* something."

Aiden blows out a breath, his expression softening, and he takes a step toward me. I cross my arms in defiance. "Addison, he has *a lot* to think about. I know you're having to deal with new feelings for a brother and a niece that you didn't know you had until a few hours ago, but everything can't be dealt with today." He grabs my arm, unwrapping it from my body, and then my other arm. He pulls me into him and rests his forehead on mine. "Let me have tonight to celebrate that I'm not the father. Tomorrow, after Brooks has time to let this all sink in, we'll call him and talk some more."

I close my eyes, feeling like shit now. *Crap.*

"I'm sorry. I didn't think about how this has affected you." I open my eyes and gaze into emerald eyes. I rub my hand along his jawline, his five o'clock shadow rough against my palm. "Tonight, let's celebrate. No more talk about Brooks, Jessie, or Presley."

"One last thing I want to say before we *stop* talking about them...thank you for standing next to me, supporting me even when you didn't know."

"I *did* know and there isn't anywhere else I wanted to be than by your side. You've stood by me through a lot worse, even when I destroyed you with my words. You fought for me. *For us.* It was my turn to do the fighting."

Chapter seven

"I swear, I'm telling him you have gonorrhea."

Sydney, mouth full of water, bursts out laughing, spraying water everywhere. I just told her about Brooks. Everything from him being my brother to him being Presley's father. The first thing she asks is if he's single. *Really*? That's what she got out of the whole story?

"I'm totally kidding," she says through her laughs. I roll my head against the lounger, over to her direction, and push my sunglasses up, narrowing my eyes. "I am!" I shake my head, not believing her. We just finished working out and now we're lounging by the gym pool. Aiden is still working out and will bring Lexi here to swim when he's done. I figure I'll enjoy this free few minutes and soak up some sun before they come out.

"I don't believe you." I look back toward the sky, pulling my sunglasses down.

"*What?* We could be real sisters. He's also hot *and* a millionaire," she says jokingly.

"I think you have enough *men* in your life."

"Seriously, I was kidding." She leans over and hits me on the shoulder. "Anyway, I just have one *man* in my life." I look over at her again and raise my brows in surprise. She shrugs and reclines. "Damon and I have decided we are going to be exclusive."

I bolt up. "Really?" I like her and Damon together, I just didn't know if they would work out because of her hooking up with Max a few months ago.

"Yep. We've been seeing a lot of each other, and he asked me the other day what I thought about us being together. I told him I really like him. I mean, hell, I've always liked him. He's the one who couldn't commit."

"And Max?" I say, wincing, not wanting to bring it up.

"We talked about it. I told him it was a one-night stand on a drunken, emotional night and it meant nothing. Max said the same thing to him."

"Did it really mean nothing?"

Syd sighs. "Max are I are nothing alike. It was never more than a sexual attraction. I never really *liked* Max." She looks at me, waiting for a response. I just nod. I don't think that's all it was, but who am I to say anything. "I really, really like Damon."

"I know." I lean over and pick up my water bottle. The sun's heat has sweat running down my chest. After I take a much-needed drink, I continue. "I'm happy for y'all."

"I think you guys getting engaged and having Lexi around, he's starting to want to settle down, too. He's questioning where he wants his life in a few years."

"And that's with you?"

"Oh, gosh! We're still too new for *that* conversation. He's just...reevaluating his player ways."

"Well, I'm glad he's...oh!" I stop talking when I think about our wedding.

"What?"

"So, our wedding... You're my maid of honor and Max is Aiden's best man." She nods her head in understanding. "Is that going to cause any problems?"

"Hopefully since Damon will be in the wedding, too, it won't. I guess we need to have another conversation." She throws her head back and moans a little. "Why did you let me sleep with Max?"

I sit up tall again as my mouth gapes open. "Are you kidding me? When have you ever taken my advice about who *not* to sleep with? And don't act like I haven't tried to warn you. Many times, in fact!"

"Many times?" She tilts her head in my direction.

"Oh, you want me to name them? Let's start with Jack and then there's—"

"O-kay!" she says, interrupting me. "It's a little concerning that you remember names, but you don't need to continue naming my indiscretions. Just because I can enjoy a man's body and you can't—"

"I definitely enjoy a man's body," I say, interrupting her and staring at Aiden walking out, holding Lexi's hand. His hair is disheveled from working out. I admire every inch of his muscular body. His turquoise board shorts hang low on his hips, and I bite my lip to stop my mouth from hanging open.

Sydney follows my stare to Aiden. "Alright, you win." She grins. "I think I need to get in the pool to cool down," she says, fanning herself. I chuckle and stand as Aiden walks up. "Come on Lulu, let's go swim." Lexi jumps up and down and runs to Syd. I watch them jump into the pool and turn toward Aiden.

He flashes a megawatt smile, wrapping his hands around my waist. "What exactly are you winning?"

"Wouldn't you like to know."

"I already know." He wags his eyebrows, amusement dancing in his eyes. One thing is for sure, the confident man who was missing the last month is back in full force. He trails a finger down my arm and my body shivers. With a sly smile, he leans over and whispers in my ear, "I'll give you the prize later."

I try to think of a witty comeback, but all I can think about is his prize and where I plan on putting it. *Oh, my.* I turn away, hiding the flush on my face. *Not the place, Addison.* I lie back down on my towel and look out at the pool, ignoring Aiden's cocky smile and sexy body. He opens his towel and places it on the lounger next to me.

"Addie, look!" Lexi screams from the side of the pool. She does a cannonball and bobs back up from her arm floats. "Did you see me?"

"I did. You made a huge splash," I respond, holding my arms out wide.

"I considered signing her up for swim lessons," Aiden says. "I've heard they have a great program here."

"It doesn't surprise me. They have everything else here." We bought a membership last month because the boxing gym isn't very kid-friendly. Lexi loves it here. There's a huge treehouse in the kid area as well as a climbing wall, kids'-only basketball court, computers, anything a kid could want to do while their parents work out. "I think it's a great idea, especially since she'll want to use the pool a lot."

"Well, that and I'll feel more comfortable with her around the pool at the beach house if she knows how to swim."

I glance over to him as he watches Lexi swim. His hands are behind his head and his stomach muscles contract as he laughs at something Lexi does. His body is sexy, but it doesn't come close to the man he is on the inside. The way he cares for Lexi's wellbeing makes my heart happy. For a quick second, I think about ten little kids all stockpiled on top of him, laughing and playing. I shake my head clearing that image. *No freaking way.* I do not want ten kids. This is all Aiden's fault, saying he wants ten of them. He had to be kidding, *right?* I look back out at the water to Syd and Lexi as they sing "Ring around the Rosie."

Thinking of kids turns my thoughts to Presley. "Have you talked to Ryan?" I say, skirting around the real question I want to ask. *Does Jessie know we know about Brooks?* It's been three days since we visited Brooks, and I haven't brought it up. Aiden did confirm Brooks was the father, but other than that I haven't heard anything else. It's still a sore subject with Aiden, so I haven't pushed it. I tried to call Brooks, but he's not answering my calls.

"Yes," he says, looking straight ahead.

"Aiden." I wait until he turns his head in my direction. "And..." I say, wanting him to continue.

He grunts. "Jessie left the hospital a couple days ago. I guess she went back to New Haven. She knows the father is Brooks," he says. "That's about all I know. It's about all I care to know." I sink back into my chaise lounge. I wish it was that easy for me, but Presley is my niece. It's hard not to think about her wellbeing.

From the corner of my eye, I see Aiden sit up and swing his legs around. He reaches over and his hand covers mine. "I'm sorry. I'll talk to Ryan and find out how Presley is doing."

I chew on my inner cheek and nod. "Thanks," I whisper.

"Now, let's go swim. I'm burning up," he says, pulling me up, throwing me over his shoulder, and jumping in. I try not to scream, but it slips out anyway. When we surface, I hear a whistle being blown. I wipe the water from my eyes and look around, making sure Lexi is okay. It blows again. When I look over at the lifeguard, he's staring at me and Aiden shaking his head. I turn to hide my smile and splash Aiden.

"You got us in trouble," I snicker, sticking my tongue out.

"Sweetheart, you knew I was trouble the second you laid eyes on me," he says, flashing a salacious smile. My heart beats faster, remembering him walking in the door. *Trouble* doesn't even begin to cover what I thought when his emerald eyes met my turquoise ones.

Chapter eight

"Nope, we'll be home alone," I say seductively into my phone, walking up to Aiden's front door. I had planned on surprising him with dinner at his place, but right when I answered his call, the security guard downstairs said hello and Aiden immediately knew where I was. *Busted.* "Lexi is out with Sydney for a few hours." Aiden growls into the phone. "You better hurry up," I say before ending the phone call.

I'm thinking about the things we can do without having to worry about little ears as I open the door. My mind is so distracted with Aiden and what's to come, I don't register it until it's too late. Someone is standing in the entryway. Pointing a gun right at me.

"Shut the door, Addison," Jessie grates out. I quickly look her over. Her eyes dart to the door and back to me. "Now!" I flinch at her demand. There's a desperate air that surrounds her. She's rocking back and forth from foot to foot and the hand that's holding the gun shakes.

"Okay, Jessie. I'm shutting it," I say, putting up my hands. I still have my phone in one hand. Unfortunately, Aiden's not on the line. I shut the door but not all the way, hoping when Aiden gets here he'll be able to hear us before coming in. I'm also hoping she doesn't notice.

As soon as I turn around, she tells me to drop my phone and kick it away. I do what she says because it's obvious she's unstable right now. She looks like shit. Her button-up shirt is askew and her hair looks like it hasn't been washed in days. Then it hits me. *Presley.*

"Jessie, where is Presley?"

"No!" she snaps, shaking the gun at me. "You don't get to ask where Presley is at. She's not yours!" My chest tightens, worrying about the safety of Presley. Please, God, let her be okay.

"I know she's not, Jessie. She's yours." My voice is rushed as I try to placate her. "Your beautiful little girl needs you, Jessie. Just put the gun down." I take a step toward her. She straightens her arm, steadying the gun right at me. I stop moving and put my hands up again.

"That's what you'd like, isn't it, Addison? How's it feel to be at the end of a pointed gun? I can tell you, it's much better on this end." Her voice drips sarcasm as she regains a little more control. I remember how I pulled a gun on her when she ended up in Aiden's bed, uninvited. I don't know if she knows, but I've been here before and it never turns out well for the person behind the gun.

I wonder what her original plan was. She couldn't have known I was coming over. Aiden was her target, not me. *But why?* She hates me. I take a couple steps to the side, in the direction of the living room. I need to move away from the door so she's not facing it.

"Stop moving!" she yells. I immediately stop. She's pivoted enough that the door isn't in her direct view anymore.

"Jessie, you don't want to do this. Think about your little girl."

Her laugh is low and snide. "Oh, yes, I do. You have taken *everything* away from me." I feel the crease between my eyebrows form. She twists her lips, studying me. "Oh, you haven't heard? Your *dearest* brother is trying to take my daughter away from me."

"I hadn't heard."

"Liar! Who told Brooks he had a child?" She waves the gun around as her voice escalates. I keep my eyes on her trigger finger. How is it I've become a psycho magnet? "You know..." she pauses and stares at me for a beat, "...Presley wasn't even part of the plan." She shakes her head and mumbles under her breath, then lets out a small laugh. "I hadn't planned on getting pregnant," she quips. There's a small part of me that is relieved Jessie isn't that much of a conniving bitch that she'd planned on using a child for revenge, but it's a miniscule part because she *did* end up using a child.

"What exactly was your plan?" I ask, confused. I need her to keep talking. Aiden should be here soon.

"To make your life a living hell by marrying your brother." Her tone is matter-of-fact, like it explains everything, but it doesn't make any sense. That was a huge assumption Brooks would have married her. Even then, I'm not sure how marrying Brooks would have made my life a living hell. It would've sucked having her for a sister-in-law, but *living hell* is a bit of a stretch. I've lived in hell and that doesn't even come close. I think the rational part of her brain is wired wrong. "But then I got pregnant. Timing was close enough to when I saw Aiden and made Ryan think we had sex. It was like a gift from God. Aiden and I were meant to be together. But then you had to show up and ruin everything. Again." She spits.

My skin prickles from the anger of her words. I know it's about to happen before it does. The gun goes off and my whole body tenses, and I instinctively put my hands up to my head, waiting for the bullet to rip through my body.

I slowly blow out the breath I was holding and gather myself, standing up straight. I haven't been hit. Jessie, still holding the gun pointed right at me, flashes a wicked grin. "You have destroyed me. I have nothing left to lose because of you. You have taken everything from me," she seethes. Her eyes are cold and empty.

"Jessie, don't do this. You're not thinking right now," I plead. Tears well up in my eyes. I am at her mercy. I know she's past the point of reason. I send out a silent plea. *Please, God, I don't want to die.*

I close my eyes briefly and a tear escapes down my cheek. My mind races through images of Aiden and Lexi. I hope they know how much I love them. When I open my eyes, I catch a glimpse of movement toward the backside of Jessie. *Aiden.* He opens the door slowly, walking behind her.

The gun goes off simultaneously as Aiden takes a flying leap.

Darkness follows.

***

"Addison," I hear Aiden repeating my name. My head feels like a hammer is beating down on it. My vision blurs at first when I open my eyes, but everything becomes clear quickly. I bring my hand to my head. I'm lying on the ground and Aiden is crouching beside me.

"Damn, my head hurts." I try to sit up.

"Wait, let me help you." Aiden slips his arm around my back and pulls me up. I hear sirens outside. My mind grasps onto the last thing I remember.

I frantically start looking over my body, running my hands all over. "Did she shoot me?"

"You're okay, Addison," Aiden says, grabbing my hands. "She missed." He leans over and presses his forehead into mine. "Thank God she missed," he whispers. I exhale, releasing the tension in my shoulders.

"What happened," I ask, opening my eyes and staring into his.

"You passed out right after Jessie took a shot. You hit your head on the floor pretty hard."

I scrunch my nose up. "Really? I passed out?" I mean, I guess it's better than being shot, but I've never passed out before.

"Yes. I want you to go to the hospital to get checked out."

"I'm fine. I've hit my head before, worse than this. I'll be fine." I look around Aiden, wondering where Jessie is. She's sitting on a barstool, handcuffed. Her head hangs and tears run down her face. "Presley. Where's Presley?" I look back to Aiden in a panic.

"She's safe. Ryan called me earlier and said they were taking care of Presley today. He thought Jessie had a doctor's appointment."

"She's sick, Aiden." I look at Jessie with a twinge of guilt. "She needs help. She doesn't need to go to jail." I think of Presley not having her mom in her life. I know having a baby messes with your hormones, on top of the questionable state of her sanity before she even got pregnant. She's definitely not in the right frame of mind now.

Aiden brings my hands to his lips, and he slowly nods. "I agree with you. But God, Addison...if I hadn't gotten here when I did, she would have killed you." The pain in his voice is all too familiar. I say the only thing I can think of to make him feel a little bit better.

"You're my hero."

He chuckles as he closes his eyes and shakes his head. "You're a smartass," he murmurs.

The pain in my head has started to lessen, but I wince as I try to get up, still holding it with one hand. Damon and the police storm in, assessing the room before continuing to enter.

"It's clear," Aiden states. Damon and an officer walk over to us while another officer heads in Jessie's direction. Aiden informs the two officers about what happened when he got here. I fill in the rest. This is where I find out Aiden had texted Damon before he walked in telling him he needed backup. Still, Damon had no idea what was going down.

"I don't know how many lives you have, woman, but you might want to save one," Damon jokes. I hit him on the arm. The impact makes *my* head hurt.

"Ouch," I say, rubbing my head.

"I'll get you an ice pack. Get the medics in here to look her over," Aiden instructs Damon as he walks away. I look around and notice Jessie is gone. The officer must have already taken her out.

When Aiden returns, handing me the icepack, I ask him, "How did she get in here?"

Aiden shrugs. "I never changed the locks. Since she was at my place at the beach, she could have left and made a key without me even knowing, I guess."

I walk to the couch and gently sit down. Leaning back into the cushion, I close my eyes and reflect on the last half hour. I think about what happened and what might have happened. I can't believe it came to this. I hope Jessie can find help; Presley is going to need her mother.

"Did you know Brooks filed for custody?" I open my eyes and look up at Aiden. He shakes his head. "I think that's what broke Jessie. She blames us for telling him he had a baby," I say. The cold pack on my head makes me shiver. "I can't say I understand her, but I can see how that might throw her off the deep end."

"Addison, you do know none of this is your fault, right?" Damon asks, sitting down next to me. I let out a bitter laugh, thinking nothing is *ever* my fault, yet things always seem to happen to me. Same old shit, different day.

"It's not," Aiden barks out, reading my mind.

I sigh heavily. "I know it's not my fault...directly," I add.

"Not directly or indirectly." Aiden kneels in between my legs, his hands resting on the top of my thighs. "You couldn't stop the slippery slope Jessie was on. She made her own decisions and now she has to live with the consequences. Just because her decisions were based on you, you can't blame yourself."

I nod because he won't change his mind, but I'm the one who has to live knowing it's because of me Presley won't have her mom around, at least for a while.

A paramedic walks into the room, and Aiden calls him over to check me out. He doesn't think I have a concussion, which is good because I want to go home tonight.

Damon joins us when the paramedic leaves and tells me he called Sydney. He chuckles, telling me about Sydney needing to give Lexi money for the bad word jar. I think that's the first time Sydney has ever had to donate to Lexi's jar.

"She's going to keep Lulu a little longer, give you guys some time to decompress. I'm getting off right now, so we're going to take her to dinner."

"Thank you," I say softly.

"Agent Roberts," a police officer interrupts, "we're almost done here." Aiden pushes off my legs to stand up and follows the officer to the other side of the room.

"Get some rest and we'll call you when we head back your way with Lulu." Damon leans over and places a kiss on my head. Thinking about him and Sydney makes me happy.

"Oh, hey, congrats on finally pulling your head out of your ass," I joke.

"I guess I didn't have a choice if I wanted a chance with her. She seems to be in high demand."

"Don't forget that. You better treat her right or I'll kick your ass." I grin up at him.

"I promise I will."

A couple hours later, Aiden and I return to my apartment after we stopped and grabbed some Chinese takeout. Aiden spreads the food out on the coffee table while I grab a couple Coronas from the fridge. He's been quiet since we left his apartment. I know why. I just don't know what to say to make it better.

He's sitting on the floor with his elbows on the table and his head in his hands. I place the beers on the table and then run my fingers through his hair. He pushes up on his knees, turning toward me, and wraps his arms around my waist. I feel him breathe in a ragged breath. His body falls lax against me as the tension in his shoulders leaves. I can't help but feel at fault for bringing this grown man to his knees. My fingers fist the back of his hair as I swallow back the guilt. He digs his head into my stomach. "God, Addison. I love you." His voice breaks and he squeezes me tighter. When he looks up at me, I see the pain in his eyes.

The fear of losing me.

"Aiden, I'm right here." My breath hitches from the raw emotion reflecting in his eyes. I hate that I keep putting fear in them. I drop to my knees and wrap my arms around him, needing to comfort him and remind him I'm here. *Alive.* "I'm not going anywhere."

"When she took a shot and I saw you fall to the floor, I had no idea if she had shot you." His hand cups my neck. "I don't think I've ever unarmed someone and handcuffed them so fast in my life." He chuckles softly and ends his mirth with a sigh.

"I can't believe I passed out. I remember seeing you and then...nothing."

"How's your head?" He presses gentle kisses across my forehead.

"Better. I have a knot from hell on it, but it doesn't hurt too badly now. What's going to happen to Jessie?" I say, sitting on the floor.

Aiden sits down by me. "I'm sure her parents will get her the best attorney possible, which is good. He'll probably have her plead insanity."

"I don't think that is too far from the truth." Aiden nods in agreement. "Someone needs to call Brooks."

"Ryan texted me. Brooks is already on his way to New Haven," Aiden says.

"I'm surprised how much Brooks wants to be involved with Presley." Aiden looks at me and cocks his head to the side.

"We're not all assholes," he teases. "There *are* men out there who want to take responsibility for their kids."

I shove his shoulder with mine. "I *know*. He didn't waste any time trying to get custody. He's this millionaire playboy. I didn't see him as the dad type from what I've read about him."

"Well, he's about to get his wish and be a full-time dad now." It makes me respect him a little more.

"Growing up without a mom, it makes me sad." I lie my head on Aiden's shoulder. I sigh, wishing things could be different.

"You haven't forgotten she tried to kill you just a little bit ago, right?"

"I won't be forgetting anytime soon, but I know she's sick. She's being held captive in her own head. I know how it feels."

"Hopefully it won't be forever," he murmurs into my hair. He's saying it to appease me. He'd be happier if we never saw Jessie again.

Chapter nine

Aiden

elp me.

H That's the last thing Brooks texted to Addison. She'd texted him back and even called, but he didn't respond. After what she's been through a few days ago—her whole life, really— you'd think she'd be a little leery of receiving a message like that. Nope. *Not Addison.* She started packing her things up to leave. When I tried to stop her, she told me Brooks was her brother and he needed help. *Yeah, we got that part in the text.* It's the *why* that concerns me. I told her the only way she was going is if I went with her. Thankfully the sixteen-year-old who lives next door, Hannah, could come stay with Lexi on short notice.

So, here we are, walking up to Brooks's building. I don't know if this is the right place since he didn't say, but we figured this would be a good starting point. Going in blind has never been smart. I sent Damon a quick text before we left, telling him what we're doing. He's on standby. We check in with the security guard, and he tells us to go on up.

"Good luck," he says as we walk away. Addison looks up at me with her forehead creased, and I shrug. Whatever his problem is, it doesn't sound like a trap if the security officer knows. I relax a little in the elevator.

When the doors open, we're immediately assaulted with the sound of baby cries. *Deafening baby cries.* I have a feeling Presley is the reason we're here. When we knock, there's no answer. Addison twists her lips.

"Screw it," she says and twists the doorknob. "He probably can't hear us anyway."

The modern penthouse is made of mostly glass or stone and the cries echo loudly. I chuckle, thinking how out of place a baby is here. It's sterile. Clean. Everything in its spot. I don't know much about babies, except they have a lot of stuff. I've been in homes where toys litter the entire living room floor.

"Brooks, where are you?" Addison calls out.

He walks out of a bedroom. The put-together guy we saw a couple weeks ago is nowhere to be seen. His T-shirt is wrinkled and stained, his hair sticks up in all directions, and he clearly hasn't shaved in a couple days.

"Addison, please make her stop crying," he pleads.

She stares at him for a second, running her hands through her hair. "Um, I can try," she says, biting her lip. "Have you tried feeding her and changing her?"

Brooks rakes his hand over his face. "I've tried everything. She has cried for over twenty-four hours. *She won't stop.* I'm sorry I called you, I just didn't know who else I could call."

Addison's brows reach her forehead. "I'm sure you have a line of women willing to come over," she says.

"I don't trust the women I fuck with my daughter," he barks. "I know we don't know each other, but you *are* family. I have this weird sense of trust with you." His voice softens, but it's hard to hear over the cries.

Addison's lips curl into a smile. I know that goes straight to her heart. She's been yearning to get to know him. This is her way in. If I know Addison, she'll do everything in her power to help. "Okay. I'll see if I can get her to stop. I'm going to warn you, I've never been a baby person so I don't know if I can help much."

"You're a woman. Don't you naturally know what to do?"

She lets out a sarcastic laugh. "I don't think that's quite how it works," she says, walking in the direction of the cries. My ears are starting to hurt. I can't imagine listening to that off and on for twenty-four hours.

Brooks paces while we wait. The cries don't stop. After ten minutes, Addison comes out. Brooks drops his head into his hand and groans. "Do you mind if I call my best friend? She's like the baby whisperer. When she was in high school, people paid her a lot of money to calm their babies down. If there's anyone that can get Presley to stop crying, it's her." Brooks seems unsure and takes a deep breath, letting it out slowly. "She's like my sister, I trust her with my life."

"Alright. I'll call down to security so they'll let her up."

Sydney arrives in fifteen minutes. Fifteen minutes with a baby crying feels like hours. My nerves are already buzzing. If Sydney had taken any longer, I might have gone for a walk. Every man for himself at that point. Addison has been in the room, trying to calm Presley, but it hasn't worked.

"Sydney, this is Brooks," I say. He shakes her hand, and Syd gives him the once-over.

"It's nice to meet you, Brooks. I'm assuming I'm here because of the crying baby?"

His shoulders sag and he nods. Syd asks him when the last time Presley ate was, and they talk a little about Presley's schedule.

"Does she have a pacifier?"

"A what?"

"A pacifier. Something that goes in her mouth to help her calm down."

"I don't know what the hell that is. Macie just showed me how to feed her and change her."

"Where is her diaper bag?"

He points in the direction of the bag, and Syd digs through it. She pulls out and holds up a green nipple-looking thing. "Pacifier," she says, smiling and then turns to go find Addison and Presley. She stops before entering the room and looks back. "Brooks, go take a shower."

"Yes, ma'am," he replies with a salute.

Within minutes the cries have stopped. Holy shit! *Sydney's fucking awesome right now.* Addison walks out of the bedroom, her hair in messy bun and her face flushed with sweat. She blows out a breath and then comes over to sit with me on the couch.

"You want ten of those," she says, lying back against the cushions. "I don't know about that, Aiden. I think you have the wrong woman if you want me to have that many babies." I laugh. I want kids, but I don't care how many we have. I want at least two, one being Lexi. I just like fucking with Addison. Every time I say I want ten kids, her pupils dilate and she gets flustered. She doesn't fluster easily so it's fun to watch.

"They all can't be that way, right?" I ask.

"God, I hope not." *Me, too.*

Brooks comes out looking a lot better and plopping down on the other leather couch opposite us. He closes his eyes and releases an exhausted sigh. "I've missed that sound. *Silence.* Who knew this was going to be so hard?"

"Leave it to a man to think parenting is easy," Syd snickers, walking out with Presley in her arms. Brooks turns his body to look at Sydney.

"That," he barks, shooting up off the couch, pointing at Presley. "How did you wrap it so tight?"

I tilt my head and look at Sydney, wondering what he's talking about. Then I notice that Presley is wrapped in a blanket. I remember seeing her wrapped that way in the hospital and thinking that it looked uncomfortable, but she obviously doesn't mind because she's content now. She's sucks on the green thing a couple times and then stops for a few moments then does it again.

"We call it swaddling," she tells him.

"I don't care what you call it. Teach me how to do it like that."

She waves her hand. "C'mon, I'll show you."

He follows her into the room. Half an hour later they emerge again, but Brooks is holding Presley now and his body language has gone from despair to accomplishment. He stands taller and smiles down at Presley.

"I'm going to give you the name of a couple books that you should read. And I'll give you my number. You can call if you have any questions or need any help."

Addison jumps up. "I'll take Presley while you guys talk."

"Oh, now you want her," Brooks say, smirking.

"Hey! I might not have been able to calm her down, but I brought her," she replies, pointing at Sydney. He chuckles, gingerly placing Presley in Addison's arms.

"And I'll forever be in your debt."

"What? She didn't do anything," Syd says, hitting Brooks in the arm. He looks down at Sydney and smiles. Fuck, I've seen that look before. *Don't do it.*

"Are you free for dinner one night?"

I groan. "No," Addison and I both say at the same time.

Brooks looks at Addison. "I'm *really* not a bad person. I understand why *you* didn't want to date me, but geez," he says, rolling his eyes.

"It's not you. She has gonorrhea." I jerk my head to Addison, pushing off the couch to stand. *What the fuck?* Addison presses her lips together and then she and Sydney bust out laughing.

"I don't have gonorrhea, *Aiden*." Confused, I turn and look at Syd. She waves her hand around. "*Inside joke.* Anyway, thanks for the offer, Brooks, but I have a boyfriend."

"If you happen to become single, let me know," he says, winking. She looks at me, and I raise an eyebrow. She shakes her head. "What am I missing?" he asks, glancing at her and then at me.

I stand a little taller and cross my arms. "Her boyfriend is one of my best friends."

He shakes his head slowly. "Got it." We stare at each other for a couple moments before Addison pulls me to the couch. I know he's Addison's biological brother, but if I'm choosing sides, it'll always be Damon's.

"Put away your caveman cape. You didn't even get that mad when he tried to pick *me* up," she says softly, sitting on the couch. She puts a pillow under her arm to support Presley. I take a seat next to her, pulling my knee up on the couch and turning my body toward her.

I shrug. "That was *funny*, and it's not like I was worried." I lean my hand across the top of the couch and play with her hair while I stare at Presley. She's a beautiful baby. Especially when she's not pissed off at the world.

"Let's make one tonight," I whisper. Seeing Addison holding a baby awakens something deep inside me. It hits me in my core, a raw, inherent need. I feel Addison's eyes on me. I look up and she's looking at me like I'm crazy.

"What?" I ask.

"I don't know about you, but I can't forget the last forty-five minutes that easily."

I shrug. "It wasn't *that* bad."

"We were in the same apartment, right?" I chuckle and it makes Presley jump. "You wake her up and I will cut you," she warns, her voice hushed but clipped. Addison gently shakes the baby in her arms until she settles back down. Presley sucks her green nipple thing again.

"What is that thing called again?" I stick my finger inside the nipple area.

"A pacifier."

"Whoever named that thing was a genius," I say, watching in awe as she sucks on my finger.

"I'm thinking they were a genius because they *created* it," Brooks states, coming into the living room and lying across the other couch. "I plan on buying stock in the company."

Sydney leans down over the couch in between Addison and me. "I'm out of here. If you need me, you know where to find me."

"Thanks, Syd," Addison says.

Sydney says goodbye and leaves. Brooks watches Addison from the couch. He looks exhausted. "I'm sorry for calling you," he says. "I know all the shit you've been through, and I've been an asshole not calling you back. I needed time to process things. But when Presley wouldn't stop crying, I just didn't know who to call."

"I'm glad you did. This little girl has nothing to do with the decisions her mother made, so please don't think I'd ever have any bad feelings toward her." She looks down at Presley. "How could I? She's an angel."

"She is. I just panicked. I knew I was doing something wrong, but I couldn't figure out what it was. Thank you for calling Sydney."

"I told you, baby freaking whisperer. Have you heard anything about Jessie?" Addison asks quietly. Guilt riddles Addison and it'll eat her alive if she lets it. It kills me how much she blames herself for everything that happens.

"Her parents are keeping in contact with me. They are trying to have her sent to a facility in California for treatment."

"California?" I ask.

"I guess. I didn't ask questions. They want to be able to see Presley, so they are being extremely nice right now." He puts his hands behind his head and closes his eyes. He passes out cold in a matter of minutes. I grab the remote and turn the television on, putting on a college football game but making sure to keep the volume down.

We stay until Presley starts getting fussy. Addison tells Brooks that we'll stay and feed her so he can sleep a little more, but he insists that his hour and a half nap felt refreshing and he's good now.

I shake his hand, patting him on the back. "Good luck, man." I don't envy him. I want kids, but not by myself.

He chuckles. "Thanks. I think I'll need it." He looks at Addison. "Thanks so much for coming to my rescue," he tells Addison as she gives him a hug.

"Anytime," she murmurs.

Chapter ten

My head is plastered to the desk, and I slap my hands down in frustration. *How does this happen*? I know how it happens. Someone got sloppy.

"It's okay, we'll find another way," Harper says, sighing. She's as pissed as I am, she just knows how to control it better. We just received news the lab contaminated a piece of evidence we gathered last week. A very important piece of evidence: the one drop of blood that could have given us a lead on the case, but it's worthless now because someone screwed up.

I pull my head up and stare at Harper. "This day sucks." She nods in agreement. "I started my day with Aiden pushing the wedding topic again." I roll my eyes. I've been so damn busy with work and we've only just started to get into a routine with Lexi and school that I haven't even had time to think about it. I suck at being a fiancée.

"Well..." she starts.

I put my hand up, stopping her. "Don't," I say, narrowing my eyes. "I don't need to hear it from you, too. I *know* I need to start planning it."

"Just hire a wedding planner."

I let her suggestion roll around in my head. Why the hell didn't I think of this? "That is a great idea. Know any?"

Her lips twist as she thinks. "*Hmm.* No, but I think when Alyssa got married a few months ago, she used someone. You should ask her if she liked the woman." I grab a sticky note and jot down Alyssa's name and stick it on the bottom of my computer screen, pressing my finger across the sticky part so it'll stay.

"I'll call her later. Now, we have to figure out how to fix *this* problem." I pick up a folder sitting to the side and slam it down in front of me. "It's going to be a long day," I say as I open it and start reading the contents.

By five o'clock my head hurts from looking through all the pictures and evidence. The sound of a male clearing his throat gets my attention, and Harper and I look up. Aiden leans against the doorway of my office with his hands in his pockets. He's wearing a black suit and green tie that makes his eyes look even more vibrant. *Hello, gorgeous!* He's a sight for these sore eyes.

My lips slowly form a smile. There's something about him being in a suit and tie that makes my insides heat up. Memories of using those ties race through my mind. He flashes a knowing smile as he watches me cross my legs. I look away, feeling the heat in my cheeks, and start cleaning up the paperwork on my desk. Aiden chuckles. Harper stands up and stretches.

"I've been sitting in that seat too long," she says. "I guess we're done for the night?"

"Yes." I sigh. "We'll go back to the sight on Monday and see if there is anything we missed." She nods and heads to the door.

"Nice suit, Aiden. Court?" He scoots over so she has enough room to pass.

"Nah. I just like to see the look in Addison's eyes when I wear a tie." He glances at me and winks.

Harper walks off, laughing. "I don't even want to know," she yells from down the hall.

"I heard you had a shitty day." I angle my head to the side and look up at him. "Since you decided not to answer my calls today, I had to call *other* people," he elaborates, leaning over and putting his hands on my desk, getting close to my face. "I thought you were trying to avoid me because I brought up our *wedding* this morning."

"No," I sigh. He presses a soft kiss on my lips and stands up straight.

"Let me take you to dinner."

"I'm really tired, Aiden. I just want to go home." I close the case file we were working on and clean up my desk.

"That wasn't a question." He puts his hand on top of the folder, stopping me. I jerk my head in the direction of his demanding tone. "You need to eat, and I'm going to take you to get something. Sydney and Damon are taking Lexi out tonight." *Bossy much?* Our eyes lock and the intensity in his eyes tell me I'm not going to win this battle.

"Let's go," I grumble. He stands up tall again and crosses his arms, satisfied with himself.

I'm only going because I'm hungry.

"You're going because you love me." *Crap.* I smirk when I realize I didn't just say that in my head.

"I do love you, Agent Roberts, but you're being a demanding ass right now," I say with a fake smile, walking past him. I hear a low rumbling chuckle behind me. I wait for him to leave my office so I can shut and lock my door. The smell of spice, woods, and masculinity waft in the air as he moves past me. I take in a deep breath, inhaling his smell and shudder. He's intoxicating and hard to resist. *Even when I've had a horrible day.*

I huff in irritation. My body seems to have a mind of its own. I take quick strides to the elevator but hear his footsteps behind me. I watch our reflection in the closed elevator doors and look down at my jeans and flats, cursing under my breath. *I can't go out looking like this.*

"I look like shit." My hair was in a sleek ponytail this morning, but now pieces are hanging out everywhere from me pulling on my hair all day. I yank off my hair tie and comb through my hair with my fingers before pulling it back. I shrug to myself. *It'll have to do.*

"You look beautiful, Addison," he says, leaning down a little. "I have a surprise for you."

My shoulders drop and I blow out my cheeks, a little irritated he can't see that I'm not in the mood for surprises.

He leans down again, this time he's so close I can feel the warmth of his breath. "I think I need to find a dark corner and fuck you until you're happy." I sharply inhale from his hushed, raspy voice. The elevator doors open and thankfully the car is empty. His *suggestion* catches me off guard so my cheeks are flushed and I'm speechless. He reaches in front of me and hits the first-floor button. As the doors close, I wonder how serious he is. "Is that what you need, Addison?" he murmurs, turning toward me. His eyes darken and lock on to mine. The elevator feels like its walls are closing in. There's emotion behind his gaze that I can't read. The intensity forces me to suck in a breath.

My mouth opens to say *"maybe,"* but the ding from the elevator tears me out of the hold he has on me. He grabs my hand, leading me out of the building. We walk in silence toward my apartment. I can tell from his determined stride that we're not heading to dinner.

I hear the door slam shut and lock and whip around at the sound. Aiden grabs me, spinning me around and slams me into the wall. My breath catches. He grabs my hands and holds them above my head as he runs his lips along my jawline, nipping and sucking. I try to release one hand so I can feel him. Touch him.

"Don't move your hands," he demands and tightens his hold. My eyes flash up to his, surprised by the dominating heat in his voice. His thigh rubs against my center, causing me to moan, and my hips move of their own accord. He removes one of his hands, but still holding both of mine with his other. Using his free hand, he grabs my breast. Hard. He curses under his breath and then slams his mouth against mine. My feelings are at war right now. I'm pissed off because he's being aggressive, yet my body is yearning for the roughness. My head says *back the fuck off*, my body says *harder*. Why is he mad? I'm the one who had the shitty day.

I keep my mouth closed in protest, so he bites my lip. When I gasp, he slips his tongue into my mouth. It's possessive and demanding. My willpower to fight fades as I give in. My body takes over, surrendering to the desire. I rock against him and heat streaks up my body. He releases my hands but glares at me with a warning, commanding me to keep my hands there. *It's too bad I'm not always compliant.*

I run my hands through his hair, fisting it. "Never fucking listen," he growls, yanking my shirt over my head. When he has my shirt almost all the way off, with my hands up high, he stops. The wicked gleam in his eyes says he's got me. "You move your hands out of this shirt, I'm going to fucking handcuff you next." He twists the center of my shirt in his fists, tightening the hold. My hands move closer together, and he holds them against the wall. His other hand yanks down my bra, releasing each swollen breast. He flicks his tongue over my hardened nipple and my body shudders. My back arches off the wall, willing him to take it all in. Thank God he listens. He devours them mercilessly. The ache between my legs intensifies as he continues his lavish assault. His hand moves down to undo my jeans. When he has them past my thighs, I wiggle out of them and kick them off to the side, thankful I didn't wear my skinny jeans today.

He runs a finger along the lace of my panties and at the center. A deep growl from the back of his throat slips out. "You're so fucking wet," he rasps. When he moves my panties to the side, he slips two fingers inside me. I buck my hips against his fingers that rapidly move in and out. The heel of his palm presses against my clit, and I scream out. My orgasm rips through me almost instantly.

Before I can form a coherent thought, Aiden pulls me to the couch, spins me around, and pushes me down over the side arm. My ass is facing upward and the cold air blows on my wet, throbbing sex. He unsnaps my bra and takes off my soaked panties. I hear him pulling down his pants. When I look back, he's already naked. The fire in his eyes is like an inferno now. *Raging.* His jaw clenches as he looks at me. I flinch in surprise when I feel his finger graze my wetness. His other hand grabs my ass.

"Do you know how fucking bad I want to make this ass red right now?" he growls.

Excuse me? My eyes snap to his, confused. I open my mouth to ask him what the hell he's talking about, but he sticks a finger inside me again and my eyes close involuntarily as he moves it around in circles. It's clear he's running the show. He removes it and grabs my hips, immediately slamming his cock into me, burying himself inside me completely. I cry out and he stills for a moment. When I glance back, his nostrils flair and his chest heaves as he tries to regain his control.

"Don't ever ignore me again," he warns. Realization dawns on me, and I understand why he's so upset. He doesn't give me time to respond. *To apologize.* He slams into me again, setting a punishing pace. Instead, I give him what he needs.

"Harder," I moan out, pushing my ass against his groin, keeping rhythm with him. Our bodies smack together. I grasp the couch, letting go of everything clouding my head right now, and submit to the man inside of me.

The position he's in hits that perfect spot, and the ache starts to build inside me again. He leans over, his hard chest against my back, and wraps his arm around me, grabbing my breast and squeezing. I arch my back again as pleasure explodes through my body, and I pulsate, squeezing him tight. His body tightens and his hold on my hips becomes painful as his pelvis pounds into my ass. My whimpers turn to loud moans. A deep, guttural groan grinds out my name and his body convulses against me. I try to hold us both up with my arms, but they give out and we fold over the arm of the couch. I can feel the rise and fall of his chest. He digs his head into the back of my neck, his breaths hot and heavy. Both his arms wrap around me, and he lifts me to a standing position.

"I'm sorry," I whisper. I can use the excuse that I had a horrible day, but I did ignore him because I was afraid he'd bring up the wedding again. He pulls out of me and walks into the kitchen, wets a hand towel, and returns. He gently wipes between my legs, avoiding eye contact. The awkward silence makes me feel horrible. He throws the towel and it lands in the kitchen sink. The side of his mouth twitches. I smirk, knowing he's probably given himself ten points for making it. When he looks down at me, he grins.

"You're going to be the death of me," he says, kissing the tip of my nose, and then leads me to the bedroom. He sits on the bed and pulls me onto his lap. "Addison, I can't have you—" He pauses and looks down for a second. "A text would have been nice if you were too busy to take my call."

"*I know.*"

"All day long I thought you were pissed at me. *For bringing up our wedding.* Then I was furious at you and *then* at myself for thinking that maybe you didn't want to get married."

"Aiden, that's not it at all. I do want to marry you." I cup his jaw, running my hand back into his thick hair. I pull my leg over his hips so I'm straddling him. "Even when you're brooding and take it out on me while you're fucking me." I bring my lips to his and kiss him softly.

"I'm not sorry," he murmurs against my lips.

"You shouldn't be." His hands move up my thighs to my back, and he pulls me tight against his chest, deepening our kiss. Our tongues intertwine, sparking the fire that hadn't been put all the way out. My body trembles, feeling his arousal at my entrance. He lifts me and slides right in.

This time there's no angst. No demands. No submitting. It's only love. Our hearts are stripped bare, exposing two people who aren't perfect but are perfect for each other.

***

I watch him slip his arms into his white shirt. The bottom is wrinkled from tucking it in. When he pulls his tie around his neck, he looks up at me. "Can we go eat now?"

A smile tugs at my lips. The rough day I had no longer hangs in my thoughts. It's been replaced. I nod, slipping a blue shift dress over my head. I'll be damned if I go out looking like I did before. I sit down on the bench at the end of my bed to put my wedges on, and Aiden walks up to me. He runs his hand through my hair, and I let out a soft mewl. His hand gently moves to my chin and raises it so I'm looking at him.

"I don't like thinking you're mad at me." *So I've learned.*

"I didn't purposely ignore your calls," I answer apologetically.

"Which I didn't find out until four." I'm surprised he waited that long.

"I'm sorry." I stand up and teeter-totter on one foot since I only have one shoe on. He wraps his arms around my waist, steadying me. I grin. "Thanks."

He wags his eyebrows and cocks a crooked smile. "I'll always be here to catch you, sweetheart." I laugh at his comment, as corny as it might be, I know it's heartfelt and true.

"Well, thank you for taking me to a happy place."

"Any time," he says. His hands move to my ass, and I can feel my dress creeping up my legs. "Like right now if you wanted."

I slap his hand. "No. I'm starving."

"So am I," he says with a wicked smile. He shoves his hand under my dress and squeezes my ass, pulling me into his hardness.

"You're always hungry. We just had sex *twice.*" I push him away and sit back down to put on my other shoe.

"Well, since you're down there." I look up at him and roll my eyes. "Really? That's original," I joke.

He chuckles and shrugs a shoulder. "Can't blame a guy for trying."

A half hour later we walk out of my building, and I feel much better about how I look. Especially next to Mr. GQ himself. We decide to walk instead of grabbing a cab; it's a gorgeous fall evening. The leaves are changing to vibrant oranges and reds. The cool air is a reprieve from the clammy, hot summer nights.

After going back and forth about where to eat, we finally agree on Chinese. When we sit down, I clasp my hands together on the table and look at Aiden. "So, was *that* my surprise?"

"Oh, *Ms. Mason*. I need you to clarify *that*." He lifts a brow and a playful smile appears on his lips. "Because I'd hate to assume what you are referring to." *Smartass*. He only wants to hear me say sex. I return the smug smile and lean forward on my elbows.

My voice is hushed as I stare into his mischievous green eyes. "Where you fucked my pussy until I was happy," I purr. A groan comes from the back of his throat as he sits back in his chair and adjusts himself.

"No, *that* was not your surprise." He takes a large gulp of water and crunches some ice in his mouth. *A little heated, babe?* I chuckle to myself. He clears his throat. "Do we have any plans on Sunday?"

I look up and think about it. My eyes dart to his. "Um, yes. And you better not have made any plans during the football game because I'm not going to be anywhere except in front of the TV watching it," I declare. It's Cowboys versus Giants. The game that divides us as a family. As much as I love Ryker, I can't cross over. I am a diehard fan. He grins, reaching into his pocket to pull out a white envelope. He places it on the table and pushes it toward me. I pick up the envelope and open it slowly. Inside are five tickets to the game.

"How about watching it *at* the game?"

A squeal escapes my lips. I jump up and sit in his lap. "This is an awesome surprise!" I wiggle in his lap unintentionally.

His hands grip my legs to stop me. "I'm still not recovered from your dirty mouth, woman, so stop."

I laugh and give him a quick kiss before hopping off and sitting back on my chair. I pull the tickets out and look at them again. My eyes widen in surprise. "How in the world did you get *these* tickets?" I ask, holding them up in the air. First row. Fifty-yard line. Right behind the team. The *wrong* team, but I'm not complaining.

"Mack. He owns the whole first row in that section. He gives me tickets a couple times a season." He shrugs like it's not a big deal. *Must be nice.* "He knows you're a big Cowboys fan, so he called me yesterday asking me if I wanted some tickets."

"You've known since yesterday and didn't tell me."

"I was going to this morning, but ..." He trails off and arches a brow in accusation. I bite my lip. *Yep.* I'm a horrible fiancée.

"I decided to hire a wedding planner," I say, hoping it'll ease his mind that I'm thinking about it and ease my guilt. His smile grows, causing his dimples to deepen with satisfaction in his eyes.

"Can we set a date?" he asks with bated breath.

"April 29," I respond with certainty. My response surprises him. He tilts his head, and I can tell he's trying to associate that date with something of importance. It's not. I had already looked at dates in April a week ago, I just hadn't picked one. April is one of my favorite months because of the weather and all the beautiful flowers. *As long as it doesn't rain*, which is why I decided on the end of April.

"I'm not debating the date, but is there a reason?" I smile at being able to read him so well.

"No, I just love April."

He claps his hands once and grins. "That's enough for me. April 29 you will be officially mine forever." I shake my head. *Silly man.* I'm already yours, *forever.*

Chapter eleven

The face Lexi's giving me when she walks out of her room can't be good. The shirt hangs in her hand and her bottom lip sticks out. "What's up, Lulu? Did it not fit?"

We received a special delivery package. Ryker found out we were coming to the game tomorrow and sent all of us a jersey. I laughed when I pulled out the jersey for me and looked at Syd and said, "He's kidding, right?"

Lexi took off with hers to try it on and obviously she's not happy about something. I almost say, "*I'd be mad too if I had to wear that*," but I purse my lips together and just wait to see what she says.

She juts out her hand with the shirt in it. "It's wrong," she pouts.

"What's wrong with it?" I say, taking it from her and holding it up in the air to inspect.

She huffs adorably. "It has Dallas on it. I live in New York." She throws her arms out. I smile at her animated expression.

"Lulu, that's Ryker's last name," I explain.

Her expression changes to confusion. "Why do I want Ryker's last name on *my* shirt? It should be my name." She pokes herself in the chest with her thumb. "And..." she starts again. "The number is wrong. It says six. I'M STILL FIVE!"

"I can't believe Ryker forgot you were still five," Sydney giggles from my side. I shake my head. There's an unspoken contest going on between the guys and Sydney about who Lexi thinks is the best. She truly loves all of them, but it's funny to see how they try and one up each other. I don't think it matters, though; Max will always be her number one.

"I know," she huffs again, crossing her arms.

I turn and look at Sydney, glaring so she'll stop, then look back to Lexi. Her defeated little face was so excited about the jersey when it got here.

I pick her up, putting her on the barstool, and spin her to face me. "Ryker's football number is six." She starts to say something but I shush her. She looks at me with wide eyes and waits for me to continue. "A team jersey has a player's name and number on it. Usually you wear the one with your favorite player on it." She tilts her head and thinks about it.

"Ryker is my favorite player." I nod. Ryker is the *only* one on the team she knows.

"He's so excited we're coming to his game, he wanted you to have this." I place the jersey in her lap. "There will be so many people wearing his jersey all around us because they love him."

"I love Ryker," she says, hugging the jersey. Then she stares at me.

"What?" I can see the wheels turning in that little head of hers.

"Don't you love Ryker?"

"Of course, I do. He's one of Aiden's best friends."

"I heard you say you'd never wear his jersey to the game."
Shit. I need to learn she's always listening.

I open my mouth to explain and then snap it shut, changing my mind. "When I was little..." I point to Syd, "...we grew up in Texas. We loved the Dallas Cowboys and would go to the football games all the time and cheer them on. We are still big fans." I open my arms as wide as they'll go. She giggles. "And that is who the Giants are playing tomorrow. I can't go against my favorite team. Aiden will be wearing a jersey just like you, though," I add, hoping she'll be satisfied with that.

"And Damon," Syd says, walking over to the bar. She reaches for her bottled water and takes a quick drink.

"So, it'll be us against you guys?" She puts her hands on her little hips and smirks. *She learns quickly.*

"Yep, and we're going to take you down." I tickle her belly, and she squeals.

"*Noo.* We're going to take you down," she says between her giggles. I laugh. Aiden is going to love this.

***

"Tater Tot! Where's my girl?" Aiden yells. She must not have heard him come in because usually she's out here the second she hears his voice. They have become quite the pair. I adore the special time they have together. Hearing him talk with her about her dad and the special things they did makes my heart swell and always brings tears to my eyes. He doesn't want to replace her dad, he wants to share the space with him in her heart.

"Aiden!" she screams, running from her bedroom. She runs into his arms, and he swoops her up. "We match." She pinches her jersey and holds it up to his.

"Yes, we do." He holds up his hand and she high-fives it. "There's a traitor among us," he says, eyes narrowing. She tilts her head with a look of confusion.

"What does that mean?"

He laughs. "Someone doesn't love Ryker." She nods her head in understanding, narrows her eyes like he did, and they both glare at me.

I shake my head at Aiden. "Would you stop saying that? I do love Ryker. I don't love the team he's playing on."

"Our team is going to win," Lexi says with a cute, competitive voice.

"You think so, huh?" I laugh at the dynamic duo. "We'll see."

Aiden has Lexi on his shoulders as we walk into the stadium. This is my happy place. The fans' excitement is infectious. My nerves tingle as my heart beats a little faster, adrenaline running through my veins. I thought about doing sports medicine just so I could experience this over and over. It was a fleeting thought because I had already decided my path.

"I can't believe we both ended up with Cowboys' fans," Damon jokes as we walk through the tunnel to our seats. Syd hits him on the arm.

"I could say the same for you," she giggles. "I'm sleeping with the enemy."

He playfully growls and grabs her waist, leaning down and attacking her neck. She laughs as she pushes him off. "And you love it," he chuckles.

"Look at what she's wearing," Aiden says, eyeing me up and down. "You think I give a..." he stops himself and glances up to Lexi. She's not even paying attention. She's looking at everything. He looks back at Damon. "*Yeah*, I don't care. That's one of my favorite outfits *ever*." He wags his eyebrows and smirks. He's especially fond of the boots. Heat spreads low in my belly, thinking about the times he's demanded I keep the boots on while I *ride him*. A salacious grin spreads across his face as if he can read my mind. Who am I kidding? *He knows*.

Syd and I are wearing the *uniform* we wear whenever Dallas plays. Jean cut-off shorts, cowboy boots, and our Cowboys jerseys. We're a little out of place here, but it doesn't matter to us.

When we walk through the tunnel to the open stadium, Lexi's eyes double in size. "Wow!" she beams. "It's so big in here. Look, a balloon!" She points up to the sky.

We all look up. "That's a blimp," Aiden says. "It's like a balloon." She nods and moves on to the next thing. Aiden flips her over his shoulders so she can walk down the stairs. She slips her hand in his, and we walk down to the first row of seats. I'll admit, I'm feeling special right now. We've never sat this close. The team is right in front of us. The reporters line the field, taking pictures of the players practicing.

"These seats are incredible," squeals Syd. She bounces on her toes and gives me a hug. "Thanks for inviting us."

We look up the stadium seating at all the people. Other Cowboys fans wave down to us, and we wave back. "It figures Mack would give his seats to Cowboys fans," a male voice from the seats behind us says. We look at him and politely smile.

"You gotta have some winners on this side," Syd says in her sweet, southern drawl. He smirks and shakes his head. Aiden and Damon introduce themselves to the guy. I guess he's some big wig in the tech industry. I stop listening and turn to face the field. We got here a little early because I wanted to make sure Lexi experienced the entire thing, so we watch some of the Giants players practice.

When Ryker comes out on the field, the place erupts with cheers and whistles. Lexi looks at me wondering what's happening. I point to Ryker. She jumps up out of her seat and yells for him, waving her arms around.

"Well, at least one of you girls has it right," Jack, the tech guy, jokes. Lexi spins around and gives him a huge smile.

"We're going to take them down," she says, pointing to me, repeating my words from yesterday. I burst out laughing.

"I like the way you think," Jack says, holding his hand out for a high five. She gives him one and turns back around. "Good thing she's taking after her dad."

Lexi turns back around to Jack. "Aiden's not my dad. My mom and dad were killed. Addison is my foster mom," she says matter-of-factly. "But Aiden will be my foster dad soon." She jumps in his lap and gives him a big hug. He returns it, but all of us sit still, wide eyed over what she just said. I turn and softly smile to Jack. He's not sure what to say either. He smiles back and nods. There's nothing *to* say. When Lexi jumps out of Aiden's lap and resumes screaming for Ryker, I link our fingers together and squeeze. It's intriguing and mortifying the way a child can be honest without any emotion.

Her truth isn't the way she feels, it's just truth. She loves Aiden like a father, but he isn't her father. *At least not yet.* Aiden picks up my hand and kisses my knuckles.

"She loves you," I whisper. I don't want him to be insecure about what he means to Lexi because of what she said. It's the first time he's heard that. I've had time to deal with hearing it for a few months. It's gut wrenching at first until you realize that kid's actions speak so much louder than words.

"I know," he replies. He takes a deep inhale and blows it out his nose, nodding that he's okay, and sits forward in his seat. He positions Lexi between his legs and points out random things to her, explaining the game. I sit back and watch them. A couple guys on the team notice Aiden and wave to him. *Hmm...I wonder how many guys he knows on the team.* Lexi gets super excited, thinking they're waving to her.

I watch one of the guys walk over to Ryker and point at us. Ryker looks and his smile grows. He jogs over to us and jumps up on the bars in front of us. "Lulu!" He picks her up into his arms and gives her a big kiss on the cheek, ignoring the fans cheering behind us.

"Ryker, look, I'm wearing your jersey," she says excitedly.

"It looks better on you than it does on me." Her face beams. He puts her down and looks at me, shaking his head. "You're killing me, Addison." He grips his heart. I roll my eyes. My feet are up on the bar and his eyes move down my legs. "If it weren't for those legs, I might be mad." He winks at me.

Aiden growls. "You better go before I break your throwing arm," Aiden jokes. I think he's finally figured out that Ryker likes to mess with him by flirting with me.

"No," Lexi says. "You can't break his arm. He's the dollarback."

We bust out laughing. Lexi looks at us perplexed, wondering what we think is so funny.

"Tater Tot, he's not *that* important," Aiden chuckles. "He's just a *quarter*back."

"Hey, Lulu, look at Addison." Ryker points to me. When Lexi turns and looks at me, Ryker flips off Aiden. He laughs again and blows him a kiss. When Lexi figures out there's nothing to see, she shrugs and spins back around. "Alright, Lulu, I expect to hear really loud cheers from you. It'll help me win."

"I'll be the loudest," she promises. He fists bumps her and hops down to go back to practicing.

From the "National Anthem" to halftime, Lexi never sits down. She cheers, yells, sings, and dances the entire night. At halftime, we take a quick bathroom break and grab some food just in time to start all over. Lexi's like the band director. She stands on her seat and directs everyone to get out of their seats and cheer. Our section follows her like the Pied Piper, and she's eating it up. By the end of the third quarter, the Cowboys lead by two touchdowns, so the crowd has quieted a bit. *Except for us Cowboys fans.*

Lexi is sitting in Aiden's lap and she seems to have stopped ticking. I look over and she's dead asleep, her head resting on Aiden's chest. Her hair is in French braids, except for the few errant hairs stuck to her face from either sweat or cotton candy.

"I think she cheered herself to sleep," I say, smiling at her. Aiden nods in agreement.

When the fourth quarter starts, Ryker glances our way and sees his biggest fan conked out. He shakes his head and chuckles before putting on his helmet and running onto the field. Not two plays later, he throws it for a touchdown and the crowd goes crazy.

Lexi sits straight up and looks at Aiden. "What did I miss?"

"They just scored a touchdown," he says. She jumps up and hollers, waving her arms around. Her little body must have needed to refuel because she's up and raring to go again. And she stays that way until the very end.

When the Giants win.

***

"Knock, knock." I look up from my files at Bryn standing in my doorway.

"Hey, girl. Come on in." Harper and I just got back from being out in the field all day, and I'm going over my notes. She sits down in one of the chairs in front of my desk, crosses her legs, and reclines. "What's going on?" Bryn doesn't normally visit with me during work hours, so I have no idea why she's here, but her smile tells me whatever it is, it's good.

"Have you looked at Page Six today?"

I stare at her with confusion. "Why would I have looked at Page Six today?"

"You'll want to see today's paper." I cock my eyebrow. *I doubt that.* "No, really. You do." Her persistence has me wondering what it could be. I know that Brooks is in Page Six a lot with the title of "Sexiest Bachelor Single Dad." I roll over to my computer and type in the website. Page Six is the celebrity, music, and entertainment section of the *New York Times.* When it pops up, I gasp and cover my mouth with my hand.

"Oh. My. God. You've got to be kidding me." I look at Bryn in shock, and she shakes her head. I look back to the website and the first thing that shows up reads *"Who's Ryker Dallas's New Girl?"* and it has a picture of him kissing Lexi on the cheek at the game. I immediately start reading the article.

Giants' golden boy, Ryker Dallas, seems to have a new girl, but this one is cute as a button and seems to grab the attention of everyone around her. (We watched her more than the game.)

I click the *read more* link and it opens the article. I skim through it. They mainly talk about Ryker's stats and his record-breaking season. It's not until the end that they talk about Lexi again.

We don't know who she is, but we can say when she passed out in her dad's arms (did we mention he's gorgeous) it was

*the sweetest thing ever. When we asked about her, Ryker
ignored the question.*

I finish reading the article and I'm speechless. I'm not sure
how I feel about Lexi's picture being on a gossip website. I look
at Bryn stunned.

"Wow," I say, shaking my head.

"I know! And if that isn't the sweetest picture ever," she
says, pointing to the screen. I look at it again. *It is sweet.* She
sits back and groans. I look at her. My head tilts to the side,
confused about why she seems upset. She rolls her eyes and
huffs. "Why does he have to be charismatic, *hot*, a perfect
gentleman, and now this..." she says, throwing out her arms. I
furrow my brows. What the hell is she talking about? "I mean,
my ovaries see that and they go spread eagle and say 'come feed
me'."

I slap my hand to my forehead and chuckle. "I did not need
that image in my head." She laughs. "Where is this coming
from?" I finally ask.

"We kind of hooked up the night of your party, before all
hell broke loose." I nod. I heard that through the grapevine
so I'm not surprised. "He's called me a few times since and
we've..." Her voice trails off, but the blush creeps up her face.

I cock my eyebrow. This, I haven't heard. I lean forward on
my desk. "Have y'all seen each other again?"

"No. We've just talked on the phone." She bites her lip and
starts fanning herself. "It got hot in here suddenly."

"*Mmm-hmm*," I say. Seems they did a little more than talk
on the phone.

"Anyway, he's just not boyfriend material. But he keeps
making me question things." Her head jerks to the screen. "He
really adores Lexi." She sighs.

"He does." I want to tell her that he's a good guy, but he is a total playboy. I understand her hesitancy. Guys like that don't like to settle down, so I stay quiet.

"I kind of wish he was an asshole. Then I wouldn't have to be thinking *what if.* It's not like I'm going to see him anytime soon."

I bite my cheek. *Oh, it might be sooner than you think.* I plan on asking Bryn to be a bridesmaid, and of course, Ryker will be a groomsman. *And* we planned on pairing them already. I'm not sure telling her will help the situation, so again, I keep my mouth shut. She'll find out soon enough when I ask all the girls.

When she leaves, I pull out my phone and text Aiden.

Me: Did you see Page Six today?

Aiden: I did.

I look at his response. *That's it?* I wait a minute to see if he writes anything else. When he doesn't, I respond.

Me: And ...

Aiden: I'm gorgeous and I'm the dad :) It's a win-win for me!

I roll my eyes. *Seriously?*

Chapter twelve

"**F**irst question, when's the date?"

It's Saturday morning and I'd much rather be out with Aiden and Lexi doing fun things. Instead, I'm here with the wedding planner, Ava. She's a serious, straight to business, no bullshit kind of woman. *I like her.*

"April 29."

She stares at me and blinks. I bite the inside of my cheek, second-guessing my date. "I know it's far away, but I don't want to get married in the winter," I say, defending my date. She snickers at my response.

"Far away?" she replies. "I was thinking that it was *too* soon."

My eyes widen. "It's almost seven months away."

"*Exactly.*" She flips open her laptop and starts typing. She looks over my head and says, "Most women start planning their wedding at least a year in advance. Especially if they expect to get the venue they want."

"A year?" my voice breaks. *Holy shit.* Why would I want to spend a year of my life planning a wedding?

"It'll be okay. I think I can make do with seven months. Especially if Ryker Dallas will be there." My eyebrow quirks.

Why the hell would that make a difference? We had to give her the names of our party when we filled out our initial questionnaire. She obviously went over that.

She waves her hand in the air. "Venues always love when celebrities attend because it gives them free advertising. Have you thought about where you want to get married?" I guess that makes sense.

I tap my fingers on the table as I think about it. "*Hmm...*" I can't think of anything. "We don't need to get married in a church." I'm happy giving her a specific detail, but she crushes it when she replies.

"Addison, have you thought about *any* of the details for your wedding?" *I thought I just gave you one.*

"No," I sigh. "That's why I hired you."

She stares at me for a beat and then nods like she's answering her own question. I'm getting the feeling I'm not her typical bride.

"Okay," she says slowly. "I just need to ask this before we proceed. Do you want to get married?" Her voice turns serious as she sits back in her seat and crosses her arms.

I laugh out loud and lean forward on the table. "That is the only thing I'm sure of. Listen, I just need my wedding to go off without anyone ruining it. The details aren't the most important thing. As long as we're married in the end, that's what matters most to me."

"That I can do." She smiles.

"I'm warning you, *that* might sound easy, but you don't know how much Fate likes to screw with me."

She sits up tall and her smirk tells me she's up to the challenge. "Addison, I promise you that you and Aiden will be married on April 29." *Yep, I like her.*

The next couple hours are spent going over detail after detail. I'm blown away by some of them. What the hell is a groom's cake for anyway? I tell her I want simple. *Classy, but simple.* I don't need over-the-top decorations. I don't even care if my girls' dresses match.

"There's a website that you pick the color of the dress and the girls can choose between over a hundred designs," Ava says, writing down the website for me.

"Sydney will love that." I take the paper from her and put it in my pile of things to do. She pulls up the website and turns her laptop around so I can see. We go through the colors, and I finally decide on burgundy.

"What will the guys be wearing?"

I hold up my hands and shake my head. "That's a question for Aiden." He can make some of these damn decisions, too. If I knew I'd have to make this many decisions, I would have had him here with me. My head hurts. I get up and grab a water for us as she clicks on her keyboard, hopefully writing out a list for Aiden. I twist the cap off and take a long drink. My mouth is dry from talking so much.

When we return to the subject of venues, I have no freaking clue. She goes over some of the popular ones around New York City. When she talks about the Central Park Boathouse, I stop her.

"I want it there," I say quickly. Central Park is one of my favorite places ever.

She twists her lips, tapping her pen against them. "It usually books up fast, but I'll check it out. I need a couple other options just in case it isn't available." I nod and we continue to pick a couple more places.

By the time she leaves, I feel like I've drained every cell in my brain. I mindlessly go through my to-do list, which needs immediate attention.

Tell bridesmaids and groomsmen they are in the wedding. Find a dress.

I drop my head onto the kitchen table. I've officially been thrown into wedding planning hell. Time to get the girls together for a dinner.

***

"I'm so glad you set this up," Macie says, sitting across from me. Her smile reaches her eyes. "I needed a girls' night out. And I have news."

We all stare at her expectantly. She waits for the waiter to put all our waters in front of us before she continues.

"I'll be right back with your drinks, ladies," our waiter says before walking away. We politely thank him and turn back to Macie.

"I'm pregnant," she beams without hesitation, clapping her hands together.

"That's awesome news," I say, standing and running around the table to hug her. Aiden told me she and Ryan have been trying for a while, so I know how much this means to her. Bryn, Sydney, and Harper congratulate her, and we do a toast when we get our drinks. Of course, Macie toasts with a Shirley Temple. Now I know why she didn't order an alcoholic drink.

"*Oh, no.* Can you eat something here?" I ask, concern in my voice. Had I known, I wouldn't have picked a sushi restaurant.

She waves her hand. "Yes, it's fine. I'll just get a roll with shrimp in it."

Syd bounces in her seat. "I'm so excited for you, Mace. Has Ryan told the guys?"

"He's going to tonight. You guys couldn't have planned this night any better! We were so excited that we could tell everyone in person."

Aiden and I each planned a dinner out with our friends to check off the first thing on our to-do list. Hannah took Lexi to a new Disney movie so it worked out perfectly. *Oh, shit.* I start counting months in my head. My fingers move as I count each month.

"We're due at the end of May, first of June," Macie says, finishing my calculation for me. I wonder how she's going to feel being eight months pregnant in the wedding. I hold off asking so we can enjoy her excitement for a little bit.

The waiters place our food in front of us. My mouth waters just looking at it. My rolls are filled with shrimp, crab, and tuna with a creamy wasabi sauce on top. My nose tickles in anticipation of the wasabi. I break apart my chopsticks and pick a slice up. Dipping it in soy sauce, I bring the roll to my mouth and savor the flavors in each bite. My nose burns and my eyes water from the heat; that short burst of burning is why I love wasabi.

We chat about everything while we eat with lots of laughs in between. By the time dinner is done, I'm rubbing my sore cheeks. I take a quick drink of my wine before talking.

"Okay, ladies. There is a reason I asked y'all to come to dinner." Syd flashes a knowing smile. She already knows what I'm about to say. I hate that Katie isn't here, but I talked to her right before dinner. She screamed through the phone in excitement. I'm surprised I can hear out of that ear.

Butterflies flutter in my stomach, and I'm not sure why I'm so nervous. I clasp my hands together and say, "We set a date, April 29."

"Finally," cheers Harper. I roll my eyes, but laugh. I know I've been avoiding the planning stage, but it hasn't been *that* long.

"And I'd like it if you all would be my bridesmaids," I say shyly. My heart beats fast, and I can feel my face flush. My feelings catch me off guard. I don't know if I'm afraid they're going to say no or I just don't like being in the spotlight.

Cheers and yesses are repeated around the table. I let out a soft breath and fan myself. Syd looks at me, shaking her head. I stick my tongue out at her. She's always been the social butterfly out of the two of us. She craves the spotlight, while I try to keep out of it.

I glance at Macie who's biting her lip. "I know you'll be eight months pregnant, but that's okay, right?" Aiden won't let Ryan back out, so if Macie doesn't want to be in the wedding I'm going to have to find someone else. And I don't have anyone else, so I'm hoping she says yes.

"If you don't mind a huge whale in your wedding." She scrunches up her nose.

I slam my hand down on the table, glasses clink together. *Crap.* I grasp the round table, steadying it. "What! You worked hard for the baby, you better be showing that belly off loud and proud. And you'll be adorable pregnant."

She smiles and her eyes well up with tears. I blink back the tears threatening to form.

"Y'all are making *me* cry," Sydney says.

"*Sorry.* These damn hormones. Yes, I'd be honored to be in your wedding," she says, blotting the tears with her napkin.

"Yay!" I clap, looking around the table. "Thank y'all for being such good friends. You've been there for me for so much, and I love y'all."

"This isn't helping me," Macie cries and laughs at the same time.

"Dessert, ladies?" the waiter says.

"Yes," everyone replies at once.

A few minutes later, we're all staring at the decadent chocolate cake in front of us. "Holy mother of chocolate," Syd says. The cake's icing looks like hot fudge, smooth and silky. Strawberries line one side of the cake, laying in melted chocolate. The other side has a scoop of vanilla ice cream, drizzled in the chocolate. My taste buds are already buzzing, telling me to hurry the hell up and take a bite. I bring a forkful to my mouth and as soon as the rich, warm chocolate hits my tongue, I close my eyes and drown in chocolate-induced euphoria.

Bryn clears her throat. I open my eyes and glare at her. She's ruining the moment. *This better be good.* She laughs at me. "So..." She pauses and looks around the table. "Who am I going to be paired with?"

"After you just interrupted my chocolate orgasm, *who do you think*?" I say, jokingly. She is with Ryker but that decision was already decided.

"Really? Can't I be with Max?" she whines.

Harper figures out what's going on and jumps in. "I don't mind being with Ryker," she boasts as she brings a forkful of chocolate cake to her mouth. She lets out a moan when she pulls the fork out. "This cake is amazeballs," she mumbles.

"Max is the best man so he'll be with Syd." I shove a piece of cake in my mouth before I have to talk again.

"Then I'll be with Damon."

I sigh. "Bryn, he'll still be there whether you walk down the aisle with him or walk in front of him." She rolls her eyes over the brim of her wine glass.

"Bryndle," Syd says slowly with a mischievous grin. "Is there something you need to share with the group?" I glance at Syd. *Is that even her name?*

Bryn scrunches her nose at Syd. "No, *Sydney*, there isn't anything to tell." She picks up her glass of wine again and downs the rest of it, filling it right back up with the bottle on the table. "I just don't want to be the one with the *'famous football player'*." She uses air quotes.

"For the wedding or *ever*?" Harper asks, eyeing Bryn.

"You guys! Nothing is going on with us. We've talked a couple times on the phone." She glares at me as I start to say something. I snap my mouth shut and grab my wine. I still don't believe it was just *talking*.

"The lady doth protest too much." Syd laughs.

"Fine," she huffs, surrendering. "I'll be with him. *At the wedding*," she clarifies.

"Ryker really is a good guy," Macie says, putting her hand on top of Bryn's.

Bryn lets out a heavy sigh. "*Yes, he is*. That's the problem. Why can't I meet a normal, boring guy? My life is boring. I'm a freaking accountant, for God's sake. I just don't want to be in the spotlight." *I certainly understand that.*

I start to wonder if there is more to her story. I've only known Bryn for a little over a year, but she's never talked about her past. I've never noticed until now. She has a strong personality, but she's struggling with this. She could easily tell Ryker no, but it's obvious she likes him. What's holding her back? I know we all have skeletons, but I hope hers don't have a tight hold on her. She picks up her wine and takes another drink.

I softly smile at her. She's clearly flustered. I don't want her to be uncomfortable at my wedding. "I can put Ryker with Harper," I say, hoping it'll help her calm down. With her elbow on the table and her glass in the air, she closes her eyes briefly and lets out a heavy sigh.

"No. I'm sorry," she says. "It's fine. I'll be with Ryker."

"You sure?"

"Yes. Now let's talk about what you have to do next."

I mentally file away that I need to talk to Bryn more, make sure she's okay with this. She clearly wants to move on, so I tell them about the website they need to go to and what color the dress should be. They're excited they don't all have to wear the same dress. They all have different body types so they start discussing what they like and don't like in a dress. I'm excited hearing them talk about their dresses. I tell them a few details that Ava and I discussed and where we're trying to book for the ceremony and reception.

"That sounds amazing," Macie says. The last few days, I've imagined my wedding at the Boathouse and I'm hoping we get it. Regret bubbles up inside of me, thinking I should have started planning it sooner. Aiden is getting a kick out of this.

"My next to-do is to go wedding dress shopping. I have an appointment in two weeks, so if you can be there, I'd love it because I'm going to need all the help I can get picking out a dress."

I'm relieved when everyone agrees to come and help me. They all start throwing out descriptions of dresses, what I might like or not like. *Holy shit, I'm scared.* Can't I just say a white dress and be done with it?

Chapter thirteen

"**I**'m so excited I finally get to meet Presley," Lexi says, bouncing on her toes.

I knock on the door and smile down at her. Brooks invited us to dinner last week, and Lexi has been counting down the days. Truth be told, so have I. I've talked with Brooks a couple times since he sent out an SOS, but I want us to get to know each other better.

"Just remember, she's a baby and you need to be careful with her, okay?" I'm a little afraid she's going to think she's here for a play date. This whole week I've tried to prep her that Presley is only two months old and all she does is eat, sleep, and poop. Her reaction? She was *more* excited, saying her Baby Alive poops and she knows how to change diapers.

The door opens and the person behind it isn't the person I was expecting.

"Melanie?" Aiden and I both say simultaneously. I look down at Lexi and back to Melanie. *Goddammit.* I'm not sure how I feel about Lexi meeting Travis. *Brooks could have warned me.*

Melanie reads my hesitancy and says, "Don't worry, I'm here alone."

I angle me head. While I'm relieved, I'm confused. Why would Melanie be here without Travis? I haven't seen her since my *stay* at Travis's. I enjoyed talking with her during that time because she knew my mom, but she runs Travis's house so it's weird she's here and he's not.

"It's good to see you both," she says with a genuine smile. "Come in. Brooks is changing Presley, so he'll be right out." She opens the door wider to let us in. Aiden weaves his fingers through mine as we walk into the penthouse.

Lexi takes off in search of Brooks and Presley. When Melanie shuts the door, I turn in her direction. "Melanie, what are you doing here?" My question comes out snarkier than I mean it to. "I'm sorry. I didn't mean that to sound so rude. I'm just surprised to see you here. Especially without Travis."

She softly smiles and clasps her hands in front of her. "It's okay, Addison. I know the last time we saw each other it wasn't under the best of terms." Her voice is warm as she looks from me to Aiden. "You had your reasons to be there, and I might not have agreed with them but I understood," she says to Aiden. "When Travis told me you two were together, I was elated. Life's journey is a wondrous thing." She brings her folded hands to her chest, releasing a soft sigh.

I'm not sure I agree with my life's journey being wondrous. *More like turbulent.*

"Addie, Addie," Lexi says, running out of a bedroom. "Brooks let me help change Presley."

She wraps herself around my leg. "Was it as fun as changing your Baby Alive?"

Her nose scrunches up, and she shakes her head. "Noo. It was stinky." She waves her hand in front of her nose. "And it was everywhere. I don't think I want to help again."

We all laugh at Lexi. "But you were so good at it," Brooks jokes, walking out of the same bedroom, holding Presley in his arms. A cloth hangs over his shoulder as he taps her back, his whole hand covering her body. He could easily be the poster child for hot, single father. His heather gray fitted shirt stretches perfectly over his slim but muscular physique, and his dark jeans rest low on his hips. I chuckle to myself.

I'm sure he won't be single long.

He looks relaxed and in control holding Presley. He must be getting the hang of it. "Here, I'll take Presley so you guys can talk," Melanie says, holding out her arms. Brooks effortlessly hands her to Melanie. Melanie cradles Presley and looks at Lexi. "Lexi, would you like to help me feed her?"

Lexi looks up at me. She's unsure of her. I don't know why she hesitates with a sweet old lady and not Brooks, whom she's never met. I'm going to have to watch her around men. "Lexi, this is Melanie," I say, introducing them. Lexi looks her way and smiles. "It's okay, you can go help." Lexi nods and releases my hand, following Melanie out of the room. Once I see they are out of sight, I turn to Brooks who is shaking Aiden's hand.

"How do you know Melanie?"

"I've known Melanie since I was eighteen. She's kind of been my go-between with Travis. When I got custody of Presley... well, you know how I was. Way out of my comfort zone. Melanie called me to see how I was doing..." He pauses, running a hand through his hair. "It was better than when you were here, but it still wasn't good, so she came to my rescue. At least until I can hire a full-time nanny."

"This is probably a lot easier than managing a house full of men," Aiden says, chuckling. "She's a good person. I'm glad she's here to help."

I nod in agreement. "How's the full-time nanny search going?"

Brooks rolls his eyes and subtlety shakes his head. "It's ridiculous. Most of the women who come for an interview are obviously not here for Presley. It pisses me off. Every. Fucking. Time." He grates out each word between clenched teeth.

"I'm sorry, women suck," I say, my tone serious. It pisses me off too that women can be so shallow. "I'm assuming you're going through an agency? Maybe tell them that all the applicants have to be over fifty."

"Well...I wouldn't mind having someone around who's not bad to look at." He shrugs, flashing a wicked smile.

My mouth gapes open, and I shake my head. "I take my comment back. Men suck." I scoff at him. Aiden laughs out loud and grabs me around my waist. "Oh, don't you dare agree with him." I jab my finger into his chest.

"What? I would never," he says innocently. "But it is kind of nice having a beautiful woman to look at every day." When I open my mouth to tell him he's an ass, too, he cuts me off by slamming his lips onto mine. I try and fight the kiss, but it's a lost cause. When I finally find the strength to pull back, I slap his shoulder.

"You don't play fair."

He leans in close to me again. I can feel the warmth of his breath on my cheek. "You know I always play to win, sweetheart."

I take a step backwards to gain control of my senses. "You're about to win a vacation from sex until the wedding if you keep it up," I warn. He returns a smirk, glancing at Brooks and then back to me.

"I think that would be more of a punishment...*for you.*"

My eyes widen. "You're kidding, right? You think I can't go five months without sex. That I would cave before you?" The fact that he thinks he can go five months without sex is hilarious.

"You both are crazy. You would never find me taking *that* bet," Brooks jokes as he walks to the kitchen. I lift my brow, waiting for Aiden to back down. There is no way he would last. Five months? *Never.*

I cross my arms and glare at him, challenging him, calling him on his bullshit. He twists his lips and assesses me, probably wondering how serious I'm being. *Try me, buddy.* I narrow my eyes slightly and wait. His lips curl up to a smile, and he yanks my arm from my chest, pulling me to him. "You're so sexy when you're being feisty," he says. I laugh, nodding my head. He wraps my arm around his waist while grabbing the other one. "Woman, I've tried staying away from you. *Numerous times.* And I've failed miserably every time. You're like my kryptonite. I get weak when I'm around you."

"Oh, so you're Superman now, huh?" I smirk.

"That's right, sweetheart. And you're my Wonder Woman."

I roll my eyes and push him off me. "That was probably the cheesiest line *ever.*" I laugh again, walking away from him toward the kitchen.

He follows me. "Faster than a speeding bullet?" He continues with his Superman jokes. I stop and look back, biting my lip. *I wish.* He barks out a laugh. "*Okay.* I could never be faster than *your* bullet, but I can suck and lick you like a fucking lollipop." He leans down and whispers into my ear. Chills run down my spine from the heat of his words. My knees weaken and I grunt, wishing my body wouldn't turn into a pile of melted desire at his beck and call. I spin in place and slap my hand against his chest, staring up at him. A smug smile rests on his face. I open my mouth to say something, but I'm not even sure how to respond. "Tell me I'm wrong," he taunts, grabbing my hand off his chest and kissing my open palm. He sticks out his tongue and flicks the padded area of my palm and then sucks. Heat bursts throughout my body, thinking about his tongue and the things he can do with it.

I yank my hand out from his. "You're not wrong," I murmur, moving away from him and his skillful tongue. *Dammit, Addison, think of something else.*

"What are you cooking?" I ask, walking in the kitchen while I fan myself.

"Are you hot?" Brooks looks at me from the kitchen sink. *On fire.*

"It just got a little warm in there," I respond. Aiden walks in, snickering. Brooks's gaze jumps from me to Aiden and back. He shakes his head, laughing, and looks down at the dish he's washing.

"We're having lasagna," Brooks says.

"Wow. Do you cook a lot?" I'd be impressed, but I glance around the spotless kitchen and see polished steel appliances that look like they've never been used. There's no way he cooks very much in here. I pull out a barstool and slide into it.

He grabs a towel and dries off the dish, placing it on the island. "I've probably had five meals in this kitchen and none of them were cooked by me. But I do know how to boil water, so I could live off mac n' cheese if I needed to." He shrugs.

"You've got Addison beat already," Aiden teases. I turn and glare at him.

"I'm getting better," I huff.

"Well, I didn't make this. Melanie did."

"Is that her famous lasagna?" Aiden moves to the oven and opens it, inhaling. I cock my head back, surprised, but then I remember he lived with the woman for two years when he worked for Travis.

Aiden wasn't kidding. That was the best lasagna I've ever had. After dinner, we sit around the table chatting. Melanie takes Lexi back to the theater room so they can watch a movie and we can talk without little ears hearing everything.

"Have you heard anything about Jessie?" I ask. I feel Aiden tense next to me. She's still a sore subject with him.

He nods. "The DA agreed to a plea bargain that she'll do a year at a psych hospital of her parents' choice. They picked one in California." I'm relieved she won't go to jail, but surprised they want their daughter on the other side of the country.

"What's with California?"

He shrugs a shoulder. "I'm not sure, but her dad comes from old money so I'm thinking they are trying to quietly get her help, away from home."

"What's going to happen when she comes back?"

Brooks's finger taps the table and sighs. "I don't know. We'll cross that bridge when we get there."

I want to tell him that Presley will need her mom and I hope they can work it out, but I stay quiet. It's obvious neither of the guys want to talk about her anymore.

Brooks looks down the hallway where Lexi and Melanie went. "What's going on with Lexi?"

"We're going to apply for adoption, but not until after the wedding. I can only handle one huge, life-altering event at once. And it'll probably help our chances if we're married."

"She's an awesome little girl. Big personality."

"That she is," Aiden replies, smiling.

Speaking of adoptions, I ask Brooks, "How did you find out that Travis was your father?"

He sits back in his seat, splaying his legs out. "I always knew I had been adopted. When I turned eighteen, I received a trust fund. My parents weren't poor, but there was no way they could afford giving me that much money."

My mouth opens to ask how much, but I close it. It's none of my business. I nod and let him continue.

"I demanded answers from my parents, and they eventually told me. So, I went to meet him."

"I bet your meeting went better than mine." The words slip out of my mouth before I can catch them. Aiden glances at me, lifting a brow.

"Isn't that when you two met?"

I nod slowly. "We did." Aiden stays quiet but sports a lopsided smile, and I bring my glass of wine to my lips.

"It couldn't have been all that bad."

I swallow the sip of red wine in my mouth before I choke on it. I clear my throat before continuing. "Travis held me prisoner for a week. I was handcuffed to a bed for most of it. Aiden was the guy assigned to watch over me so I didn't escape."

Brooks's eyes widen. "What the hell? I thought you were FBI?"

"It wasn't really that bad," I say, holding my finger up. It sounds much worse than it was. Brooks looks at me like I'm nuts. I retell the story and he listens intently the whole time.

"He thought you would stay there, huh?" Brooks asks, flicking his hand open on the table.

I shrug. "I *guess* I understand. Not that I would have ever stayed, though."

"So, Aiden got you out of there?"

Aiden barks out one laugh, shaking his head. "No. Addison had *other* plans." Brooks cocks his head and looks at me.

I run my hand through my hair. I always hate this part. I feel bad every time it passes my lips. "I shot Aiden in the arm and ran." Brooks's brows shoot up before he starts laughing, slapping himself in the chest.

"Damn, I have a bad-ass sister."

I smirk at his reaction. This is the first time he's referred to me as his sister. It feels weird and exciting at the same time.

"You should have known that the first time you met Addison," Aiden says.

"No." Brooks shakes his head. "You don't want to know what I thought of her. It's illegal in most states."

I slap my hand to my head. "Maybe you should keep that to yourself," I say.

Aiden stands up and walks to the counter, grabbing the wine bottle. He refills our glasses and sits back down. We continue talking about our lives, where we grew up. It's weird how alike we are. Traits that I thought were learned from my environment make me think they were more innate and the environment just brought them out. He's only eight months younger than me. Melanie joins us, taking a seat at the table. Brooks gets up and gets her a glass, filling it with wine and placing it in front of her.

"Thanks," she takes a quick swallow. "Lexi fell asleep on the couch watching *Tarzan*."

I slap Aiden on the chest. "It's your favorite movie." He smirks.

"What can I say, you bring out the animal in me." He wags his brows. I giggle, rolling my eyes. He's on a roll tonight with cheesy lines.

"She's a doll," Melanie says. I turn my gaze to Melanie and my lips curl into a smile. "Travis told me what happened. She was a blessing given to you. I know you may not want to hear this, but Travis is so proud of you." Her words are soft but hit me hard. I take in a deep breath and blow it out my nose.

I've always wondered what it'd be like having a father who looked at me with unconditional love. Ted took on that role, but I was almost an adult already, so it's not the same. He loves me, but if something were to happen with Amy, I don't know if he'd keep in touch. I hope so. I don't know how to respond to that, so I just smile and nod.

"What's up with Travis having two kids within a year?" Brooks states, clearly trying to move on from that topic. He glances at me with a slight nod of his head.

Melanie grunts. "That man..." she groans, taking a quick drink of her wine, "...he was heartbroken when your mom left. I told you he went wild." She looks at me. She did tell me that, what she didn't tell me was that I had a brother out there in the world. "Unfortunately, Brooks was a byproduct of that wildness."

"Hey," Brooks interrupts, holding out his arms. "I'm sitting right here."

She looks at him warmly, like a grandparent would. "You know he's extremely proud of you and has never regretted having you. That's why he handpicked your adoptive parents. It was because of you that he pulled his shit together."

I jerk my head to Brooks, wondering if this is news to him. He nods. "I knew. Like I said, when I turned eighteen, my parents told me everything."

"Travis is a good guy. He's just caught up in a bad business. He was born into it, and he wanted to make sure his son wouldn't have the same upbringing he did, being burdened into taking on the family business." When she talks about Travis, it's obvious that she loves him. Her eyes shine bright, the lines around her eyes wrinkle from her smile.

She tells us stories from when Travis was a child and teenager. I can't help but grin, listening to the things he did. She talks more about his and my mom's relationship. That she never saw him act that way toward a woman before or after my mom.

By the time we leave, I feel so much closer to Brooks. We agree that we want to be part of each other's life. Especially since he has Presley.

He wraps his arms around me when we get to the door. "Travis and I have lunch every three or four months...if you'd like to join us," he says. That must be why Travis was in the city when he dropped by to see me a few months ago.

I look over at Lexi sleeping in Aiden's arms and then back to Brooks. I think about the scars on my wrists caused by being Travis's daughter and even though they are almost completely gone on the surface, the emotional scar will never fade. And I can't bring that world into Lexi's.

"I can't," I murmur. "I have too much to risk."

He nods. "I get it. I just wanted to put it out there so you didn't think he was picking favorites." He laughs to lighten the mood. My competitive side wants to say he'd pick me, but I keep my mouth shut. That's one race I don't want to enter.

Chapter fourteen

"Wake up, birthday girl."

Lexi rolls over, looks at me, and then puts her arms out into a stretch. "It's not my birthday yet. My birthday is November 10," she says, yawning. She sits up in bed. Her bed hair is crazy. It looks like a caramel poof of cotton candy.

"I know that, but we're celebrating all weekend." Her birthday is officially tomorrow but this is her first birthday without her family, and I want to make it extra special for her. "So get up and let's eat so we can go have some fun," I say, leaning over and tickling her. Her eyes widen.

"Fun? Where are we going?" She jumps up on her bed. I stand and start walking out of the room.

"You're just going to have to get up and see."

"Wait for me!" She jumps off her bed and comes running after me. I run into the living room where Aiden waits with her first surprise.

A squeal so loud I'm certain it just woke up every neighbor I have comes out of her mouth. She takes a flying leap and lands on the human-size, white teddy bear. "I love it," she says, her voice muffled from her face being buried in the belly of the bear.

When she digs her way out of the bear she jumps into Aiden's arms. "Thanks, Aiden."

"You're welcome, Tater Tot." He kisses her on the head. "You need to eat so we can go ride some rides."

She jumps up and down. "Are we going skydiving?" I laugh out loud. *That would be a no.*

"Lulu, do you know what skydiving is?" I ask.

She nods her head. "It's a ride and we fly through the air." She has pictures from when Aiden and I went, but I guess she doesn't realize how far *up* we were. Aiden's sitting on the couch with his fingers over his lips, contemplating something. If he thinks we're taking Lexi skydiving, he better think again.

"You do fly through the air, but you jump out of a plane." Her eyes widen in surprise.

"Like Max's airplane?"

"It was out of Max's airplane, but a different one than you've been on," I reply.

Her mouth drops open and her little brows furrow. "I don't think I want to go skydiving."

"Tater Tot, it's so much fun. Flying in the sky like a bird." I glare at Aiden. *What is he thinking?* I just had her convinced it wasn't a good thing. She glances at Aiden. Her lips pucker as she thinks.

"I can't fly like a bird," she says, her tone serious. "*I've tried.* I hurt my knees." She points to her knees.

"*Yeah, Aiden*, she can't fly. She's too young," I say through gritted teeth so maybe he'll get the hint and stop trying to convince her. Instead, he winks at me and flashes a mischievous smile as he stands up. I narrow my eyes and shake my head.

"No, we're not going skydiving. But I think you'll love it when you do go." He picks her up and throws her in the air like a ragdoll. She yelps on her way down. When he catches her, he says, "Today, we're going to Coney Island." She throws her hands in the air and screams in excitement. Then wraps her arms around his neck and squeezes.

"I haven't been there before, but my brother went last year. I wanted to go so bad, but my mom said I was too young."

"You're a big six-year-old now," Aiden says. "You're definitely old enough."

She grabs his face with her hands and whispers, "I'm not six until tomorrow."

He leans his forehead against hers. "*Shh.* Nobody has to know that."

Great. Now he's encouraging her to lie. *We're going to make fantastic parents.*

When we pull out of the parking garage, I glance back at Lexi in the backseat. She's flashing a grin as big as her face. She's bouncing with excitement. Her smile is infectious. I love looking at her little face.

The drive isn't too long. Lexi and Aiden sing to the music on the radio. It melts my heart to hear them together.

"Tater Tot, if you look over there you can start to see a roller coaster," Aiden says, pointing out my window. Lexi squeals and claps. "Look, you can see the ocean, too."

"Are we going to swim in the ocean?" Lexi asks excitedly.

"The water is too cold," I respond.

"Okay," she sighs.

"But I brought a picnic and a blanket so we can eat on the beach and find some shells."

"Yay!"

The sound of roller coasters and the smell of carnival food greet us as we walk toward Luna Park. Lexi skips between us, holding our hands. Her random squeals when she sees a new ride she wants to try only adds to my own excitement.

***

It's hot for November. Dozens of rides later, we're ready for lunch. Aiden volunteers to go back to the car to get the blanket while Lexi and I hang out at a restaurant on the boardwalk. I'm sitting down enjoying a Dr. Pepper, and Lexi is skipping around.

Can I please have some of that energy?

People walk up and down the boardwalk in droves. This is the place to people watch. To our left there's a group of people dancing to the restaurant's blaring music. Lexi joins them and they all cheer her on. I laugh as she tries to mimic some of their moves, like the robot and the running man. I look down at my watch. *Why is Aiden taking so long?* I'm hungry. He needs to hurry his ass up. I glance in the direction he'll be coming from. *No Aiden.* I sigh. I should have gone.

I look back to my left at Lexi.

Where did she go?

"Lexi," I call out. I'm sure she's behind someone and I just can't see her. I wait a few seconds before calling her name again, but I still don't see her.

I jump out of my seat as my eyes dart from spot to spot. Panic shocks me momentarily so I have no idea what to do. My throat constricts as I stand frozen in place. Finding my voice, I yell out "Lexi" over and over and run to the people who are dancing. "Where...little girl. Where did she go?" My words come out jumbled. I hold my hand to her height. "Did you see where the little girl who was dancing went?" My voice is rushed. The people shake their heads and look around too when they sense my panic.

"Lexi!" I scream. I grab my phone and try to call Aiden, but my mind and fingers aren't working on the same wavelength. I keep hitting the wrong buttons. Frustrated, I shove my phone in the back of my pocket and continue to look in between people. There are so many people here. Where can she be? I scream her name again. *And again.*

My heart drops into my stomach each step I take. Every scream I yell. Every second I can't find her. I'm so frantic my eyes can't stay in one place for more than a second. By now I have more people's attention. A few men come up to me asking what she looks like, what's she wearing. I squeeze my eyes shut. What is she wearing today?

"She's wearing..." *Fuck!* Why can't I remember? "Oh! She's wearing black shorts and a turquoise blue shirt. Her hair is in a ponytail. Blondish brown. She's five and her name is Lexi." Her description rolls off my tongue as my memory clears the panic for a second.

When I hear "Addison," I spin around, hoping someone found her. Then I remember I didn't give anyone *my* name. Aiden. I run toward him, and my heart plummets. *I lost Lexi.*

"Aiden, she's gone," I cry and then quickly spin around to keep looking for her. "I only took my eyes off her for less than a minute and she wasn't there." I can't breathe. I grab my chest.

"Where was she last?" When I don't answer him, he yanks on my arm to get my attention. "Addison, where was she last?" I point to the spot where she was dancing. "It's okay. We'll find her. You go that way, I'll go this way." He points in the direction he wants me to go. I nod my head and start walking and looking. *But what if we don't?*

I find my voice again, but my frantic cries grab the attention of more and more people. Soon there are at least a dozen people searching for Lexi. I hear my name again, and I turn in the direction it was called from. Aiden is yelling and waving his hand.

Please tell me he found her. He gives me the thumbs-up, so I take off in a sprint.

Relief spreads over my body the second my eyes lock on to her. I fall to my knees and grab her in a tight embrace. "Lexi! Where did you go?"

"I just went in the ice cream shop," she says quietly. I pull back and look at her and then up at Aiden. He's holding an ice cream cone; it's dripping down his hand.

"How did you get ice cream?" I ask slowly, looking back at her. She looks down and her shoulders drop. I grab her hands, squeezing them so she looks at me. "Lexi, it's okay. I just need to know how you got the ice cream."

"I was looking at all the flavors and the worker asked me if I wanted one."

I take a deep breath, trying to keep my emotions at bay. "Lexi, you know better than that."

When she looks back at me and notices my watery eyes, her huge eyes fill with tears and her top lip starts to quiver. "I'm sorry, Addie," she cries, wrapping her little arms around my neck. "I didn't mean to make you mad. I'm sorry." Her back shakes with sobs. I pick her up and hold on to her tight.

"I'm not mad, sweet girl. I was just really scared because I couldn't find you."

I watch Aiden walk to the trashcan as he throws away the melted ice cream. A police officer intercepts him as he's coming back. I don't want Lexi to hear Aiden talking to the officer, telling him what happened, so I walk her back into the ice cream shop.

Lexi's face is still tucked into my neck. I can feel the wetness and heat from her tears on my hair. "Lulu, do you want another ice cream?" I ask softly, feeling bad she's so upset.

She looks at me with red-rimmed eyes and nods. I order her another ice cream while I tell her to sit down at the table so I can have a chat with the worker.

I narrow my eyes at him while I decide what to say. His eyes dart to Lexi and back to me. He must know immediately that I'm not happy. He can't be older than eighteen.

He holds his hands in the air. "She said she was allowed to have ice cream. She was singing while she was looking at the flavors and I thought she was a cute little kid, so I gave her a scoop. I'm sorry," he says quickly. I watch him fidget with his apron strings. I can tell by the way he's so nervous that it was an innocent gesture. "Please, don't tell my boss, he'll fire me and I need this job."

"I'm not going to tell your boss," I say. "But it's probably a good idea not to be handing out ice cream to kids without their parents around."

He nods and apologizes again. While he scoops her ice cream, I look back at Lexi. She's resting her head atop her hands on the table. Her little lips curl up on one side as she looks at me. I smile at her pitiful look.

The door jingles and I look back, thinking it's Aiden. A mother with two girls comes in. She softly smiles at me and then at Lexi. She instructs her kids to go sit down by Lexi. One of her girls looks to be around the same age as Lexi. The mom comes and stands by me.

"Are you okay?" she asks sympathetically, softly placing her hand on my back.

I take a deep breath in and blow it out. "Not really." I look back at Lexi, and she is smiling now, talking to the girls. Coming down from my adrenaline high is making my stomach twist, and I feel like I'm going to be sick. I'm handed Lexi's ice cream and I take a bite, hoping it'll calm my stomach. Guilt starts to spread inside me. They'll never give her to me if they find out that I lost her.

"Don't beat yourself up over what happened to your daughter. It can happen to anyone. I'm pretty sure I've misplaced mine a time or two." I don't know why, but I feel a little better having a mother validate me and not judge me. Before Lexi, *I would have*. I would have been the one to wonder how a mother can lose her kid that easy.

I sigh. "Thank you."

I motion to Lexi to come get her cup of ice cream and she skips over. As soon as I hand it to her, she skips back to her new friends. I gaze at her, thankful she's okay.

I hear the door jingle again, and Lexi jumps out of her chair. The scraping noise echoes off the glass tile walls. "Aiden," she screams and runs into his arms. He lifts her up, and she wraps her legs around him. "Are you mad at me?"

"Tater Tot, *never*. But I don't want you to ever take off without telling us again," he says, pulling his head back so he can see her face. She nods with wide eyes.

"I won't. I promise."

Aiden looks at me. "Are you ready to go?"

"We're not going to the beach?" Lexi whines.

"How about we go another day. I think we've had enough fun for today." Our eyes meet and I nod in agreement.

"Okay," she says, sticking out her bottom lip. "It's my fault anyway." Her shoulders slump and she leans her head on his shoulder.

Aiden grabs her chin and lifts it. "Hey! Everyone makes mistakes. We just need to make sure we learn from them." She nods her head again, and he kisses her on the forehead before putting her down.

While Lexi tells her new friends goodbye, I step in front of Aiden. "Can I breathe now?" I whisper. My voice hitches with emotion. "I feel like I've been suffocating the last half hour." A tear falls down my cheek. His hand cups my face, and his thumb wipes away the tear. I lean into his palm.

He pulls me into him, and I grab onto his shirt. "It's alright. She's safe," he murmurs. His arms wrap around my shoulders, and he digs his face into my neck. Time stands still as we hold each other up. Moments in time flash through my head, replaying today's events. I need to let go of the *what ifs*. They didn't happen. Lexi is safe. I exhale, releasing the anxiety inside of me. When little hands wrap around both of us, I feel complete. My world is put back on its axis.

For now, *I can breathe again.*

***

When we walk into the apartment, I notice Lexi being unusually quiet as she heads to her room. I tilt my head as I watch her walk to her room. Her head is down, and it looks like she's crying. It's been a long day for all of us, but I don't know why she would still be crying. I follow her and when I enter her room, she's on her bed, facedown. Her little shoulders shudder as she lets out a little cry.

"Lulu, what's wrong?" I ask gently, sitting down beside her. I rub my hand on her back. She rolls over and it breaks my heart to see her tear-filled eyes. She sniffs and her upper lip trembles.

"Are... are..." she stutters, "...are you going...to send me away?"

What? Why would I...What the hell? Her words catch me off guard and it takes me a second to respond. "Lexi, why would I send you away?"

"Be-be-because I did something really bad. You might not want me anymore." She sniffs again. Picking my heart off the floor because it just shattered into a million pieces, I pull her up into my arms and hold her tight.

"Lexi. No matter what you did, I would not send you away. I love you," I say as tears roll down my face. "So much, sweet girl."

"I'm sorry, Addie," she cries into my chest.

I pull back so I can see her eyes. "Stop apologizing, Lexi." She nods her head slowly. "Why would you think I would send you away?" I wipe a few tears away that have run down her cheek. I know I'm her foster parent, but I've never given her any reason to think her stay here is temporary.

"Some kids at school said I don't have parents," she says quietly and looks down. "They said you can send me away if I'm bad." My mouth drops open in shock. *What the hell kind of devil kids go to that school?*

"Those kids are assholes." The words are out of my mouth before I can stop them. I cover my mouth with my hand, and Lexi smiles softly.

She nods. "They are," she whispers. I bite back a smile and pull her into a hug again.

"Lexi, this is your home. I don't want you to ever worry about if I'm going to send you away because I'm not. Okay?" I feel her head nod.

"I love you, Addie."

"I love you, too, Lexi."

After she showers and I tuck her in bed, her words stick in my head. *Give her away?* Is that always in the back of her mind? My stomach knots at the thought. *Those fucking brats*, putting ideas like that in her head.

I walk into my bedroom and spot Aiden on the bed. He's relaxing on my bed, reading something on his phone. I let out a small growl in frustration and slam my phone down on my dresser. He lowers his phone and stares at me.

"What's wrong?" he asks slowly and sits up. I shut the door so Lexi can't hear me talking.

"I'm seriously about to go ape shit on some five-year-olds."

"Do you need backup?" He smirks.

"This isn't funny," I snap. He holds his hands up to say sorry, but I'm so furious that I don't wait for his apology. "Some little shits from school told Lexi that she didn't have parents and that we were going to give her away if she did something bad." Aiden's eyes bulge open, and he does a double-take. *My thoughts exactly.* I start pacing the room, wrapping my arms around my stomach as my emotions start to bubble up. She's not here temporarily, dammit. Why hasn't she talked to me about this?

I stop walking, lean against my dresser, and dig my palms into my eyes. I don't hear Aiden get up, but I feel his arms wrap around me. He buries his face in my neck. I take a few deep inhales and exhales to gather my thoughts.

I can fix this. "I want to start the adoption process," I whisper into his ear. He pulls his head back and smiles down at me. His eyes shine from the light of the lamp. He wants this, too. I'll make sure she knows she's ours. *Forever.*

"I'll have Jaxon start the paperwork."

"And on Monday, I'm going to need backup."

Chapter fifteen

Aiden

I'm a man.
I'm a *fucking* FBI agent.

I've been in some of the worst situations undercover and still stayed in control. Even when the words *"she's gone"* came out of Addison's mouth, I didn't panic. I can't say I wasn't scared because I live in a world where I see the worst in people. I see the people who prey on the innocent, hiding in corners, waiting for the perfect moment to inflict their worst pain. But I remained calm until we found her.

Not now. I've been brought to my knees with three little words out of the mouth of a five-year-old. *Give her away.* Someone kicked the ground out from underneath me and the control that I crave came tumbling down with me. My initial thoughts were to go hunt down some five-year-olds. Make them pay for the pain they caused Lexi. *Irrational*, I know. If it hadn't been for the hurt in Addison's eyes, I would have been on a mission. Like I said, *no control.*

What kind of *shit nugget* kids say that anyway? The ones who grow up and hide in corners, that's who. They're just starting early in life. I haven't stayed the night at Addison's place when Lexi has been there, but tonight I'm making the exception. If I leave here, I can't promise I won't go hunt down some little people.

So, here I lie on the couch, my feet propped up on the end of the armrest, and I can't sleep. I hear cars randomly drive by as I stare up at the ceiling. My thoughts keep taking me to how I'm going to deal with the shit nuggets. One thing is for sure, I'll be making a visit to my favorite principal on Monday.

Tomorrow, though, I'm going to make sure Lexi knows that she's wanted and loved. And when she falls, I'll always be there to catch her. I wish I could tell her the only thing we're *giving away* is the word foster and replacing it with forever. That would fix a lot of insecurities she's feeling. I sigh, running my hand through my hair. Jax tells me not to because of all the due diligence crap that goes along with adoption and the possibility that we won't be approved. For that reason alone, I won't be the one to give her false hope. It will crush her if it doesn't happen. For now, we're just going to have to show her how much we love her.

***

"Why don't we just keep the door open?" I ask Addison. Every time we shut it, there's a knock at the door and I have to stop what I'm doing and go answer it.

"Because I don't want random people coming in here."

"Who walks into a little girl's birthday party in the middle of the day, uninvited?" We're in Addison's apartment, and we gave the approved guest list to security so they are only letting them up so it can't be just *anyone*. And there are two FBI agents, an ex-agent who looks like the Hulk, a cop, and then *there's Jaxon*. Four out of the five us are carrying a gun. I think we're safe in here.

"I would just feel better keeping it closed." She bites her lip, worry still reflected on her face. I can tell by the circles under her eyes she didn't get much sleep last night either. I pull her into my chest and wrap my arms around her.

"Sorry," I whisper.

"I know I'm being a little overprotective, but I can't stop." She pulls back and peeks up at me.

"You don't need to explain," I assure her. I wipe a streak of blue makeup off her cheek. I show her my blue thumb and she chuckles. The knock at the door makes her smile.

"I'll get it," she says.

"No, you go take care of that hot mess," I say, pointing to Lexi and her three little friends putting on makeup and dressing up. "I'll take care of the door." She flashes a wicked smile.

"Scared of a few little girls, *Mr. I Want Ten of Those*?" She hits me on my arm and smirks. I swat her ass.

"Woman, that is your job. I don't do makeup and girly things."

She twists her lips and shakes her head. "We'll see about *that*, Agent Roberts." She saunters away. Damn, her ass looks amazing in those jeans. It's Sunday, which for Addison means Dallas Cowboys attire. Her loose gray shirt with a blue star hangs off one shoulder and matches her gray furry boots. I love when she dresses up, but her casual look is one of my favorites, *not including her naked*. Because *naked* Addison will *always* be my favorite. I'm preoccupied staring at her ass and thinking about her naked that I forget about the door, until they knock again. Oh, shit. I have a job. I glance at the girls and their colorful painted faces that almost resemble clowns. I turn quickly to get the door so Addison doesn't fire me and decide to give me a new job with *them*.

Addison's apartment fills up quickly. The whole wedding party is here, minus Katie and Ryker. The both of them wanted to be here, but work got in the way. Brooks is here with Presley, who (by the look on his face as he watches the squealing girls) is terrified of what's to come. *You and me both, brother.* Lexi's friends' moms are all here and talking with the women while us guys watch the football game. I thank God that Addison is a football fan. She doesn't mind that we're watching. She even slips away to catch the score every now and then. When she sits on my lap, I can't help but think about our future.

Surrounded with friends and family, I never imagined wanting this. Now that I have it, I'll stop at nothing to make sure it stays this way. Lexi comes and sits on my other knee. Her frilly princess dress drapes over the chair, and she waves her wand around.

"Why is Ryker wearing a different number?" she asks, staring at the game.

The guys all laugh. "That's not Ryker," Jax says.

She looks at him, her face scrunched up. "It's not? Where is Ryker then?"

"Ryker plays for a different team. They play tonight," I explain.

Her eyes open wider. "Are we going?" She bounces on my knee in excitement.

"Nope, we have other plans." Addison jerks her head in my direction and her brows furrow. I wag mine at her.

"What are we going to do?" Lexi asks, clapping her hands.

"Yeah, Aiden...what are we going to do?" Addison turns her body so her legs are in between mine, and she stares at me with confusion.

I tap them both on the nose. "I'll tell you after our friends leave." Max looks over at me and shakes his head. Addison sees it and narrows her eyes.

"You know, don't you?" She points at Max. He shrugs, smirking. She's about to say something when Lexi's friends decide to all come over to see what Lexi is doing. Addison pushes off my thigh and stands up, corralling them back to the kitchen table. Squeals of excitement echo in the room when she mentions cake and ice cream.

Max gets up from the couch and slaps me on my shoulder as he passes me. "You know she hates surprises." I nod slowly. Oh, I know. That's what makes this so fun.

"Where are you going?"

"To get some cake and ice cream," he says, looking at me like I'm crazy for even asking.

I hear Lexi giggling behind me, so I look back. Max has her on his shoulders, and he's telling her he gets to be first for cake and ice cream.

"No, Max, it's *my* birthday. I get to make a wish and blow out the candles *and* get the first piece of cake." She leans over his head so her head is upside-down in front of his. Lexi's friends cheer her on and attack Max. He picks up all the girls, bouncing them up and down. Their giggles fill the room. I look at the moms, and they all have hungry eyes. One bites her lip and the other two whispers back and forth to each other, blushing.

Jaxon stops and leans down. "Max needs to find someone to settle down with." I nod as we both watch him entertain the girls. I sigh, knowing him better than anyone. Unfortunately, he did find someone. She's standing just a few feet away from him, in the arms of one of his best friends. He'll never admit it, but I see the clenched jaw, the quiet sigh whenever she gets close.

He hides it well. I know he's fighting with himself internally, so I keep my mouth shut. Someone will come and replace those feelings; he just needs to find the right someone.

The next hour is entertaining. Not because the girls put on a fashion and talent show for us, which of course Lexi stole the show with her singing, but it's the sideways glances Addison gives me or the puckering of the lips with her eyes narrowed. It's killing her that she doesn't know what I have planned. Who knew this would be so fun? Max catches the looks she's giving me and laughs out loud, which pisses her off even more.

She even has Sydney ask Damon, but he tells her he has no idea. He's a great liar. But then that's our job. It's not until the girls leave that she runs and jumps on me, demanding that I tell her what we're doing.

"You know I hate surprises," she says, digging her fingers into my side.

"I do," I say, grabbing her fingers, pulling them to my mouth and playfully biting them. "That's what makes this so fun."

She huffs. "You're evil!"

I growl into her ear. "The good kind of evil," I whisper and bite her bare shoulder. Her body shudders and my cock feels it instantly. I keep my lips on her soft skin, wishing I could feel the rest of her. I breathe in her unique scent. Fucking delicious.

"Aiden," she says slowly.

"What?" My lips move against her skin. I can feel her body move as her breathing deepens. Her hand squeezes on my inner thigh.

She leans back with her back to my chest and rolls her head against my shoulder, looking at me. "You better stop," she giggles, regaining some of her control.

"Stop what?" I shrug and her brow rises.

She wiggles her ass on my hard cock and I lean my head back, trying to hide the moan that escapes my lips. "*Hmm*, I guess you weren't doing anything." She shrugs.

The little she-devil continues to find reasons to grind her ass against me. My balls are bordering on painful, but fuck if it doesn't feel good. After I can't take it anymore, I grip her hips hard.

"You're evil," I rasp.

She licks her bottom lip, biting it right after, and then she leans back again. "Yes, but *it's the good kind of evil.*" She leans in, running her lips along my jaw, nibbling it a little. Then she stands up and walks off. *Jesus Christ!* I sit forward on my knees as the ache in my balls rolls through my stomach. Max is sitting on the other side of the couch, laughing his ass off. I pick up a pillow and launch it at him.

"Fuck off," I say through gritted teeth, not even caring if Lexi is in the room. I'll just hand her my wallet.

He *tsks* me. "Someday you'll learn not to mess with Addison. She'll have you by the balls. Every. Time." He couldn't have said truer words.

Thankfully, I'm able to stand without seeing stars when Lexi comes running into the living room. "Aiden, my friends are gone!" she exclaims, jumping up and down. "You can tell me now. What's your surprise?"

"Tater Tot, I'm taking you skydiving." Her eyes open so wide, I think they might pop out.

"Aiden," Addison says, standing behind Lexi. Her voice is clipped as she stares at me with hands on her hips. "Can we talk?" It's not a question. It might sound like one, but I'm not stupid. I can read between those lines. What she is really saying is *fuck no*, but I expected this.

159

I look down at Lexi, and she still hasn't moved a muscle except her smile has faded. Shit! This is not the reaction I was expecting from her. I was planning on messing with Addison a little longer but seeing the fear radiate off Lexi, I squash that plan.

"Tater Tot, I thought you wanted to go skydiving?" I say, squatting down in front of her.

She slowly shakes her head. "I don't think I want to jump out of a plane for my birthday. Maybe my next birthday?" I chuckle at her attempt to negotiate.

I pick up her hands and squeeze them. "We are not jumping out of a plane today."

Her eyebrows scrunch together. "I thought you said we were going skydiving?"

"We are, but it's called indoor skydiving. You get to feel like you're flying, but you're just a few feet off the ground." I look up at Addison and smile wide.

"You better be glad I like those dimples that you're flashing," she says, rolling her eyes.

"Do we all get to go?" Syd says from the kitchen.

"Yep, our ride should be here in..." Max looks down at his watch, "...twenty minutes."

"Brooks, I'll stay here with Presley if you want to go," Macie says. She has Presley in her arms and she's asleep.

"Are you sure?" He stands up, walks over to where she's sitting, and gently runs his hand over her head, admiring her. "You must be tired of holding her by now."

"Are you kidding?" She swats his hand away. "I could never get tired of holding this sweet baby. And anyway, I need all the practice I can get. As long as Addison doesn't mind that I stay here?"

"Oh, my gosh, not at all. Feel free to use my bed if you want to lie down with her. Or whatever you need."

Brooks shows her where everything is in the diaper bag while we all get ready to go. I'm shoving a piece of cake in my mouth when I feel a tug on my pocket. I look down at Lexi's concerned face. I lick the icing off my finger before grabbing a napkin. I swing a chair around and sit down, pulling Lexi in between my legs.

"What's up, Tater Tot?"

"I'm scared."

I flash her a lopsided grin and pull her up onto my leg. "Lexi, I'll have you the whole time. And I promise that I'll never let you go." *Ever.* My words remind me of what those shit nuggets said. "I want to tell you something. Are you sure you're listening?" She nods. "Addison and I love you. You mean so much to us. If you are ever afraid because of what someone says to you, for whatever reason, I want you to talk to us." Tears pool in her eyes. "Those..." I swallow the words that want to come out before I continue, "...*kids* were wrong."

"You can call them assholes. *They are,*" she sniffles. I hear Addison gasp. I look over at her and she has her hand over her mouth, stifling her laughter. I chuckle and look back at Lexi.

"Yes, *they are.* They are bullies. Kids are bullies because they are jealous of what you have or who you are. They make themselves feel better by making others feel bad. Don't let their words make you question our love for you." She nods again and the movement causes tears to fall down her face. Her arms wrap around me, and she digs her face into my chest. I embrace her tiny frame, resting my head on hers. The heat from her little body wraps around me, and I can feel the grasp she has on my heart. She has embedded herself inside, staking claim to a piece of it.

I will give you the world, Lexi, and all I ask is that you hug me like this forever.

"I love you, Aiden," she murmurs into my chest.

"Tater Tot, I love you, too."

She releases her hands and looks up. Her eyes are wide as she sniffs back her tears, trying to dry them up. "I'm ready to go skydive now. *But not out of a plane,*" she adds, squinting her eyes and puckering her lips.

I tickle her and the sound of her giggles makes everything better. "Not this time. But someday I'll get you up on that plane." I lift her off my leg, putting her back on the floor. "Go get some tennis shoes on so we can go." She runs to her bedroom with her arms out like she's an airplane. I take a deep inhale and let it out slowly before finding the eyes of everyone in the room pinned on me.

Sydney is looking up, blinking back tears, and Addison's wiping hers away. Harper and Bryn softly smile. I clear my throat, standing up. *Everyone, stop fucking staring at me.* I spin around and shove another piece of cake in my mouth, chomping down on the sugary substance to avoid all the hormonal stares. Hands wrap around my waist. Addison leans against my back, resting her chin on my shoulder.

"You're going to be an amazing father. It *almost* makes me want to give you ten kids."

I turn around in her arms. "Almost, huh? So...are we talking about nine, then?" I lift a brow and smirk. Her beautiful blue eyes sparkle from residual tears. The corners of her mouth turn upwards, and she shakes her head.

"You're relentless."

I shrug. "Just motivated. The more kids we have, the more sex we'll be having," I whisper.

She snorts out a laugh. "Well, you'd better enjoy those years because if we have ten kids, I'm pretty sure I won't be wanting sex anymore after that. I'll be begging for a chastity belt."

A few people from the peanut gallery laugh with her. "I can be pretty convincing," I say, wagging my eyebrows. She rolls her eyes.

"Let's focus on making sure we get that one." She tilts her head in the direction of Lexi's room.

"Oh, *sweetheart*, I am laser focused when it comes to Lexi. Stop worrying about it. They have no reason to deny us," I say, mainly to reassure myself. That small percentage that they could come back and deem us unworthy parents eats at me, too, but I choose to focus on the positive. She bites the inside of her cheek.

"*I know*. Just don't be too crazy with her with this indoor skydiving thing. We don't need her to get hurt on top of what happened yesterday." I can see the guilt written all over her face. She blames herself, no matter how hard I try to convince her that it wasn't her fault. I thought today would be fun and not as emotion-filled as it's been.

"I promise, I won't let her get hurt. Like I told her, I'll have hold of her the entire time."

She nods, exhaling quickly. "Where is this place, anyway?"

I tell her where we're going and pack everyone up. When we file out of Addison's apartment building, I'm holding Lexi's hand. Lexi squeals as she runs in place. My eyes have to adjust to the hot pink Hummer limo parked right in front of us. I jerk my head in Max's direction.

"You didn't?"

"I did," he boasts. Lexi screams and runs to Max. He flings her in the air. "Only the best for my Lulu."

"Max, I love it!"

Addison walks up to my side. "Wow, that's pink," she says, staring at the big blob of pink. It's so obtrusive in the street, I can't stop looking at it either. We don't notice that everyone has climbed into the limo until Max yells at us.

"Sweetheart, your chariot awaits," I chuckle.

"*Hmm.* Please, don't ever think I want you to get me a pink limo, okay?" Never crossed my mind. "It makes me think of Pepto-Bismol," she quips. It makes me a little nauseous.

"Addison, look!" Lexi says excitedly as we climb in. "There are pink lights, too."

"I see," she says, trying to sound excited. I glance at Max, and he flashes a cocky smile, proud of himself. "Max, where in the world did you find a pink limo?"

He lifts one shoulder. "I have my ways." Hell, he probably had this limo painted just for Lexi. I'm a little jealous I didn't think of it first. I told Max to find us a limo so we could all go together. I never thought he'd find a huge, pink one.

"Thank you, thank you, thank you, Max," Lexi says, hopping in his lap.

Lexi jumps around from empty seat to empty seat, having to try each one as we make our way to the skydiving place. She touches every button to see what it does and when she finds the radio, she stops so she can dance around. I feel like the bad guy telling her she needs to sit down while we are moving. It doesn't help when Jaxon and Max boo me, telling me I'm a spoil sport. *Assholes.* Addison gently squeezes my leg and smiles up at me. Then she kicks Max.

God, I love you.

"Ow! What was that for?" She glares at him without saying anything. "Wow, you've got that mom look down perfect." He

barks out a laugh when she acts like she's scratching her nose...
with her middle finger.

We pull up to the place and everyone hops out. Everyone
but Bryn is excited to try indoor skydiving. "C'mon, Bryn, live a
little," I say, throwing my arm around her.

"That's exactly what I'm trying to do. *Live.*" She blows out
her cheeks slowly. "With both feet on the ground."

"You'll love it and one of the guys will be in there with you
so you don't slam yourself into the wall." She glances up at me,
eyes open wide, and I smirk.

"Well, that sounds lovely."

Addison stops at the door and reads the sign. She turns
and looks at me. "Did y'all rent the entire place out?" she asks,
pointing at the sign. It says they are closed from four to six for
a private party.

"Something like that," I reply, grinning. Max owns this
place. He bought the franchise about four years ago. When
the concept came out, he jumped at the chance. We also get to
come here and play around without having to take the plane up
in the air. He has a manager whom he trusts that has been here
the entire time to run the place so he doesn't have to deal with
anything except the money part.

After everyone watches the video, we put our jumpsuits on.
Everyone except Max. He doesn't fly in front of a lot of people.
He's not a showy type of guy. Damon, though, has no problem
showing off.

He jumps in first and shoots all the way up the tube. Lexi
jumps up and down, giggling, and runs to the glass to look. He
comes back down, headfirst, and stays that way in front of Lexi
for a couple seconds. She yells his name and claps. He continues
to show off moves that we've practiced numerous times. It's all

about body control and displacing the air pressure with slight movements. He's only in the tube for two minutes. When he comes out of the door, Lexi runs up to him.

"You *are* Peter Pan!" she exclaims. He belts out a laugh along with everyone else. "Only Peter Pan can fly like that." She points to the tube.

"Lost Boys can fly, too."

"*No, they can't.* Tinkerbell only gives pixie dust to Peter Pan," she says defensively. She puts her hands on her hip, waiting for him to argue with her.

"Okay, you win. I'm Peter Pan," he says, throwing his hands in the air. "Alright, Tinkerbell, let's go show them how to fly." He points to Syd, and she jumps up off the bench.

One by one, either Damon or I take each person into the tube. Max is stationed at the controls, making sure the wind is just right for each person. Lexi and Addison are all that is left in this round.

"Who's next?" I say, looking at both of them.

"I think I'm ready to go," Lexi says, walking over to me. Her steps are slower than normal, but she's putting on a brave face.

"Come on, Tater Tot. I've got you."

"Are you going to let me go?" She slips her hand in mine.

"Only if you give me the thumbs-up. Okay?" She nods in agreement. "After I let you fly for a few seconds, I'm going to fly with you, and we'll go up there." Her eyes widen as she leans on the glass and looks up at the tunnel. "It'll be fun, I promise."

I'm so freaking proud of her when she stabilizes herself. She listens to all my cues, and she's sticking her thumb up in no time, allowing me to let go so she can fly on her own. When she sees that I'm not holding her, her smile grows. The wind puffs out her cheeks so she looks like a chipmunk. I glance at

Addison and she's clapping. Lexi waves to her which causes her body to move out of control. I grab her and she puts her hands back in the correct position. She's still smiling. That's my girl.

I grab a hold of her suit and nod at Max to turn up the wind. As it increases, I'm able to lift my feet. I make us spin and move up and down in the tube. I have a feeling Lexi is screaming, but I can't hear anything. *Probably a good thing right now.* She remains calm, so I continue to have some fun with her. She's light and easy to maneuver.

When we exit the tube, everyone cheers and Lexi smashes into my legs, wrapping her arms around them. "That was so fun! I want to go again!" she shouts. I stick my arm out against the glass, so I don't go flying back.

"We will," I smile. "First, I have to take Addison." The adrenaline running through her little body makes her a live wire. I'm afraid she's going to explode with all that energy. Her arms flail at her sides as she talks to everyone about what we did. She's talking so fast people just nod and laugh. Then she moves to her next victim. "Watch her," I tell Damon. She's jumping off the bench, trying to mimic what we did. Damon grabs her and puts her on his lap.

"I think you're going to create an adrenaline junky," Addison says as we watch her.

"She's going to crash hard later," I say. "Sweetheart, it's you and me now." I grab her hand and lead her to the doorway.

"Don't think of doing any of that crazy shit." She motions to Damon. My mouth twitches thinking of things I wish I could try while skydiving with Addison. Not sure any of it would be doable, but the wicked thoughts are still there. "Aiden..." she says slowly.

"Don't worry, none of the things I was just thinking can happen in here," I whisper. Her cheeks redden as she hits me in the stomach. I laugh at her disapproval of my sexual thoughts. *I can't help it.* If she only knew the places I've thought of fucking her, she'd think I was crazy. When it comes to her, I'm certainly *crazy horny.*

I walk into the tube and let her fall in, catching her in my arms. Since she's a beginner, the main goal is to fly by yourself, so I don't try anything crazy. After thirty seconds, I do the same thing with her that I did with Lexi. Hold on and spin.

Everyone goes three more times before we finish, each time getting more and more comfortable flying. Brooks tells Max that he'll pay him to take him skydiving out of his plane. Max said anytime, but he doesn't want his money. One taste and it's addicting.

Just like Addison.

Lexi bounces all the way to the pink limo. "This was my best birthday ever!" she exclaims. My smile widens hearing this. We knew the first birthday without her parents might be hard on her, but kids are resilient. They move on too quickly, and sometimes it saddens me. I think that's why I bring up her father frequently. I want her to remember him. I want her to know that he didn't leave her by choice and he loved her. I don't mind being the host for her father's love. I'll make sure she knows how loved she is every day of her life.

Chapter sixteen

"Ugh! If any more snot comes out of my nose, I'm going to cut it off," I murmur into the Kleenex I'm holding up to my nose. It's so sore and raw that I'm barely touching it.

"You need to go to the doctor," Syd says. "You've felt miserable for the past week, and you're still not better. We leave this weekend for Vegas. Go. To. The. Doctor." She pokes me in the arm as she says each word.

I throw my head back into the cushion. I feel like shit. My chest hurts from coughing, my nose burns from constantly blowing it, and my voice is hoarse from my sore throat. The last thing I want to think about is my bachelorette party. In. Six. Days.

Just kill me now.

"Fine, I'll go to the Minute Clinic."

Sydney jumps up and puts on her shoes. "Great! Let's go," she says with a little too much excitement.

"I didn't mean right now," I whine.

"No, we're going right now. You need meds. I'm going to make sure you get them. Now, let's go." She reaches for my hand and pulls me up. I blow out an exasperated sigh to show my annoyance but it makes me cough, which pisses me off even more.

Two hours later and an incessant need to take a shower and wash off the germs from the millions of other sick people at the clinic, I'm loaded up with meds with a diagnosis of bronchitis and a sinus infection.

Syd makes me some chicken noodle soup and sees to it that I take the meds then sends me to bed. I'm sure this is not how she imagined the beginning of her spring break. I'm supposed to be flying to Texas right now to drop off Lexi with Amy and Ted for the week since it's her spring break, too. Max and Aiden go instead. The air pressure from the plane would have made my head explode, so I stay home.

When my head hits my cold pillow and my sick body relaxes into my soft bed, I pull my comforter around me and send up a silent plea that I start feeling better soon. My mind starts thinking about the wedding and Lexi. It's hard to believe Lexi has been with me for almost a year already. Somedays it's hard to remember what it was like before she came to live with me. Jaxon is still working her adoption case. Lexi's social worker makes frequent visits, and I was elated when she told me she thinks Lexi belongs here with us. Now to prove it to the judge. We have perfected our schedule over the last few months. The months have flown by without any incidents, surprisingly. We constantly ask Lexi if kids are being assholes, but that seems to have stopped after Aiden went and had a meeting with the principal.

Seeing Christmas through the eyes of a child made me love it more. I'd never seen Aiden more excited than when he dressed up as Santa. There have been a lot of firsts for us, and I cherish all of them.

My eyes droop as the medicine takes affect. My chronic cough has kept me up for nights, so I'm exhausted. The inhaler the doctor gave me has given me temporary relief from the cough from hell, so I quickly fall asleep.

***

"Are you sure this looks okay?" I ask, spinning around, looking at myself in a full-length mirror.

"Are you serious?" Syd asks. "You look stunning in that, and Aiden will love it." I turn back to Sydney, who is sitting on the couch in the dressing room area.

"You really think Aiden will be okay with this number..." I sweep my hand down my body, "...when I'm not with him?"

Sydney has dressed me in a short, black sequin dress. I don't even think short is accurate. It's *if I bend over my ass is going to show* short. The back of the dress is open, draping down to my ass.

She waves her hand around. "The only thing he's going to think about is that you'll end the night in his arms, wearing *that*." She points at the dress. She doesn't know Aiden very well, then. "It's Vegas! Live a little!" Syd jumps up and walks over to me, spinning me around to face the mirror. "You look gorgeous. If I had legs for days like you, I'd be showing them off all the time."

"You have zero problem showing yours off," I joke, hip bumping her. She looks at me and wags her eyebrows. I glance at the mirror. I'm just glad I'm not sporting the Rudolf the Red Nose Reindeer look anymore. The meds worked wonders and after three days, I started to feel human again. We leave tomorrow afternoon, so Sydney and I are getting some last minute shopping in. I already had a dress picked out to wear Saturday night, but when we walked past the boutique, Sydney saw this dress on the mannequin and here we are.

"Fine, I'll get it." It does look good, and I know Aiden will love it...*when I'm with him*. I might have to get ready after the guys leave and make it a surprise for when we meet up after the festivities. I have just the right shoes to go with it. Excitement for this weekend starts to bubble up inside me. The last two weeks I've been sick. I couldn't think about anything other than trying to breathe.

"I can't believe you get married in a month." Syd wraps her arm through mine as we walk out of the store. "I was sure I'd get married first."

I nod my head. "I did, too. I can't believe we're actually *getting* married."

Syd whips her head to me. "What?"

"I mean...it seems like it's the world versus Addison and Aiden. And we are *not* in the lead."

"What are you talking about? You're together. After everything the world has thrown at you, nothing has come between y'all. I'd say you're the winners." We weave in and out of people leaving work and head to meet Aiden and Damon for dinner. I bust out laughing when she starts singing "We Are The Champions" by Queen. People stare as she belts out the song. The only thing I can do is smile and shrug. She drags out the last line about champions. The sound of clapping behind us sends us into a fit of laughter. "Look for me on Broadway," Syd yells out.

"You're nuts," I say in between giggles.

When we walk into the restaurant, the heady smell of curry greets us. My mouth waters as I inhale the smell of lemon grass and ginger. I've never been so thankful to breathe again. We're meeting the guys at my favorite Thai restaurant.

"Hey there, Soon-to-be Mrs. Roberts," Aiden says as he stands and draws me into his chest. His lips graze mine. They're cool to the touch with the taste of beer still lingering on them.

"Y'all been waiting long?" I ask, looking down at the empty beer glasses.

"About twenty minutes. We had a long day and needed beer. In fact, we need more..." He eyes the place for our waitress.

"Hey, shorty," I hear Damon say to Syd. I look over and he kisses her. It's a funny sight. She's standing next to him while he's still sitting, and she's only a couple inches taller than him.

"Let's not talk about short stuff," she says, pulling back. "I don't want to embarrass you."

"Woman," he growls and pulls her onto his lap. "You weren't complaining last night about it being short. In fact, you were having a little trouble—"

Syd gasps and puts her hand over his mouth as he mumbles the rest. "Nobody needs to hear the rest of that sentence," she says, blushing.

That is for damn sure.

He licks her hand and she squeals, moving it away right before he pulls her in for a kiss. My heart is happy seeing them together. I can't believe they have been together for almost seven months. They're starting to talk about moving in together. Syd and I have always dreamed of our kids growing up together like we did. I think about all the stages in our lives that we've been through together, and I can't wait to move on to the next one with her by my side.

"What's on your mind, sweetheart?" Aiden whispers in my ear. I look over at him and I grin. He sweeps my hair behind my ear.

"Just thinking about how happy I am."

"You don't know how much I love hearing that."

"Are y'all ready for our Vegas weekend?" Syd jumps out of Damon's lap and sits in the chair next to him.

"I still can't believe we're all going," Damon complains. "I mean, this is *supposed* to be your last night of debauchery before getting married. It's not supposed to be done *together*. That defeats the whole purpose."

"I don't need a night of debauchery with the boys. The only person I want to debauch is this woman right here." Aiden yanks my chair closer to him then playfully pulls my hair back to bite my neck. I push him away, shaking my head and laughing. Aiden was very adamant that he didn't need a bachelor party. I didn't care to have a bachelorette party either. Syd and Damon weren't happy about that, so we compromised. We all go to Las Vegas at the same time. We're going to start our night out apart and end it together. Everyone in the wedding party is going except for Ryan and Macie. Her doctors don't want her traveling, and he's being a supportive husband by staying with her.

***

"Vegas, here we come," Sydney says as we walk through the hangar. The sun shines bright once we emerge from the shadows, so we both pull our sunglasses down from the top of our heads. We've yet to see anyone else other than Aiden and Damon. Katie is meeting us there because she's flying in from Florida.

"Hey, beautiful ladies," a southern voice purrs from behind us. We stop and turn as Ryker walks up to us. He plants himself in between Syd and me and wraps both arms around our shoulders as we continue walking toward the plane. "You both ready for some wild fun?"

"See? This isn't fair," Sydney whines. "You guys are going to get VIP treatment everywhere because of you." Syd pokes Ryker in the ribs.

He shrugs a shoulder. "It's not my fault people love me." I roll my eyes. How is it I used to have a fan-crush on him? I thought Aiden was an egotistical ass when I met him, but Ryker...he's in a whole new category. I can't help but laugh. He tightens his hold around my neck. "What are you laughing at?"

"They must love you for your humbleness," I say sarcastically.

"They love me for more than that," he says, winking at me.

"How about you not talk about your dick when you have my fiancée in your arms," Aiden barks from the top of the stairs. Ryker's head falls back as he laughs.

"I'd screw with you a little on this one," Ryker jokes, looking up at Aiden, "but I have a feeling you'd really kick my ass."

Aiden smirks. "Try me, brother."

"Nah. I'm good keeping my front teeth. I have this smile insured." He flashes a shit-eating grin.

I lean over and look at Sydney, laughing. *I knew it.* His trademark smile is notorious for getting him out of trouble—or *into* trouble, depending how you look at it. Ryker lets go of me, and I walk up the stairs, wrapping my arm around Aiden's waist. I stand on my toes and bring my lips to his, biting his bottom lip. My jealous man, *what am I going to do with you?* He growls against my lip.

"Mine," he murmurs, devouring my mouth possessively before moving me inside the cabin of the plane. I touch my swollen lips, wondering if he'll ever feel comfortable with Ryker around me. He's getting better, but I can see his body tense every time Ryker is near me, even though he knows Ryker flirts with me just to get a rise out of him.

Bryn, Harper, Jaxon, and Damon enter the plane and not too long after we take off. Aiden comes back from the bathroom, chuckling. I cock an eyebrow, wondering what he finds so funny.

"Hey, asshole, what's up with the locked door?" He slaps Max on the shoulder.

Max shrugs. "There were some issues that needed immediate attention."

"What issues?" he asks.

"There was a bed in there."

I feel a blush burn my cheeks, and I look down to avoid questioning eyes. Aiden laughs, sitting down next to me. "You think we have to have a bed?" I cover my eyes with my hand.

"Hence, why it's locked."

"Way to go, Roberts. Ruin it for the rest of us," Damon says.

"Okay! We can stop talking about this now," I run my hands through my hair. I fidget in my chair while everyone finds this amusing. "Who are we meeting there again?" I ask, changing the subject. Aiden lays his hand on my thigh. It's such a natural reaction for him to always be touching me. I cover his hand and thread our fingers together.

"Drake Webb. He was with us at Quantico, but was sent to the Las Vegas office," Aiden says.

"I just received his RSVP last week that he's coming to the wedding. He's the one hoping to bring a plus one but can't promise anything."

The guys chuckle. "That sounds like Drake," Damon says.

Chapter seventeen

"Come on out, ladies," Syd screams from the living room. We're staying at the Aria in a two-bedroom penthouse in one of their sky suites. This room is crazy huge. It's bigger than my apartment. We had booked a normal two-bedroom suite, but when they saw we were with Ryker Dallas, we were upgraded. I guess Syd was right about them being VIP everywhere they go. I am a little jealous of that.

The guys were already booked in one of the penthouse rooms, so they are across the hall from us. We heard them leave earlier. I glance down to my barely there dress, noticing more cleavage and legs than fabric. I yank on the hem of the dress, trying to get another inch of length, but it shrinks back up as soon as I stand tall. I blow out a defeated breath. Why did I let Syd talk me into this thing?

Syd pokes her head into the bathroom. "C'mon, woman. Get that beautiful butt of yours out here so we can take a shot."

Let the fun begin.

"Okay, ladies, listen up," Syd says, hushing everyone. "Here's to Addie. My beautiful friend, whom I didn't think would ever get married."

"Gee, thanks," I respond.

"I mean, I didn't think you'd ever find a man who could challenge you enough to keep your interest." I nod. "You do have a history of getting bored in relationships," she says in a matter-of-fact tone. She's right. I think back to my past relationships, and they all ended the same way: me bored, walking away.

"You found the most amazing man who has proven that he loves you time and time again. I couldn't be happier for you. And I'm so excited to be standing here alongside you. But first..." she holds her shot in the air, "...we need to say goodbye to your single life. To a night of fun with all you crazy ladies!" Syd holds her shot higher, and we lift ours and clink our glasses together. The golden warm liquid fills my mouth and burns my throat on the way down. I shiver, looking around for a chaser. I haven't even swallowed the sip I took from my screwdriver before I'm being handed another shot.

"Y'all are going to get me drunk before we even leave this room," I say, taking the shot from Harper.

"This is it until we get to the club." Harper smiles wide. This time I keep my screwdriver in my hand, ready to take a drink after the shot. The second one doesn't go down as harsh as the first.

"We have to leave here in fifteen minutes, so let's get moving," Syd says while she turns up the music. She dances as she walks away. "Sexy Back" from Justin Timberlake blasts from the speakers throughout the penthouse. Bryn and I start dancing, swinging our hips to the music. When I dance lower to the floor, Bryn busts out laughing. I look down and notice my dress has shimmied up my thighs and is showing my thong. I'm pretty sure my ass is out for all to see, too. I join Bryn laughing, feeling the effects of the shots already, and stand to pull my dress down.

Damn Sydney! Don't dance low tonight, Addison.

I hear my phone ding as I'm finishing up my makeup. "I bet I know who that is," Syd says, standing next to me, putting on her mascara. "Damon said he was moping around before they left because he wanted to come over and talk to you. They wouldn't let him." She giggles. I smile, imagining how that conversation went. After we checked into the hotel, everyone (except Aiden and me) agreed we wouldn't see each other until we meet up later. We both *agreed* our friends are all assholes.

I grab my phone off the bed and look at the text.

Aiden: This is stupid! I had to sneak off to the bathroom to text you.

I giggle to myself. I'm almost positive they know what he's doing.

Me: I'm glad you did.

Aiden: I love you. See you tonight, sweetheart.

Me: Love you. Don't let them buy you too many lap dances!

Aiden: The only person that's going to be in my lap tonight is you ;)

Warm tingles spread throughout my body just thinking about being in Aiden's lap.

Me: I'll give you a lap dance you won't ever forget :o

Aiden: Fuck, Addison, now I'm hard.

A laugh escapes my lips. I see the little dots telling me he's still typing.

Aiden: Just make sure I'm the only lap that you're in tonight.

Me: You're the only one who will mean something.

Sydney comes and stands by my side, reading my texts. "You are so asking for it," she jokes.

Aiden: Addison.

Syd and I both wait for him to add to his response but he doesn't. *Oh, shit.* Syd's phone starts to ring, and we glance at each other with wide eyes. She picks it up and we both look down and see that it's Damon.

"Hey, babe, what's up?" she answers.

"She was kidding." She rolls her eyes. I can't hear Damon, but I can assume what he's saying.

"I won't. Tell him to calm down. Go buy that boy a shot...or three." She looks at me with amusement and shakes her head. "Okay. Love you."

She hangs up and throws her phone on the bed. "Thank God we didn't tell him where we were taking you." I raise a brow in question.

"Where exactly are you taking me?" Our entire night is top secret. No one will spill.

"Don't you worry about it. We'll make sure you stay out of trouble." The mischief in her voice is slightly concerning. At least I can look forward to the end of the night, knowing I'll be falling asleep in Aiden's arms. We have a little secret, too. We have our *own* room for later. Syd starts digging around in a bag on the bed and pulls out a white sash that says *bachelorette*. I roll my eyes.

"I can't believe you're going to make me wear that."

"Hey, just be glad I didn't do the veil with dicks all over it," she laughs while putting it on me. I look up thinking about that. She's right; I'll take the sash.

We walk out of the hotel and spot our ride, a Hummer limousine. I chuckle to myself that it's not pink. Neon lights and a small disco ball spins on the inside roof of the limo.

"Fancy," Bryn says, hopping to one side of the limo. Music fills the air when we start to move. A loud pop has me turning toward Syd. She's pouring champagne into flutes, passing them out. After another round of cheers, Bryn sits up on her knees and opens the moon roof. "Oh, my gosh, I've always wanted to do this!" She stands up on her feet, fitting through the open window. "Addison, get up here with me."

I push off my seat and squeeze in with her. The warm air hits our faces as we slowly make our way down the strip. Lights from cars litter the streets every direction I look. Guys holler and whistle as we pass. Bryn and I wave even though we don't have any idea what they are saying because it's so loud. We start dancing to the song coming out of the limo's speakers. I've never been to Las Vegas, so I take in all the blazing lights beaming from the hotels. We pass the Bellagio and the fountains are on. I lean my ear in the direction of the music to see if I can hear what song is playing, but it's useless. My friends are loud.

"Our turn," I hear Katie say as she pulls on my dress. Bryn and I duck down into the limo and Katie and Harper take our place.

Syd is texting on her phone when I hop in the seat next to hers. "Who are you texting?" She yanks away her phone, hiding it from me. She smiles, biting her lip. She's up to no good. I cock an eyebrow. "What are you planning, Sydney?"

"I'm just setting some things up."

"I can see that. What *things* would those be?"

She looks down at my bare legs. "That dress is a *little* short," she says. I look down at my dress. Again, it has crawled up my thighs. Dammit! I tug it down and glare at her.

"This is your fault. I swear, you'd think they could have spared just a couple more inches of fabric on this thing." Syd giggles. "I hate you." I grab a glass of champagne and lean back against the seat.

She rests her head on me. "No, you don't. You love me."

"I do. But right now I don't like you," I joke and lean my head on hers.

A few minutes later our limo stops in front of the Hard Rock Hotel. Syd grabs my hand and pulls me out of the limo. When I stand, I make sure the small scrap of fabric called a dress is covering all the right places.

"Why are we at a hotel?" I ask Bryn as we're walking into the lobby.

"You'll see," she answers with a large smile. She and Harper wrap their arms through mine, and we follow Katie and Syd through the casino. I look around at the constant sounds of dinging slot machines and cheering off in the distance. The machines I look at confuse me. I've never played slots before, but I always had it in my head there were three wheels and you match the cherries or something simple like that. These machines are *complicated.* There are tons of lines crossing each other in every direction. I watch a person play for a second and wonder how they know they won. Syd pulls me away as I'm trying to figure the damn things out. We walk out of the sea of machines toward the side of the casino. The bright sign catches my attention.

Magic Mike Live. My eyes go wide. I whip my head around to Sydney. Her smile reaches her eyes as she waits for my reaction. She knows I secretly love that movie. We watched it five times while it was at the theater, but I would never admit that to anyone.

"Is Channing here?" I ask excitedly.

A girl who overhears me steps beside me and says, "Nope, I hear he rarely comes to these."

"Well, that sucks," I reply.

"It does, but don't worry, there are sexy-as-hell men in there who will light your panties on fire. They'll make your fiancé seem *mediocre*." She obviously doesn't know what she's talking about. Aiden could very easily be a stripper. I laugh at my thought. The drinks are making me silly.

"Girl, I have a man who looks like those guys," I say, pointing to a poster of the Magic Mike guys. "*Aaanndd* he's FBI."

The girl looks at Syd for confirmation, like she thinks I'm lying. Syd nods. "Lucky woman! Most of the guys I date are losers."

"Hey, me, too," Bryn says loudly to the girl. "These two have freaking gorgeous men with guns, literally." She points to Syd and me while she laughs at her own joke and ends up snorting. Her hand quickly covers her mouth, and we all start giggling at Bryn as her cheeks redden. I wrap my arm around her and hug her.

"Don't worry, Bryn. We're going to find you one," I say. "You just need to stay away from Ryker."

The girl's eyes widen. "Ryker who?" she says slowly. I smirk and nod, confirming what she must be thinking.

"Holy shit! Ryker Dallas?"

Bryn rolls her eyes at the girl's overzealousness. "He's not all that," she says pointedly. "Just another loser." Her arms flail out.

"I wouldn't even care if he was the biggest loser ever, I'd still ride that boy, given the chance."

Bryn quietly snickers at the girl. "Be careful what you wish for," she murmurs and then walks toward the entrance of the club, leaving us behind.

"We are so hanging out with you guys tonight," the girl says. Harper introduces us all as I walk over to catch up with Bryn.

"You okay?"

"Yes. I promised myself I wouldn't let him get to me on this trip, but seeing him today..." She pauses and lets out a moan. "Why does he have to be so gorgeous and *nice to me*?"

I tilt my head and laugh. "I'm going to kick his ass for being nice to you," I say sarcastically. "What's really wrong here, Bryn?"

"He says he wants to take me out on a real date." I don't know what I was expecting her to say but that wasn't it. I stare at her, waiting for her to continue, but she doesn't. "And?" I finally say.

"And look at me?" Her hands flow down her body. "A guy like that would never settle for a girl like me."

"Are you kidding me? You are gorgeous and he'd be one lucky guy to have you. You're smart, independent, and have a lot to offer a man."

She sighs. "He's...*Ryker Dallas*. I'm just Bryn the accountant. He'd get bored with me within a week. Hooking up at a party was okay, but now he wants a *date*."

"Where is the confident woman I know? Where is all this self-doubt coming from?"

"Ugh. I don't know. I've seen the girls he's dated before. Models from freaking Australia. I can't compete with those types of women."

"Have you ever thought those were the *types* of women he gets bored with? Maybe he needs more out of a woman than just looks. Ryker is a good guy. I don't know if you should go out with him, but I don't think you should say no because you think you're not enough for him...because that is bullshit."

"You're just saying that 'cause you're my friend."

We move up and I catch the bouncer's eye. "Hey, what do you think of my friend here." He looks Bryn up and down. She's as tall as me and lean but has great curves. She's wearing a dark blue fitted dress that accentuates her body, but it isn't too revealing or too short. *Unlike mine.*

"She's gorgeous," he says and winks at her.

She huffs. "He's just saying that because he works here."

I stare at her. "I'm going to hit you."

The bouncer leans over and whispers something into her ear, causing her to blush. Her lips curl into a smile, and she shakes her head. "Thanks," she says, looking away. She starts to fan herself, and he laughs loudly.

"Okay. Are we ready to go in?" Bryn squeaks, avoiding the bouncer's heated stare. She blows out a breath. "It's really hot in here. I need a drink."

I laugh at her while grabbing the girls to come inside. Finding out what he said is a conversation that will happen later. We walk through a small gift shop before getting to the front doors and then we're escorted to our seats. Couches surround the stage and there's a row of tables with chairs right behind it. That's where we are. Our new friends just happen to be sitting to our left. Harper pulls their table closer so they can join us. We find out their names are Coryn and Abby.

I run my hand across the red velvety couch in front of us. *Fancy.* Sitting down, I watch as the crowd fills the room. Coryn orders a lemon drop shot for everyone as soon as our waiter comes and introduces himself. *Trey.* Trey is freaking hot. I'm wondering why he's not one of the guys on stage because he *certainly* could be.

We talk with our new friends, waiting for our drinks and for the show to start. Syd keeps smiling at me. I can feel it. She's planned something, and I'm sure I'm not going to like it. She knows if I get dragged on stage, she's going to die. *A slow and painful death.*

"You know, payback is a bitch, right?" I say, glaring at her.

She bursts out laughing. "Just remember, I love you." She blows me a kiss. I itch my nose with my middle finger.

A couple shots later and after downing a fishbowl drink called XXL Voodoo, with glowing ice cubes, the lights begin to dim. You'd think we were out in the wild with how many women start howling and screaming. It's like their mating call. *My friends?* They're the loudest of them all.

Strobe lights spear through the fog, permeating the air from the ground up. Heavy bass music blares all around us, and I can feel the vibration deep inside me. Syd bounces in her chair, her hands in the air as she screams. I can barely hear her over the music. When the screams elevate to a deafening level, I turn toward the stage. The lights go out. When they turn back on, ten beautifully sculpted men are dancing on stage.

Right in front of me. Holy hotness.

Everyone is up on their feet, including me. I can't help it. I move my hips to the music while I watch their bodies move around on stage. One guy drops down, walks in front of me, and runs his hand down my face. "Hey, beautiful," he whispers in my ear. *Oh, hell.* I should not be getting goose bumps from the heat of his breath. Before I can regain my senses and back away, he's moved into the crowd. Thank God!

"He was hot," Harper screams. I nod and smile wide in agreement. That same guy brings a woman from the crowd onto the stage, and I blow out a sigh of relief that it wasn't me. The guys surround her on stage, each one taking their turn with her. Then she starts talking about safe words and unicorns. Nope, not a random girl. She must be the MC.

As the show progresses, the level of heat in this place rises. Between the gorgeous men and the show they put on to the drinks I'm inhaling, I'm feeling really good...*and turned on.* I clench my crossed legs, watching a number where a woman and man are on the stage with water falling on them.

I lean over to Syd. "What's the name of this song? Because the next time I'm in the shower with Aiden, I want it to be playing," I say, fanning my face.

"I don't know, but when you find out, please share." I nod and go back to watching the erotic scene in front of us.

The songs continue and each time a guy hops off stage and walks in our direction, my heart starts to beat faster. I turn and look at one of the girls. *Don't make eye contact,* I keep telling myself. I *really* don't want to go on stage.

Then it happens. Two guys are on stage dancing and both hop off and head right for us. I do my normal, look away routine, but when I look back he's standing right in front of me with a sexy ass grin.

It's the same guy who called me beautiful at the start of the show. "Come on, beautiful, you can't ignore me anymore," he says, pulling my hand. The other guy walks Syd on the stage, too. She's certainly more willing than I am. She practically jumps into his arms. We're seated on two wooden chairs opposite of each other on the stage. The guys dance between us. I glare at Sydney and shake my head. I knew I should have had more to drink.

I have my legs crossed so I don't flash anyone, but Mr. Hottie comes and uncrosses them, straddling me. Oh, God. I'm holding on to the chair for dear life.

"Relax," he breathes into my ear. "I've got you." No. No, you don't have me. My heart is beating so fast I can't relax even if I wanted to. Between my nerves, the music, and the man rubbing his groin on my lap, I think I might have a heart attack. I take a deep breath and blow it out slowly. God, I hope no one is getting video of this; Aiden would hunt this guy down.

Mr. Hottie grabs my hands and puts them around his neck. His hands glide down my sides. Oh. I bite my lip. Oh, SHIT! He grabs my thighs and picks me up.

"Wrap your legs around me. Don't worry."

Don't worry? That's easy for him to say. My crotch is going to be rubbing against his cock and only my panties are going to be between us. *Oh, no.* This is not good. I'm going to kill Sydney. I wrap my legs around him because I start to slide down his sweaty body. I close my eyes and try not to think about what's happening right now. It'll be done in a minute. He nuzzles his face in my neck.

"I need you to hold on. We're about to go up," he whispers. Go up? *Go the fuck up where?*

I don't have time to resist because he jumps up on a ladder. Whoa! He gyrates against me and flashes me a wicked smile. I laugh at the insanity of all of this. Next thing I know, I'm on the floor and he's dancing over me, on me, against me. My body starts to tingle from the heat coming off him. Our eyes lock for a few seconds.

"Goddamn, you're gorgeous. Too bad you're getting married," he says into my ear, all the while dancing on me. Wait, what? Do they normally say that kind of thing to the girls? *Yes, they do. This is all part of the show*, I tell myself. I shrug and smile. "Find me after the show," he says, finally bringing me to my feet and walking me back to my chair.

Okay, *that* was not part of the show.

When the show ends, I practically drag the girls out of there before Mr. Hottie can *find me*. I don't know if he was serious, but I don't want to find out.

"I think I need to change my panties," Syd says as we walk out. "Why are you rushing to get out of here?" She looks at me.

"Did your dancer friend tell you to find him after the show?" Her eyes widen. "Um...no."

The girls all whistle and moan. "You guys were hot up there. I felt a little weird getting excited," Katie jokes.

I whip my head toward Katie. "This does *not* get repeated to Aiden. Ever. That goes for all of you." I point to each girl.

"Is your fiancé the jealous type?" Coryn asks.

All the girls bust out laughing. "He is definitely an alpha male," Syd says.

"*Mmm*, he sounds hot," Coryn purrs. I lift a brow to the girl who is still a stranger to me. I don't know why her comment rubs me the wrong way, but it does. Syd notices my expression and jumps in between us.

"Alright, girls, next stop!" She gestures for us to start walking. She walks beside me and leans into me. "We can ditch the new girls if you don't want them to come."

I exhale. "No, they seem fun. I think my nerves are just overstimulated, and I overreacted to her comment." I look down at her, eyes narrowed. "And you are going to pay very, *very* badly for that back there." I point back to the club.

She beams. "It was hot."

Okay, I'll admit it. It was a little hot.

***

The blue ambiance of the club glows from down below. It seems Ryker called in a favor and we were escorted up to the VIP section. Our hands are never with an empty glass either. I'm sure everyone up here wonders who we are. We only have an hour left before we meet the guys at a different bar. I'm excited to see Aiden, put my hands and lips on him. Since we left the Magic Mike Live show, I've been horny as hell, and I'm looking forward to our time tonight more than ever.

A remix of the song "That's What I Like" from Bruno Mars starts to play. "Let's go down there," Syd screams, pointing to the crowd. I nod my head and grab her hand.

We tell the other girls we're going to dance. Harper comes with us, but the other four stay to watch from above. We hang onto each other's hands, weaving our way onto the center of the dancefloor. I put my hands up in the air, moving my hips to the beat of the music. Syd looks at me and giggles before bringing my hands back down. I feel my dress creep up and tug it down. I mouth *thanks*. No need to say it, she'd never hear it.

It's probably the first time I'm thankful I'm wearing just a scrap of fabric. It's so freaking hot in here. I look around at all the bodies. It's packed. Sweat drips along my brow. I wipe it away and take a few breaths, blowing it up into my face. I'm not drunk but I'm feeling good. A glass of water sounds great right now, though. I lift my thumb and pinky and do the universal sign for "I need a drink." Sydney and Harper both nod in agreement.

Harper goes first, then me, and Sydney behind. I have Syd's hand in mine. When I feel it drop, I turn around. Some guy is holding her around the waist, trying to get her to dance with him. She rolls her eyes and tells him no thanks. When she tries to keep walking, he tightens his grip on her. Come on, fucker. She said no. I walk back and grab her hand.

"She doesn't want to dance, dude," I scream and pull her out of his grasp. He pins his gaze on me. His eyes creep down my body and back up, meeting mine again. There's heat in them now. I shake my head. Not going to happen. We start walking again and the asshole flings his arm around my waist and slams me into his hard chest.

"It looks like you want to dance with me," he hisses.

"No, asshole, I don't," I snap, trying to get out of his grasp.

"I think you do." He runs his other hand down my side and moves his hips to the rhythm of the song. I take a couple deep breaths, trying to calm my anger. I attempt to move again, but this time he grabs my ass. "Your ass is gorgeous."

Red. Flaming red is all I see. The stench of cigarette smoke and sweat makes me feel sick to my stomach. I can't even tell if it's reality or a flashback. I can feel his hand grabbing my ass. My mind turns off and my automatic defense mechanism kicks in. I grab the hand holding me and ram my elbow back as hard as I can. When he lets go, I turn and bring my knee up to his groin and then punch him right in the face. He goes down and everyone steps to the side. You'd think I would have stopped; he's down, but the rage running through my veins doesn't let me. I kick him, making sure to move my pointed heel to his groin area. He screams out in pain. I'm pulled off him by a very large bouncer. Max-sized bouncer. I fight him until my brain kicks back on and I'm able to process the situation.

I'm hauled outside. "What are you kicking her out for? That asshole was sexually assaulting her, and she was defending herself!" Syd screams as she follows us outside.

"Stand there and don't move," he demands, looking down at me. I glare back at him until he goes back inside.

I look down at my hand and it's red and swollen. Shit, that's going to hurt when my adrenaline calms down. I pace along the sidewalk, my body trembling with anger. I groan a few times out of frustration.

"Addie, are you okay?" Syd asks.

I don't answer because I'm not okay. I continue my path, back and forth, taking deep breaths in and blowing them out. I take off my shoes and throw them against the wall. The large bouncer is still not out here, but another one stands to the side, watching me. Breathe in, breathe out. It's all I concentrate on. I'm safe. He can't hurt me.

Ten minutes later a cop car pulls up and a cop gets out and walks over to me. Thank God they called the cops. That guy can't get away with grabbing women however the hell he wants.

"Miss?" he asks.

"Addison Mason."

"Miss Mason, are you the one who attacked the guy in there." He points to the club. I'm caught off guard by how he used the word attacked.

"I defended myself from being sexually assaulted," I deadpan.

"That's not what he said. He said he asked you to dance and you attacked him out of the blue."

"That is not what happened," Sydney sneers and jumps in between us.

"Ma'am, please stand aside," the cop says as he puts his hand on his gun. I look up for a second. Shit!

I pull Sydney behind me. "Syd, I got this." I glare at her and hope she listens.

"Officer..." I pause and look at his badge, "...Romero, that isn't what happened." I try to sound calm.

"We have other witnesses who tell the same story."

"*Other witnesses*? It happened fifteen minutes ago. How can you have already talked with other witnesses?" So much for being calm. This asshole cop is lying, and I'm not sure why.

"Ms. Mason, please turn around. You're being arrested for aggravated assault."

"What?"

"Don't make me use force, Ms. Mason."

I can't believe this is happening. By now the bouncer has come back outside with my friends. They are all freaking out. I have a feeling if I don't go, someone is going to get hurt. I turn around and put my hands behind my back. I'm facing the girls and most of them have tears rolling down their faces. The cop tugs on my hands more than necessary and I let out a grunt.

"You're going to regret this," Syd warns. "You don't know who she is." I look at Syd like *what the hell are you doing?* That is not going to help this situation.

The large bouncer steps forward. "Officer, I can tell you it wasn't her fault," he says in a deep voice.

"Well, she can tell it to the judge," he responds. The bouncer's expression turns hard at the officer and softens when he looks back at me. I mouth *"thanks."* The asshole cop pushes me toward the car.

"Can I at least get my shoes?" I ask, walking barefoot on the cement. Now that I'm able to form a coherent thought, it's gross thinking about not wearing shoes. He doesn't reply, just pushes my head down into the back of his police car. By now a crowd has formed and many are taking video of the whole thing. Aiden is going to have a heart attack if he sees that video.

I'm taken into custody at the Las Vegas Detention Center and escorted into a holding cell—at least they gave me some flip-flops—and have a seat on the long bench off to one side. The cold steel hits the back of my legs and I shiver. I pull down my dress a little and curse Sydney at the same time. There is another long bench on the other wall where a woman sits. Must be a slow night for only one person to be in here.

"What are you in here for, hun?" she says, popping her gum.

"Defending myself." I wrap my arms around my chest. It's freezing in here and it stinks like urine. I glance down to the floor and can see stains of God knows what. I don't even want to think what I could pick up with one little swab.

Her snicker makes me look back up at her. "That's what they all say." I tilt my head, wondering what the hell she's talking about.

"I was," I say.

"Oh, I believe you, sweetie," she says in an accent. It sounds southern, but not like Texas southern. "I'm just sayin', that's the first thing someone says when they're caught."

I can't even comprehend that answer. Caught from what? I look away from her over to the passing guards. A couple of them look over and smile at as they walk by the cell. I roll my eyes and look back to her.

I sigh. I guess talking to her is better than sitting her doing nothing. "So, what are you in for?"

"Defending myself," she says, her tone serious. I chuckle awkwardly. She's a weird one. "I know what you're thinking, our stories are *exactly the same*. We need to stick together. Girl power." She throws her fist in the air. I'm not sure if she's drunk or high, but she's not right. I look closer and her eyes are dilated, which tells me she's on something. This keeps getting better and better. I hope Syd finds Aiden soon. "Did you run over your husband, too?" My mouth gapes open before I snap it shut. I giggle to myself, wondering what she would say if I said yes. She stares at me with a serious gaze.

"Um...no." I shake my head. "I didn't. I kicked some guy's ass who sexually assaulted me."

"Good for you." She jumps up on her feet. I sit up straighter against the cold cement wall, wondering if she's going to come over to me. "See, us girls need to stick together. Men are all assholes," she yells down the hallway.

"Sit down, Barb," a male's voice says from around the corner.

"Fuck you, Nate," she replies and sits back down.

I know I'm going to regret asking, but it seems I don't have anything better to do. "So, Barb, tell me why you ran over your husband."

Chapter eighteen

Aiden

"Come on, Aiden, just one lap dance," Damon says, holding up some dollar bills. He's been begging me for the last hour. Like I told Addison before, she's the only woman I want in my lap tonight. Seeing these naked women hasn't changed my mind. "We just have half an hour left before we have to meet the women."

I groan and look up to the ceiling. He's never going to shut up. "Fine. One dance." I hold up my finger. Max chuckles and shakes his head. "What, asshole?"

He shrugs. "I just remember a time when you couldn't get enough of that..." He points to the girls.

I nod my head and smile. "Times have changed."

He grabs my shoulder. "That they have, brother." I look around and see Damon talking to a brunette woman. I can't deny that's she beautiful. Beautiful boobs and a great body, but she doesn't even come close to how beautiful Addison is. I make a mental note to take a shower before we go to *our* room tonight.

I see Max pull out his phone and his expression hardens. "Max!" Ryker screams at us from across the room, throwing his hands out. A girl grinds against his lap. He looks bored, obviously more interested in Max than the girl. "We said no phones until we meet up with the girls."

"We have to go. Now." He stands and pulls out his wallet.

"What's wrong?" I say, standing. He pulls out five hundred-dollar bills and throws them on the table. When he looks back to me, he shakes his head. "That's not a fucking answer, Max."

The other guys have stood up and are waiting for Max's answer, as well. Damon pulls our waitress over and tells her we're leaving. Ryker adds a few more hundred-dollar bills to the stack. The waitress picks up the money, blows a kiss to Ryker, and walks off.

"The girls are waiting outside for us." My eyebrows shoot up. *Why?* He's not going to tell me, so I take long strides toward the front door. Something's wrong, and I need to find out what it is. Now.

I slam the front door open and walk out into the open air. It's not any better out here than it is inside. At least inside it's air conditioned. I spot the girls in a huddle. There are two who I don't recognize. The only one I don't see is Addison. What. The. Fuck.

"Where the hell is Addison?"

Syd jumps at my voice. "Aiden, calm down." I look at Syd's tear-streaked face, and I stop walking.

"Sydney," I warn. The guys catch up and stand around the girls. I look at Sydney's hands and she's holding Addison's shoes. I fist my hand. "Tell me. Now!" I demand forcefully. The new girls jerk back.

"She's okay," Max says to my side. I glare at him.

"How the fuck do you know she's okay?" I seethe.

"I texted him," Syd says, stepping forward. Damon looks at her, hurt. "I tried to call you, babe. I tried to call you, too," she says, looking at me. I exhale loudly and nod. I guess it's a good thing Max didn't listen to the *"no phones"* rule.

"Addison got arrested," Syd says, wincing. I straighten my back and cross my arms, looking down at Syd.

"What? Why?"

"The details are still a little unclear."

"What the hell does that mean, Sydney," Jaxon says.

"We were dancing. Some guy grabbed me and Addison pulled me away." She stops and watches me closely. I nod for her to continue. "As we were walking away, he grabbed her and pulled her into his chest." I close my eyes. Please tell me she didn't kill a guy. When I open them, Syd continues. "He wouldn't let her go. So...she kicked his ass."

I stare at her, waiting for more. "She didn't kill anyone?" Syd shakes her head and looks at me like I'm crazy. "Why was she arrested then?" I ask slowly.

"That's where we're not sure. The cop pulled up about fifteen minutes after it happened and said that the guy and numerous witnesses stated she assaulted the guy for no reason and he arrested her for aggravated assault."

"Let me get this straight," Jaxon says, trying to wrap his head around this. "Addison was assaulted, she defended herself, and then *she* was arrested? Did she tell the cop that she was defending herself?"

"Yep. I did. She did. The bouncer did. His response...tell it to the judge." She puts her hand on her hip, pissed off. Max holds out his phone for me to hold.

"You should watch this," he says. Syd grabs it out of his hand before I can get it.

"Um...no. No, you shouldn't." She holds the phone close to her chest and takes a step back.

I keep my hand out and tilt my head. "Give me the phone, Syd. I'll see it one way or another."

She rolls her eyes but smacks it into the palm of my hand then shoots eye daggers at Max. Max chuckles.

"Tink, it was just a matter of time before he saw it." She huffs and walks to stand by Damon. I press play on the video. It's hard to see her because the video isn't in focus, but I can hear it clearly. Drake comes and stands beside me to watch. When I hear her grunt, I grit my teeth together and say a few curse words under my breath. I've heard enough when she asks for her shoes and the douchebag doesn't let her get them. I press pause and look at Drake.

"Who is that?" I say through gritted teeth.

"It's hard to say, but he doesn't look familiar. Max, mind if I send that to someone since it's already up on your phone?" Max shakes his head. I slap the phone on Drake's chest. He grabs it just as I walk away. I need to do something. I reach up and drag my hand through my hair. I swear this woman is going to be the death of me. I bite back a laugh. She's definitely going to keep me on my toes. I shake my head. She's sitting in a jail cell right now. At least she's safe. I'm not worried that she can't hold her own against other women. At least there's that. What a fucked-up night this has turned into. I take a few calming breaths and walk back to the group.

"I made a call. Seems Addison kicked a cop's ass," Drake says, sporting a grin. I slap my hand to my forehead. *Figures.* "The arresting cop is his buddy. I called their lieutenant and sent him the video. He's looking into it but said we can meet him at the detention center. It's not far from here." He points his head to the left.

"Who are you guys?" I ask the unfamiliar girls standing with Harper. One of the girls can't stop looking at Ryker, which isn't surprising. Ryker has a hat on, trying his hardest to be incognito but failing miserably. She turns to me as a deep red creeps up her face from being caught staring.

"This is Coryn and Abby. We met them at..." Syd pauses and twists her lips, "...a club." I narrow my eyes at her and chuckle.

"No need to lie, Syd. I mean, look where you just pulled us out from," I say, pointing to the neon sign flashing behind her.

"She's not lying. It was a club," Bryn adds, giggling. I glance around at all the girls; the smiles on their faces tell me it wasn't just a club. A tinge of jealousy surges through me, but I knock it down. Fuck, I almost had a naked woman dancing on me, which is probably more than Addison had at her club.

I stick my hand out to the new girls. "Well, it's nice to meet you, Coryn and Abby. I'm Aiden." I introduce all the guys, including Ryker. A couple small squeals slip from the back of their throats when they shake his hand. I'm impressed they keep their excitement contained, though. It would've irritated me if we would have had to deal with obsessed fangirls right now.

"I brought them along just in case we needed more people who witnessed how that asshole cop treated Addison," Syd explains, standing in Damon's arms. I still can't get over the stark difference in height between those two.

"I think the video does a good job of that," Drake says.

"We didn't know there was a video until we were on our way over here," Katie chimes in. She's been quiet the whole time, standing with Jaxon. Looking at Katie, my lips turn down as I really look at her the first time tonight. Jaxon's hand is on her hip, and she's leaning against him.

"Did you forget the rest of your dress, Katie?" She's wearing a black dress that shows a little too much for my liking. I remember a time when she wouldn't wear dresses. Can we go back to those days?

"Oh, Big Brother," she says, shaking her head, laughing.

"I think you look gorgeous," Jaxon says as he wraps his arms around her.

"Jax, you're not helping." He shrugs. Asshole. "*She's* my little sister. I don't want to imagine men lusting over my sister... dressed in *that*." I shake the thoughts from my head.

"If you think that's short—"

"I think you guys should probably go get Addie," Syd says, interrupting Coryn. She glares at Coryn for a second before turning back and flashing an innocent smile at me. I look between the two girls wondering what I just missed. Women and their secret code. I need a decoder ring to figure out half the shit that comes out of their mouth.

"She's right," Drake says.

"You guys go back out. I'll get Addison. I have a feeling she won't want to party anymore after this," I tell the group. "We'll text you when we get her to let you know she's okay."

"You better text me first," Syd demands. Her voice is serious. I nod, knowing how concerned she is. She comes over, hands me Addison's shoes, and gives me a hug. "Just...don't be mad at her for anything. She's had a pretty messed-up night so far." She catches me off guard. Why would I be mad at her? I pull my head back and look down at her.

"I could never be mad for what she did, Syd. She was protecting herself." The side of her lip twitches and she nods. When she walks away, I wonder if there is something else that happened tonight. I stand there and my eyes scan the other girls. They all look away from my questioning gaze except Katie.

Katie softly smiles and blows me a kiss and mouths, "*Don't worry, it's nothing.*" Her words calm my wandering thoughts *slightly*.

Drake and I head over to the detention facility. I'm quiet the entire ride. My mind is reeling from the last thirty minutes, the video, and the fact that we haven't had one moment of celebration that hasn't ended badly. I close my eyes and lean my head back on the headrest. I'll make damn sure our wedding goes off without a hitch. Addison is going to start fucking questioning Fate again. I wonder what she'd do if I drove her to the Little White Chapel here in Las Vegas and we got married. I chuckle. She would think it was a horrible idea. And Lexi isn't here so it wouldn't happen. I rub my jaw and exhale. God, I hope she's okay. For her to kick a guy's ass like that, something triggered her. It kills me to think what it could have been. I want to rip the guy's hand off for even touching her.

We exit the taxi as soon as it stops and walk up the stairs. I have a flashback from the last time we were at a jail. Each step I take reminds me of that day. The day she found out my dad killed her mom. The day she was kidnapped. The day my heart stopped beating.

Dammit, that's not today, Roberts.

"You alright there, Aiden?" Drake asks.

"Yeah, just having some fucked-up memories."

Drake stops walking and puts his hand on my shoulder. "I don't know Addison other than the obvious... She's beautiful, but is she worth it? She seems to come with a lot of baggage." His words hit me in my gut. What the hell? I fist my hand and my expression turns hard. "Aiden..." He puts his hands up.

"We've been friends a long time. I just want to make sure you're not thinking with the wrong head when it comes to Addison." I release my fist and relax my shoulders. To most outsiders I'm sure our relationship looks like a never-ending whirlpool and we're going to eventually drown. Drake doesn't know the whole story, and I'm not about to tell him. I can stand back and see where his concern is coming from.

"Drake, she's owns my heart and my mind. Every piece of me belongs to her. I don't know how else to explain it. I couldn't live without her."

He nods and pats me on the back. "That's good enough for me. Let's go spring her out of jail."

I glance at the name on the badge as we sit down. Lieutenant Graves. "Agent Webb, it's good to see you," he says, sitting down behind a desk.

"Lieutenant Graves, this is Agent Aiden Roberts." He leans over and we shake hands. I sit back in the wooden chair, rest my leg on my knee, shaking it, and wait to see how this is going to play out.

"I'm just going to cut out the bullshit. Our guys screwed up. There's going to be an internal investigation about what happened. I apologize. We don't condone what happened here in this office ever. Both officers will be placed on administrative leave." I'm relieved. He looks over at me with a grin. "I can tell you that Ms. Mason broke Officer Mace's nose, and he has a nice puncture wound in his leg from a heel, pretty close to the groin area." I try not to smile. "But from what I hear, he deserved it. There were numerous witnesses who came forward to tell us what *really* happened when they found out that Ms. Mason had been arrested."

"Your girl is a wild cat," Drake jokes, holding his hand over his groin. I chuckle. *If he only knew.*

"You're fiancée is definitely the talk of the night around here." The lieutenant smirks.

"Can I go back there with you when you release her?"

"You have your badge?"

"Of course," I say as I lean forward to grab my wallet from my back pocket.

"Let's go." He stands up and we follow suit.

"I think you can deal with it from here," Drake says, patting me on the back again.

"Thanks, man. It was good to see you." We shake hands. "Will we see you at the wedding?"

"I wouldn't miss it."

I follow Lieutenant Graves out back, flashing my badge to security. He points where I need to go while he delivers her release papers. I hear a woman talking, rather loudly, in the direction of the holding cell. Then I hear Addison's voice. A weight inside me releases when I hear her laugh. I walk slowly and revel in the sound of it. Listening to her talk strips away any anxiety that I was feeling. *She's really okay.*

Chapter nineteen

Barb is an interesting lady. I'm still not positive what she's in here for. One thing I know for sure, she didn't run over her husband. That was blatantly clear when she changed his name three times during her story. She's been entertaining, so I've indulged her.

The second I see Aiden walk around the corner, though, my mind stops hearing Barb and it focuses solely on Aiden. His perfect fitting dark jeans and navy dress shirt, sleeves rolled up to show off his muscular forearms, makes one thing come to mind. *Mine.*

His eyes catch mine and his lips curl into a slow sexy grin. When I stand up, his eyes rake down my body and back up. When they reach mine again, his expression has changed. His jaw clenches and the hardness in his eyes catches me off guard. My brows furrow and I look down, wondering why his expression did a one-eighty. An awkward giggle escapes my lips as I tug my dress down an extra inch. It's a lost cause. I don't know why I think pulling it down will make it any longer. It didn't the other hundred times I tried.

"I wore it for you," I say, attempting to defend myself. He's clearly not happy with my outfit choice.

He grabs hold of a couple of the bars and leans forward. "You weren't with me, Addison," he sears. "What the fuck do you expect wearing that? You might as well be naked."

His words leave a bite on my heart, and if he doesn't stop now, they might leave a scar. I straighten and glare at him. I open my mouth and then snap it shut, afraid of what might come out. The cell feels like it's closing in and suffocating me.

"What?" I grit my teeth together. "Even if I was naked, no man has the fucking right to touch me."

Aiden immediately recognizes his fuck-up. His eyes soften and his shoulders droop. "Addison, I'm sorry."

Too late.

I look up to the dingy ceiling. Anger is replaced by hurt. Tears burn my eyes, and I blink them back. I glance at Aiden and see the regret in his eyes. "Aiden, please go. I'll meet you back at the hotel," I say quietly.

"Addison, I didn't mean it like that."

"If you didn't mean it, why did you say it?" barks Barb. I turn my head in Barb's direction and nod once before turning back to Aiden. I look at him expectantly. *Yeah, what she said.* His eyes shut for a beat.

"I'm sorry," he repeats.

I chew the inside of my cheek and nod again but stay silent. Crossing my arms, I turn around and sit back on the cool metal seat. I welcome the cold and intentionally don't try and pull my dress down. I watch him walk away until he's out of view before sighing loudly. Deep down, I know his response is from a place of jealousy, but what he said hurts deeper than that. It touches a place I keep hidden for a reason. I don't need reminders. He should know that.

"He seemed genuinely sorry, hun."

My head rolls to the side in Barb's direction. "He is."

"And he was damn mighty fine."

I chuckle. "He's that, too." He's also an asshole right now. I wonder how much longer I'm going to be in here. If Aiden was here, I must be getting out soon. About fifteen minutes go by before I hear anything.

"Ms. Mason." I glance to the cell door and there's an older gentleman in a uniform, standing there. "I'm Lieutenant Graves. You're free to go," he says, opening the door. The way he says it, with sympathy, I'm not sure if he heard Aiden or if he knows that his cop arrested me without any reason and he's afraid of the recourse.

I stand and turn toward Barb. My lovely government-issued shoes squeak on the laminated floor. "Barb, it's been nice talking to you."

"You, too, hun. And hey, go enjoy that jealous, alpha stud muffin. He seems like he loves you." I laugh at her description of Aiden. It's pretty spot-on.

As I walk through the door, the lieutenant guides me into an office. He gestures for me to sit down in the chair across from his desk. I sit and watch him round the desk and take a seat, too. He plops his elbows on the table and links his fingers together.

"You've definitely made my night interesting," he says, blowing out a breath through his nose. I glance down at my sore hand, opening and closing it a couple times. Damn, that hurts. "I hear you pack a hell of a punch. And kick." I look back up to him. He smiles and sits back in his chair.

"It probably wasn't hard enough."

"I think he'll remember it for a while," he says. "We heard from actual witnesses about what happened and they say he deserved it." I nod in agreement. He definitely did. "Do you know anything about the guy?"

"He was a drunk asshole."

"He was *that*. But did you know he was a police officer?" My eyes widen in surprise. "And the arresting officer was his buddy." Now it all makes sense. "We put both officers on administrative leave while IA does an investigation, but we have enough proof that you shouldn't be here. If you want to file a sexual assault report, I would fully understand."

I think about it for a few seconds. As much as I want to walk out these doors and never have a second thought about what happened tonight, can I? I look at the lieutenant. "I feel he got what he deserved and his decision might cost him his job even without my report." I take a deep breath. "Lieutenant Graves, to be honest, my past has a habit of coming back to haunt me and I'm tired of being on people's revenge list. I would just like to go take a shower right now." I wrinkle my nose. The stench in the cell seems to have seeped into my clothes. He chuckles and nods.

"Well, we're sorry for what transpired tonight. I'm sure Agent Webb will follow up on things on behalf of you and Agent Roberts." Agent Webb? I tilt my head, unsure who that is. "Agent Drake Webb," he says slowly.

"Oh, Drake. Sorry, I didn't remember his last name."

"I went to retrieve your things, but they told me you didn't come with anything?" He gives me an unsure look. I think about my shoes and my purse, hoping they made it back with the girls.

"Nope. Would you like your shoes back?" I ask, lifting my leg and flopping my shoe against my foot.

His laugh echoes in the tiny office. "No, you can keep those courtesy of the Las Vegas Police Department." He stands and walks around his desk. "You'll find Agent Roberts outside, waiting on his Cinderella." I look up to him and my brows furrow. *Cinderella?* What is he talking about? He flashes a lopsided grin and shakes his head. "You'll understand," he says as he ushers me out.

As I walk outside, the heat hits me and helps thaw the cold from my bones. The building's lights shine bright against the pitch-black sky. I don't have a clue what time it is but it has to be after one in the morning since I was brought in around eleven. I can't believe that asshole was a cop. I can't believe I was arrested. I can't believe the words that came out of Aiden's mouth. *Damn this night.*

Looking around, there are only a few people walking around out here. For a town that never sleeps, it's awfully quiet right now, or maybe it's just the part of town that people avoid. I find Aiden sitting halfway down the stairs, hunched over with his elbows on his knees. A lone heel sits beside him. I snicker. *Cinderella.* Where the hell is my other shoe?

I walk down, taking each step slowly. The hurt left by his words hasn't dissipated. Time has allowed me to understand his frustration. I know he's a jealous man, but I will not accept him talking to me like that.

I sit down next to him, stretching my feet out in front of me so I don't flash anyone walking by. That's all I need right now. "Have you found her yet?" I whisper.

He turns his head toward me, lifting a confused brow.

"The one who fits the shoe. Isn't that how the story goes?" It's been a long time since I saw the movie *Cinderella.* I was never into princess movies, so I could be wrong. I've seen current movies with Lexi, but the classics...it's been awhile. He turns his head to his other side, looking at the shoe. He chuckles softly, picking it up.

"They say the woman it fits will forgive her prince for being a jealous asshole."

I run my hand through my hair, looking up at the sky. I sigh heavily. "I can handle you being a jealous asshole. I've come to terms with that." I turn back to meet his pleading eyes. I can see he's sorry and I'm sure he'll do anything to make it up to me. "But your words cut right through me tonight, hitting a target that they should never have been pointed at. Especially by you."

"I'm sorry," he says, blinking back his tears. His hand scrapes over his jaw. "I shouldn't have ever said that. You know I don't think that way." He reaches for my hand. "I just..." He pauses, shaking his head. "There's no excuse. Nothing I say will justify my actions."

After a few silent beats, I let out a long exhale. "It's been a long night. Let's go back to the hotel." I stand up and wait for him. He pushes off the cement, grabbing my shoe. He shows it to me as if to ask if I want it. "I'm a little afraid to ask, but where is my other one."

He looks toward the dirt field across the street. "I threw it over there," he murmurs. It's pitch black over there. There is no way we're going to find my shoe tonight.

"Well, it's a good thing I was given some shoes, then." I step down a few stairs and notice Aiden isn't walking with me. I look back up at him. He's staring at me with one hand stuffed in his pocket and the other holds my shoe. "Are you coming? Because I need a shower." He nods. My heart hurts from the sad look in his eyes but my mind tells me he deserves it.

The taxi pulls up in front of our hotel. A valet opens my door, and I slip out while Aiden pays. I look down at my lovely orange flip-flops, waiting. The valet looks down too and cocks his head, staring at them. When his eyes meet mine, I slightly narrow my eyes at him. "You've had some of these, haven't you?" I chuckle, holding my foot up a little.

He laughs and holds his hand up in the air. "I plead the fifth."

When Aiden exits the car, he notices the valet and puts his arm around me. *Really? Now is not the time for your jealous bullshit.* I look up and glare at him. He removes his arm from my waist. I shake my head in disbelief and walk into the hotel, proudly displaying my orange flip-flops, and feel Aiden walking behind me. I wait for him to pull out his room card to show the security guard so we can pass to the hotel elevators. The security guard catches a glimpse of my shoes and cocks his head, assessing me. Aiden whips out the card and ushers me past the asshole security guard. He can take his judgmental stare and fuck off. I'm not in the mood tonight.

I kick off my shoes the second we walk into the room. Next stop, shower. My dress slides down my body easily, and I'm about to step into the shower when Aiden appears.

"Wash off and I'll run you a bath."

I manage a soft smile. I scrub the grime and stink off my body. I blow my nose, trying to get the smell of urine out of it. When I'm done, Aiden has left the bathroom, but my bath waits for me. After braiding my hair, I sink down into the hot water and listen to the television that Aiden has on in the next room. My eyes drift shut as my body finally relaxes.

"Addison." I open my eyes and Aiden is sitting on the tub. "You should probably get out now." I move my arms out of the water and look at my wrinkled fingers. My knuckles on my right hand are already starting to bruise. Aiden stands up and holds out a towel for me to step into. He dries me off and I'm taken back to the first night we had sex. Goose bumps spread over my body. He pauses for a beat, noticing them on my legs, but continues just drying me off. He wraps the towel around me and lifts me, carrying me to bed. He's already turned all the lights out except a dimmed lamp on the nightstand.

The only thing he has on are basketball shorts. When he tucks me in, he slides in on his side then turns off the light. I quietly sigh, rolling to my side and stare at him. It's pure blackness in here because of the thick curtains, but I have a feeling he's looking at me, too. I blink a few times, wondering if I should say something.

I close my eyes when I feel his hand on my cheek. His thumb caresses it. I turn and kiss the palm of his hand. He scoots over, pushing me over and lying on top of me. "I'm sorry," he repeats as he presses his lips up and down my neck.

"Shh," I finally say. "I know."

His mouth captures mine and he pours his apology into his kiss. I skate my fingers up his back and weave them through his hair. When he pulls down his shorts, I help him slide them down his legs with my foot. "I love you," he whispers on my lips as he enters me and I moan into his mouth. Our rhythm is slow and sensual. We're chest to chest, heart to heart. There are no words, just the sounds of our heartbeats. His telling me *he's sorry* and I'm saying *I forgive you.*

Was that my phone? I rub the sleep from my eyes and open them to a dark room. Slits of light squeeze around the hotel curtain. I groan from the headache wreaking havoc in my brain right now. Rubbing my temples, I roll my head to an empty bed.

"Aiden?"

The only thing I hear is the air conditioner. I sit up and pull the cool sheets over me, covering my naked breasts. I squeeze my eyes shut, wincing. Maybe I sat up too fast or maybe I didn't and just sitting up makes my head feel like it's splitting open. My phone dings again, reminding me of what woke me up in the first place. I lean over to grab it and find a note from Aiden right beside it. He's left me Advil and a bottled water with a demanding "take these" note. I drop my head on his pillow, taking deep breaths through the pain.

Take the pills, Addison. Forcing myself back up, I swallow the pills and the entire bottle of water.

Memories from last night flash through my mind and my eyelids fall heavy as I drift back to sleep. My phone rings, pulling me out of my sleep. I look around the still dark, cold room. No sign of Aiden. Reaching for my phone, I already know who's calling because of the ringtone.

"Good morning, Sydney," I say, my voice raspy from sleep.

"Good morning? It's almost noon, girlfriend." *Noon?* I sit up and run my hand though my hair. The Advil did its magic, but I wonder where Aiden is. "I've tried texting you, but you didn't answer so I had to resort to calling you. Wake up," she snaps into the phone.

I chuckle into the phone. "I'm up."

"We're all meeting for lunch at one. We have some news for you." I hear one of the girls in the background telling Syd to be quiet.

"News? What news? Please, don't tell me anyone else went to jail last night?"

Sydney giggles. "Nope, you're the only jailbird in our group. Drake ended up meeting back up with us and telling us the whole story. Addie, *only you.*"

"I know, right? A freaking cop," I say, shaking my head, still not believing the turn of events last night. "Okay, when I find Aiden we'll meet y'all downstairs at one."

"Oh, he's with Damon working out." Figures. I'm glad someone feels well enough to work out because I sure as hell don't.

I hang up the phone then stand and open the curtains. Sunlight pours into the room. The heat from the windows feels good on my cold body. I wonder what news they have for us. I can't even imagine with that group. After grabbing a pair of panties and a bra, I head for the shower.

Aiden should have been back by the time I was out of the shower, but I walk into an empty room. I pick up my phone off the bedside table to see if he's texted me, but the only one I see on the screen is the one from Sydney earlier. Should I call him and tell him I'm up? He's with Damon so I'm sure he already knows we're meeting at one. Screw it, I'll just start packing up and finish getting ready.

Half an hour later, my hair is dried, my bags are packed, and I'm about to get dressed when Aiden walks in. Those gorgeous green eyes lock with mine. He's wearing blue basketball shorts that hang low on his hips, and his sculpted, sweaty chest is begging me to touch it. He's got his shirt gripped in his hand. My eyes slowly rake down his body. When I make my way up to his face, his tongue darts out to lick his lower lip. Desire tickles deep down in my stomach, and he flashes a knowing smile.

He stalks over to me like he's going to swallow me whole and throws his shirt on the bed. "That look will get you fucked. Every. Time." I gasp when he picks me up.

"Looking like that, I'll let you," I say flirtatiously, wrapping my legs around his waist. My eyes are hooded, and I bite my lip as my pulse starts to quicken. The look of raw, unadulterated lust and desire in his eyes makes heat streak up my body. I cup his neck and pull his lips to mine, demanding the feel of him. He growls into my mouth, taking back control with his tongue. His hand moves down my back and traces the lace on my thong, down my ass. He stops and flirts with my puckered entrance through my panties.

"Fuck, I want to take you here, Addison," he says, his voice a rasp against my lips. He presses more into me and my fingers grip his hair as the sensation deliciously burns through me. The heady feeling that he wants me everywhere makes me lose all sense of what is normal or taboo, pushing every inhibition I have out of my head.

"Yes," I breathe out. My voice is full of need. He groans as he tugs my panties aside and two fingers glide inside my sex. I'm drenched and throbbing. I rock against his fingers, begging for relief.

"Jesus Christ," he pants, "you're so perfect."

He pulls his fingers out, and I bite his lip. He chuckles and smacks me on the ass. "Lie on the bed with that beautiful ass in the air," he demands, walking us to the bed. When he puts me down, he spins me around, laying his hand on my back, pushing me to bend over. My face hits the cool comforter. My breathing is erratic. He unclasps my bra and it droops down in front of me so I pull my arms through it and throw it to the side. He presses his pelvis against me and leans over, kissing my back as he reaches around and pinches my nipple. I buck my hips against him and a sharp moan slips from my lips. "Don't move," he whispers into my ear.

I hear him digging into a bag from behind me. Anticipation of what he's going to do has me gripping the comforter, my nerves humming. I want to look what he's doing, but he's back quickly. He drags his fingers down my back, hooking them under my panties and slowly pulling them down my legs. I shudder when his tongue trails from my clit to my ass. My legs start to shake from tensing them up.

"Put your knees on the bed." He guides me forward, and I do what he says. I moan again, feeling his tongue circle my clit. His nipping, biting, and sucking has me screaming and my body jerks with spasms in a matter of minutes. He grips my hips so I can't move against his punishing tongue. Before I can stop spinning, he's at my entrance and pushes in slowly until he's fully sheathed inside of me. He grunts, squeezing my thighs. I arch back against him, sticking my ass higher in the air, wanting to feel him deeper.

"Fuck, Addison," he hisses. "You're going to make me come."

"Isn't that the point," I mutter, grinding my hips against him.

He grips my hips, stopping me. "Not yet," he growls loudly. I hear a bottle pop open and feel wetness go in between my butt cheeks. I fist the blanket, waiting. Something foreign touches me, and I jerk my head around. *What is that*? Aiden holds up a butt plug.

"It's just this. I thought we should start small," he smirks and winks at me. He pistons his hips once, and I cry out as he reminds me how *big* he is. *I'm good with starting small*. He goes back to rubbing the plug against my ass.

"That better be new," I murmur. Where the hell did he get a butt plug?

I hear him snicker behind me. He throws down something by my head. I glance and see it's my bullet. *Someone has been digging in my drawer.* "You know what to do with it," he commands softly. I pick it up and put it on my clit. Aiden starts to thrust his hips as he nudges the plug against my ass. He slowly slides it in, allowing me to get used to the feeling before going any farther. The initial pinch subsides quickly. When it's all the way in, the sensations from the nerve endings back there make me gasp audibly. I arch my back, letting out a cry as he starts moving his hips. I can tell he's losing control when his pace becomes almost frantic, filling me completely. He grunts under his breath every time he feels the plug rub against him. "Fuck," he roars.

"Oh...Oh...Aiden!" I scream out in ecstasy as the most intense orgasm explodes inside of me. The delicious burn is almost unbearable. Heat runs down his cock, and I bite down on the blanket to muffle my cries. He grips my hips again, thrusting one last time before his body tenses and he roars my name as we ride out our orgasms together.

He falls forward on me, his chest heaving against my back. His body pushes the plug in, and I moan out in pleasure.

"Holy shit," he pants. "That was...amazing." He kisses my back. "You're amazing," he whispers against my skin. I search for the bullet still buzzing somewhere under the covers. I press the little button on the back of it, turning it off when I find it. When Aiden pulls out, I still feel full, which is weird. *Hmm...*I'm not sure how I feel about this *after* the fact. It's really awkward, actually. The sex haze has lifted, and I still have a butt plug in my ass.

"Come on, gorgeous. Let's go take a shower. We have people to meet."

I hold up a finger as I stand up and pinch my lips together. "Let me go to the bathroom first." He arches his brow. "Everything okay?" he asks, his voice worried.

"Yes. I just need to take care of this myself." I point down toward my pelvis area, assuming he'll know what I'm talking about. I can feel the rush of heat, slowly making its way to my cheeks.

"Sweetheart, you don't have to be em—"

I put my finger to his lips and shake my head. "Don't. I'll let you know when you can come in." I walk backwards toward the bathroom, and Aiden drops his head and shakes it.

Chapter twenty

Aiden and I spot our friends huddled in the lobby. As soon as Sydney sees us coming, she breaks out into "Jail House Rock" by Elvis Presley.

I sigh and roll my eyes. *Why do I feel like I'm in a constant musical around these people?*

"Not funny," I say.

She stops singing and wrinkles her nose. "It kind of is." She shrugs and laughs.

"Well, I'm glad I had crazy Barb to keep me company." *I wonder if she's still there?* I tell the group about Barb and the stories that I'm positive she made up.

"Guess who left together last night," Bryn says. I look at her and then the rest of the group. I'm a little afraid to answer that. I recount the hookups between the eight of them. I know Jaxon and Katie are out. Sydney and Damon are out. I stare at Ryker, Max, Harper, and Bryn, debating who it might have been. "No! Not any of us," she states. Ryker clears his throat and Harper blushes, hitting him on the chest. "I mean..." She stops and flusters. "I mean Drake and Coryn."

"That's not all that happened last night," Syd says in her singsong voice. I raise a curious brow.

"I'm starving, let's eat first," Katie quickly says. I, again, look around the group and wonder what they aren't telling us.

"Katie? What are you hiding?" Aiden says from behind me. I turn and look at him, his eyes narrowing at her.

"Um...well...I...we..." she stutters and looks to Jaxon for help. The carefree smile on his face doesn't reflect the same trepidation Katie has on hers. He looks down at her and winks. I feel Aiden tense behind me.

Jaxon stands taller and confidently says, "We got married last night."

My eyes widen in surprise, and I do a double-take. *Did I just hear that right*?

"What the hell did you just say?" Aiden grinds out. Oh, shit. I spin and put my hand on Aiden's puffed out chest. He looks down at me, his face tight with anger, whips around, and stomps away.

I hear Katie sigh. "That went well." I turn back toward them and my lips curl into a smile.

"Oh, my gosh! I want to hear all about it, but I need to..." I point behind me and she nods. I squeal and give her a quick hug. "Congratulations! *I think*. Is it for real? How drunk were you?" I have so many more questions.

"Go calm my brother down. We'll tell you all about it at lunch," she says. Her voice is giddy, so I know she's happy about it. Jaxon wraps his arms around her and kisses her.

I head in the direction Aiden walked and look around. I see him pacing down a hallway, muttering things I can only imagine. I lean against the wall and give him a couple minutes to wrap his head around this before I say anything.

"I know that was a knee-jerk reaction." He doesn't stop pacing, so I continue. "Seems you've had a lot of those lately." He stops, whips around, and pins me with his angry eyes.

"Addison, she's my sister." He says it like it allows him to be an asshole.

"*And*? Jaxon is one of your best friends, and I thought you had accepted them being together." He grunts and runs his hand haphazardly through his hair, making it stand on its ends. "Tell me what you're thinking," I say, walking toward him.

"I'm angry they did it, here in fucking Vegas, probably drunk as hell." I nod in agreement. I have no doubt they were drunk. "I'm hurt because we weren't there. She's my little sister. I should be there when she gets married." He looks away from me as my eyes soften. When he turns back, he pulls me into his embrace and rests his forehead against mine. "I'm also jealous that they're married," he says, his voice just loud enough for me to hear.

I look up into his eyes. "You're such a man," I say. He shrugs his shoulders and grins. "Can you at least admit that you're happy for Katie and Jaxon?"

"I am. But I'm still hurt they didn't wait for us to be there." He places a soft kiss on my forehead.

"I'm sure with that crew, there was a lot of drinking and not a lot of thinking last night. I mean, I doubt they got a marriage license, so it's probably not even legal."

"Addison, you underestimate Jaxon. He's a high-profile attorney. I'm sure he found a way."

I link my fingers through his and squeeze. "Can we go back? I'm kinda of starving." He nods as he tugs me in their direction.

The guys decide we need to eat at a buffet, so I slide my tray down each side, looking at the different food. None of it is appetizing. Maybe I should start with a salad. My stomach rumbles in defiance. I need a fat, juicy hamburger. I look around to see if there is anything remotely close.

"I know you're not picky," Aiden says, walking up to my side, looking down at my tray that only has some fruit on it.

"I want a thick hamburger," I whine. My eyes widen when I look at his tray. He has two plates full of...*everything*. Just the thought of all that food makes my stomach twist. I hate buffets.

"They have a menu. I'll just order you one." My lips curl into a smile. *Perfect*. We walk back to our table and place our trays down.

"I know you're not on a diet," Max says from across the table, motioning to my fruit. What is with everyone being worried about what I'm eating?

"No, I just want—"

"A juicy hamburger," Syd finishes my sentence. *Exactly*. The day after a drunken night, the best thing in the world is to eat a hamburger. At least, I think so.

Aiden flags down a waitress and orders. "Make that two," Max says, smirking. I look over at his food piled high and shake my head. These guys are going to get their money's worth. "What? It does sound good." He rubs his hands together and picks up a rib, taking a hefty bite. Judging by his tray, it seems everything looks good to Max.

"Let's hear about last night," I say, poking Katie next to me. "It's not legit, is it?"

"Too Legit To Quit" from MC Hammer comes out of Damon's mouth and Syd adds the "heeyy heyyyya" part. My head tilts to the side as I stare at the two across the table.

"I can't take you guys anywhere. Y'all are nuts," I say, chuckling. It's not until Aiden starts beat-boxing next to me that Damon starts rapping the lyrics. Max starts playing the drums with his silverware on the table. I think they've all lost their freaking minds. I shrink down in my chair and glance around the restaurant. All eyes are on us. Please, make it stop soon.

Katie leans over and whispers into my ear, "Now you see what I've had to put up with for years. Welcome to the family," she giggles. I should be used to it by now because of Syd. But this is a whole new level. *We've got a band now.*

When they finish, I clap and tell Aiden, "I'm so glad Audacious Babes are getting back together." Aiden shakes his head and chuckles.

"Who the hell is Audacious Babes?" Max asks, putting down his silverware drumsticks.

I do my best confused expression that I can muster. "I thought that was the name of y'all's band when you were kids?"

"You told her about that?" Max says, belting out a laugh. Aiden leans over and wraps his arm around my chair, kissing me on my temple.

"I did," he answers. "But I did not tell her our name was *Audacious Babes*. That's her own spin on that story."

I shrug. "It's better than *Paperback Boys*," I say dryly.

Ryker and Jaxon burst out laughing. "Paperback Boys? Why haven't we ever heard this story," Ryker taunts. Max throws a roll at him and hits him in the head.

"That was a long time ago," he answers and looks at Aiden with a lopsided grin. Max knows the pain Aiden went through from the death of his mom. Pain that left an unspoken promise to never talk about the past. Aside from the teasing, Max seems genuinely happy that Aiden told me.

The pieces of our lives that we hid from the world because of the deaths of our mothers have slowly surfaced. I lean my head on Aiden's arm and reflect how far we've come. Our instant attraction that turned into a deeper love than I ever could have imagined has shaken my whole world and that world is being rebuilt with Aiden as my foundation.

"I love you," Aiden whispers. The rasp of his voice pulls at my insides. I glance up at him and softly smile. He can sing every love song or dance with me every night but nothing will elicit the same heartfelt response than hearing those three simple words.

A plate is placed in front of me, pulling me from my deep thoughts. I politely thank the waitress as I stare at the delicious hamburger. My mouth waters and my stomach grumbles in anticipation.

As I bring the hamburger to my lips and take too big of a bite, the waitress says, "What male revue do you guys work at?" I try to laugh but my mouth is too full so I end up choking it down. The other girls break out in giggles at the absurd remark. Tears run down my face as I reach for my water. Aiden helps by patting my back.

"What?" Damon says, sitting up taller in his chair.

"What show are you guys from," she says in a hushed tone. I look around the table and I can see where she might think that. All the guys at the table are very built and are wearing T-shirts that show off their muscular arms. They're hot a*nd they seem to be okay with entertaining people.*

"We're FBI," Damon states matter-of-factly, holding his arms out.

"Oh! I bet that is a *hot* skit. So, all of you come out on the stage in uniform?" She starts fanning herself with the menu she has in her hand. My hand is on Aiden's leg, and I squeeze it while I try and stifle my laugh. The waitress is young, maybe twenty at the most, and she is dead serious.

"You think this is funny?" Aiden says, poking me in the waist. I double over and laugh, thinking about Aiden being on stage dancing like the guys the other night. Don't get me wrong, it'd be hot, but I just can't see him *wanting* to do that.

"At least I wouldn't have to stuff my thong," Damon busts out proudly.

"Oh, baby," Syd snickers. "I've seen you dance. You need to keep your day job."

This is too much. I can't stop laughing. The waitress looks around the table. Her lips twist. I think she's starting to question if they really are part of any show. But then again, if I were her, I wouldn't believe they were FBI either.

Damon jumps up and straddles Syd. She squeals, sitting all the way back in her chair. He wraps her hands around his ass as he grinds his hips on her lap. This is happening. In a restaurant. People are going to think we're crazy. The waitress watches while the table roars with laughter. When he's done, he flashes a confident smile as if he thinks he's proven Sydney wrong. Her face is red from laughing so hard.

"So...you're not dancers?" the waitress comments after he sits down. Aiden slaps his hand down on the table and throws his head back, laughing. Damon laughs but flips off Aiden.

"No. I'm Ryker Dallas," Ryker says, standing up and taking off his hat. The waitress's eyes widen. Her face flushes from embarrassment. "I am definitely *not* a stripper."

"*Oh, my God.* I'm so sorry." Her voice raises a couple octaves and her face flushes. Ryker politely smiles and puts his hat back on.

"It's okay..." he glances at her name tag, "...Lindsay." His southern drawl is sexy as he says her name. An awkward giggle escapes her lips, and she looks down briefly before looking back up. I chuckle, thinking back to when I first met Ryker. I know exactly how she feels right now.

"So...um...if you...um...need anything..." her words come out jumbled, "...just let me know." She spins on her heels and walks away quickly. I watch her walk to the waitress stand, lean against the counter, pull a phone out of her pocket, and type so fast it's like her life depends on it. So much for being incognito. *Way to go, Ryker.*

"Are y'all done singing and dancing now?" I look at the guys, my eyebrow arched. "I'd really like to hear about the wedding I missed last night." I take a quick bite of my hamburger before turning to Katie.

"There's really not a lot to tell. We got married," Jaxon says, shrugging. I lean over Katie and hit him in the chest.

"Don't ever retell your wedding story like *that*." I glare at him. He puts his hands up in the air as Katie glares at him, too.

"Baby, I didn't mean to make it insignificant," he says, backpedaling. "It was truly the best night of my life." Katie's glare softens and her lips curl into a sweet smile. He grabs her hand and pulls it to his mouth, kissing it.

"Do y'all remember any of it?" I ask, interrupting the love fest going on. I get a chuckle from the table.

Katie's head bobs a little. "Most of it."

"Okay, so tell me!"

"After Aiden and Drake left to go get you, we all went to a bar. Lots of drinks later, we thought it would be a good idea to go break you out of jail." She smirks as I shake my head, wondering who thought that was a good idea.

"Just for the record, I never thought that was a good idea," Max chimes in.

"Whatever, Rambo, you said you were going to take a bazooka and blow up the place," Ryker jokes.

Max shrugs and grins. "I don't remember that." *Way to plead the fifth, Max.*

To keep the conversion moving, I say, "Okay, then what? Obviously you didn't break me out of jail." I motion with my hands to continue.

"When we got to the jail, Drake was coming out and told us everything, so we started to leave and I saw a sign that said: *Marriage License, open until midnight.*" Katie bites her bottom lip and grins. Sydney jumps in during her pause.

"It was so romantic," she says, holding a hand to her heart. "*Aww.* Did Jaxon ask you to marry him right there?"

Jaxon chuckles and shakes his head, looking at Katie. She blushes and looks away from his shit-eating grin. "No, I asked him," she says, biting the inside of her cheek.

Aiden had stayed quiet *until now.* "What the fuck, Jax? You married my sister and couldn't even do it right?"

"Hold up," he says, putting his finger in the air. "How many times have I asked you to marry me?" He sits up in his chair and angles his body toward Katie. All eyes are on Katie.

"Three times," she says.

"Exactly. You can bet your ass that when she asked me to marry her, I took her up on that offer."

"You were drunk!" Aiden snaps. "And didn't the first three no's tell you something?"

Jaxon's smile turns into a frown and his expression hardens. "Aiden," he warns with a chill in his voice.

"You two stop," Katie says, putting a hand on Jaxon's chest. "I didn't say no to him all those times because I didn't want to marry him. *I did.* I just wasn't ready to uproot my life."

I look at Aiden and his eyes soften, and he slowly nods. "You are now?"

"I am. I have been for the past six months, but he hadn't asked me again, so I wasn't sure if that is what he still wanted." Her voice trails off.

"What?" Jaxon murmurs, grabbing her hands into his. "I would have asked you the second I knew you were ready." They embrace and kiss and sighs are murmured around the table. The love between the two of them is so evident, I knew it was just a matter of time, especially after Aiden came to the realization that he couldn't stop it.

When they pull back, Aiden says, "Welcome to the family, brother," with resignation in his voice. He scoots his chair back, stands, and pulls Jaxon into a man hug.

"Ry Ry," I hear a high-pitched voice say from across the restaurant. Ryker mutters a curse word and drops his head. All our heads turn in the direction the voice came from. We watch a gorgeous blonde wearing white shorts and a bright pink ruffled shirt that hangs off her shoulders walk effortlessly in five-inch wedge shoes. She waves as she walks toward our table and smiles. Aiden groans as he sits back down in his chair. *I agree.* I knew it was just a matter of time before crazy fans started to come out of the woodwork.

"Ry, baby! I heard you were in town. I was hoping to run into you." Ryker stands and gives the woman a hug.

"Hey, Ray," he replies in an annoyed voice. She beams at him, either not noticing the undertone of his voice or not caring.

"I've tried calling you. Why haven't you returned my calls?" Her whiney voice makes fingernails on a chalkboard sound like music.

He glances down at Bryn and genuinely smiles. "I've been busy."

She looks at Bryn. Her top lip pulls up and she huffs. It seems she is more than a crazy fan, she's a crazy booty call. I'd rather it be a crazy fan. Bryn's wearing denim shorts and a gray T-shirt that says *Happiness is when debits equal credits*. I still laugh when I read it. It's definitely Bryn. Her hair is in a messy bun, and she doesn't have any makeup on but she's naturally gorgeous. She might not be as thin as Barbie, but if I were a man, I'd take Bryn and her curves over that cheap looking booty call any day.

"*Really?*" the crazy girl says, her voice condescending. I angle my head. Who the hell does this girl think she is?

Bryn rolls her eyes and stands up. "I'll be back," she says. She glances at Ryker then with a slight shake to her head, she turns and walks away. Ryker's jaw clenches as he watches her leave. I stand up and toss my napkin on the table.

"I don't know who you are, but you don't get to come here and interrupt our lunch and be a bitch to my friends." Aiden's hand grabs hold of my back pocket. Her eyes meet mine, and I cross my arms. She narrows her eyes and moves her gaze down my body. They land on Aiden's arm holding me back then follows the path to the man the arm belongs to. Her sour expression changes to excitement as soon as her eyes meet Aiden's.

"Aiden!" Her eyes widen in recognition. I feel a slight sting in my stomach. My arms drop to my sides as I look from Aiden to Psycho Barbie. "It's been a long time," she purrs. My eyebrows shoot up, and I look at Aiden. The grip he has on my shorts tightens before he stands up. The apologetic smile he gives me doesn't help how I'm feeling right now. A flash of heat runs through my body.

"Rach," he says, with a nod.

"It's Raquel now," she replies with the wave of a hand. The more she talks, the more I dislike her. "You're still looking good." This girl can't be serious. I'm standing *right here*.

Aiden's hand releases my back pocket, but he wraps his arm around my waist—tight. "Rach, this is Addison, *my fiancée.*"

She flashes me catty smile. "Fiancée? *Hmph.* I figured you would have eventually ended up with that Jessica girl," she says, lifting her brow. Her intentions hit their mark. Dead center. My body tenses, my pulse quickening. She knows it, too, so she continues and her claws come out. "That girl would have done anything for you. Even wait for you to finish having *your fun.*" She winks at Aiden. My stomach churns at the insinuation of that comment. The fact that she seems to know both Ryker and Aiden very well leads me to believe she's been with both. My mind takes me back to when Aiden told me they've shared women at *the same time.*

Bitch, I have claws, too.

I manage to fake a smile. "I feel sorry for you." She sighs and rolls her eyes. "I mean it must suck to find out that men only want to fuck you. And it must not even be that great since they don't keep you." She gasps, but the words roll off my tongue and I keep going. "I'm not a gambling person, but I would bet everything that you saw a tweet just a little while ago that Ryker was down here so you got all dolled up to come find him only to be rejected. I'm not sure what's more humiliating, that you keep trying and he *clearly* doesn't want you or that he just rejected you in front of everyone just now. *It must be lonely in your world.*"

Her face turns beet red. She tugs her purse strap on her shoulder and glares at me. I wait for a comeback, but instead she huffs, whips around, and stomps off. The adrenaline from my anger has me shaking. I open and close my hands and shake them out. I look down at my half-eaten hamburger and sigh.

"I'm not hungry anymore," I say, grabbing my purse and walking away. I don't bother waiting for anyone to speak. I just leave. Aiden grumbles something, and then I hear his heavy footsteps behind me.

"Wheels up in two hours," Max says from behind. I throw up a peace sign, acknowledging him.

While I'm waiting for the elevator, Aiden stands behind me. He's not touching me, but he's close enough I can feel the tension between us. "I don't want to know anything about her. I read between the lines, loud and clear." He stays quiet but exhales heavily.

When we get to the room, I pace around, checking to make sure everything is packed. I already know it is, but it gives me something to do. Aiden sits on the bed with his hands together, leaning on his knees, just watching me. I glance at him a couple times and our eyes catch, but I look away quickly. I can tell he wants to explain himself, but I don't want to hear it.

Finally, I break the awkward silence. "Aiden, I know you have a past. It's not your fault *that* happened. I'm not mad at you, *per se*..." he lifts a brow, "...I'm more mad that you didn't have better standards back then."

He chuckles and nods softly. "She didn't mean anything to me."

I lean my hip against the desk. "I know."

"She and Ryker have messed around since—"

I hold my hand up. "I *really* don't want to know." Because I already know how this story ends. The image of the three of them together is burned in my mind, so I don't need confirmation. "As far as I'm concerned, I've never met Psycho Barbie."

He flashes a lopsided grin and stands up. "She didn't used to be so—"

"W-h-y," I say, extending the word, "must you keep talking about her?"

He grunts and runs his hand through his hair. "I don't know, I feel I need to defend myself."

"No." I shake my head. "No, you don't. I'm sure I've been with guys that would make you wonder '*what the hell was she thinking?*' too."

A growl erupts from the back of his throat as he takes two long strides to reach me. My breath catches in surprise as he grabs me and walks me back to the bed. I can't do anything but grab hold of his arms. When the back of my legs hit the mattress, he lays me down on the made bed. His thigh presses down in between my legs as he gets close to my face.

"You made your point," he says, his voice curt. I stare up into his intense eyes. "I don't need a reminder that you've been with other guys." *What?* That wasn't my point. I let out a bitter laugh and push him off me. His hands have a firm grip on me as he rolls to his back and I land on top of him. I sit up and try to move but his hands on my hips keep me in place.

"Aiden, you don't get to be a jealous asshole right now. Not after what just happened. I now have a threesome with you fucking Psycho Barbie seared in my brain," I snap. He grimaces. "I didn't say that to get back at you, but if you want to compare notes of who's been with other people, I think I win, hands down."

He closes his eyes, taking in a couple deep breaths. When he opens, his emerald green eyes look defeated. "I'm sorry," he murmurs. "I can't help this intense feeling of jealousy I get when I think of you and *other* people."

"You need to trust that I am yours and only yours. That won't ever change." I lean down and brush my lips against his. He sighs against my lips.

"I trust you, Addison. *I really do.*" He brings his hand around my neck, his thumb gliding over my bottom lip.

"I know. You can't help being Tarzan." I smirk.

He beats his chest. "*Ahahahaaahaaa.*" I laugh out loud. He slaps his chest and says in his deepest voice, "Me Tarzan..." and then puts his hand on my chest, "... you Jane." I roll my eyes but grin.

"Come on, Tarzan, we have a plane to catch."

Chapter twenty-one

I suck in a deep breath when I exit my building. I love the smell of rain. It's the cleansing of the air, washing away the grime and stink that usually wafts around the city. After last night's rain, I'm surprised that New York City is still above sea level. I'm glad my apartment isn't on the ground level, just in case it ever floods.

My feet pound the wet pavement, moving to the song "Thunder" by Imagine Dragons. I needed this run especially after all the crap I've been eating. My dress comes in tomorrow, and I hope it fits. I'm still not feeling one hundred percent from being sick a few weeks ago. Maybe the fresh air filling my lungs will make me feel better. Aiden's back at the apartment with Lexi. Sunday mornings are officially their time to hang out. She looks forward to it every week.

I run around the Reservoir at Central Park, my favorite path. The spring air has brought everyone out this morning. Finishing my run, I take the East Drive path so it'll take me by the Boathouse. I can't believe I'll be getting married there in two weeks. The last seven months have gone by so fast. Jaxon called the other day, telling us we were able to move up our court date for Lexi's adoption to this week. We're hoping to have it official by the time we get married. We have it all planned how we are going to tell her.

I'm running behind a group of guys who are training for a marathon. I overhear them talking about it. You will never find me running twenty-six miles. Six, *maybe*. They slow down, and I run around them. I'm almost finished, and I'm already feeling better. The Boathouse comes into my view, and I smile to myself. I'm so glad Ava booked the wedding there. As I get closer, I narrow my eyes at a huge sign hanging across the front of the restaurant.

"What the hell?" I mutter. Looking at the sign, I'm not paying attention to where I'm going. "Shit!" I yell on my way to the ground. My foot catches on something and my ankle twists. Then I fall. My hands break my fall, and I roll on my side, grunting.

"Are you okay?" I look up and the group of guys that I passed has stopped. Pain shoots through my ankle.

I groan, trying not to beat my hand against the cement like I want to. I look at the sidewalk where I tripped and there's a crack in the cement with an inch lip sticking up. I try to stand, but my ankle won't hold my weight. I shrink back down.

"Here, let me help you," one guy says. He reaches a hand out. I study him for a second and he looks innocent. *So did Marco.* I don't have a choice if I want to get off the ground, though. I stick out my hand, and he pulls me up, letting me lean against him as he puts his arm around my waist. He walks and I hop on one foot over to a bench. I look down at my ankle and it's already starting to swell. *No, no, no.* This can't be happening.

"Thanks," I say to the guy. Another bends down and picks my ankle up. I hiss out in pain. *What is he doing?*

"I'm an orthopedic surgeon, I promise," he adds when I narrow my eyes at him. He touches a couple spots and I flinch. "Does this hurt?"

"Yes," I cry out. *It fucking hurts,* is what I want to say.

He sighs and looks up at me. "You definitely sprained it. You might want to go to a doctor to get an X-ray to make sure it's not broken." I look up to the blue sky and groan.

"Do you need help getting somewhere?" Dr. Ortho asks. I think about the phone that is lying on my kitchen table because I decided not to bring it with me, thinking I wouldn't need it. I can see the top of my apartment building from here.

I sigh. "Can I borrow your phone?" He pulls it out of his arm band and hands it to me. I try to call Aiden, but it goes to voicemail. Sydney is too far away to get here anytime soon. I stare down at the phone. *Dammit.* I don't know anyone else's phone number by heart.

"If you need help getting somewhere, I don't mind helping you," he says when I hand him his phone.

"No, I think I'll be okay," I say, pushing myself off the bench. I blow out a breath. I can do this. *It doesn't hurt that bad.* "Ow, ow, ow." I wince, sitting back down to take pressure of my ankle.

"Look, here's my card so you know I'm not lying," Dr. Ortho says, pulling out a business card from his armband. "I'm Jake." He hands me the card.

I glance at the card and hold it up with an eyebrow raised. "Carry these just in case?"

He shrugs. "You never know when you're going to need to hand one out." He motions to my ankle. "You really shouldn't put weight on it if it hurts. How far away are you?"

I point to my building. "Just right over there."

"Nice! I wish I lived this close to Central Park. Let me help you walk there. I swear, I'm a good guy," he says, holding his hands up in the air.

"I'm pretty sure that's what they all say."

His friends all vouch for him. It's just a block away. I look up at him and say, "Okay, but just so you know...my fiancé is FBI and I work for NYPD."

He grins and looks me up and down. "You don't look like a cop."

"That's because I'm not. I'm CSI," I reply.

"Wow. I bet you two have a lot of interesting bedtime stories."

I smirk. "You could say that."

Jake bends over, helps me up, and wraps his arm around my waist. We start slow as I bounce on one foot. He's around six foot with a slender build but muscular. When his friends take off, my anxiety begins to simmer, my heartbeat quickening. It's just us and I'm not very mobile right now, but it's daylight and there are people everywhere. I let out a long breath, calming my nerves.

"I'm Addison, by the way."

"Nice to meet you, Addison. Do you run here a lot?" I turn and stare at him. "Just small talk. I'm not stupid enough to try and pick up an FBI's girlfriend." I smile and return to concentrating on each hop. My thigh is starting to burn on my jumping leg and we're not even half way there. Jake must feel my body tense. "Alright, Addison, this isn't working. It'd be easier if I just carried you." He doesn't give me time to answer before he swoops up my legs with his other arm. I grab ahold of his neck in surprise.

"You could have given me a little warning, Jake."

"I had a feeling you were going to say no." *You think?*

He carries me with ease as we walk down the street. I ask him questions about being a doctor just to make this awkward situation go by faster. When we get to the front lobby of my apartment, he softly puts me down. The security guard sees me and rushes over.

"Ms. Mason, do you need help?"

"Is Aiden back?"

"Yes, Agent Roberts and little Lulu got here about five minutes ago. Do you want me to have him come down here?"

"Please," I respond. He walks off to his desk and calls upstairs. There are a few chairs in the lobby, so I ask Jake to take me over to one. As soon as I sit down, Aiden and Lexi come running out of the elevator. Lexi rushes over and gives me a big hug. When she pulls away her eyes are concerned.

"Addison, what happened?" Aiden asks.

"I fell and twisted my ankle." He looks at Jake and then back to me with a questioning look.

"I'm Jake." He holds out his hand. "Me and my friends were behind her when she went down. She took a pretty hard fall. I think it's just a sprain, but she might want to get it X-rayed."

"Aiden," he says, shaking his hand. "So, is that your professional opinion?" Aiden asks sarcastically. *Knock it off, jealous man.* I hit him in the leg.

I glare at Aiden. "Jake is *actually* an orthopedic surgeon."

Jake nervously laughs. "No worries. Addison told me all about her FBI fiancé. I was just helping her get home because she couldn't walk." Aiden's demeanor softens, and he smiles down at me.

When he glances back at Jake, he smirks. "Sorry. Thanks for helping her get back here."

"Like I said, no worries." He looks down at my ankle and then me. "If you need an orthopedic doctor, I know a really good one. I can probably get you in for an X-ray tomorrow."

"You have to go to the doctor," Lexi asks.

"It looks like it," I sigh.

"If you could get her in tomorrow, that'd be great. I'll bring her in." I jerk my head in Aiden's direction, surprised he's not demanding that I find a different doctor—one who didn't carry me home in his arms.

"Sounds good. You have my card," he says, motioning to my hand. I hold it up. "Just call my office in about a half an hour and they'll confirm your appointment."

"Thank you for all your help," I say. He flashes me a smile and nods. He tells me to ice it and keep it elevated until tomorrow and not to put any weight on it until they find out how bad it is.

Aiden thanks him again, and they shake hands one last time before Jake leaves. My ankle is propped up on a chair, and Aiden squats down to inspect it. His lips twist as he looks at me. "Am I going to have to roll you down the aisle?"

I gasp and grab Aiden's arm. "Give me your phone," I demand. I hold out my hand, and he stares at me, motionless. "Now!" He takes out his phone and slowly puts it in my hand then pulls back quickly like he's afraid I'm going to bite him. I scroll through his contacts to Ava's number and hit send. I squeeze my eyes shut. *Please be wrong.* Each ring that she doesn't answer I feel my heart skip a beat. On the fourth ring, she answers.

"Hi, Aiden."

"It's Addison. Please, *please,* tell me it's wrong," I plead. Aiden looks at me with his brows furrowed.

"I guess you heard," she murmurs into the phone. I drop my head into my hand. This can't be happening. *Not now.* "Addison, I'm working on getting it booked somewhere else. I will fix this."

Tears start to burn my eyes. Words escape me. When Aiden asks me what's wrong, I just shake my head. He grabs the phone from my hand and puts it to his ear.

"Ava, what's going on?" I can't hear what she's saying, but I know. I saw it. That's why I tripped. The Boathouse is closed. I knew something like this would happen.

"Okay, let us know what you find out. I'll make a few calls, too." They hang up and Aiden stands over me, running his hand through my hair.

"Sweetheart, we'll find a different place." I look up at him with tear-filled eyes.

"It's two weeks away," I whisper. My voice shudders. Aiden bends down and puts his hand on my thigh. "And now this..." I point to my foot.

"It'll be okay, Addie. I'll go get you some ice," Lexi says, hopping out of my lap and being extra careful not to hit my leg.

"That's a good idea, Tater Tot. Let's take Addie upstairs." He picks me up the same way Jake did and carries me to my apartment, setting me down on my couch. Lexi runs to the kitchen and fills up a bag with ice. She brings it to me and her bottom lip is out, pouting.

"I'm sorry you got hurt, Addie. I can kiss it and make it better," she says. I chuckle.

"Thanks, sweet girl, but I'm all dirty. How about you just give me a kiss. It'll still make me feel better."

She leans over, kisses me on the cheek, and then hops up on the couch next to me, snuggling close. Aiden pulls the coffee table closer to the couch and props my foot on a pillow on top of it. When he puts the ice on it, I jerk at the coldness.

"Shit. That's cold," I snap. I feel Lexi giggle next to me.

"It's okay...you're hurt," she says. Aiden and I laugh. She's getting more lenient with the swear jar the longer she's here. She'd never let me have a hall pass before.

"What did Ava say happened?" I look up to Aiden.

"The storm last night made the roof collapse. They'll be closed for at least a month." I lean back against the cushions and wonder how the hell we're going to change everything last minute.

I squeeze my eyes shut. "Maybe we should postpone the wedding." My stomach twists saying it, and I don't want to open my eyes to see Aiden's reaction.

"Hannah, can Lexi come over?" My eyes fly open when I hear Aiden's voice. He's obviously not talking to me. "Thanks," he says and ends the call.

"Hey, Tater Tot. I need to talk to Addie. Hannah is going to come get you. I'll come over and get you in a little bit."

Her little lips twist, worrying about me. "Are you going to be okay, Addie?"

"I am, Lulu. You go have fun with Hannah. I'll be here on the couch all day, so we can hang out later, okay?"

Her smile brightens and she jumps off the couch. She loves hanging out with Hannah, especially when they play makeup and hair. A knock at the door has Lexi running toward it. She hops on each foot, waiting for Aiden to open the door. As soon as she leaves, Aiden comes and sits on the couch where Lexi was.

"Do you trust me?"

I dart my head in his direction. "Of course, I do."

He picks up my hand and traces his finger on the inside of my palm, remaining silent for a few moments. It tickles so I squeeze my hand into a fist around his finger. His gaze meets mine and his expression turns serious. "We're getting married on April 29, Addison."

I chew the inside of my cheek. "But—"

He puts his finger on my lips. "Trust me?" I nod. "Don't worry about anything except getting that ankle better." My chest rises with my deep inhale. I lean back and deflate, blowing it out.

Stupid ankle. Stupid rain.

"Is that why you tripped? You saw the Boathouse."

"Yes." I sigh.

"Why couldn't you have tripped in front of a group of women?" I glare at him, shaking my head. He belts out a laugh and stands up. "I'm kidding. Jake seemed nice."

"He was. Can you call the office and get my appointment? Oh, and I need some Advil. Badly."

"Shall I get you a bell, too, madam?" he asks in a British accent, taking a bow.

My eyebrows shoot up and my mouth hangs open. I huff. Is he insinuating that I'm acting like a Queen? "That's okay, I'll do it myself." I pick my foot off the pillow and swallow the pain that shoots through it as soon as I put it on the floor.

"Stubborn ass woman, I was kidding." He pushes me back on the couch and elevates my foot. He puts his hand on the couch to the side of my head and leans over. His lips sweep over mine. "I like taking care of you," he murmurs against my lips. When he pulls back and stares into my eyes, the warmth of his breath hits my check. "Now, sit your ass down and don't move. If you need to go to the bathroom, let me know." He taps my nose with his finger and stands up. I watch him walk into my bedroom.

Staring at his gorgeous backside has me biting my lip. Broad shoulders all the way down to his sexy ass. I don't know why he would ever get jealous of another man. I may find other men good looking, but none come close to the attraction I have for Aiden. One look at him and my heart beats faster, my skin tingles. My body reacts only to him. He must see that by now.

I'm still staring at the doorway when he reappears with my Advil. Our eyes lock as he struts over. He puts two pills down on the side table with a bottle of water and leans over to me and whispers, "I love you, sweetheart, but stop looking at me like that."

"What?" I feign innocence.

He grabs my hand, shifting it to his obvious bulge. "This is *what*. I told you already, I can feel when you get excited. It's like my dick is a fucking remote control toy and your pussy is the remote." I feel my face flush with heat. *Yep, he sees it.*

***

"Good news," Jake says, walking into the room. He sticks an X-ray on a light box hanging from the wall. He flips the switch to on and it illuminates my X-ray. "Nothing is broken."

I blow out a sigh of relief. *Thank God!*

"You have an inversion ankle sprain." He picks up my foot and points to the outside of my ankle. "You have lateral ligaments right here that were stretched too far. Since you can walk on it a little today, that tells us it's probably a grade-two ankle sprain."

"Okay, Jake. I have two weeks until my wedding. I need a plan of action so I'll be able to walk down the aisle, *not on crutches*. And I'd *like* to wear heels."

He crosses he arms and stares down at me. I feel like a little kid sitting on the table, patiently waiting for the doctor to tell me if I can go to school or not. "Two weeks is not very long." I laugh bitterly. *You're telling me*. We don't even know where we're getting married at this point.

"I'll do everything you tell me, exactly," I say. This time Aiden chuckles. I glare at him.

"You've never done anything you were supposed to do *exactly*," he says sarcastically.

"Shush." I point at him and then look back at Jake. "Don't listen to him. He's just mad I've never promised that to *him*." Jake chuckles. Aiden mumbles something under his breath about handcuffs. I can imagine what he's thinking. I roll my eyes, shaking my head slightly. *Can we move on?*

"I'm going to give you a splint to wear. I want you to use crutches until the swelling goes down. By the end of this week, I'll have you start physical therapy to speed up the healing process. You can do the exercises at home, but it'll help having a therapist making sure that you're doing them correctly." I nod, agreeing with everything he's saying. "I can't promise anything. Everyone heals at their own rate. But since you're already physically fit, I don't see it being a long-term problem."

Half an hour later, I'm sporting an ankle brace and hobbling out of the doctor's office on crutches. "I need to go back to the office," I say, trying to hold my foot up, keep the crutches under my arms, and wave down a taxi. When Aiden doesn't say anything, I look back. He has an *I told you so* expression. "What? I can keep my foot up at the office, and I'll be at my desk the rest of the day. I can't take off the next two weeks, Aiden."

"Remember, we have Lexi's adoption court date tomorrow."

My eyes widen and the hand I'm holding up in the air falls. *Oh, no.* Lexi. My eyes start to blur from tears. I grasp the sides of the crutches and lean on them so they're holding me up.

"I can't go in there like this," I cry, pointing down to my wrapped ankle. Emotions that I can't control bubble up inside me. "They'll think I'm an unfit parent. They'll take her away from us, Aiden." The words tumble out of my mouth before I can stop them. I hear myself saying it, but I don't recognize the desperate tone in my voice.

Aiden stares at me, dumbfounded. I wipe the tears that have escaped my eyes. "Addison," he says slowly, "they are not going to take Lexi away from us because you're clumsy."

"You don't know that."

"Are you feeling okay? Did you by chance hit your head yesterday?" He chuckles.

"Stop, it's not funny." I hit him on his arm. His eyes scan the area before making it back to mine. He cocks his head, running his hand over his mouth while accessing me. "I'm fine," I say. "You're right, it'll be fine. I need to get back to work."

I hurry and wave down a taxi, so I can escape the awkward moment I just created. "Meet you at my apartment after work?" I ask. He nods and places a quick kiss on my lips before helping me into a taxi. As we drive away, I lean down into my hands.

What the hell just happened? I must be emotionally exhausted from the last couple days that I'm starting to act crazy. My phone dings. I dig for it in my purse and pull it out.

Aiden: Make sure Dr. Jekyll comes home tonight.

That's what I'm hoping, too. Seems I'm losing control of my sanity.

Chapter twenty-two

A loud noise jolts me from my sleep. I glance at my nightstand and see it's only five-thirty in the morning. As I sit up, I wonder if I dreamed the noise because I don't hear anything now. I should check on Lexi. Make sure it wasn't her and she doesn't need something. When I'm tightening my robe, another noise comes from the living room. It sounds like someone's groaning.

I rush to grab my gun, but it's not there. Where the hell did it go? I frantically look around the room, wondering if I moved it and just don't remember doing it. I know I didn't. Another groan. I run out of the room, not even thinking. I need to make sure Lexi is safe.

I stop. Frozen in place. Staring at the man tied to a chair in my living room, hunched over with blood running down his face. My heart stops.

Aiden.

"Aiden!" I scream and run over to him, trying to lift his head. It falls right back down. Then I hear a laugh behind me.

A laugh I used to have nightmares over.

A laugh that could bring me to my knees.

A laugh I thought I'd never hear again.

I jerk my head in his direction and shake it repeatedly. "No, you're supposed to be dead," I whimper, pointing at him. Everyone told me he was dead.

"Well, princess, I'm alive and well," Joe says, standing up from the barstool. "You looking for this?" He holds up my gun and waves it in the air.

I look back to Aiden. "Aiden, wake up. Please, wake up," I say in a panic as I shake him. Each step Joe takes, my heart skips a beat. My hands shake as I try to untie him, but I can't make them stop long enough to do it. The sound of Joe's footsteps suffocates me.

"You had to know I'd come back for you, princess."

"Stay the fuck away from me!" I snap, taking a few steps away from Aiden. Away from *him*. Memories flood my mind, reminding me of the hell I was in when I was his prisoner.

"You are mine and always will be," he grates out. When he reaches Aiden, he brings my gun up to Aiden's head. No. No. No. *Don't kill him.*

"Stop! I'll do whatever you want. Please, don't kill him," I beg. My fear of Aiden being killed far outweighs my fear of what Joe can do to me. I survived once, I can do it again.

"Oh, you'll do whatever I want whether he's alive or not. *And I choose not.*" His laugh echoes off the walls. I gasp, my chest burning as I try and find the strength to breathe.

BANG!

I scream at the sound.

"Noo! Aiden!" I run over and fall to my knees at his lifeless body. "Noo!" I scream out over and over. "You can't leave me," I cry.

Chapter twenty-three

"Addie, wake up."

"No!" I hear myself yell. "Don't leave me."

"Addie, it's me, Lexi."

I feel little hands on me, shaking me. I gasp and bolt up in bed. My eyes dart around the room. They land on Lexi who is sitting in my bed, staring back at me with concerned eyes. Oh, my God. I hope Lexi didn't see Aiden. I throw the covers off me, wincing when I put weight on my bad ankle but push through it and rush into the living room.

The living room is pitch dark, other than the soft glow coming from the windows. The only thing I hear is my heartbeat. I turn my head toward the living room and everything seems normal. All four chairs are properly pushed in at the kitchen table. Then I glance at the clock. Twelve-thirty. I grab my chest and close my eyes. It was only a nightmare. Tears flow down my cheek as the feeling of relief spreads throughout my body.

"Addie, are you okay?" A warm little hand slips into mine and squeezes. "You were having a bad dream."

I wipe my tears and look down at her. Her big, caramel eyes look at me with worry. "I'm much better now," I say and manage a weak smile. We walk back into the bedroom, and I sit on the bed, grabbing my heart, trying to control my erratic heartbeat. She crawls up on the bed beside me and leans her head on my arm.

"I heard you screaming, and I didn't know what to do."

I grimace and my shoulders slump. Wrapping an arm around her, I say, "I'm so sorry, Lulu. I didn't mean to scare you."

She shrugs. "We can't help what we dream about." Her arms wrap around my waist. "I'm just glad you're okay."

We stay like that for a few minutes. I can feel her body getting heavier, sleep pulling her under. "Hey, sweet girl, let's go back to bed."

"Can I sleep with you?" She yawns.

When I nod my head, she crawls up my bed and wiggles her body under the covers. I look around once more and then reach behind my side table to feel for my gun. My fingers graze it, and I let out a sigh of relief.

It was a dream, Addison. A fucked-up dream.

It takes Lexi mere minutes to fall back asleep. The dream sits at the forefront of my mind and still feels too real for me to go back to sleep. I grab my phone off the table and turn it to silent and then open the text app.

Me: I need to hear your voice. Are you up?

When I don't receive an immediate response, I lay my phone on my chest, close to my heart. It's like my lifeline to Aiden right now. I can feel the thumping of my heart and glance at the phone every couple seconds to see if he's responded. I softly moan. He's not going to wake up to my text. Maybe I should just call him. When I see the three little dots, I close my eyes and send out a silent *thank you.*

Aiden: I'm up. Call me.

I look over at Lexi again before slowly pulling the covers off and slipping out of bed. I wobble into the living room, grab a throw blanket, and sink into the couch. With my feet tucked under me, I try and take a few calming breaths before calling Aiden so I don't sound too freaked out.

"What's wrong, sweetheart," Aiden's concerned voice greets me.

"I just needed to hear your voice." My voice shakes with emotion. So much for not sounding freaked out.

"Addison, what's wrong?"

I draw in a ragged breath. "I had a nightmare about Joe."

"Oh, baby. I'm sorry. I promise he won't ever hurt you again."

"It wasn't me," I whisper. *It was you.*

"Addison, he won't hurt anyone ever again."

"How do you know? He was supposed to be dead before and he wasn't." Seeing him in my nightmare has brought back the fear I've held onto for so long. *He's still alive.*

"Because I know."

"Aiden, what if he escaped—"

"He didn't," he says confidently. "I know he didn't because I was the one who took the shot." An audible gasp escapes my lips. "I made sure he would never hurt you again."

"Aiden," I say slowly.

"Sweetheart, I have no regrets. I'd do it again. That bastard deserved more than he got," he growls.

I let out a soft sigh and run my hand through my hair. "Thank you."

"I'm sorry," he mumbles. I hear his sheets rustling, like he's sitting up. His apology catches me off guard.

"Why are you sorry?"

"That I didn't tell you before. And I'm sure this is happening because of what I said." His comment about my dress crosses my mind.

"I think it's a little of everything. Everything keeps going wrong the closer we get to the wedding. I'm so afraid it's not going to happen, and we still haven't heard back from the judge about Lexi's adoption." I pull my legs out from under me and lie across the couch, spreading the blanket over me. I stare up at the ceiling, wondering if there will ever be a time in my life that's *easy*. The court date we had went well, so I don't know why we haven't heard back yet, but it's killing me, not knowing.

"Oh, our wedding will happen, even if I have to whisk you away to elope. We will be married by the end of the month." His confidence helps calm my irrational thoughts. "This...won't ever happen again though," he growls.

"This?"

"Calling me in the middle of the night, needing to hear my voice. It's killing me that I'm not there holding you right now. Addison, it's taking every ounce of self-control I have to not get out of bed and come over." I can hear his hand run over the stubble of his jaw. "Fuck, I want to be there for you."

"You are. God, Aiden, you have been here for me through so much." My voice shakes as tears well up in my eyes. "I couldn't have gotten through the past year without you. Whenever I felt like I was losing control, you were always there to ground me. Like right now," I add. Tears break free and run down the sides of my cheeks. "I wish I could express how much I love you."

"You are...by marrying me," he murmurs. "For better or worse, till death do us part."

Chapter
twenty-four

Aiden

"**E**verything set for the wedding?" Damon asks from the passenger seat. I nod, not taking my eyes off the road. We're on our way to question a guy who called in a tip regarding a child's murder that happened last week.

"We just have to get the band there, and we'll be good."

"How's Addison's ankle?"

"It's getting better. She's pushing it, probably too much, but you know Addison. She doesn't listen to anyone."

"Sounds like someone else I know," he chuckles. I take my hand off the wheel and flip him off. I'm assuming he's referring to when I was shot. *That was different.* Addison's life was in danger.

I talk about some of the details of the wedding and what time we're heading up there. We're going up the night before. I want to make sure everything is perfect. Addison's so stressed with everything going on, I will kill anyone who messes up our wedding. Max has his whole crew working security, so I'm not worried.

Travis called the other day, asking if he could come see her the day of the wedding. My mouth opened to say "*fuck no*," but who am I to say Addison can't see him. I think, deep down, she wishes there could be more, but she knows he can't be a part of her life. At least at Max's place, we'll be able to slip him in and out without anyone noticing.

"She still acting weird?" he asks, looking over at me. I told him about her random breakdown about going to the court on crutches. I seriously thought she was kidding until tears started to roll down her face. And then her nightmare about Joe. After we hung up, I was so on edge that I went to her apartment and kept watch from outside in my car. If I could kill the asshole again, I would have. I grip the steering wheel, remembering the terror in her voice on the phone.

"Today she seems to be okay, but that doesn't mean anything. She's all over the fucking place. I've never seen her so emotional."

"It has to be from stress. Have you heard back from the judge?"

"No," I murmur. "Jax thinks it went really well, so he doesn't think we have anything to worry about. He said it takes time, but Addison thinks it means we're not going to get approved."

"If you guys need any help with anything, let us know."

"Sydney has been a lifesaver, helping Ava set up the wedding. I didn't know what I was supposed to be doing." Addison was hesitant to let me plan the wedding. She had good reason to be because when I figured out *where* it was going to be, I had no idea what to do next.

"I guess she'll know what to do with her own, then," he says.

I jerk my head in his direction. My brows lift over my sunglasses. "Are you about to start planning one?" I ask then turn my head back toward the road.

Addison will be ecstatic. The bond between those two has always scared me a little. Damon and I are close like brothers, but we're not dependent on each other like they are. Maybe it's a girl thing, but I've been a little worried about how the dynamic will be when we get married. But Sydney getting married will help ease my concern because she'll have *someone* else and not depend on my wife. Call me an asshole for being selfish, but Addison will officially be mine. I chuckle to myself. If Addison could hear my thoughts, she'd rip off one of my balls. I wince and adjust myself just thinking about it.

"*I hope so.* Can you believe it?"

"Fuck, if I'm getting married, nothing surprises me anymore."

He slaps me on the shoulder. "That's for damn sure." I laugh, knowing all the guys thought I'd never settle down. "I have a plan, but it involves you guys." I glance his way.

"Is this going to be payback for making you sing 'You've Lost that Lovin' Feeling'?"

"No. But *someday*…it'll happen." He chuckles. "I want to know if it'd be okay if I ask her at your reception."

I scratch my chin, thinking I don't care. Will Addison? *No.* She'll love the idea that she can share her day with Sydney. "Are you sure she's going to say yes?" I joke. I know I asked Addison in front of every friend we have, but I wasn't going to take no for an answer.

"I wouldn't be asking if I wasn't sure," he responds.

Pulling into the driveway, I put the car in park. I survey the property and then turn to Damon. "You have our blessing." I squeeze his shoulder. "I'm happy for you."

Max isn't going to be, but that's on him. He needs to move on. I'm glad he hasn't made it known how he really feels. This would be one awkward situation. *Well, more than it already is.*

When we leave the house, we're not sure what to think of the guy's tip, but we get a good laugh. After we get back to the office, we do our report and head out for the day. As we're leaving our building, the guy we talked to earlier starts walking toward us. *Here we go, this guy is a nut.* Damon's talking and doesn't notice. I tap his arm once and motion with my head in his direction. We stop walking. I stand with my legs wide apart and my arms tight to my body so I can reach for my gun quickly if I need to.

"Mr. Shoemaker, what can we do for you?" I ask.

He tugs at his earlobe and his eyes bounce from me to Damon. "I feel...I feel you didn't take my tip seriously earlier..." He stumbles on his words. His pupils dilate and he tugs at his ear again. He wasn't this nervous at his home.

"I can assure you, Mr. Shoemaker, that we take all tips seriously," I respond with a calm voice. This guy calls in a tip, saying that he saw the murder happen in his dream. He gave us a very detailed description of the man.

He fidgets again, his eyes scanning the area. My heart thumps quicker. I feel Damon's body tense next to me. He feels it, too. This guy isn't right.

"Are you...are you going to look for the man? I can't sleep at night knowing what he looks like and knowing that he's still out there." Every time he jerks his hand to his ear, my finger flinches.

"Mr. Shoemaker, we gave your description to a sketch artist. We'll call you when he's finished so you can confirm that the sketch is correct," Damon says.

Mr. Shoemaker's posture slumps a little as he blows out a breath. "Okay. Okay..." He nods his head a couple times. "I'll look forward to hearing from you then." We both nod as he turns and staggers away. I don't take my eyes off him until he rounds the building.

"Something is up with that guy," I say, exhaling loudly. "You're such a fucking liar." Damon lets out a quick, loud laugh. There's no composite sketch being done.

"There's a reason he's adamant we focus on this person he *dreamed* of. I think we need to delve into Mr. Shoemaker's life."

"I couldn't agree more."

"Sydney's working late tonight, so I'll just go back up and start pulling some data."

"Alright. Let me know if you find anything. I'll see you in the morning."

***

I throw my keys on the kitchen counter and scan the apartment. The emptiness of it causes mixed feelings. I hope Addison likes it here. She told me she loves this area, and I couldn't pass up this deal anymore. The four-bedroom penthouse is the perfect size for us, but will she be pissed I made this huge decision without talking with her? I wanted to surprise her, but now I'm starting to second-guess my decision.

It's too late, Roberts.

Grabbing a beer out of the refrigerator, I take a long swallow, pushing the thoughts of regret out of my mind, and get to work unpacking. I have five days until our wedding. I don't know how the hell I'm going to keep this a secret. Hopefully Addison doesn't decide to just pop over. I've told security to call me immediately if she shows up. I'm not sure how I'll explain the empty apartment.

The movers will be at her apartment right after she leaves

for Max's on Saturday. Sydney knows about this, so she'll let me know as soon as they leave. I've left detailed instructions on where all the furniture should be placed. Cheryl, our receptionist from work, told me she would come and make sure everything was running smoothly before driving out to the wedding. The painters will be here this week to paint Lexi's room. I hired the same ones who did her original room, and I instructed them it needs to look identical to that one. Lexi loves her room so much, and I want her to feel comfortable here. She's had so much change this past year, I'm afraid if it's different, she might not adjust as quickly. I'll let Addison decide on the rest because I don't have a clue.

My job is to make this place feel like our home, and I have five days to do it.

Chapter twenty-five

"Look at the directions again. This has to be wrong." I lean forward against the steering wheel, looking out the windshield. Trees. All I see are freaking trees. I *had* to have missed a sign somewhere. We haven't passed a car in miles. We made a wrong turn. *I know it.* I'm positive we didn't go this way when Aiden and I come here to skydive. Granted, I didn't see his house either so who knows where it is on his property.

"Google Maps is telling me we're going the right way," Syd says, shoving her phone close to my face. She's getting annoyed because this isn't the first time I've asked. More like the fifth.

"It'll be my luck that I'm late to my own wedding." Aiden gave me his car to drive since I don't have one, and I'm determined we don't see each other until I walk down the aisle. I never saw myself as superstitious, but I'm staying as far away as possible from anything that might bring me bad luck. All the guys came out yesterday. Harper and Bryn are driving together. They shouldn't be too far behind us. Macie is picking up Katie from the airport on her way here. Lexi is with Amy and Ted. They came out last night, as well. They wanted to give me a night to myself to get ready for today. Although I'm glad they did, this is a big day for Lexi, too. I can't wait until she sees her surprise. I smile to myself, thinking about it. Everything is coming together. *Except I can't find the damn place.*

"Relax, Addie. We have plenty of—" she stops midsentence because once we clear the trees, she can tell we're not going the wrong way. "Holy mother of huge. *That*'s Max's house?" she exclaims, pointing to the mansion we're headed straight for. It's a colonial-style house that sprawls across an immaculate green lawn. It must have at least one hundred windows just in the front. Painted gray with white trim, it reminds me of Aiden's beach house—if you add an extra few thousand feet. I can't even imagine how many bedrooms this place has.

I can't take my eyes off the house as I take my foot off the gas pedal to slow down. "Um...*I think.*" I glance over at Syd who has the same amazed look I have and shrug. "I mean, we shouldn't be surprised. He does own his own plane. Oh! *And* has a runway and hangar *somewhere* on this property."

"What does a single guy do with all this *house*?" Syd spreads her arms across the car. I push her arm out of my view. I want to know who cleans it, because it sure as hell isn't Max. As we pull through the black wrought-iron gate and make our way up the long driveway, I notice a building next to the house. It's a five-car garage with two black SUVs sitting outside of it. They resemble FBI-issued vehicles.

"He owns his own security firm. Maybe this is where he does his business." I can't believe I've known Max for over a year now; I feel like I should have known all this already. "When Aiden told me we were having the wedding at Max's house, I was a little concerned, but it's *beautiful* out here," I say, looking around at all the scenery. The front yard has been freshly mowed and is outlined with small bushes and flowers.

"That it is. It's a beautiful day outside, too, perfect for an outdoor wedding," Syd says excitedly, clapping her hands. She tilts her head forward, looking up. "And not a cloud in the sky." I breathe a sigh of relief. My anxiety is at maximum high right now. I know something is going to go wrong. It wouldn't be *normal* for me if it didn't. My ankle only hurts when I overdo it, but I'm not using crutches and I can wear heels...at least walking down the aisle.

I drive around the circular drive and put the car in park. A man in a valet uniform smiles as he approaches my door. I glance at Syd, surprised.

"Valet?" she says, shaking her head. "The guys went all out." She laughs as she gets out of the car.

"Miss Mason?" the valet asks.

I giggle, thinking it's funny having a valet at someone's house. I certainly wasn't raised with the rich and famous. "Yep, that's me."

"Mr. Owen will be right out to let you know where to go." He holds his hand out, and I drop the key into his palm.

"I have to get my stuff out first," I say, walking to the trunk.

"That's okay. One of my staff will grab everything and bring it up to you." *Staff*? How many people does it take to park cars?

"Thanks," I say, walking past the trunk to Syd.

"Fancy." Syd giggles. She hooks her arm in mine, and we walk up the stairs to the front porch. The front door opens and Max strides out before we make it to the top step.

"Ladies," he says. "Glad to see y'all made it okay."

When I walk up to him, I slap him in the arm. "Why didn't you tell me you lived in a mansion? Holy shit, Max, this is huge! And beautiful!" His laugh booms and ricochets throughout the porch. "And a staff of valets? Please tell me that's not normal." I turn and point to Aiden's car being driven away.

"I do have a staff, but the valets aren't normally here. I don't have a place to park a lot of cars without walking across a field."

He lifts one shoulder in a half shrug. "I figured people probably wouldn't want to do that."

"Well, I'm impressed," I say and give him a hug. "Thank you."

"You know I would do anything for you and Aiden." With his arm around my shoulder, he glances at Syd and smiles. "Hey, Tink." This never gets any less awkward for me. It pisses me off because they act like nothing ever happened between them. If they don't feel weird, why should I?

"Hey, Max," she replies. "Nice place you have here."

Max stands a little taller and smirks. "Thanks. This used to be my dad's house. Everything has been remodeled, though," he says proudly. "It was a little dated when I got it."

"It's gorgeous. I can't wait to see the rest of it," I say.

"Then, let's go," Max says, directing us into the house. "The women will be upstairs and the guys are in the guesthouse."

I stop dead in the doorway and spin around to Max. He puts his hands on the doorjamb to stop himself from running into me. "What in the hell do you need a guesthouse for?" I muse. "It's not like you don't have room in here for guests."

He chuckles. "My dad didn't like visitors too much, so they got their own space." He twirls his finger in the air, gesturing for me to turn around.

"I'm going," I murmur. When I spin around, the beautiful grand entryway greets me. The floors are a honey-colored wood that has a rustic feel, but the rest of the house is decorated with more of a simplistic style. Looking straight ahead, I can see the sparkling pool through the French doors. The stunning spiral staircase runs along a white wall with colorful, abstract artwork. The reds, oranges, and blues stand out against the stark white walls, but it's like they bring life to the place. It surprises me to see them. I turn my head and look at Max. "I'm assuming those were your mom's?" I ask, pointing to the pictures.

He crosses his arms and smirks. "No, I bought those." My brows lift. He laughs at my obvious state of surprise. "I have a friend who painted them," he responds, looking at them.

"They're beautiful. I'd love to have one of her pieces in my home," I say, looking back at them.

"I'll try and make that happen. Now get upstairs before I carry you. I have stuff I need to do."

"I'm going," I say. "It's not my fault this is the first time I'm seeing your house and now that I see it, I'm intrigued."

"Well, start yourself a list of questions and I'll answer them later." He groans and pushes me toward the stairs. Right as my foot hits the first step, the front door opens and in walks Bryn and Harper.

"Holy shit, Max, do you live here?" Harper says, putting her suitcase down and looking around. Max rolls his eyes and looks up at the ceiling.

I giggle. "That's exactly what I said! Who knew?" I throw my arms out.

Max shakes his head. "Yes, women. I live here. Any other questions?"

"Well, now that you're opening the question box..."

His eyes go wide and he bites back a grin. "You better be glad I like you."

We all start laughing. "Come on, girls, I've heard our room is upstairs," I say and stick my tongue out at him.

"Finally," he murmurs as we walk upstairs.

Our chatter about how impressive his house is doesn't stop. I'm not the only one surprised by Max's house. He stays quiet behind us while herding us to our room. I bet he'll do anything to get out of coming back here next time. We stop at the top and let him by so he can lead us to which door is ours. I look down both hallways and all I see are closed doors. *A lot of them.*

"Max, what do you do with all these rooms?" I point down each hallway.

He shrugs. "I find things to do with them." He winks and turns to leave. I lift a brow. *Things?* Well, shit, now I'm interested in these *things.* "You all are in this room," he says, opening one of the doors, pulling me from my detective tendencies.

Focus, Addison, you're getting married today.

We walk into a room filled with *white.* Everything is stark white, like a canvas begging to have color splattered on it. It's probably the biggest room I've ever seen with a bay window spanning almost the entire length of the room. This must be two rooms combined. The sunlight reflects off the white and it's blinding.

"I think I need sunglasses in here," I say, laughing and dramatically squinting my eyes. Max takes out a pair of sunglasses from his shirt pocket and slips them onto my face. His smart-ass grin spreads across his face.

"Your wish is my command," he says, sarcastically.

I grin, pushing them up to sit on top of my head. "You're like a Boy Scout, always prepared." He laughs out loud when I hold up three fingers. "I bet you even know the Boy Scout Oath." I cock my head a little, taunting him. When I lived with my mom, my neighbor was in Boy Scouts and he would make me test him on the oath.

He puffs up his chest. "Aiden and I had more badges than anyone," he boasts. I drop my head in laughter and hear all the girls giggle.

I look up to him, shaking my head slightly. "I was kidding, but I'm not surprised." I take off the sunglasses and hand them back to him. Two guys walk into the room carrying Sydney's and my stuff, including my wedding dress. They hang my dress off the bathroom door and place the rest of the stuff on the bed.

"Ladies, if you need anything, let us know," one of them says.

"We need some orange juice," Syd quickly replies, walking to her bag. She pulls out a bottle of champagne and a smile spreads across her face. "And some glasses."

"Let the festivities begin," Max says, chuckling as he walks out the door behind the guys.

There is a sitting area with a couch and two chairs. The girls take a seat, chatting about the drive here. I walk to the bay window, which looks out to the pool.

My breath hitches. "Oh. My. God." I say, stunned.

Syd jumps up. "What? What's wrong?" she says, coming to the window. I turn and look at her with wide eyes. The girls jump to their feet right behind her. I can't even talk. My mouth hangs open as I take in the back of Max's house.

"Wow," Harper and Syd say in unison.

The pool, of course, is gorgeous, but it's what is past the pool that has me speechless. Max's land backs up to a very large lake. I can just make out a couple of houses on the other side of the lake, but it's mostly land. Some steps lead down a hill to a white tent where we'll be having our reception and it's right in front of the lake. We can see people coming and going from underneath the tent, getting things ready. To the left of the tent, white chairs are lined up in a semicircle facing the lake. Workers set flowers all around the area.

Tears sting my eyes as I watch my wedding come together. I can't believe Aiden did all this. *For me.* Sydney wraps her arms around me and leans her head on my shoulder. "You deserve this, Addie." I sniff and wipe away a tear that escapes down my cheek. I grab her hand on my waist and squeeze. "I can't wait to stand by your side and watch you marry the man who was meant for you. Fate couldn't have led you to a better man."

I laugh and cry at the same time. "The journey to get us here..." I pause to sniffle, "...it's definitely been a twist of fate."

"I know it's been a long journey, hun, but right now down there is all that matters." She points to a small house nestled between the trees to the left of the main house. That must be the guesthouse. I nod in agreement and close my eyes momentarily, basking in this feeling of euphoria.

"Alright, ladies, I have orange juice," a male voice says. I open my eyes and turn my head to see one of the guys from earlier putting glasses and a carafe of orange juice on the dresser. "Anything else you need, I put my phone number on this napkin. Just text me." He smiles and walks out.

I turn back to look out the window one more time and scream, jumping back against the wall, out of sight. I hold my chest as my heart just exploded.

"What in the world," Harper says, looking out the window.

"Aiden," I say, breathing heavy with my hand on my chest. "He's down there." All three girls look at me like I've gone crazy. "We can't see each other," I stress. They still stare at me and blink. "Why are you guys staring at me? You know it's bad luck if we see each other on the day of our wedding."

Bryn twists her lips and then says, "Is it bad luck if you see him but he doesn't see you? I'm fairly certain he couldn't see you up here."

I start second-guessing. "I know he can't *see me*, I guess I'm assuming I can't see him either," I say with uncertainty.

Harper pulls out her phone and types something. "How did we live before Google?" she murmurs. "Oh, found it." She waves her phone around before looking at it again. "It says here that it's bad luck for him to see you before the wedding, not the other way around. So, I think you're good." My shoulders relax as I blow out a breath. I cannot have anything go wrong today. I look up and send out a silent plea for Fate to be on my side today.

A loud pop grabs my attention. The girls cheer as Syd makes mimosas for everyone. She picks up four glasses and passes them around.

"Alright, gir—"

"Wait!" Katie says, darting into the room, interrupting Syd's toast. "You can't toast without us." She drops her bags on the floor, and Macie comes waddling in after her.

"I'm going to kill whoever decided we should be on the second floor," Macie says, breathing heavily.

I scream with excitement and run over to them. "I'm so glad y'all are here." After giving them a hug, I place my hand on Macie's belly. "Is he kicking much?" My eyes widen when I feel him move. "Oh, my gosh, that's crazy feeling that!"

"Yeah, just think how it feels from the inside." She rolls her eyes. "He thinks he's a Kung Fu champ. I swear he's going to break a rib."

"Have you all been here long?" Katie asks. She takes the mimosa Syd hands her. Syd gives Macie a flute of just orange juice.

"Nope," Bryn says. "We've been here long enough to see the backyard and learn about superstitions on wedding days." She giggles as Katie looks around the room.

"Superstitions?" she says, glancing at me. "You don't seem like the superstitious type."

"I'm not, but I'll be damned if I don't try everything I possibly can to make sure nothing goes wrong."

"Let's get this toast out of the way so we can drink our mimosas," Syd says, holding up her flute. We hold ours up, too. "To my best friend, may the day be as amazing as you are." My lips curl into a smile and my eyes start to water.

"My turn," Katie says. "Here's to you, because you now have to deal with my brother every day...and to me for gaining a wonderful sister." The tears start flowing again. *Shit*, how am I going to get through today with all these emotions?

By the time Bryn, Harper, and Macie toast to me, I'm a sobbing mess.

"Thank you all for being here and celebrating this day with me," I hiccup through my tears. "Each of you are so important to me, and I cherish our friendships more than you know."

We raise our glasses and clink as we say "Cheers." Syd downs hers before I even bring mine to my lips. I take a drink as she says, "I think I'll just drink the champagne." A thought crosses my mind, and I immediately spit my drink back into my glass. *Dammit!*

When I look up, five sets of eyes are staring at me. "Something wrong with your mimosa?" Syd asks slowly. *Shit. Shit. Shit.*

"No," I squeak out.

"You love mimosas." I do. I *love* them. The tangy taste of orange juice with the sparkling crisp taste of champagne. They were meant to be had together. It's one of my favorite alcoholic drinks. But I can't drink it. *Not now.*

"Um..." I pause for a beat and crack my knuckles. Sydney narrows her eyes at me. She knows when I'm nervous. "So...*I'm pregnant.*" My voice cracks. The foreign words coming out of my mouth surprise me. It's the first time I've said it out loud.

"Oh, my gosh!" Sydney places her drink down and grabs mine out of my hand, placing it on the coffee table then wrapping her arms around me. She pulls back and asks, "When? *How?*" She knows how neurotic I am about taking my birth control. I have never missed a day. *Ever.*

I sigh. "Antibiotics."

"Oops," Harper murmurs.

Syd's eyebrows rise and I nod. I don't need to explain. Every woman on the pill should know antibiotics could make the pill ineffective. *I should have known.* It's been forever since I've been sick though, and when I have been in the past, I guess I was never with anyone.

Syd watches me for a moment before saying, "How do you feel about it?" Her voice is tinged with apprehension. I'm not good with surprises. *And this is a big one.*

What haven't I felt? Since taking the test last night, my emotions have gone from one extreme to the other. I look away from her inquisitive eyes. Tears pool in mine as I think about the baby growing in me.

"It'll be okay," Bryn says, grabbing my hand. Her words come out soft and tender. I glance at my wedding dress hanging off the door and focus on it while blinking back my tears. A soft laugh escapes my lips when I look back to the girls.

"No, I'm fine," I whisper and squeeze Bryn's hand. "I'm excited. I'm scared. I'm nervous. You name it, that's me." I take a couple deep breaths. "I know Aiden will be ecstatic. Hell, he wants ten kids." I roll my eyes.

"Oh, dear God," Harper says, giggling.

"I know, right?" I reply. *Not going to happen.* "I just took the test yesterday, so I'm still working my way through the shock."

"Have you told Aiden?" Katie asks.

I shake my head. "I plan on telling him tonight," I say, walking to my purse. I pull out a gift-wrapped box and show the girls. Syd claps excitedly.

"Lulu will be a great big sister," she says. I smile. She'll be amazing.

"And I'm going to be an aunt to two kids!" Katie says, jumping up and down.

The happiness in the room is contagious. Excitement bubbles inside me. I'm having a baby. Aiden's baby. *Our baby.* Sharing this wasn't planned. I wanted to tell Aiden first, but I didn't think about having to hide the fact that I can't drink. I look around the room.

"Y'all have to help me tonight. If I don't drink, people will notice," I say and pick up a flute holding it in the air. Syd snatches it out of my hand and downs my mimosa then she fills it with orange juice and hands it back to me.

She swipes her hands twice and smiles wide. "We gotcha covered," she says. "We'll make sure to hand you either cider or water throughout the night so it'll look like you're drinking."

"Well, don't make me look like a lush," I say, laughing out loud.

"I thought you wanted to make sure it wasn't obvious."

"Ha, ha, funny girl." I push her shoulder.

"I've got some people who I think belong up here with you girls," Jaxon says, tapping on the door and walking in. Katie does a little jig and runs into Jaxon's arms. He lifts her up in his embrace and kisses her deeply. It makes my heart so happy to see them together. They have been flying back and forth this month, working on getting her moved.

"Move, you two love birds. I have work to do," Cherrie says, strutting around them in her five-inch heels. Her flaming red hair and brightly colored one-piece jumpsuit stands out against the white in the room. I have a feeling she stands out anywhere. I chuckle to myself. A couple more people file into the room behind her and start setting down their cases full of makeup and hair stuff. Cherrie has done my hair since I moved to New York, and she made me promise to use her and her people for my hair and makeup. I told her she didn't have to when we moved the wedding here, but she insisted.

"Addie, baby, you are glowing," she beams.

I gasp, wondering if she can tell I'm pregnant. My gaze darts to Jaxon, but he's in his own little world with Katie right now. I look back and shrug. "It must be the wedding glow," I say awkwardly.

Her brows furrow and her head tilts to the side. "It sounds like you're nervous, sweetie."

Syd comes to my side, wrapping her arm around my waist. "No, she's just ready to get things moving. Cherrie, do you want a mimosa before we start?"

Her lips curl into to a smile and her eyes brighten. "I would love one, but just tell me where and I'll get one. I like it *heavy* on the champagne side," she says, winking.

"Me, too, girl," Syd chuckles. "It's over there." Syd points to the table, and Cherrie heads in that direction. "*Calm down.* Nobody can tell," she whispers in my ear. I close my eyes briefly and exhale. She's right. I need to relax. I look over at her and nod. "We got this. Now let's get you married before you inadvertently end up telling everyone *except* Aiden."

"Someone tell me about the gorgeous man who lives here and is he single?" Cherrie's voice radiates from across the room.

"That's my cue to go back to the guys," Jaxon says and leans down to give Katie a quick kiss. We laugh at how fast he exits the room.

A second later he pokes his head back into the room. "Oh, Addison, you are definitely glowing." He smiles and winks then disappears.

Shit.

"Addie!" Lexi comes running into the room, straight to my arms. I hold her and take in a deep breath. She doesn't know this day is about her, too. The love in my heart for her spreads warmth throughout my body.

"Hi, sweet girl. Are you ready for hair and makeup?" I run my hands through her caramel-colored hair. Her eyes go wide, and she shakes her head up and down quickly.

"Can I get pretty blue on my eyes and red lipstick?" she asks, sweeping her finger over her eyelids and lips. I laugh at the thought.

"Oh," Cherrie says excitedly, "a girl after my own heart." *Oh, dear.*

Chapter twenty-six

"**Y**ou look stunning, Addison," my aunt says from behind me.

I stare at my reflection in the mirror, and I almost don't recognize myself. The woman looking back is radiant and mature. *It's you*, my brain reminds me. I run my hand down my stomach. The delicate lace from my dress is soft to the touch. I wonder about the baby growing inside of me. *Are you a boy or a girl? Will your eyes be emerald green or turquoise blue?*

I glance at Amy in the mirror and guilt rushes through me because I wish my mom were here to see me. My vision blurs as my emotions get the best of me. *Again*. I blink repeatedly to dry up the tears. Cherrie will kill me if I ruin my makeup before the wedding even starts. Blotting the corner of my eyes with my fingertips, I laugh.

"I wish she was here," I admit.

"Addie, I do, too." She stands beside me and links her fingers through mine, hanging our hands at my side. "You look so much like her. I was going through some old photographs and came across this." She pulls out a photo from her dress pocket. I carefully take the photo in my hand. It's a picture of my mom and Amy in front of a building that looks like a dorm.

"Were y'all in college?"

"Mmm-hmm. That was our graduation day. We left for Mexico the day after."

I look over at her and she flashes a knowing smile. "When she met Travis?" She nods. I look back to the picture. Two beautiful women in *short* shorts and crop tops. I tilt my head, studying it. Running my finger over my mom's image, I certainly see our similarities. I glance at myself in the mirror and then look down again. I inhale deeply and blow it out slowly.

"Thank you," I say handing the picture back to Amy.

She pushes my hand back. "No, you keep it to remind you that she's with you today."

I hold it over my heart. "I'm so glad you're here with me. I don't want you to ever think because I miss her that I don't appreciate everything you've ever done for me."

"Addie, I don't ever question the love you have for me."

"And I don't think I could have taken in Lexi without the devotion you have shown me most of my life," I say, looking at her in the mirror.

"I don't believe that." She places her hand over mine as I hold the picture against my heart. "You have a huge heart, guarded a little, but when you finally let people in, you keep them in your heart and hold on tight."

The love between us reflects in the mirror. The love of a mother and daughter on her wedding day. Someday this will be Lexi and me, and I can only hope that our connection is this strong.

"I love you, Amy," I whisper.

"I love you, Addie." We stay silent for a few more moments. She stands tall and squeezes my hand before releasing it. "It's almost time. You are marrying a wonderful man. And he's getting quite anxious, so take a few minutes and then come downstairs." She kisses me on the cheek and walks out of the room.

I stare at the picture in my hand. "You gave me the perfect person," I say to my mom.

"I agree." I jump at the sound of a man's voice behind me.

Spinning around, I pick my dress up so it comes with me. Turquoise blue eyes meet mine. "Travis." He's leaning in the doorway and his smile reaches his eyes.

"Wow. You look...gorgeous," he says, stuffing his hands into his pockets.

"Thank you," I say, looking away, feeling shy suddenly.

"I didn't know if I should come," he says, his voice hushed. "I'm not staying, though." I look up to him, and he pushes off the doorframe, walking toward me. "Aiden knows I'm here."

My brows crease and I nod. "It's okay. I'm happy you're here." Seeing him here causes guilt to build inside me because I didn't ask him to walk me down the aisle. He didn't expect that, did he? While Ted hasn't been in my life except the last nine years, he's still been more of a father than any other man. Including the one standing in front of me right now.

But he is my father.

I peek down at the picture in my hand. "God, she was beautiful," he rasps. "May I?" I look at him and he sticks his hand out. I place the picture in his hand gingerly, like it's going to break if I'm not careful. He takes a deep breath and exhales as he stares at the picture. His eyes gloss over when he hands the picture back to me, which makes mine tear up. I look up to the ceiling. I'm going to need to stuff my bra with a freaking box of Kleenex if I can't get my emotions in check.

"I have something for you," he says, bringing my attention back to him.

"Is it going to make me cry?" I blot my eyes with my fingers, drying the tears. His eyes dart around the room, not knowing how to answer. I shake my head. "I was kidding, Travis. Everything seems to be making me cry today."

"I can't promise it won't, then," he says, his lips lifting into a half smile, shrugging. He reaches into his pocket and pulls out something. "I don't know if this is considered something old or something new, but..." He holds his hand out. I place my mom's picture on the table and hold out my hand. He places a small black jewelry box in my palm. "I bought these for your mom. She left before I could give them to her. I've kept them all these years because they represent the love that I had for her." I slowly open the black velvet box. "I want you to have them."

I let out an audible gasp. The most exquisite earrings catch the sun's light making it dance around the room. Each earring has a round diamond encased in platinum and a teardrop diamond hanging from it. By the size of the diamonds, I can tell these earrings were very expensive.

"They're flawless, just like your mom."

"Travis..." I pause because it's hard to stop gazing at them. I manage to look away and up to Travis. "They're beautiful. I don't know what to say."

"You don't need to say anything. Just cherish them as much as I did your mom."

"I will." I sniffle. The tears that I've tried to keep at bay finally spill over. Travis sweeps them away softly with his thumb. The fatherly touch that I've craved my whole life churns inside of me, and I lean into his hand. I close my eyes and revel in the feeling momentarily until I catch myself. *It's Travis.* We can't have the father-daughter relationship. I sigh and straighten my back. He softly smiles and returns his hands to his pockets. I turn toward the mirror and take out the earrings. When I stick them in my ears, I look at myself quickly before turning back to Travis, smiling sincerely at him.

"Addison, since the day I found out about you, I had hoped that someday you would be wearing those. They're perfect. You're perfect..." He chokes back his emotions, clearing his throat. "God, how I wish things were different."

"Me, too." I cry as a flood of emotions runs through me. I wrap my arm around my stomach and think of the child growing in there. I can't allow his world to affect my children. This is why we can't have a relationship.

"Addison, what are you doing in here, woman," Syd says walking into the room. She freezes when she sees Travis. "Oh, sorry."

"It's okay, Sydney," Travis says as his eyes remained pinned on me. "I was just leaving. Congratulations, Addison."

My heart moves my body before my brain catches up, and I jump into Travis's arms. I wrap my arms around his neck and his arms wrap around my waist. "Thank you," I murmur into his shoulder.

"No, thank you." He squeezes me a little tighter. He releases me and leans down to kiss me on my forehead. "I'll see you around. Oh, Frankie said to tell his Add Cat congrats, too." I chuckle while wiping the tears off my face.

I watch him walk out of the room as Syd scoots over to let him pass. She walks in with a sympathetic smile on her face. "You okay?"

I sigh and softly nod. She grabs some Kleenex and blots my face. "Let's touch up your makeup. If Cherrie sees you..." I laugh, knowing exactly how Cherrie would react. She leans down and picks up some powder off the table of makeup, sweeps the brush through it, and glides it across my face. "The earrings are gorgeous. I'm assuming Travis gave them to you?" she asks quietly.

"Yes. He bought them for my mom. Just never got the chance to give them to her." Syd smiles and continues to touch up my makeup. I blow out a heavy breath. "When he's around, I always think maybe we could have a relationship. But that's stupid," I say, throwing my arms up in the air. "*We can't.* Especially now with Lexi and..." My voice trails off as I look down at my stomach.

"Addie, you have to take it for what it is. You *know* how dangerous Travis's world is, but you can't keep getting mad at yourself for longing for the father you've always wanted. *Especially your biological one.* I think right now your hormones are getting the best of you."

I snicker. "You think?"

"Yes, but what I really think is that you need to get your butt downstairs before your groom thinks you've changed your mind."

"Are you kidding? If Aiden thought I changed my mind, he'd be up here handcuffing me to the bed and bringing the pastor with him to say our vows."

"I could totally see that," she says, laughing. She grabs my hand and pulls me.

"Wait," I say, stopping her. I turn back to the table and reach down to grab my mom's picture. Folding it in half, I place the picture inside my dress, over my heart. "Can you see it?" I turn to Syd.

"Nope. Are you ready?"

I am. It's time to marry the man I was meant to marry. I've never been one to believe that there is only one person in this world meant for you...until I met Aiden. The deep bond we share is so tightly woven inside of us, it's hard to imagine the force needed to break it. I don't think I could ever love another man more than I do Aiden.

***

I watch each of my girls go out one by one. Ava quickly closes the door behind them so Aiden can't see me. After the third time, I giggle to myself thinking it must be driving Aiden mad seeing the door close each time. Lexi comes up and slips her hand in mine.

"Is it my turn yet?"

"Almost, Lulu. Are you ready?" She bounces on her toes. I look at her white dress that falls just below the knees swish as she moves. The burgundy sash around her waist makes a big bow in the back. I squat down, which is a little difficult in this dress. "I love you so much, Lexi. You look beautiful."

Her little arms wrap around me, and she hugs me. "I love you, too, Addie. I love Aiden, too," she adds.

"And he loves you."

"Okay, Lexi, you almost ready?" Ava asks. She fluffs her dress out so it's not crooked anywhere. "Just remember, go slow, okay?" Lexi nods her head and straightens her back. "Just like we rehearsed," she reminds her, and Lexi nods again. The door opens and the sound of the music floats around the room. Again, the door shuts and silences the music. We're in the guesthouse because the double doors lead right out to the chairs. The windows have all been blacked out so no one can see inside. The guys' belongings are draped over every chair, couch...you name it, there's a piece of male clothing on it.

Geez, they're worse than women. The table is littered with shot glasses and bottles of alcohol. It's a good thing I don't see any *empty* bottles.

"You're up," she says to me, interrupting my perusal of the messy room.

I take in a deep breath and slowly let it out. I stand in front of the door, and Ava adjusts my dress so the train is spread out. Ted is standing on the other side of the door, waiting to walk me down the aisle. I look down and grasp my bouquet in my hands. White roses bound tightly with burgundy satin ribbon, tiny burgundy and blush-colored flowers arranged between the roses, which stands out against the white. I hear a guitar start playing, and I look at Ava. Her smile beams and she shrugs. This wasn't part of the plan. She swings open the door, and I squint so my eyes can adjust to the bright light.

When they do, I see Aiden at the end of the aisle, standing with a microphone in front of him and his guitar strapped around his tuxedo. The lake is right behind him. The sun's reflection causes a yellow glow. I can't move. I'm mesmerized. When the first word comes out of his mouth, his voice cracks. He stops playing and clears his throat, flashing me his sexy half smile with a subtle headshake. He mouths, *"Beautiful,"* before his fingers begin to move across the strings again. I look up at the blue skies, trying to stop the tears. *Why am I even trying? It's pointless.* I step out into the brightness, and Ted hooks his arm though mine. He leans over and kisses me on the head.

"I think *I* have a man-crush on your guy," he whispers into my ear. I laugh through my tears. "You look gorgeous, Addison. You ready to go?"

I glance at Aiden and my smile beams. "As I'll ever be."

Aiden sings "Marry Me" from Train. His deep, sexy voice reverberates against my beating heart and goose bumps spread across my body. My chest rises and falls as each word he sings wraps around me and pulls me closer to him. I feel like I'm floating. I don't hear or see anything except Aiden.

When Ted and I stop at the end, the song is almost over, but Aiden stops playing and takes his guitar off. He hands it to Max and looks at the pastor and says, "I'm sorry."

I feel my forehead crease, wondering why he's saying sorry. He walks over to me and a salacious grin spreads across his face. He stops in front of me and looks at Ted, who's standing there as baffled as I am.

"Sorry, this can't wait," he says, his voice raspy from singing. He pulls me into him, slamming his lips down on mine. I open, letting his tongue explore my mouth. I feel Ted let my arm go. I'm holding onto my bouquet and my other hand drops to my side. Hoots and hollers spread behind us. He bites my lip as he pulls back. "Marry me?" he sings.

"I'm trying," I say, gripping his arm while I regain my composure. A smug smile plays on his lips as he runs the back of his finger over my shed tears.

"There are so many firsts for me at this wedding, this shouldn't surprise me," the pastor jokes, walking up to us. "Are you ready to start?" We both look at him and nod.

The pastor begins and the ceremony moves quickly. We kept out the *does anyone here object to this marriage* because it wouldn't matter and *hello*, that's asking for trouble.

We wrote our own vows, so as we get closer, I start to struggle with nerves. Thank God we decided to keep them short. Aiden is so much better at telling me and showing me how he feels than I am. He squeezes my hands and winks at me. I softly smile up at him.

"Aiden and Addison chose to write their own vows," the pastor announces. "Aiden." He nods his head for him to proceed.

Aiden clears his throat and looks down for a beat before his eyes find mine. His emerald green eyes shine from the sun's glow. "Addison, the first time I saw you, your eyes hypnotized me, your independence challenged me, but it was your heart that finally broke me. You shattered the shell that I had crawled into and set me free. You made me feel things that I didn't even know I was capable of feeling and it scared the hell out of me." Our eyes lock with one another and tears roll down my face. He lets go of my hand and sweeps his thumb across my cheek, catching some of my tears. "But it was how I felt when you weren't around that scared me more than anything. You were the North Star to a man without direction, and I know as long as I look to you, I'll never be lost again."

"Oh..." I mumble through my tears. I let go of one of his hands to fan myself. I can't breathe. I look up to the sky to try to catch my breath. My heart drums in my chest. His words were perfect. He reaches for my hand and lifts our joined hands to his lips. "Wow," my voice shakes. He closes his eyes with his lips pressed to my hand.

"I love you," I whisper. His lips curl against my fingers.

"Okay," I say, taking a sharp exhale. He grins, knowing this is hard for me. "Aiden..." I pause as I collect my thoughts. "I've always blamed Fate for everything that has gone wrong in my life. But here I am, marrying the only man who can complete me. And it was all because Fate led me to you. *Twice*." I laugh softly. Aiden's smile pulls at the corner of his mouth as he tries to blink away his tears. "You've been there at my worst and guided me to my best. Our love story isn't perfect, but the love we have for each other is. I love you, Aiden, with all my heart." My voice trembles by the time I'm done. I'm not sure I could continue even if I had more to say.

I take in a deep breath and let it out slowly. Aiden squeezes my hands and mouths, "*I love you.*" I nod and bite my inside cheek, trying to control my emotions. I pull out a Kleenex from my bra and blow my nose. Aiden quietly chuckles.

The pastor allows us a couple moments to gather ourselves before we continue. After we exchange rings, we turn to the pastor. I hang onto every word that comes out of his mouth. "... the giving of these rings and the joining of your hands, I now declare you husband and wife." He looks at Aiden and smiles wide. "Congratulations, you may *now* kiss your bride."

He sweeps me into his embrace and his soft lips capture mine. It's not like the kiss before that was rushed and demanding; it's slow and passionate. The crowd erupts. Whistles and clapping envelop us. I can't believe I'm married.

"We did it," he mumbles against my lips.

"We did."

He pulls back and looks down at me. "Ready for the next thing?" he asks. My lips curl up to a smile that reaches my eyes.

"Yes."

He glances at the pastor and nods.

"Would everyone please take a seat," he says, trying to quiet everyone. He gestures with his hands for everyone to sit down. Confused faces look around, wondering what's going on. I look over to Syd, and she can barely contain her excitement. Once everyone quiets, the pastor says, "Today we witnessed a man and woman come together as one. But they are not completely whole yet." He smiles brightly at Aiden and me. "Alexandra Jade Collins, will you please step forward."

I turn to look at Lexi and her eyes widen. She looks around, unsure. I flash a smile and nod, gesturing for her to walk toward us. She walks slowly to the middle of Aiden and me. I can hear sniffles in the crowd already and it's not helping to keep mine at bay. I have looked forward to this moment since we received the official paperwork from Jaxon. I want her to know she's so special to us and we felt this would show her. She places her little hands into our hands and stares up at us with questioning eyes.

Aiden squats down and kisses her on the forehead. "It's okay, Tater Tot."

"Alexandra—"

"You can call me Lexi," she says innocently, interrupting him. Chuckles are heard coming from behind.

"Okay, Lexi. Do you know why you're here?"

"I'm the flower girl," she says excitedly.

"Yes, and you did a great job."

Her face lights up. "Thank you."

"But that isn't the only reason why you are here today." She looks up at me and then to Aiden with confusion. We both smile down at her, reassuring her that it's okay. The pastor talks again and she looks at him. "You're here because you are very important to Addison and Aiden. They would like to tell you something." She nods her head.

We stand in front of her and kneel. Aiden helps me down because of the confines of my dress. I adjust myself, making sure everything is still in its place.

"Lexi," I start. "I can't imagine a life without your bright smile and beautiful voice. You have lit up my world, helping me in so many ways." Tears roll down my cheek.

"You helped me, too, Addie," she says, her eyes filling up with tears. I'm sure she doesn't even know why.

"Tater Tot." She looks at Aiden. "Before I met you, I didn't even think I wanted kids. But now I'd be happy to have ten just like you." Oh, God. *Stop with the ten!* I glance at Aiden and narrow my eyes. He laughs out loud. "Lexi, the love we have for you is unconditional. We want you in our lives forever, and we would be honored if you would be our daughter."

"Do you mean you want to adopt me?" she says, jerking her head in my direction. I nod as my emotions take over. My face twists, as I'm sure I'm about to ugly cry. "So, you'll be my Mommy and Daddy?" *That did it.* I choke on my tears.

"Yes," I cry out. "If you'll have us." Aiden sniffs and I look at him. Tears run down his face. His lips curl up to a smile.

Lexi jumps into my arms almost knocking me over. Aiden wraps his arms around Lexi and me as we embrace. "Yes, yes, I want that," she cries into my chest.

I pull back and wipe the tears away from her face and kiss her forehead. I watch Aiden's hand reach into his pocket as he pulls out a ring.

"Lexi," the pastor says. She looks up at him with red eyes. "Aiden has a ring that represents the love between all of you. There are three hearts on the ring, each representing one of you. They are interlinked with no end. That means your love will go on forever. Can you hold out your hand?"

She sticks out her hand and looks at Aiden with anticipation. We had the ring custom made so we know it will fit her. As Aiden slips it on her right-hand ring finger the pastor says, "Lexi, do you take Addison and Aiden to be your mother and father."

She bounces on her toes again. "Yes." Aiden pushes the ring on her little finger. We know the ring won't fit for very long, but she can do whatever she wants with it when she outgrows it. It's more the gesture than the ring.

"Aiden and Addison, do you take Lexi to be your daughter? To love her unconditionally and give her a home she can call her own forever?"

We both look at Lexi and say "I do" at the same time.

"Aiden and Addison Roberts, I now pronounce you parents," he says joyously. Lexi jumps up and down, hugging both of us. Everyone gets to their feet, cheering and clapping again. Aiden helps me off the ground and then picks Lexi up. With his other hand, he links it through mine.

"I present to you for the first time, Mr. and Mrs. Roberts..." the pastor says loudly over all the loud cheers. "...and Lexi Roberts." Now the crowd is roaring. Music fills the air and we make our way down the aisle. People pat us on the back or squeeze our hands as we walk past them.

I hear Cherrie say, "I think everyone needs to refresh their makeup," as I pass her. I laugh and nod. Although, I'm sure it's a lost cause for me. I'm on an emotional high, and I'm not coming down anytime soon. The pieces of my puzzle have just been glued together.

Chapter
twenty-seven

The DJ announces each couple in our wedding party. We've just spent the last hour taking pictures, and I'm tired. My feet hurt and I'm dying for an alcoholic drink or a nap. Neither would be a good idea right now. We're standing behind a closed curtain, waiting for our turn. Except for glimpses, I haven't had a chance to see under the tent. The sun is slowly melting in the sky, leaving behind a beautiful pink sunset as a backdrop to our reception. You can hear the frogs down by the lake starting to come out and play.

"I can't believe you did all this," I say, looking at Aiden, running my hand up his lapel. He looks gorgeous in his tux. He's loosened his tie already. I'm sure he's ready to lose the jacket, too.

"I can't believe you doubted me." He puts his hand on his heart and drops his head to my shoulder dramatically.

"Thank you," I whisper in his ear and then nip his earlobe. "It was amazing." I kiss his neck and run my hand up through his hair. I can feel the movement of his chest increase as I kiss him along his jaw. His hands glide down my sides before wrapping around me. He pulls me into his hard body and tilts his head to find my lips. Warmth spreads throughout my body.

A moan slips from my mouth when his lips trail down my neck to the hollow spot behind my ear.

"Fucking hell, I want you so bad right now," he growls into my neck. My whole body shudders. "When I saw you standing there waiting to walk down the aisle, I about lost my shit and ran to you." I giggle. I can imagine him doing that. "And now I have to wait for who knows how long before I can have you." He stops his assault but his hold on me is tight. I can tell he's trying to regain control.

"They are about ready to introduce you," Ava says, coming from behind the curtain.

Aiden takes a deep inhale and exhale. "Give me a minute," he says to her from over my shoulder. "I guess I shouldn't go in there with a hard-on, huh?" he whispers in my ear. I look up to the sky and laugh. When our eyes meet, he leans his forehead against mine. "I love you, Mrs. Roberts."

I smirk. "You like the sound of that, don't you?"

"There isn't a better sound." He flashes his signature sexy half-grin. "Except when you're screaming my name," he adds.

"Are you ready yet?" Ava asks, impatiently. Aiden moans. "When is Katie moving here for good?"

He narrows his eyes at me before releasing his arms. "Yep, we're ready." I laugh out loud. I knew that would help his *situation*.

We hear our name and Aiden links our fingers together as we walk in. Our friends and family cheer and clap with our entrance. Tables lined with white cloths surround a dance floor. Decorations of burgundy are placed all over. Lights are strung over the entire ceiling, dancing around from the light breeze coming in. A band is setting up to play, higher up on the stage, but right now the song "At Last" by Etta James plays over the speakers.

I glance at Aiden and raise a brow. "Did you pick the music, too?"

He grins and gives me a carefree shrug. "Maybe one or two songs."

We make our way to the dance floor and grab the microphone from the DJ. Looking around the crowd, I'm in awe at the amount of love I feel right now. It's consuming. I feel my face flush, and I look away from everyone. I hate being in front of crowds. Especially being on display. Whew, it's hot in here. I fan myself and Aiden looks down at me with a concerned look.

"I'm okay. It's a lot to take in," I say quietly. He smiles and kisses me on my nose.

"I'm right here, sweetheart."

I nod and turn back around. He brings the mic to his gorgeous lips and says, "Wow. Can you believe she's finally mine?" Whistles and clapping drown out the music. "We want to thank everyone for being here. Our new journey begins today and with all of you by our side, we can handle anything that comes our way." He briefly glances down at me and winks. "Now, let's celebrate. Someone bring my *wife* a drink!" He throws the mic to the DJ and swooshes me up in his arms and swings me around. "My wife." His face beams as he says it again. He sets me down, and Syd comes to my side with two flutes of bubbling champagne. I look at her with wide eyes.

She forgot already.

"Here are your drinks, love birds," she says, first handing one to me. Well, I *guess* I can have a sip and then get something else in a minute.

"To my gorgeous wife," Aiden says, lifting his glass.

"And to my perfect husband." I bring my glass up to his and clink it. He downs his whole glass before mine has even made it to my lips. When the bubbling liquid hits my mouth, I can immediately tell its cider. My shoulders relax, and I swallow the entire glass, too. The cool liquid moves down my throat and it feels amazing. I didn't even know I was that thirsty. I look at Sydney and smile wide, mouthing, "Thank you." She blows me a kiss and takes our glasses.

"I'll get y'all another one. Be right back."

The next half hour we make our way around the room, talking to everyone. My cheeks hurt from smiling. Harper brought me some flip-flops so at least my feet aren't hurting anymore. Lexi has been by our side, her small hand in mine, the entire time. Seeing her smile and her excitement about being adopted has shred every doubt that I might have had. There will always be a small part of me, hidden deep down, that thinks she lost her parents because of me. But I silently vow to them that I will give her the best life I can offer.

We're talking to Brooks and his nanny, Robin, when my stomach rumbles. I grab my stomach. Aiden looks at me and smiles. "I guess I need to feed my wife."

Instantly, I feel nauseous. "Oh, my God. I'm going to be sick," I say, putting my hand in front of my mouth and running to a trashcan. Please, don't throw up. *Please*, I beg my body.

"Addison, what's wrong?" Aiden says from behind me as he rubs my back. I try to take in deep breaths and slowly blow them out. My stomach rumbles again. Shit! My mouth waters and I squeeze my eyes shut, waiting for something to come up. How freaking embarrassing to throw up at your wedding.

"Addison, eat these," I open my eyes and see Bryn standing beside me holding out some crackers. I grab them and stick them in my mouth like I've been without food for days. The memory of when I was starving flows through my mind. I shake my head, forcing that memory out. That will not taint my wedding day. Bryn hands me some Sprite to wash it down. I stand by the trashcan, thinking I'll probably throw it right up, but I start to feel better as quick as I felt sick. I look at Bryn and her soft smile tells me everything. Oh, no. *I just got morning sickness.* At my wedding. I glance around the room and there are a few concerned faces watching me, one being Aiden.

"Sweetheart, are you okay?" he asks, still rubbing my back.

"Uh, yeah. That was weird. I think my blood sugar was low since I haven't eaten in hours. I guess maybe we should eat."

"Okay. Are you sure you're feeling alright?"

"I promise I'm fine." *I'm just growing a baby inside me, and I guess he's hungry.* He nods slowly, still unsure about what just happened. I would tell him, but I'm not ready to tell everyone. If I tell Aiden right now, everyone will know.

Aiden wraps his arm around me like I'm going to fall as we walk to the head table. Pulling out my chair, I take a seat and look up to him. "Aiden, I already feel much better. Stop worrying. I just need food."

"Maybe you shouldn't drink anymore," he says. I bite my lip to hide my laugh. Sydney hits my leg with hers under the table. I look at her and she shakes her head and chuckles. I look over at him when I feel him sitting down. His leg brushes up against my dress.

"I'll eat before I drink anymore." I smile wide and he returns it, satisfied with my answer.

Throughout dinner, glasses clink, which seems to be the cue for us to kiss. Usually I wouldn't mind kissing Aiden, but this steak is *incredible.* And every time I hear someone clink a glass, Aiden gets excited and I get irritated. Damn people, can't you see I'm starving?

I accidently huff out loud when I hear another clink, and Syd shakes from laughter. I glare at her and then I notice her half-eaten steak. "Are you going to eat that?" I ask sweetly. My mouth waters just looking at it. When I steal my gaze away and look back at her, her eyes are wide. "What?" I whisper. "I am freaking hungry." This baby isn't anything but a bean, but he obviously has a major appetite.

Harper leans forward on the other side of Syd and quietly says, "It must be a boy." I jolt upright and I peek at Aiden, hoping he didn't hear. *People*, this is supposed to be a secret! Aiden's busy talking to the guys, so I turn back.

"Why?" I whisper.

"Because you're craving meat."

"Huh." I rattle that around in my head. A boy. *A little Aiden running around.* I softly sigh and unconsciously run my hand over my stomach. Syd elbows me and I jerk my hand away. *Shit.* Thank God I'm telling Aiden tonight.

"Thanks," I lean over and say.

After eating half of Sydney's and my dinner, the nauseous feeling has subsided and I feel more energetic. Aiden's staying close by my side, still concerned. Amy has been keeping an eye on me. Every time I glance her direction, our eyes meet and I awkwardly smile. When I sneak away to go to the bathroom, she corners me when I come out of the stall. She leans against the wall while I wash my hands. I quickly peek at her in the mirror and look away to dry my hands. I feel like I'm a teenager again and she's using the silent treatment until I break down and confess.

I blow out a breath and then turn to face her. "I'm pregnant," I blurt out. *Damn it.* It works every time.

"I knew it!" she says vigorously, grabbing my hand and pulling me into a hug. "Congratulations, Addison." She steps back but holds my hands. "Were y'all planning it? When did you find out? How far along are you?"

I laugh and squeeze her hands. "Okay, stop!" I say.

"Sorry," she winces. "I'm just so excited for you."

"I just found out last night. It definitely was not planned." She tilts her head. "I took antibiotics last month because I was sick," I explain. She nods slowly in understanding. "Nobody knows except for the girls in the wedding party, and now you."

"Aiden doesn't know yet?"

"No." I throw my arms out. "I'm planning on telling him tonight. He was supposed to be the first person I told, but not being able to drink and getting sick out of the blue has given it away."

"I promise I won't say anything." Her eyes soften and she smiles, the soft wrinkles around her eyes deepening. She brushes an errant piece of hair behind my ear. "Let's get out there before someone comes looking for you."

I put my hand on her upper arm, stopping her from turning around. "I'd like my kids to call you grandma..." I grin, tearing up, "...if that's okay with you." I was never able to call her Mom, even though that is what she is to me in every way possible. She respected my decision and always knew how much she meant to me. I want her and Ted to be a part of my children's lives. They will be the only *grandparents* our kids will have.

Amy chokes back her tears. "I would be honored." Her eyes gleam as she cups my face. "You've brought so much happiness to my life. *A lot* of worry in between all that," she adds, chuckling, "but you have filled my life with more love than I could ever have imagined." My nose runs from tearing up, and I have to keep sniffling.

I wave my hand in front of my face. "Okay. We need to stop or I'm going to be a blubbering mess." I wipe the tears from my cheek and walk into a stall to grab some toilet paper. I grab a handful for Amy, too. With one last hug, we walk back out to the reception.

"There she is," a voice announces, coming from the speakers. It's Aiden's voice, so I glance toward the stage. When our eyes meet, he says, "Hi, sweetheart." His voice is raspy and sexy as hell. I lick my lips, watching him up on stage. His sleeves are rolled up and his tie is loose. He flashes his panty-dropping grin. Both dimples are on display, causing my stomach to flutter.

That gorgeous man is mine.

"Aiden, stop staring at Addie," Lexi whispers, forgetting she's at a microphone. Her small voice breaks our connection, and I laugh with the crowd. I hadn't noticed her up there. I was too busy ogling Aiden. My heart beats differently when I look at her. The beat is a slower, patient beat filled with adoration. She smiles at me, lifts her arm, and waves. I wave back and blow her a kiss. The little girl who looked up at me through frightened eyes when I opened her closet door that horrific day has stolen my heart. When I let go of the guilt that followed the death of her parents and brother, I knew Lexi's place in my life would be permanent. I was relieved when the courts agreed.

Aiden strums his guitar once. "You ready, Tater Tot?" He looks down at her, and she nods her head quickly. Her small hands wrap around the microphone. "This song was for Addison, but I think I'm singing it for both my girls."

I can tell how much she adores Aiden by how she looks up at him. Her smile is contagious. He winks at her before his fingers move across the strings of the guitar. The drums and piano play behind him. Lexi sways to the beat. She's so freaking adorable on stage.

Aiden's deep voice fills the air with the words from "You'll Be in My Heart" from Phil Collins. A song from *Tarzan*. *Fitting for Aiden*. He looks down at Lexi when he sings the first part. When the chorus starts, Lexi joins in and they both look at me. Her angelic voice is wrapped around his raspy voice, creating the perfect storm of melody.

My body is shaking with so much feeling I don't even know what to do with it. I cover my mouth as tears stream down my face. Up on stage is my heart and soul. Their words burn into my heart, leaving a permanent mark. It's the birthmark of our family.

Someone hands me a Kleenex, and I blot my face and nose. I try to bottle up my breaths and attempt to calm down, but I just end up suffocating myself. They take turns singing then come back together. My eyes move around, catching glimpses of people with tear-stained faces. When they finish the song, everyone is on their feet. Including me. I clap and then bring my hands back to my heart, staring up at them. Lexi jumps into Aiden's arms as soon as he puts his guitar down.

When they come down from the stage, the band takes over again. I'm waiting for them when they walk down the stairs. "I loved it," I say, squeezing them. "Y'all were amazing together."

"We make a good team, don't we, Tater Tot?" Aiden says, pressing a kiss on her cheek.

The best. I rest my head on Aiden's shoulder, watching the two rehash about singing together. They tell me about practicing on Sundays when they were having their special time. I knew they had to have practiced. They were too good for it to have been spontaneous.

"Hey, little rock star, do you want to dance with me before you become too famous and forget you even know me?" Damon asks Lexi, reaching his hand out.

"Let's go, Peter Pan." Aiden places Lexi down, and she dances away with Damon.

Aiden's fingers slowly scrape up my arm, making my body shiver. His eyes follow the path of his fingers, and he inhales deeply, letting it out slowly. When his eyes meet mine, they're so intense. I tilt my head, wondering what he's thinking. His thumb outlines my collarbone before moving up and cupping the back of my neck.

"God, you're beautiful, Addison." I softly smile. He draws me to him and claims my mouth before I can say anything. I grip a handful of his shirt to hold on. My mind turns dizzy as I'm consumed by Aiden's mouth. When he releases me, we're both breathless. "I need to step away from you or we're going to need to leave our wedding early," he growls. I nod, still trying to catch my breath. *That's probably a good idea.*

He spins around and starts to walk away. "Thanks for the song," I say. He looks back and nods.

"Wait until you hear the next one," he says with a sly smile. I bite my lip, watching him leave, wondering what he plans on singing.

"Dance with me?" Max asks from behind, startling me.

I wrap my arm around his, and he leads me onto the dance floor, pulling me into his very large chest. We two-step around the floor. He doesn't say anything, just leads me. It's an awkward silence. One I've never had with Max. I can tell he has something on his mind.

"So..." I bite my inner cheek. He looks down at me and waits for me to continue. I didn't have anything specific to say, I just wanted to break the silence. "Cherrie's cute," I blurt out.

He arches a brow and grins. "That she is."

"Y'all seem to have hit it off."

He smirks. "Something like that." I've always appreciated Max and his simple, no bullshit talks, but he's holding something back and it's irritating me.

I nod and go back to concentrating on dancing. I look around, even though I still feel his eyes on me. Finally, I glance at him. "What, Max? Just say it."

"You'll be mad at me." Whatever he thinks I'll be mad at doesn't stop him from flashing a Cheshire Cat grin.

"Max, I could never be mad at you." He looks down at me, and I shrug. Okay, that's a lie. "Tell me."

He leans down and whispers in my ear, "Congratulations."

I whisper back in his ear, "Thanks." I shake my head at the weird conversation we're having.

"I'm talking about being pregnant."

What the ever-loving hell? My foot stumbles, and I trip on Max's foot. He catches me and continues two-stepping without missing a beat. I regain my footing and stare up at him.

"Max, how in the world do you know that?" I say through gritted teeth. I am going to kill someone. I asked for one night of secrecy. One. Fucking. Night.

"Calm down there, Annie Oakley," he chuckles. Using the nickname he gave me the day we met doesn't calm my rage. "I heard Harper at the dinner table."

"You did not. She didn't say it loud enough." I narrow my eyes at him. His smirk tells me everything. "Asshole. You read her lips." *Goddammit.* At this rate, everyone is going to know I'm pregnant *except* Aiden. "You're a Nosey Nelly, Max." He laughs out loud.

"I promise I wasn't trying to be nosey. I just happened to look over when Harper leaned forward. I still wasn't sure but then remembered you running to a trashcan to lose your shit, so I put it together."

I sigh and look up to the white tent ceiling, lights twinkling all around. I tap my finger against Max's back, wondering if I should just go find Aiden and tell him right now. If he hears it from someone else, I'll feel like the worst wife ever.

"Addison," Max says, pulling me from my thoughts. When our eyes lock, he softly smiles. "He doesn't know. And I'm sure as hell not going to tell him."

"Dammit, Max. I was planning on telling him tonight, but my plan was also for him to be the first to know and now the whole place seems to know."

"No, they don't." That's easy for him to say. He's not the one going to let Aiden down when he hears the news secondhand. "You only have an hour left. Keep to the plan."

I nod and take in a deep breath. "Thank you," I say, looking at him. He winks and smiles.

"Remember, you said you'd name your first son Maximus."

I laugh, remembering the first time we met and how that wasn't how the conversation went. "I think that was your idea, and I don't remember agreeing to it," I say.

He shrugs. "I knew you two would end up together. There was never a doubt in my mind. I never saw Aiden look at someone the way he looked at you. I'm glad someone finally made the asshole wake up."

I lean my head down on his chest. "I can't say that I never doubted that we would be here, because...*well,* you know. But I knew that I had never felt like this for anyone else from the moment I saw him as *Jett.*" He chuckles at the name.

"I think the love you have for each other will outlast anything thrown your way. Just don't forget that." He leans down and kisses the top of my head. "Congratulations, Addison." My heart warms from his tender touch. Max and I have forged a deep bond from a dark place in my life. He will always be my hero.

"Thanks, Max...for everything. It makes my heart happy that you're part of the package deal with Aiden. And you're going to be the best uncle to our kids." He squeezes his arm around my waist and softly nods.

As soon as the song ends, Aiden stands behind me. "Alright, I think you've taken enough of my wife's time."

Max releases his hold on me and pats Aiden on the back. "You did good, brother." Aiden pulls him in for a tight hug. They give each other a silent nod that says so much. The love and friendship between them rivals mine and Sydney's. There isn't anything that could come between us.

"Okay, you two newlyweds, we're going to take Sleeping Beauty here to bed," Ted says, holding Lexi. Lexi yawns and puts her head down on Ted's shoulder.

"You've had such a big day, Lulu, you've been a trooper," I say and push a piece of fallen hair behind her ear. She manages a small smile. Her eyes flutter as she tries to hold them open.

"You can put her to bed in her room," Max says from behind us. We all look at Max and stare at him. *Her room?* I glance up to the house and wonder what the hell he's talking about.

He shrugs. "I had a room set up for her." He's very factual about it...like we should have already known. Lexi's head bobs.

"I have my own room?" She perks up, wide eyed and awake.

"Just for you, Lulu," he says. "I also thought about getting a couple horses." She gasps and I look at him. How often does he plan on us being here? He lives in a freaking different state, for God's sake.

"Can I bring Ketchup up here?" Her hands clap.

"Ketchup has to stay in Texas, Lulu," I say quickly before Max can say yes. The horse that helped both Lexi and I during our time of healing is currently a therapy horse on Amy and Ted's ranch. Amy works with a team of therapists who bring their clients to the ranch for animal therapy. The work they do there has a special place in my heart. I made a huge donation when Amy started up the nonprofit business.

"Oh," Lexi says, disappointed.

"Sweet girl, you know Ketchup is helping a lot of kids, just like he helped you."

"I know," she pouts. "I just miss him."

"Tater Tot, I'm sure he misses his girl, too." Aiden pokes her nose. She softly giggles and nods her head. We've talked a lot about what Amy is doing on the ranch and how important it is.

"How about you go with me to pick out a horse that'll be just yours?" Max says.

I hit Max on the shoulder. "Max! Would you stop spoiling her?"

Lexi reaches her hand over and puts it across my lips to silence me and giggles. "He's not spoiling me. *It's just a horse.*" I roll my eyes. "Please, let Max get me a horse?" she says, her innocent eyes plead.

I sigh. Like I can say no. I'll forever be the villain who didn't let Max get her a damn horse. I look at Max and narrow my eyes. He laughs out loud. *Oh, you can laugh now, Max, but later we are having a little talk.* I hear Aiden chuckle, too.

"You are in so much trouble," he murmurs to Max. That makes Max laugh louder.

"Lulu, right now, let's just worry about getting you into bed," I say. Brooks walks over and joins us.

"In my new room?"

I look at Aiden and he shrugs as I look up at the ginormous house. We're not staying here tonight, so I don't know how I feel leaving her here. What if she gets scared or has a bad dream? Will she ever be able to find Max?

"Robin is up there with Presley in one of the rooms. I'm sure she wouldn't mind watching over Lexi, too," Brooks says.

"The room is actually right by Lulu's," Max adds. Lexi looks at me with hopeful eyes.

"Okay," I resign. "But Amy and Ted will come get you later to take you back to their hotel since we're not staying here tonight." I look at Max, biting my bottom lip. I hope he doesn't think I'm being a bitch by not letting her stay here. "It's unfamiliar—"

"It's alright, Addison. I understand," Max says, stopping me. His lips curl into a smile and he nods, reassuring me that it is okay.

"Okay, Lulu, let's take you to see your new room." Ted puts her down, and she hops over to me, slipping her little hand into mine.

"It's three doors down from where you were today," Max explains.

"So, top of the stairs, do I go left or right?"

"Left," Max and Aiden say simultaneously. I quirk an eyebrow, looking between the two.

"Secret spy business on the right. Got it." I chuckle.

The guys smile, but don't confirm. *Or deny.* Aiden and I walk up the hill with Lexi, the three of us linked hand in hand like the ring on her finger. I hope she knows that even when we have a baby, the love we have for her won't ever change. She will forever be our first child.

She excitedly runs down the hall, counting doors to find hers. When she does, she looks back at us before entering. We nod, giving her confirmation, and hear her squeal before we make it to the room.

My mouth falls open and I gasp as soon as we walk into the room. I slap Aiden on the chest. "You thought I was bad?"

Aiden chuckles and shrugs. "I didn't know what kids liked then."

I watch her run up the stairs of a princess castle with a play area on top and a bed on the bottom. She slides down the slide on the other end. It's a freaking playhouse. Feeling slightly jealous that she loves it so much, I turn to Aiden and say, "Couldn't he have just bought her a normal bed?" He wraps his arm around my waist and pulls me into his side.

"Don't be jealous, momma bear." I pinch his side, hating that he can read me so well. "You know Max would do anything for Lexi. This shouldn't be a surprise," he says, leaning his head on top of mine.

I wrap my arms around him, and we stand there watching Lexi go up and down over and over. It doesn't take long before she wears herself out.

"You ready to get your jammies on?" I ask when she falls on her bed. Her eyes start to droop again, and she nods.

Aiden and I sit beside her when she's all tucked in. Robin sticks her head in and lets us know she'll text us if Lexi needs anything.

"It's been a long day for you," I say, moving her hair out of her face.

"Thank you," she says softly.

"For what, sweet girl?"

"For adopting me. I want to be with you forever." Tears automatically pool in my eyes.

"Oh, Lulu. You have made our lives better. We love you and now your ours. *Forever*." I sniff.

"Do I have to call you Mom and Dad?"

"You can call us whatever you want. Whatever feels comfortable to you," Aiden says, rubbing her stomach.

"I want to call you Mommy and Daddy, but it feels weird," she says, scrunching up her nose. My heart beats faster hearing those words. I smile at her.

"How about we take it slow. Today is the first day we are officially a family. There isn't any need to rush if it feels uncomfortable. Whatever you decide won't hurt our feelings, just remember that. And you can always talk to us about how you are feeling, okay?" She nods and I lean down and give her a hug, kissing her on her forehead before standing up. Aiden does the same thing.

"We love you, Tater Tot. We'll see you in a week. And then we'll go on our *familymoon*," Aiden says. I giggle at the word. We had to explain to Lexi what a honeymoon was, so she coined the phrase familymoon when we decided to take her somewhere to celebrate her adoption after we get back.

When we reach the door, she says, "I love you, too, Mommy and Daddy." I hold a hand over my heart, knowing how hard that must be for her to say. It's been a year since she lost her parents, and I can't imagine how confusing it is for a six year old to say that to someone else. My smile reaches my tear-filled eyes. Aiden squeezes his hand around mine, and I watch him blink back his tears. We blow her a kiss and turn the lights off. I roll my eyes when the ceiling twinkles with pinhole lights resembling a star-filled night.

She audibly gasps. "Look at the stars," she exclaims.

"I see it," I say, trying to sound excited. Aiden laughs. *Damn Max*! She's not going to want to come home.

Chapter
twenty-eight

"Aiden," I say, laughing. "You better behave down there."
"*Sweetheart*, there are no rules when I'm down here."
He winks, flashing a wicked grin. I'm sitting on a chair in the middle of the dance floor and he's on his knees, slowly lifting my dress. Whistles and laughter cheer him on. I can feel the blush creeping up my face, as his fingers graze my bare legs, moving higher and *higher*.

I laugh awkwardly and grab his hands, which are now above my garter. "Stop," I whisper-yell.

He leans forward, his mouth close to my ear. "I fucking love it when you blush." I shiver from the warmth of his breath that's laced with the smell of whiskey. To the outside world, he's just showing me love. They can't see his fingers continuing their ascent to my center. He glides a finger across my silk panties. I glare at him with wide eyes and sit up taller to move away from his fingers.

"*Stop*. Or I'm going to give you the worst case of blue balls you've ever had," I whisper into his ear. His laughter rings out as he sits back on his feet. "Now do your job without getting touchy feely." I lift my dress and motion with my head toward my leg.

"Yes, ma'am." A devilish glint in his eyes tells me I probably shouldn't have said that. He dives in headfirst under my dress. I can feel his teeth score my thighs as he slowly pulls off my garter with *his mouth*. I cover my face with my hands, hiding. When I feel him remove it from my foot, I lower my hands. The crowd goes wild. He's dancing around with it in his mouth, showing off his handiwork. *He's thirty, right?*

"Let's get all the single men on the floor," the DJ announces. *Thank God that's over.* I stand and scurry off the stage. Sydney comes and stands by my side, giggling at me. I slap her arm and glare at her.

We stand there and watch the guys get ready. Some crack their knuckles, others stretch. You'd think they were getting ready for a football game. Aiden holds up the garter and looks at me, wagging his brows. I roll my eyes. *Just throw the damn thing.*

He looks at all the guys and spins around as the DJ starts the music. Aiden plays around with where he's going to throw it before he launches it. The guys crowd around where it falls, fighting for it. *They make great actors.* Damon breaks free and waves around the garter, pointing at Sydney. Her arm is wrapped through mine, and she laughs.

"Well, crap, now there's pressure. I'll be the smallest one out there."

I look at her through the sides of my eyes. "You might be small, but I'm positive that's not going to stop you," I chuckle.

"That's right," she says, hopping from foot to foot. "I'll cut a bitch." I burst out laughing. I hold my stomach because it starts to hurt from laughing so hard.

"I'm serious. I'll take someone down." She punches the air like she's boxing. Oh, my gosh, it's hard to breathe. Tears running down my cheeks.

"Stop," I say between laughs. "You're going to make me bust, little bean."

The DJ calls me to the dance floor. I blot the tears from my eyes and take a couple of deep breaths. I hear Syd say behind me, "I got this." *Yes, you do, Pixie.*

The girls crowd the dance floor. My eyes go wide. I thought the guys were intense. I'm a little afraid of the mob behind me. I glance at Aiden, worried our plan isn't going to work. These girls have serious game faces on. They are here to win. I grasp my bouquet in my hand, eyeing the dance floor of hungry woman before I turn around. *Three...two...one.* I toss it over my head and whip around to see the melee ensue.

In the end Sydney holds up the bouquet in triumph. She looks like she's been in an actual fight. Her face is beet red, hair falling out of her side bun, and her dress is askew. But her smile reaches her sparkling ice blue eyes when she spots Damon. She waves the bouquet around like she's saying *"look what I got."* He smirks.

He grabs a chair and slides it onto the dance floor near where I'm standing. My nerves are crackling, I'm so excited. I reach up and give him a hug. "Good luck," I whisper in his ear and stroll to the side of the dance floor. Aiden comes to my side, wrapping his arm around my waist as we watch our best friends. Out of the corner of my eye, I catch someone leaving. Max is walking to the bar. I elbow Aiden and jerk my head in Max's direction. Aiden sighs and shrugs.

"Maybe this is what he needs to move on," he leans down and says in my ear. I watch Cherrie walk over to him and whisper something in his ear. He glances at the dance floor, downs a shot, and they walk into the darkness, outside the tent. When the music starts, I turn my focus back to Damon and

Sydney. I hate that Max is upset, but there isn't anything I can do. It's been almost a year since he and Sydney spent the night together, and he made it clear that it didn't mean anything.

The DJ plays "Bad Boys" by Inner Circle, and I giggle, knowing that is Damon's ringtone on Sydney's phone. Damon points at Syd and curls his finger. She saunters over and he reaches for her hand as soon as she gets close enough, helping her sit down. Damon twirls the garter on his finger and kneels, grabbing Sydney's leg. He drags the garter up her leg. When he pulls it over her knee, Jaxon yells out from the crowd, "Keep going." Sydney looks in his direction and laughs. The song quickly changes to "A Thousand Years" by Christina Perri. When Sydney looks back to Damon, he's holding a ring up in between shaky fingers. Sydney gasps, covering her mouth. Tears burn my eyes and my nose starts to tickle again. I pull out a tissue from my bra. Aiden's arm tightens around me, and I lean my head on his chest, trying to fight the tears but failing miserably.

It's hard to hear what Damon's saying over the music even with the silent crowd. When she nods her head and holds her hand for him to put the ring on, the crowd goes wild. Damon pulls Sydney up into his arms, and they dance to the rest of the song.

Aiden and I sway to the song, and I think about our lives. How intertwined our worlds have become. People slowly make their way to the dance floor, joining Damon and Syd, dancing next to them. Ryker pulls Bryn to the dance floor. Ryan holds Macie's *very large* belly as they dance. Jaxon and Katie whisper back and forth, embraced in each other's arms.

This is our life.
This is our family.

This is what Fate has given me. *Love.*

A tear rolls down my cheek. I place my hand on my chest as warmth spreads through my body. The euphoric feeling makes my nerves tingle. My heart has never been so full of love.

"Mrs. Roberts, you ready to join them?" Aiden says, glancing down at me. His emerald eyes gleam, reflecting the love that I'm feeling. I wipe the tears that have fallen, smile, and nod. His fingers slide between mine, and we move to the dance floor.

When the song ends, I smack a kiss on Aiden's lips and run to grab Syd. She squeals and jumps into my arms. "Congratulations," I say, squeezing her.

She pulls back. "Are you okay with this?" I jerk my head a little, taken back by her question. She knows that I love her with Damon. "I mean him asking me at your wedding," she explains.

"Are you kidding? I'm more than happy to share the spotlight with you. And Damon had already asked us before the wedding just to make sure." I snatch her hand to see the ring. Damon wouldn't let me see it earlier. "It's beautiful, Syd. I'm so happy for you."

All the girls from the wedding party come over to congratulate her. We start dancing to a rock song when Aiden and Damon bring a tray with flutes of champagne for all of us. My eyes go wide, looking at Syd. *Shit.* There's no way for her to run off and change my drink. I'm sure there are numerous eyes on us so it's not like I can dump it in other glasses without getting caught.

I swallow. *It's just a drink,* I remind myself. Aiden moves the tray around for everyone to grab a flute. Once I have one, he takes the last one and passes the tray to a random person walking by. His hand slinks around my waist, and he pulls me into him.

"We couldn't be happier for you two," Aiden says, smiling at the happy couple. "Congratulations and all that other shit." He laughs, holding up his glass. Glasses clink with cheers all around. I brink the flute to my mouth and take a sip. Tiny bubbles dance on my tongue, the crisp taste of fruit fills my mouth before the warmth moves down my throat. *Mmm.* It tastes...like the forbidden fruit. I lick my lips, still tasting it. I'm staring at my glass debating if I can have one more sip when Aiden asks me if I'm okay. *Yep, don't mind me. I'm just getting your child drunk.*

The song for the electric slide begins to play. Sydney excitedly yells my name, takes my drink, and hands it to Aiden before whisking me off to join in the line dance. Sydney to the rescue. She looks at me when we move to the left, rolling her eyes, knowing that we both hate this dance.

"Thanks," I say, moving back a few steps. She nods, dancing in front of me. "I swear I banned this song." When we turn, I catch a glimpse of her giggling. I wince, my ankle reminding me that it hasn't healed all the way and it's time for me to sit down. I look over at Syd when we're side by side again. "I'm done. My ankle is starting to hurt." I lift my dress and can see it's beginning to swell.

"Sit," Sydney barks. "I'll go find you some ice."

Chapter twenty-nine

Aiden

I glance around the room and my eyes freeze when I see Addison. Sydney is putting some ice on Addison's ankle. I stop a coworker who's rambling on about something that I'm not even paying attention to. "I need to go check on Addison," I say, pointing in her direction and walking away.

"Hey, gorgeous." I lean down and kiss her. She's sitting in a chair with her foot propped up. She looks up at me and frowns. "Seems you overdid it." I lift off the ice to see how bad it is. Not too bad, but bad enough that I'm ready to take her home. *Almost.* One last thing to do. "I'll be back in a little bit. Stay here."

"Yes, sir," she says. My smile grows wide. *Fuck*, I like hearing her say that. She narrows her eyes at me, and I laugh. I've had submissive women before, not really my thing. Give me a strong-willed woman who will take charge and ride me like a superstar, now *she's* my thing. Addison fits that bill to a T.

I walk away before my semi-hard dick goes full Monty. I roll up my sleeves, walking to the stage. This is the last song of the night. At least for us. Then I'm going to take my wife to our new home. I shake my hands out, nerves getting the best of me.

I hope she doesn't freak out about the apartment. I'm not sure what I'll do if she doesn't like it.

Hopping up the three steps to the stage, I grab my guitar. The guys are just getting done with a song, and they see me coming from the side. I nod, telling them it's time. This was already planned ahead of time. I walk to the mic and clear my throat. Damon whistles and Sydney hollers. Attention turns to me, and I smile and wave. "I'm sure you're getting tired of hearing me," I chuckle. "But I have one song left. Now that the little ones have gone to bed, this one's for you, sweetheart." I give the audience the once-over and then pin my gaze on Addison. I won't see anyone else the entire song. Her smile reaches her eyes, and she blows me a kiss. The look of worship she gives me when I'm on stage is the most heart-pounding rush. It's fucking intoxicating.

At the wedding, when the door opened and I saw her standing there, my words slipped from my mind. I was stunned stupid at how beautiful she looked. I don't remember how I found the words, they just came out.

I know *exactly* what I'm want to say now. The band begins to play behind me, and I grip the microphone and close my eyes, letting the melody soak in. When I open them, I sing directly to Addison, singing "Slow Hands" by Niall Horan. Whistles with whoops and hollers fill the whole room. Addison blushes and covers her face with her hands for a few beats. I grin, loving making her flustered. She leans over and grabs a napkin, fanning herself as I tell her I want to take my time and I will certainly have slow hands.

I couldn't have picked a better song. It's what I want. *Right now.* I don't know what it is about her today, maybe it's the wedding dress, but I've been hard more times than I can count.

Her smell is different and it's making me want to ravage her. As I sing, I watch her morph from her flustered self into her confident, sexy self. She licks her lips and then bites her bottom one, flashing her "come fuck me" look. *At least, that is what I'm imagining she's saying.*

Baby, I'm coming.

I look over at the lead singer of the band and nod. I'm done looking at my wife. I need to feel her. I hop off the stage and the lead singer takes over where I left off. I grab Addison off her chair and move to the dance floor with her.

"Your foot okay for one last dance?"

"By the sound of your song, this is definitely not the last dance of the night." The heat in her eyes shoots right to my dick, lighting it up. I pull her in closer.

"It's the last one you're going to be dressed for," I say, leaning down and kissing her neck. She tilts her head, giving me better access to her silky smooth skin. A moan slips from her throat, vibrating against my lips. Fuck, I want her.

Our bodies move in sync to the beat of the song. "I liked it when you were singing," she whispers.

"I like it better when you're in my arms."

"How about you sing to me while I'm in your arms?"

She doesn't have to ask me twice. I will do anything for this woman.

When the song ends, I pick her up, swinging my arm under her knees, and carry her off the dance floor. *It's time to go.*

We thank everyone for coming and say our goodbyes. I stuff Addison and her dress inside the limo and crawl in behind her. "You could have let me take off my dress," she giggles, trying to push it over enough for me to sit by her.

"No." I shake my head. "I want to be the one to take off your dress." I lift her hand to my lips, kissing her palm. "And it'll be a good deterrent until we get home."

She cocks her head to the side, the line in her forehead creasing. "Home?" I nod. "We're going back to New York City tonight?"

"Yes." I chuckle as her eyes widen.

"Couldn't we have stayed at a hotel close by?" she asks, trying to turn her body toward me. She pushes up and twists her dress with her as she sits facing me.

"No." Her shoulders slump when I don't explain.

She scoffs and hits me in the shoulder. "You sound like Max." I bark out a laugh. "I can't believe you're going to make me wear this dress for two hours in a car."

"We're taking Max's jet," I say, wrapping my hand around her neck and bringing her lips to mine. I kiss the corner of her lips and work my way to the center. Her mouth opens for me and I can't help but crush my lips onto hers. One taste and I can't control myself. *Which is why she's wearing her dress.* I knew I'd never make it home without tasting her *everywhere* and our home is the first place that I want to make love to my wife.

Unfortunately, I haven't been able to keep my hands to myself, but I have kept my dick in my pants. This only frustrated Addison more and more by the minute. She was so mad, she shooed me away on the plane and took a nap. She looked exhausted, so I let her sleep. She's going to need her energy for tonight anyway.

The town car pulls up to my apartment building, and Addison's eyes light up. "Finally," she says, running her hand in between my legs. I grasp her hand. My dick has been on the starting line, waiting for the go signal, all day long. I'm not going to be able to hold back much longer, especially if she's touching my dick.

"Someone's anxious," I say, flashing a wicked smile.

"You sing a song to me about slow hands and taking me home, get me all hot and bothered, and then tell me we have to wait an hour." She throws her arms out. "Yes! I'm anxious."

I hum. "I love getting you hot and bothered." I stare into her eyes.

She cups my jaw lovingly and then grabs my cheeks. Hard. "Then get out of the car," she demands. I throw my head back, laughing.

I open the door and help her and her dress out. I swoop her up into my arms, and she squeals, holding onto my neck. The bellman comes behind me and grabs our bags. The doors are opened for us when we walk in, and we're greeted by security.

"Good evening, Agent Roberts and Mrs. Roberts. Congratulations." My smile stretches across my face hearing those words. *Mrs. Roberts*. When we get on the elevator, I press the button for the eighth floor and put Addison down. She cocks her eyebrow up.

"As much as I love that terrace, *Agent Roberts*, unless you plan on sticking your cock inside me out in the open, now is not a good time." I chuckle at the seriousness in her words.

"I just need to show you something really quick." I wink at her.

The elevator rises and with each floor, my nerves start to get the best of me. Addison hates surprises and this is a really big one. I close my eyes and take a calming breath. When I open them, the elevator dings. We're *home*.

"Aiden, you okay?" Addison stares up at me.

I stand taller and crack my neck. "Yes." I swallow once and lead her to the foyer. "We're not up here to go out onto the terrace." Her eyes dart around as she looks confused.

Just do it, Roberts.

I grab her hand and pull her to the front door. *Our front door.* When I unlock it and open the door, I glance back at her and smile before pulling her in behind me. I watch her reaction as she takes everything in.

"That looks like..." she says, pointing to her couch but stopping herself, and looks around again. "Is that my..." She stops, taking in her kitchen table. "I'm so confused, Aiden. This looks like all my stuff." She spins around to me.

My smile grows. "That's because it is."

Chapter thirty

I can feel him behind me, watching me stare out the window. "Do you like it?"

I slowly turn. The *swoosh* of my dress is the only thing I hear. "What is there not to like?" I reply. I reach down and pick my dress up so I don't trip and saunter toward him. "Aiden, this place is remarkable. I can't believe it's ours. I can't believe you did all this." I chuckle when his brows shoot up. "I shouldn't be surprised. This is just...wow," I say, looking around. "Didn't Mack live here?"

"He did," he replies. "He's always offered to rent out this place to me since he's never here and I watch over it anyway. He offered it to me again when he found out we were getting married. We don't have to stay here if we don't want to. I only signed a year lease. We can sell our apartments and then decide what we want to do."

I look at everything. It's weird seeing my furniture in here. I can't believe they moved everything today. Aiden walks me from room to room. When we get to Lexi's, my hand goes over my heart. He made it just like the one at my place. Even her corner with pictures of her parents and brother. "It's perfect."

His arms wrap around my waist, linking his fingers at my stomach. I look down and slide my hands on top of his. *Baby, this is your daddy.* It's time to tell him.

"Aiden—"

"Wait, there's more," he says, stopping me and pulling me back to the living room. He walks me to a set of sliding glass doors. The darkness makes it look like nothing is out there. Aiden holds up a finger and runs to grab a remote. The boyish grin on his face warms my heart. He's so excited about this place. When he presses a button, lights brighten the other side of the glass doors.

I gasp. "Is that the terrace?" He nods and unlocks the door, sliding it over. We walk onto the same terrace we were on months ago, just through a different door. Nothing has changed out here. It's the same furniture and decorations. The only thing that's changed is it's ours now.

I squeal and jump into Aiden's arms. "I love it!"

"I'm so relieved to hear that."

I pull my head back. "Did you think I wouldn't?"

He shrugs. "I was hoping you would."

"Everything about today has been amazing." I shake my head in disbelief. Nothing went wrong. "It's been unbelievably perfect." Aiden walks inside and I follow, closing the door behind me. *We are definitely having some parties up here*, I say to myself, looking back outside as I lock the door.

"Well, at least no one showed up saying I was the father of their child," he says, sarcastically.

My eyes go wide and I bust out laughing, unable to control the giggles coming out of my mouth. I anchor myself on a table with my hand to keep from doubling over in hysterics.

"It wasn't that funny?" His eyebrow rises and he stares at me, confused.

I take a few breaths and bite my lip so I don't break out in a fit of laughter again. It seems now is the perfect time. I walk over to my purse and pull out a small, pen-sized box. It's wrapped in silver with a shiny blue bow on top.

"I have something for you, too," I say, holding out the box. His head tilts slightly to the side and the corner of his mouth curls up to a sexy half smile. It's that damn smile that started this whole thing. Every time he flashes it, heat sears through my body. He takes the box and shakes it. I smile and nod for him to open it. His fingers move slowly as he carefully unwraps it. Right before he opens the box, I say, "The night isn't over yet."

He looks up and our eyes lock for a beat, confusion still in his, before he finishes opening the present. He pulls out the positive pregnancy test and holds it between his thumb and finger.

"Does this...is this...*how*?" he stutters, not able to form a whole sentence as he holds up the test. His eyes gleam as he looks at it again.

"It's what you think," I nod as my eyes start to fill with tears. "I guess I forgot antibiotics decrease the effectiveness of the pill." I shrug one shoulder.

He looks back to me. A smile spreads across his face and his emerald green eyes sparkle. "We're having a baby," he boasts. I'm swept off my feet, and Aiden spins me around. I wrap my arms around his neck. When he puts me down, he drops to his knees and rests his head against my lace-covered stomach. I look down and watch his hand stretch across me, slowly caressing my stomach.

I didn't think I could love this man any more than I already do, but my heart grows watching him. I place my hand over his and close my eyes, reveling in this feeling. *The feeling of being complete.*

When I open my eyes and look back down, he's smiling up at me. Humor crinkles in the corners of his eyes. I tilt my head slightly, wondering what he's thinking.

"Eight more to go," he beams.

THE END

Author's note

I can't even put into words how excited I am for Aiden and Addison to finally have their happy ever after. The ending is bittersweet for me. I loved writing their story and I hope you have stayed with me for the ride, because it's been a turbulent one with a few gut-wrenching drops. But their love was strong enough to withstand everything, and in the end it was beautiful.

The next few pages are the epilogue. I highly recommend that if you're on a *happy ever after* high, to come back in a few days to read it. *Unfortunately*...Fate doesn't stop at happy ever after's.

XO
Tina

Epilogue

One Year Anniversary

I look out the window where we stood a little over a year ago to say "I do." Now, a couple of empty chairs sit facing the lake. Sun peeks through the cloudy sky, reflecting off the silent water. I startle when I feel Aiden's hand wrap around me, stopping on my stomach.

"You doing okay?" he asks, nuzzling my neck.

It's a phrase I've heard too many times this year. His patience and understanding is ironclad, and I'm grateful for it. He can read through my lies when I say that I am okay. The response is so automatic now, I'm starting to believe it. I slide my hand on top of his, linking our fingers and lean back into his body.

"I can't believe it's been a year," I whisper. It's funny to hear those words come out of my mouth because *during* the year it seemed liked everyday went by like a dripping sink. Painstakingly slow. I tried not to think about. I tried to keep myself busy taking care of Lexi and growing a baby inside of me, but a day hasn't gone by that I haven't thought about her.

"I know," he murmurs.

"Jett finish eating?"

"Yep. As soon as he was done, Katie grabbed him." I smile. Jett loves his Aunt Katie. I've loved having her close this year. She's been one of my lifelines this year. "Did you see Lexi riding?"

"I did. She's doing really well," I respond proudly. We arrived at Max's a little early before everyone else arrived so she could ride. Max kept his promise and bought her a horse. He had a barn with stalls built and has since bought a few more horses. I've just started to ride the last couple times we've come out because Aiden forbid it when I was pregnant.

"I think someone is getting sleepy," I hear Katie say, walking into the kitchen. I release Aiden's hand and turn. Jett's rubbing his eyes but when he sees me his smile lights up and his green eyes shine.

I return his smile and walk over to them. "Is my big boy getting sleepy." He lifts his arms for me to take him. He's almost four months and the happiest baby ever. After all the heartache we've gone through, I was sure he would end up being a grumpy baby.

I reach for him and bring him in close to me, kissing him on his head. He lays his head on my shoulder, and I sway my body. Aiden rubs his hand down his back. I take in a deep breath, loving the smell of him. It's a calming smell I crave these days. "I'll put him in his bed," Aiden says.

I can feel Jett's body already relaxing against me. His arms haven't gone limp yet, so I know he's not all the way out. I kiss him and pass him over to Aiden. He snuggles into Aiden's neck, and I can't help but smile at the love between the two. I watch them until they disappear out of the kitchen.

Aiden is an amazing father. He still makes special time just for Lexi. He never wants her to think that just because Jett is our biological child that he is more important. They are both perfect in every way.

"Where's JD?" Jaxon says, walking into the kitchen with us.

"You just missed him," Katie responds. "Off to take a nap."

Jaxon pulls Katie into him. "Can we go take a nap," he jokes, kissing her neck. She slaps him on the chest, pushing him back.

"No." She laughs. "Everyone is going to start showing up soon."

Almost everyone.

I sigh. Katie peeks at me, sympathetically. "I love you, Sis," she murmurs, giving me a hug.

"I love you, too," I reply. "Can you do me a favor and go check on Lexi? I need to use the restroom."

"Of course." Her voice raises. "I've heard she's getting good at riding."

"She's a natural," Jaxon says. "Max is going to have her barrel racing soon."

I laugh, knowing that is something Max would do. When they walk out of the kitchen, I make my way up the stairs. My hand runs along the wooden banister. I don't need to go to the bathroom. I just wanted to see the room where we all got dressed for the wedding. It's my favorite room of the house. I can still feel her energy in there.

Max hasn't changed a thing in here. The bright room is blinding, but I'm used to it now. I stay for only a short while because I know the house is going to be full any minute. As I'm about to walk down the stairs, the sound of a door opening stops me. Stone is coming out of a room to the right of the stairs. I've asked Max repeatedly what he keeps in those rooms and the only answer he gives me is "stuff."

I smirk, walking toward Stone. "Hi, Stone," I say, flashing a sweet smile.

"Hey, Addison. How's it going?" His hand is on the doorknob, and he clicks it shut.

"Good," I reply. I tilt my head. "Stone, is that your room?"

He shakes his head. "Nah. I live in the guesthouse."

"So...what's in there?"

He cocks an eyebrow. "Nothing," he says slowly.

I narrow my eyes. "I don't believe you. Show me." He starts to shake his head. "Please?" He stares at me for a beat and then sighs.

"Just a peek." His voice is hesitant as he looks around first. The excitement in me bubbles over. Max is always so secretive about everything and now I get to see a little bit of it. When he opens the door, my eyes go wide.

One wall has at least ten monitors on it, all playing different locations of God knows where. It's surveillance feeds. I catch a glimpse of a wall of pictures, which I assume are their cases. There are probably a hundred photos. I push open the door to get a clearer view. One picture in particular makes me freeze.

Stone holds onto the door, guarding the room so I can't go in any farther. I lean my head closer and squint my eyes to focus on the picture. "Is that—"

"Fuck. Time to go," he says, interrupting me. He pushes me out the door.

"Stone!" I say trying to get past him. He's too big for me to move.

"Addison, don't ask questions. I'm not going to answer them," he states matter-of-factly. "Just forget you saw anything."

I stomp my foot. "Really? How the hell do I forget what I just saw? Never mind! I'll deal with Max." I fly down the stairs and go straight to the kitchen. Stone follows me downstairs; I feel him on the heels of my feet. I hear him mutter a few curse words under his breath. My insides burn with anger; I can't even talk. I snag a couple beers and head outside. I need to think and calm down before I rip Max's head off. I hear Aiden call my name but my body keeps moving forward. I head down to the water to the empty chairs and sit down.

I've drunk the first beer by the time Aiden joins me. The Corona went down so fast, I don't recall tasting it. That's not how I wanted my first taste of liquor since that small sip of champagne at my wedding. I wanted to savor it. I've missed it so much. There were many moments over the last year that I've wanted nothing more than to get wasted to *forget*.

Aiden kneels in between my legs, his hands on my thighs. I look over his head at the water, avoiding eye contact.

"He did it for you," he murmurs. My eyes snap to his.

"Me?" My face twists. "He didn't do it for me. If he had, he would have told me." I look away and swallow. "You know how many hours I spent looking. Wondering. And he knew this whole time!" I take the cap off the other beer and take a quick drink. Aiden's head drops. "Did you know?" I whisper.

He looks up quickly. "No. Stone just told me." I stare into his eyes, looking for the truth. *Shit.* I forget who I'm married to sometimes. "I swear, Addison, I would have told you." He squeezes my thigh.

"Why didn't Max?" I cry out. Tears burn my cheeks.

"I don't know. You're going to have to ask him that." His eyes focus over my head, and he nods at someone. I'd look behind me, but I know Max is there. "I love you, baby." He kisses me softly on the lips and pushes off. I manage a smile before he disappears behind me.

The chair creaks as Max sits down. I can feel the tension between us on my chest. I take another drink, trying to swallow the lump of anger I want to spew. My thoughts take me back a year, to the day we got back from our *familymoon* with Lexi.

Aiden's phone started blowing up that morning. At first he didn't answer because we had just got back, but it continued. His boss called. Max called. Jaxon called. Something was wrong. I remember the second he found out what was wrong. His knees gave out and he fell to the floor. His world had just shifted underneath him, crippling him.

His best friend was dead.

We found out that Damon had been shot two days earlier. He was working a child murder case. He and Aiden had been working on it together before we left. I had to put the pieces together, but what I gathered was one of the tips they were given ended up being the suspect. When Damon and his team went to arrest the guy, the guy opened fire and hit Damon. He died while in surgery. Aiden blamed himself because he wasn't there to help. I felt conflicted. I felt like I had to choose. The two most important people in my life just lost someone important, and I didn't know how to comfort them both at the same time. I tried to be there for both of them, but I didn't try hard enough. I failed Sydney.

She was there for me without any hesitation my entire life, whenever I needed her, but I couldn't do the same for her *the one time she needed me*. I beat myself up every day knowing she left because of me. She left the day after the funeral. No goodbye. *Nothing.* The part of my heart that was dedicated to only her was crushed. I looked for her for months. I didn't ask for help because of the guilt I carried. I didn't want to burden anyone for something I caused. Her father passed away a couple years ago, so I thought she might go live with her mother for a while. Her mother hadn't heard from her either. She was closer to Amy than her own parents, so I wasn't surprised.

Every day I wrote her a letter, hoping that would be the day I'd find out where she was so I could send it to her. I have three hundred and sixty-four letters waiting for her. Today is the anniversary of Damon's funeral. We're celebrating the life of a loved one who was taken away from us too soon. I'm also mourning the loss of a sister who is still here but has left me.

Jett's middle name is Damon. All the guys call him JD. When we were deciding on a name, I threw out Jett. Aiden thought I was kidding. *I wasn't.* My first love was named Jett. Damon was a given for the middle name. Both names changed our lives for the better. So, our baby boy became Jett Damon Roberts.

I sigh and finally look over at Max. "How long have you known?"

His body tenses and I see him open and close his hands. "The whole time," he mutters, looking down at his hand. I draw in a ragged breath, looking away from him.

"You knew, Max..." I choke back my tears "You knew what her leaving did to me." I push off the chair, walking to the edge of the water. "Why didn't you tell me?" I whisper. I doubt he heard me. I jump when I feel his hands on my shoulders.

"She told me not to," he says, folding his arms around my chest. I cover my eyes with my hand and cry. *She hates me.* "She called me the day after the funeral, asking me if I could fly her to California." I drop my hand. *California?* "I tried to get answers. Told her not to go. But she said it was something she had to do." I pull his arms off my chest and turn around. His jaw is clenched as he runs his hand behind his neck.

I take a couple deep breaths. "It's time," I declare. "It's time to bring her home."

"I don't know if she'll come."

"I need you to try." My voice shakes. I can taste my tears on my lips.

He closes his eyes for a moment and nods. "Okay."

Acknowledgements

Y'all! I can't believe I'm done with Addison and Aiden's story. I'm a little sad. I've lived in their world for the last two years so it's bittersweet. How many of you hated the way the epilogue ended? C'mon! I warned you! Obviously, Sydney's book is next. I haven't started writing it yet, so I can't even guess a date right now. There is another book that is screaming at me to write it so it might come first. It's going to be a standalone and the title is *Blinding Echo* (well, that's the title for now). Make sure to like my Facebook page, Instagram, or sign up for my newsletter to stay informed of future books.

If you're reading this, I can't thank you enough for following me on this journey into the writing world. It's been a surreal experience. I've been humbled by the outpouring of support and love from friends, family, readers, bloggers and other authors. I still can't believe I've published three books.

To my alpha/beta readers—Tiffany, Lori, Traci and Michelle—you guys are my rock stars. Your thoughts and opinions have helped me make the Twist of Fate trilogy what it is today. Thank you, thank you, thank you!

Max and Elaine, I couldn't have done this without you two! Max, you bring life to my words and Elaine, you make them spotless. Thank you both for sticking with me while I was learning and my last minute tendencies. I promise, I'll get better at that.

To my wonderful husband, you definitely win husband and dad of the year. Thank you for your patience when I had deadlines and your support throughout this whole process. It means the world to me. Love you!

Of course, to my readers and bloggers. You are the Nutella to my banana (in my world there isn't anything better!). Thank you for all your kind words and for reading my books! Y'all ROCK! Last, but not least, thank you to the girls I found on Facebook and messaged asking if you'd answer some questions about places I'd never been but needed to know about, you're awesome for helping me out.

About the author

Tina Saxon lives in Dallas, Texas, with her husband and two kids. She's not afraid to try new things because it's outside the box of typical housewife. CEO of her home is by far the most rewarding job she has ever had. Her jobs include, but are not limited to, seamstress, carpenter, craft extraordinaire, PTA President, chauffeur, dance mom, mediator—of mentioned kids—and author. Once upon a time she was a Financial Analyst but traded in budgets and forecasts for diapers and bottles. The former was definitely easier but the latter more fulfilling.

Tina's love for reading surged into her passion for writing. Wanting to bring the reader an intriguing story that's hard to put down with steamy love scenes that heat you up, she's always thinking of the perfect way to take you down that path.

For more information about Tina and her books, visit:

https://www.tinasaxon.com/
https://www.goodreads.com/author/show/
16743159.Tina_Saxon
https://www.instagram.com/authortinasaxon/
https://www.facebook.com/authortinasaxon